# CHAOS MODE

Piers Anthony is one of America's bestselling science fiction and fantasy authors. His popular series include *Incarnations of Immortality* and *Bio of a Space Tyrant*. This is the third volume in the ground-breaking *Mode* series. He lives with his wife in Inverness, Florida.

By the same author

SCIENCE
FICTION
FANTASY

# PIERS ANTHONY

# Chaos Mode

HarperCollins*Publishers*

HarperCollins Science Fiction & Fantasy
An Imprint of HarperCollins*Publishers*
77–85 Fulham Palace Road,
Hammersmith, London W6 8JB

This paperback edition 1994
1 3 5 7 9 8 6 4 2

First published in Great Britain by
HarperCollins*Publishers* 1994

ISBN 0 586 21348 1

Set in Times

Printed in Great Britain by
HarperCollinsManufacturing Glasgow

# Contents

# 1

## *Contact*

It was the strangest creature Darius had seen. 'Uh-oh,' he heard Colene say.

The four of them stood by the anchor, gazing out onto the world it showed, and the thing that hovered in the foreground. The world was ordinary: a gently rolling countryside, patches of flowering bushes, and trees beyond. In the distance were blue-gray mountains. He had seen many realities like this. But the creature was something else.

It was about the size of a calf, maybe the weight of two solid men, and roughly oval in cross section. At the top was what looked like a stout elephant's trunk, but it connected to no elephant's head. Instead it seemed to thicken, and then condense into another trunk pointing the other way. Two or three projections sprouted from its center, moving sinuously, as if snakes were poking their heads out of small tunnels. The double trunk might as well have been the snout of a dragon, ready to belch fire fore and aft.

The main body was odder yet. It was covered with stubby projections and with holes. Air was being sucked into those holes and evidently blown out below, because –

Because the thing was floating just above the ground. He stared, but saw no sign of legs or feet. Yet it did not seem to be magically levitating. Instead the body was hovering on a cushion of air. Its base seemed to be a curtain to enclose that air, and sections rippled as gusts moved out.

*Its mind is blank to me.*

Darius became aware of his companions. Beside him on the right stood Seqiro, the massive horse . He was their most intimate companion, because of his powerful telepathy. With him, all of them seemed to speak the same language,

7

and could share feelings directly if they wished to. It was Seqiro who had spoken − or rather, who had projected his thought.

'It is an alien creature,' Darius said. 'It will take time to fathom its mind.'

He spoke in his own language, but knew that the others heard it as their own, because of the linkage. Colene had set out across the Virtual Mode to join him, and he had set out similarly to join her. They had met more or less in the center, where they had encountered complications. But she had met the horse first, and that had turned out to be a wonderfully unifying thing, because of the ambience of their shared thoughts. Now, with fair luck, they would resume their trek across the Modes and reach Darius' reality. There they could settle down to a satisfying existence. If they didnt get stuck along the way. If they could work out their personal problems. If a thousand unlikely things did not happen.

'It's our new anchor person,' Colene said. 'It has to be, because here we are facing a new reality, and there it is facing us. So we'd better talk to it fast, before it decides we're its next meal.' She nudged Darius. 'Can you do your thing with it?'

'Transfer?' he asked. He had the ability, in his own reality and in some others, to drain the emotion from a person, and then to broadcast it to everyone in the vicinity. That was his job, at home, as the Cyng of Hlahtar. Or, as Colene put it in her idiomatic thought, King of Laughter. He made people happy. But he hadn't been able to do it in Julia, the Mode they had just left. Each reality seemed to have its own mysterious rules of magic, science, or whatever. 'I can try. But who − ?'

'Not with me!' Colene protested. 'I'm full of depression. That thing's depressing enough, without adding to it.'

That was of course her tragedy. Instead of being a vessel of job, she was a vessel of dolor. Except when she was close to him; then her love blotted out the pain. Their shared thoughts revealed it all. It was one of those problems they had to work out.

'But Nona is the only other human person here,' he said.

Colene thought of the way he drew emotion, and he followed her thoughts to their inevitable conclusion. He had to get as close as possible to the other person, and that other person was Nona. That was disaster, as Colene saw it. 'Skip that for now,' Colene decided. She faced Nona, the fourth member of their party. 'What about you? Can you work your magic here?'

Nona considered. She was verging on eighteen years old, and absolutely beautiful in face, feature, and mind. Her thick cloud of brown/black hair framed her head and shoulders and full bosom in a manner that was endlessly becoming. Darius knew that Colene feared she would never be able to match that sort of appeal. All this and magic too!

Nona gestured. Nothing happened. She concentrated, her face as lovely when frowning as when smiling. 'My magic has no effect,' she reported. 'I can not levitate, or move objects, or transform them to other forms or substances. I am not in a position to attempt healing, and I am not yet sufficiently adept at changing my own shape to know whether I can do that here. There does not seem to be sufficient magic power here for me to draw on.'

'How about illusion?' Colene asked.

'Oh, that's not magic,' Nona protested innocently. 'Anyone can do that.'

'Anyone in your Julia set,' Colene said wryly. 'The rest of us can't.'

Nona concentrated again. A faint haze appeared above the horse. That was all.

'What about a familiar?' Darius asked. 'That's not physical magic.'

'But for that I must touch an animal.'

9

Colene looked at the monster floating patiently before them. 'Is that an animal?'

'I couldn't touch that!' Nona exclaimed, horrified.

'Well, we have a choice, here,' Colene said, exhibiting some of the qualities that made her a much more significant person in her own right than she believed: intelligence, initiative, and courage. She was only fourteen, but much like a full woman in respects. 'This has to be our new anchor person, and it has to have had really good reason to latch on to our Virtual Mode. So chances are it's either a scientist or a felon. We can't shut it out from our Mode. So either we try to ignore it, or we try to come to terms with it. Me, I'd rather know something about it before I relax.' She nerved herself. 'So *I'll* go touch it. If it eats me, the rest of you get away from here in a hurry.'

Nona smiled ruefully. 'I will touch it, Colene. Perhaps I can indeed tame it as a familiar.' She stepped forward.

Colene thought to protest, but Seqiro's thought restrained her. *I will work with her, as I have before. Perhaps together we can relate to it.*

Nona's magic and the horse's powerful telepathy. They could indeed work well together. Seqiro could help Nona without getting in range of the weird creature. 'Thanks, horseface,' she said, reverting to one of her immature facets. The irony was that she appealed to him this way, too. He loved her as she was, with her internal conflicts and all.

Nona approached the creature somewhat diffidently. Seqiro suppressed her natural fear, so that she could be objective. Seqiro could if necessary take over a person's body, if the person let him, and make him or her do things impossible to manage alone. Probably he could enable Nona to leap away from the creature with inhuman speed and strength. If she needed to. So this was not quite as risky a procedure as it might seem.

The creature quivered on its cushion of air. Two of the upper stalks twisted to orient on her.

10

'Eyes!' Colene exclaimed. 'It's a BEM!'

'A what?' Darius asked.

'A bug-eyed monster. It's focusing its eyes on Nona.'

'Those look more like snail eyes to me,' Darius said. But he had to agree that they were orbs of some sort.

As Nona came close to the thing, they saw that knobs poked out from its rim, each on a rod, like the antennae of sea denizens. But these didn't look quite like antennae. They looked like blind terminals, in Colene's imagery. Darius lacked sufficient experience to understand the nature of the reference, but he accepted it because he had no better image of his own. He had had some limited experience with machines, while crossing the realities of the Virtual Mode, and gathered that this was a machine analogy.

Nona stopped beside the creature. Air from the thing's outflow stirred the turf by her feet. The stalked knobs reached out farther, wiggling.

Now Darius saw something else. The thing did have eyes. They were on the three central stalks. They were watching Nona. So it knew she was there. What else did it know?

Nona slowly reached out. Her left hand came toward one of the knobs.

Suddenly that knob jumped outward on its rod and smacked into her hand. Nona, still pacified by the horse, did not jerk away. She remained calm, her hand holding the knob.

Something happened. The ambience of telepathy faded. It was like stepping out of a warm chamber into the chill air of a barren plain.

Darius looked at Colene. She seemed as concerned as he was. She put her hands to her head, as if something was missing from it. Then they both looked at Seqiro.

Now the horse was just a horse. Darius noticed how Seqiro, eighteen hands high at the shoulder, dwarfed the girl, who was only fifteen hands high at the top of her head. But the horse's brown mane exactly matched Colene's brown

11

hair. They were a matched set in that respect, and in age: Seqiro was also fourteen. The girl loved horses, and Seqiro loved girls. Seqiro linked them all, telepathically, and liked them all; he assumed the qualities of whatever mind he was in touch with, borrowing its intelligence. But Colene was his first love. If there were to come a crisis, and Seqiro had to choose just one of them to save, she would be the one.

Colene spoke. This time he heard it in her actual language, without the translation to his own. Normally the horse relayed the thoughts, and each person's mind did the rendering, unconsciously; now those thoughts were not there. But Darius had spent time with Colene in her reality, when they first met, and had come to learn some of her language. He could translate it, approximately, when he concentrated.

'Seqiro — are you all right?' she was asking. Or 'Are you well?' or 'You have not been harmed?'

'He — all — well,' Darius said, picking from his memory of her vocabulary. 'He — help — she.' For he was tuning in on the horse, as he might for a drawing of emotion, and realized that there was no problem. Seqiro was merely devoting his entire mental energy to the purpose at hand: Nona's rapport with the creature. It had to be a considerable challenge.

Colene looked back at Nona, and Darius followed her gaze. The woman stood unmoving, her eyes blank, her hand on the knob. But the creature was moving, slowly: as it was settling to the ground. The swish of air diminished, and then faded out, as the bony lower fringe of the creature came to rest on the ground. The three eye stalks retracted until they were mere spots on the surface.

'Xxxx yyyyyy zzzzz,' Colene said, incomprehensibly, amazed. She was using vocabulary too sophisticated for Darius to decipher. Then, realizing, she turned back to him. She concentrated visibly, and he felt a faint touch at his mind. She was trying to use her own very limited telepathy.

12

So he stepped to her, embraced her, and focused his mind on hers, as if he were about to draw her emotion. But he only touched her awareness, without taking hold of it. That facilitated the contact, and amplified her projection.

*Innocent woman and fantasy horse*, she thought. Then, realizing that she was getting through, but not sufficiently, she clarified the concepts. *Young woman, girl, never done sex –*

'Virgin,' he said, grasping the concept.

*Virgin with one-horned horse*, she thought, then spoke the word: 'Unicorn.' *Only virgin can tame unicorn. Nona –*

He nodded. Nona, unlike Colene, was a virgin. This suggested a certain mental innocence. Sometimes only the truly innocent could approach a creature others knew to be dangerous. Somehow the creature might know, and not harm her. As he reflected, he picked up more of the background from Colene's reflections. It seemed that there was a certain ironic humor to the myth: unicorns were extremely rare. In fact they did not exist at all. The implication was that human virgins were similarly rare. That concept was tinged with grief and anger, for Colene herself had found out how a virgin lost her innocence. It had not been by her choice.

So it was Colene's judgment that Nona was taming the monster. With the help of all Seqiro's mental power. All he and Colene could do was not interfere. They would just have to wait for it to happen.

They were, in effect alone. He was holding her close. He brought his head down. She lifted her face. They kissed.

Colene had never been strong on subtlety. She grabbed on to his shoulders, heaved herself up within his embrace, and wrapped her legs around his torso – while holding the kiss. She opened her mouth a little and stuck her tongue through. He was so startled he almost dropped her. She laughed – still without breaking the kiss.

But he was learning her ways. He slid a hand down to

her upper thigh and tickled it through the cloth of her trousers. She squirmed, but he continued more vigorously, crossing the buttock, until she had to break the kiss and grab his hand. 'No fair!' she cried, trying to act outraged as he let her slide down to the ground. He needed no telepathic translation of that expression. She was still young enough to consider herself duty-bound to react to tickling, especially in places where it wasn't supposed to be done.

She made as if to punch him in the groin. He made as if to grab her by the hair. They were feinting, looking for a pretext to kiss again. Colene was also, in her fashion, trying to seduce him. Fortunately he was more experienced than she in this respect, and was countering her ploys emotionally as well as physically. He never forgot that though they loved each other, she was too young. By the standard of her culture she was not supposed to be ready for sexual interplay. That standard had been violated, and the violation had caused her much emotional mischief. He intended to see that it wasn't violated again. Perhaps when they reached his reality, it could be determined whether she could be considered a new citizen, governed by the more permissive standards his people enjoyed. So that she would be allowed to choose for herself. Because he would like nothing better than to *let* her seduce him, if –

Then Darius heard something. It was a honk. He held up a hand, flat, signaling her to desist.

She had heard it too. She looked in the correct direction. Nothing was visible.

Then they heard a faint hissing or swishing, as of moving air. Something was happening in the distance, out of sight. What could it be?

Colene was the first to catch on. She pointed to the creature with Nona. She pursed her mouth and blew air out. Then she pointed to the unseen noise. Another of that kind of creature?

Darius suspected that it was. Now he heard more hissing,

14

from another direction. Then from a third. There could be several such creatures drawing near.

The creature they had met had invoked the anchor. That could only have been for serious reason. It was possible it was a criminal, trying to flee where the local law could not follow. But it was also possible it was a martyr, deserving of assistance. Regardless, it was the anchor creature, and no one else could release that anchor, so they were stuck with it. Better to get to know it, as Colene had said.

But they wouldn't get much chance, if others of its kind came and captured it. Others were indeed coming; now he saw one steaming in from the forest, gliding across the land at what must be its traveling speed.

There was a honk from that direction. 'First blood,' Colene muttered, and again he didn't need a translation. The prey had been sighted, and soon all of them would be here. Indeed, another appeared, sliding at the same velocity. Darius judged that he could outrun the things, but he wasn't sure that they wouldn't accelerate and outpace him.

Nona and the local creature remained in their communion. What was happening between them? Would it be dangerous to interrupt? But it might be dangerous *not* to interrupt, and warn them of the approach of others.

Darius took a step toward them. Colene grabbed his arm, shaking her head no. Then she walked to the horse, reached for his head, and changed her mind. She signaled Darius, making an up motion with her two hands.

What did she have in mind? He went to her, put his hands on her hips, and heaved her up so that her head was the height of the horse's head. She was a small girl, and carried no excess weight; it was easy to lift her.

She put her face to Seqiro's left ear. 'Seqiro,' she murmured. Then, louder: 'Seqiro.' Then she put her mind into it: *Seqiro*.

The ear twitched. She had gotten his attention. 'Danger, maybe,' she said.

This time Darius heard her through his mind, with no effort. The horse had resumed the job.

'Others of this kind are approaching rapidly,' Darius said. 'We must alert this one, in case this means trouble.'

Nona looked around. She had heard the warning too. She still had her hand on the knob, but the communion seemed to have ended.

'Seqiro,' Nona said. 'Amplify me for one more moment; I must warn him and ask him to follow us through the anchor.'

The other creatures were converging. 'Do it!' Colene cried.

The ambience faded again. Then Nona withdrew her hand.

The creature infused air. Its eye stalks sprang out and waved, sweeping the horizon. The air hissed louder. The body lifted from the ground.

'Come on!' Nona cried. She ran for the anchor.

The creature followed.

The other creatures were closing in. The closest one crossed a patch of sandy soil. Its rear trunk dragged down, touching the sand. Then sand blasted out of its front trunk. The sand didn't travel far ahead, but some of the pebbles in it did. One landed not far from Darius.

'They're shooting at us!' Colene exclaimed, outraged.

'Get moving!' Darius shouted.

They ran after Nona and the creature. Nona abruptly disappeared, having stepped through the anchor. Then the creature did the same.

'Come on, Seqiro!' Colene cried. Because the horse was waiting for her.

The three of them stepped through the anchor almost together. The scenery hardly changed, but the pursuing creatures vanished. Nona and the first creature were not in view.

*We are in the next reality*, Nona's thought came. *We passed through two.*

16

'She can mind-talk across Modes?' Darius asked, startled.

'No. Seqiro can transmit across Modes, when he tries,' Colene explained. 'Especially when he knows the people. He's keeping track of Nona.'

They walked three more steps, and there were Nona and the creature, seemingly popping into existence. The Virtual Mode was like that: every ten feet, by Colene's reckoning, there was the boundary of another reality, or Mode, similar to the last but a completely separate entity. The land and vegetation changed less between Modes than the animals did, so animate creatures seemed to pop in and out against the common background. It was, as Colene also put it, weird – until a person became accustomed to it.

'Okay, Nona, what gives?' Colene inquired. 'Did you get its life story?' She gazed without complete trust at the creature, and two of the eye stalks gazed back at her. The third was watching Darius, and he was just as disconcerted as Colene was. The thing was obviously aware, and now that he knew that its trunk could hurl stones, he feared what other threats it could muster.

'No,' Nona said. 'We reached only the yes/no not-enemies stage. The rest is too complicated to assimilate immediately. This is a completely alien creature, but he means us no harm. He wants to travel on the Virtual Mode.'

'Look,' Colene said. 'This landscape is Earth. Not right around where I live, but somewhere on the continent. I know Earth when I see it. How did such freakish aliens get here? Did they conquer Earth and kill all the people? I mean, how do we know this thing isn't trying to conquer the larger universe, the way Emperor Ddwng of the DoOon Mode was?'

That was a fair question. They had barely escaped that grasping Emperor, and only by tricking him into vacating his anchor. They did not want to get into such a situation again.

'This is indeed your Earth,' Nona agreed. 'But he is not

alien. He is native. His species evolved here. And he is not an evil creature.'

'How can you know that?' Colene demanded. 'I'm sure that nothing like this has ever existed on Earth. I mean, the eye stalks are possible, and maybe the elephant trunks, and maybe the knobs. But air suspension and propulsion? No way!'

Nona shook her head. 'My understanding is as yet imperfect. But there is no untruth when I tame a familiar, and there is no untruth here. To him, we are the alien creatures. He was appalled when he saw us; it was all he could do to remain for my contact. I am the ugliest creature he has seen or imagined, let alone touched.'

Darius laughed, and so did Colene. Anyone in the universe who thought Nona was ugly was crazy.

But she was serious. 'Seqiro at least could be mistaken for a large animal, but the three of us are like demonic fantasies. It was some time before he could suppress his revulsion enough to pick up my thoughts, and it remains difficult. But this was the gamble he took when he invoked the Virtual Mode, and he has to live with it. He could not remain with his kind. I don't understand what is wrong, but he is not a bad person; it is some complex social interaction that caused him to be banished. But he can not live alone, so he had to gamble on alien contact.'

'You say his kind is native to Earth, in this reality?' Colene asked. 'Then what about our kind?'

'Our kind does not exist here. We never lived here. None of the kinds of animals we are most familiar with ever existed here.'

'You mean no mammals at all?' Colene asked, daunted. 'I know this is a different reality, and a lot of them don't have any life at all, but –'

'No mammals, reptiles, birds, fish, dragons – no vertebrates,' Nona said. 'No – what you call chordates. But there are arthropods, and sponges, and mollusks, and the plants seem similar. I think everything is much the same, except that his kind is here and our kind isn't.'

'How far back does this go?' Colene asked.

'From the time that many-celled life evolved. He thinks of three great dyings that eliminated many creatures, but his kind managed to survive the last two, and come to dominate the world.'

'From the time of multi-celled creatures?' Colene asked. 'That's the Cambrian explosion! Five or six hundred million years ago!'

'Yes, that seems to be the scale time he is thinking of,' Nona agreed. 'In my universe, it isn't the same, so it's confusing.'

'The Burgess Shale!' Colene exclaimed.

'The what?' Darius asked.

'This is a world where things changed with the Burgess Shale,' Colene said, awed.

Nona looked blank, and Darius felt the same. 'Things are obviously different here,' he said. 'But what does shale have to do with it?'

'Well, nothing, really, maybe. But it's where we discovered all the strange creatures who didn't make it. The experiments of evolution. It must be that in this reality, our phylum, the chordates, didn't make it, while his phylum, whatever it is, did. So I guess this is Burgess, and this is the world of Shale.'

Darius exchanged a glance with Nona. Even with telepathy, this didn't seem to make much sense.

'Each Mode has its own rules,' Darius said. 'Whether of magic, or science, or memory, or something else. Perhaps they all were unified once, if we could trace back to the points of divergence. This creature is surely no stranger than many others we might encounter in other realities. But surely he has a name of his own, and we should honor that.'

'What's his name?' Colene asked Nona.

'It's just an electrical identity pattern. I wouldn't know how to translate it to a name in our terms.'

'That's what I thought,' Colene said smugly. 'So we have to call him something we can relate to. So it's Burgess. The same goes for this world/reality. So it's Shale.' She faced Darius. 'You have a problem with that?'

He knew better than to challenge her on a minor point. 'I have no problem, if he does not. He can address us by electrical pulses, if he wishes, so long as we are able to tell whom he means.'

'Nah. Seqiro can render the translations. When we say Burgess, he'll hear his pulse, and when he pulses at us, we'll hear our names.'

Nona looked doubtful. 'Seqiro has not yet related to — to Burgess. He has merely amplified my power of relating to a familiar, and I have somewhat clumsily communicated. We shall have to spend a great deal more time together before we can converse at all readily. It is — it is like learning another language. For him and for me. We have been exchanging pictures.'

'Well, then maybe we should get into some safe nook and get to know him,' Colene said brightly. 'Because we don't want to have to risk another anchor change; no telling what might come up next time. And Burgess is the only one who can free his anchor anyway. So let's find out what's on his mind, and see if our purposes align, and then maybe we can travel on together.'

Darius looked around. 'This is only two realities away from — from Shale. There are probably similar creatures here, and we probably should avoid them until we know more about them. So perhaps we should travel until we find a reality that seems barren, or at least inoffensive.'

'Good point,' Colene agreed. 'Nona, tell Burgess what we're up to.'

'I will try,' Nona said. Darius had a notion what she was up against. Relating to an alien creature was no simple

20

matter, but Colene acted as if it were just a matter of translating a few terms.

Colene shot him a glance. 'No, I'm just trying to get something done, before anything worse happens.'

He tended to forget that his private thoughts as well as his uttered ones were shared with the others. Seqiro would limit communication if requested, but that would make it seem as if Darius had something to hide. So normally only his strongly sexual thoughts were excluded.

'Oh they are, are they?' Colene demanded. Darius was smart enough not to respond.

Nona put her hand on the creature's knob again. 'These are his contact points,' she explained. 'Normally he touches one to a contact point of another of his kind, and they exchange information rapidly. In the way ants do with their antennae, perhaps. But I am alien, so the exchange is difficult.'

Then the telepathy faded, as Seqiro focused entirely on Nona. Darius was alone again.

Colene, never one to miss an opportunity, stepped up to him, ready for more kissing games. Perhaps with a demand to know exactly what sexual thoughts weren't being relayed, relating to whom? But she hesitated.

'You – are – well?' he asked in her language.

'I'm not sure.' She looked around. 'Is there something coming?' He was sure he had the essence, because her gesture and expression matched what he understood of her words.

'I – see – no.' Indeed, the landscape was clear. There were only bushes and trees.

'Something ugly,' she said. 'Festering. Horror.' Or words to that effect. She kept looking around, as if expecting disaster to appear.

'There is nothing,' Darius reassured her. 'I can tell by my feel for emotion. My power is working here, I believe.'

Still she reacted. Lines appeared in her face and her lips

drew back from her teeth. 'Awful. It's coming for me. I know it!'

Then he began to sense it too. Because he was tuning in to Colene, and the ugliness was there in her mind. There *was* something – something that he had never found in her before. Not her normal depression, but something worse.

He took her in his arms. 'Use mind-talk' he urged her. 'Show me the whole of it!'

She let him have it. Her telepathy was quite limited, compared to Seqiro's, but they were in close physical contact and her emotion was strong. The ugliness expanded to foul his own awareness.

He felt frightened and ill and despairing. He wanted to flee, but couldn't. It was as if a monstrous predator had locked his gaze to its own eye and would not let go. Moment by moment, that terrible grip strengthened, squeezing his mind and soul.

He tore himself away from her, and the awfulness diminished. 'The mind predator!' he cried. 'The thing that pursued Provos, our friend who remembered only the future. Now it is orienting on you!'

'The mind predator,' Colene agreed sickly. 'Oh, Darius, get me out of here!'

He knew he had to. Because Colene and Provos had traveled the Virtual Mode together, and Colene had reported with mental pictures when they returned. The thing had threatened to destroy Provos, seeking her across the realities. They had escaped it only by fleeing through an anchor. It seemed to be a horror of the Virtual Mode, not a particular reality, and it could not pass out of its range.

He stepped to the horse. 'Seqiro,' he said into the animal's ear. 'Break contact. Emergency.' Probably Seqiro could not understand his actual words, but the sound was enough to break his concentration.

The ear twitched. Then the telepathy returned.

'Colene's in trouble!' Darius said. 'The mind predator. We must go back through the anchor immediately!'

That got the horse's instant full attention. Suddenly the horror invading Colene's mind was blasting at them all. Nona screamed and sank to the ground.

Darius fought back, forewarned by his prior encounter with it. 'Stifle! Stifle!' he cried. 'Don't relay!'

Then it stopped. The horse had damped out that aspect. In fact he had cut Colene out of the circuit. Nona climbed back to her feet, her eyes round with horror.

'Tell Burgess we must go back to his world,' Darius told her. 'Now. Before that thing consumes Colene.'

'But it's not safe there!' she protested.

'It's not safe *here!* We shall have to go through and flee the other creatures, or fight them. Hurry!'

She put her hand back on a knob. The telepathy faded out again.

Darius picked Colene up. She was like a doll, mostly limp, but her hands and feet were twitching sporadically. The mind thing was making mush of her mind. He strode back toward the anchor, carrying her. The others could follow or not, but he was getting Colene away from the monster.

# 2

## Burgess

'Burgess' was in a mixed state. He had invoked the dread Virtual Mode and suffered the touch of the monsters therein. They were alien and grotesque, yet not actually inimical. They did seem to have a hive of some sort, though it seemed distastefully limited and crude. So far only one of the four had contacted him, but she was trying to understand.

Now this 'Nona' pattern was indicating alarm. They had to go back through the anchor; the picture was clear. The aliens were fleeing something on the Virtual Mode.

Burgess would have protested, but he lacked status with this hive. So he would have to accept its mandate, and try to protect it from external threats.

This hive, small and alien though it was, had something strange and enlightening. It enabled him to seem to think for himself. Instead of merely reacting to the latest contact, he experienced the throes of a decision-making process. He was acting like an entire hive — by himself. This was so odd it was ordinarily impossible. Yet the pattern for it was with the aliens, and as he followed that pattern he became conscious of self. He was becoming an individual.

This must be a requirement of survival, on the Virtual Mode. The creatures of the Mode survived, and they had it, so it must be necessary. They touched each other only to compare strategies, not to restore their places in the whole. He would never have conceived of such a thing, had he not discovered its patterning in the Nona thing.

They had to flee into his world, and he had to help them survive it, for they did not know its ways. He had to have initiative. It was a strain in his awareness, especially when he was not in direct contact with the alien, but that was the

24

way it was. Actually he had been developing a crude kind of initiative before, fro necessity: cut off from the home hive, he had done what gave him a chance to find a new hive. It had been desperation, because otherwise he would have lost his ability to function as a member of a dominant entity, and would have regressed into animal status. But it was also initiative. He recognized that now. The alien contact had greatly amplified an ability he had not understood before.

He lifted and quested with his jet. He found several round stones, which he sucked in and held for expulsion. They would do for only token attack, but that was all that offered. Just enough to make the others pause, so that escape was possible.

Then he would have to show them the one place where the members of the hive would not go. He believed that the aliens could go there, because they used animal propulsion. They had legs, like those of crustaceans, that pushed against the ground. They seemed to take in air, but to push it out through the same orifice. That was not effective for locomotion. But in this case, their animal nature would help them.

He followed the Nona thing across the Modes. The larger animal went with them. It had four leg appendages, instead of two, but was similarly primitive about its use of air. Its surface was highly irregular, with projections that did not seem to be either eyes or contact points. But it moved well enough, its legs coordinating with bewildering finesse.

They caught up with the other two. Now there was another surprising thing: the two had merged, and were traveling on only two legs.

They plunged through the anchor almost as a group. The hive members had departed, unable to pursue Burgess through the anchor. They had seen him vanish, and they believed that he would never return. But one was watching, just in case.

Now that one saw the emerging creatures, and honked. That signaled the more distant members of the hive. Soon they would converge, as they had before. There was only limited time to reach the safe zone.

The hive member lifted a trunk. But Burgess, prepared, fired a stone first. It struck an eye stalk, momentarily blinding the hiver. The hiver retreated, unable to decide on a more aggressive course without contact with other hivers. This was Burgess' advantage, he realized with surprise: he was now able to act with minimal consultation, because of the pattern he had learned from the alien.

The aliens were hesitating. The two who had merged separated again, each using its own legs. Burgess showed the way. He set out toward the nearest section of the wilderness region. He moved as fast as he could, but it was soon apparent that the aliens' animal legs could propel them faster. That was good, because it meant that the hivers would have difficulty catching them.

But now the pursuit was manifesting. Several hivers were coming into view, converging. He would not be able to outdistance them all. Burgess had several rocks remaining in storage, which he could use to discourage too close an approach. But he would soon be overwhelmed by the greater number of hivers. He saw that clearly now that he was thinking for himself. Also, the same wilderness that blocked the hivers would block him. He could show the aliens the way to their safety, but he could not help himself. He should have remained on the Virtual Mode. Perhaps if he had been more accustomed to thinking as an individual, he would have realized that.

They were moving across the almost level land toward the adjacent river. Beyond it was the wilderness. But now he recognized another problem: the water presented a barrier for the aliens, who could not float across it. He had not thought of their limitations before. Was he leading them into a trap?

The hivers were now closing from four directions. One followed directly behind; two were angling in from the sides; one was coming along the river. The fleeing folk were ahead of three, but the one on the river was cutting them off. So even if the aliens could cross water, they would not escape.

The aliens made exclamations. Burgess suspected that these were expressions of dismay at the sight of the hiver ahead of them. Such dismay was well taken.

Burgess did what he could. He floated up to the river and fired a stone at the hiver. But the hiver saw it coming and slid aside so that it missed. Then the hiver oriented a trunk to fire a return rock.

Then a second rock flew at it — one Burgess had not fired. Surprised, he turned his eye stalks to trace its origin. There stood one of the aliens, making some kind of gesture. In a moment another made a similar gesture — and a rock flew away from it. They were firing rocks!

The hiver on the water floated away, because the rocks were too numerous for it to avoid. The aliens were taking them in their upper appendages, moving the appendages swiftly, and letting the rocks sail out. In this weird manner they were able to do combat!

But the three other hivers were approaching. Burgess floated across the water, hoping the aliens could somehow navigate it, because there was no other choice.

The aliens moved into the water. Their legs plunged through it to contact the ground below, and they maintained forward progress. They were able to cross! It was slower than on land, but adequate. Soon all four of them were on the other bank.

They moved on toward the wilderness as the leading hiver arrived at the river. The hiver on the water was now advancing again, coming to join the others. Burgess saw that the river had slowed them so that the pursuit was now much closer. They were almost within rock range. With four hivers firing, that was bad.

Burgess floated as rapidly as he could toward the trees, but he had to veer around a rocky hill. That was impassable, of course. The hivers cut across and narrowed the distance between them.

Then the aliens did something amazing. They moved up the slope of the hill! They were able to navigate it, because they lacked air cushions, which had to be almost level. But they were not safe, because the small hill was in rock range; the hivers would bombard them as soon as they finished with Burgess.

A rock came at him, and bounced off his canopy. That one did not hurt, but others would. He would have to stop and fight as well as he could against the four.

But then the aliens stopped. They gestured, and rocks started flying again. They were hurling rocks down at the hivers! Three of them were doing it, while the largest one stood and watched. Burgess realized that that one could not use its legs for this purpose; all four were confined to the ground. How did it do combat?

For a moment Burgess watched, amazed at the facility with which the creatures handled the rocks. They were not limited to small ones that a trunk could handle; they were taking larger ones and heaving them down. The rocks missed, but the hivers halted their pursuit and floated back out of range. They touched each other, getting current on the situation.

Still the aliens threw rocks. This was another surprise: the rocks were reaching the hivers. The aliens could hurl the rocks farther than the hiver could! Their seemingly awkward limbs were good at this.

One hiver was struck on an eye. Another suffered a rock in an intake hole, causing it to lose some of its flotation. The hivers retreated farther, to get out of the surprising range of the aliens.

And the aliens advanced! They continued to pick up rocks and hurl them. The hivers had to retreat, and finally

28

to flee. They could not match the rock-throwing ability of the aliens.

In this manner the aliens had saved Burgess, who would surely have had his eyes knocked out and his intakes blocked if he had been alone. He had tried to save the aliens, and the aliens had saved him.

When the hivers fled, the aliens ceased throwing rocks and returned to Burgess. The Nona creature put an appendage on one of his contact points. *Good?* she sent.

Burgess returned a picture of a placid blue sky. It was good.

They continued to the wilderness. Here the big trees spread their branches high and their roots made a lattice on the ground. This prevented any hiver from traveling through, because it was unfeasible to maintain a sufficient cushion of air to support the body. The irregular roots prevented the canopy from making even contact with the ground, and the air leaked out inefficiently. Thus the wilderness was impossible to penetrate, and no hivers went there.

The aliens, however, had no difficulty. Their legs simply stepped on the roots, or between them. They could go wherever they wished in the wilderness.

Now that Burgess had shown them to safety, he contemplated his own problem. He could not join the aliens among the trees. But neither could he return to the anchor porthole. The hivers would now be guarding it. What was he to do?

Then the aliens did the strangest thing yet. One of them touched the largest one, and separated something from it. Were they dismantling the large one?

The second largest alien took the object, which looked like a detached branch of a tree, and poked it at the ground. It sank into the dirt. Then it came up, and the dirt came up and fell among the tangled roots of the nearest tree. The alien moved the branch again, and more dirt fell. He

29

continued to do this odd series of motions, until considerable dirt was piled across the roots.

Then he moved away, and the smallest of the aliens climbed onto the mound of dirt. The legs moved up and down, and the feet landed on the dirt, making it spread and flatten.

This continued. The larger alien piled more dirt, while the smaller trod it flat. Was this some ritual of theirs? What was its point? The spread dirt was forming a channel which passed the tree and extended into the wilderness, where the ground was less interrupted.

Then the Nona creature touched a contact point again. *Go*, she sent, and made a crude map showing the dirt.

Burgess tried to convey to her that he could not go into the wilderness. But she was persistent. *Go. Path.*

Path? An awesome explanation loomed.

Burgess pumped up his air and moved to the dirt. He moved onto it. The dirt had filled in the crevices between the roots, and made a section of level ground there. He could travel on this!

He followed the path, and soon was on the other side of the tree, where the ground was navigable. The aliens had made it possible for him to enter the wilderness!

But Burgess realized that where he had passed, the hivers could also pass. They would soon be returning in force, to overwhelm him and the aliens.

After he passed, the aliens with the branch used it to scrape away some of the dirt. Now the path was impassable in that region. Burgess realized that the aliens had understood the threat, and acted to protect him. No hivers would follow them into the wilderness.

The day was declining. Now that safety had been assured, it was time for Burgess to eat. Rather than try to explain this process to the aliens, he showed them. He fired a rock up at a fruit hanging above. The fruit dropped. Then he sucked the fruit into his intrunk and ground it up with his internal teeth so that his body could absorb it directly from the reserve chamber. The irreducible husk and seeds he simply blew out the outtrunk.

Now the aliens demonstrated how they consumed food. One used its limbs to climb up into a tree — a process that amazed Burgess — and plucked and threw down several of the ripe fruit. Another caught the fruits before they reached the ground. Then the aliens brought out a sliver of stone or bone and used it to cut the fruit apart. Each piece was then put to an orifice in the upper end of the creature, where it slowly disappeared. The process seemed, on reflection, to be roughly similar to what Burgess did, but with different implements. Now he saw that there were indeed teeth in the upper orifices, which masticated the fruit. Since the chewed fruit did not emerge, it must find its way into the body. It seemed to be a workable system, crude as it was. The largest creature ate its fruit from the ground, but also had grain which came from a pocket along its side.

By now it was getting dark. Burgess simply settled on his curtain and drew in his eye stalks. The aliens were more elaborate. They gathered sticks and brush and fashioned a structure. Then they made themselves horizontal within this structure and were quiet. This, too, seemed workable.

There was a sound deeper in the forest. A kind of clicking.

Then Burgess' new syndrome of thinking for himself brought him alert again. He had been lulled into a sensation of security, because he regarded the aliens as an alternative kind of hive, and the hive was safe at night. But they were not really a hive, and this was the wilderness. It was not safe at all, especially by night.

He honked. It was a floater's signal of danger or alert. He had done it automatically, because that was the way of his kind. His new mode of thinking was merely an overlay on the conditioning of his lifetime.

The aliens reacted immediately. They scrambled out of their shelter, making exclamations. They looked around with their odd recessed eyes. One held an object which emitted a beam of light, as if the sun were inside it. The light splashed around in a circle, showing the trunks and foliage of the trees. The aliens had understood the warning honk well enough, but there was no threat near.

The Nona creature came to touch a contact point. *?*, she inquired.

Burgess tried to clarify his concern. He sent a picture of a tree of the wilderness, with a darkness looming beyond it. He made a click with the rocks in his trunk. He fashioned a bolt of fear, hoping it would be intelligible to her.

The Nona made sounds. The others responded. They seemed to have better sonic differentiation than the floaters did, perhaps because their contact points were undeveloped.

Then, so abruptly it had to be by communal agreement, they were quite silent. They remained so for some time, motionless.

The click repeated. It was followed by a rustling and scraping, some distance away but approaching.

*Describe*, the Nona creature sent.

Burgess sent a picture of a huge crustacean that dragged itself along the ground by the use of several sets of legs, with enormous pincers in front. He had seen one of these only when it was dead; it had evidently fought some other creature in the night, and been defeated, and had dragged itself out onto the plain to escape. But its injuries had been too great, and it had died there. The flying flesh-eaters had swarmed there in the morning, and a floater had investigated. It had summoned others, who had spread the news, so that soon the entire hive had the mental picture of the creature. This was a monster of the wilderness! And this was what Burgess feared was coming near, with its pincers clicking hungrily.

The aliens consulted, in their fashion. Then they went to work, in their fashion. It seemed as senseless as their prior activities with the sand and shelter, but Burgess suspected that it would turn out to be as sensible at the conclusion. The aliens might not be a true hive as he knew it, but they managed a fair emulation of hive activities.

Then they went to the largest of their number, flashing their little beams of light, and drew out more branches from its hide. Burgess realized that the complicated protrusions were actually not part of the creature; they were somehow attached to it, and could be removed. It was as if he were carrying them, without carrying appendages. The aliens were as strange in their subtle ways as in their obvious ways.

They fetched more fallen branches, and started to spread more dirt. Burgess didn't know what this dirt was for, as the ground in this glade was level and needed no path for him, but he was willing to help on the assumption that they were accomplishing something useful. He wanted to be part of the hive, as every floater did. So he went to where the larger two-footed alien was, and sucked up some dirt from the place where it was being excavated with the stick, and blew it out where it was being piled. The creature stepped back, then indicated where more dirt should go. Another creature flashed the light there, so that there was no question. Burgess was able to move the loosened dirt faster than the creature could with the stick. Soon he had moved all of the loose dirt and there was a long mound at the edge of the glade.

The creature used its stick to loosen more dirt, and this facilitated Burgess' effort. He blew it to the end of the mound, extending it. In this manner they formed a small valley and ridge that entirely surrounded the glade.

Meanwhile the Nona creature had gathered more branches, and had rolled some large stones to the glade. Now the aliens set the stones on top of the ridge of dirt, and put the branches up by the stones. They fashioned some of the branches into straight sections, and used stones to pound on these, so that they sank endwise into the ground.

Now at last Burgess came to understand what they were doing: they were making a hive-barrier! What the hivers did

33

entirely with dirt, making a mound that no hiver could cross, the aliens were doing with dirt and stones and branches. Inside the circle it should be safe.

Now the two smaller aliens returned to their shelter. The two larger remained outside it. The four-footed one merely stood silently, as before, but the other came to Burgess. It put an extremity on a contact point. Faintly its information came through. It was male. His identity was 'Darius.' He was a friend. He was watching.

Burgess sent images of his own. He was not sure how well they were being received, but there did seem to be partial communication. Now at least he knew the contact pattern of a second alien. This was reassuring.

Burgess was tired. He had alerted the creatures to the threat, and they had responded in what had turned out to be a sensible manner. He was reassured. He sank back down to the ground and retracted his eyes.

He resumed consciousness when another alien contacted him. This was the smallest one, who turned out to be female. There was something special about her; she was intense, and her thoughts forged through with sharper definition. She was 'Colene.' She was watching now.

But she wasn't satisfied just to be alert for danger. She wanted to know about Burgess. Where did he come from, why was he alone, why had he invoked the Virtual Mode? Her determination to know cut through the problem of communication. He found it relatively easy to understand her, and she was understanding him. Her pictures were coming through with increasing clarity. She let him know what her own world was like: similar plants to this one, but no creatures like him, and many variations of her type. Creatures who had ridges down their length, through which their bodily communications flowed, and four legs, and minds at one end. Strange!

He tried to clarify for her what his world was like. It was

34

dominated by a number of creatures she thought of as 'arthropods'; she knew what spiders, insects, and crabs were. But the dominance by power was the 'phylum' to which the floaters ultimately belonged: the vast array of 'triramous' animals. That was her term, and she presented it with such wonder that he had to explore the matter further. It seemed that this was the key difference between their worlds: the triramous phylum existed in one, and the 'chordates' in the other. In each, the numerically inferior type nevertheless had achived the greatest influence over other types, and had the greatest freedom of action.

The time in the development of life when their two worlds had been the same was, by Colene's reckoning, the 'Cambrian.' The records of his world had no indication of her type of creature, known also as the 'vertebrates'; the records of her world lacked indication of the triramous creatures. But surely the two coexisted in that time, 550 million years ago. The time of the great proliferation of species, most of whose phyla later was lost. Colene's kind had become aware of this early abundance by inspecting a layer of rock they called the Burgess Shale. Now her identification of his was associated with this, so that he was 'the creature of Burgess' and his world was 'the shale rock.' It was just the way she visualized it, she explained, and she intended no disparagement. She rendered this concept with such a friendly corollary that Burgess had to respond.

This 'friendly' concept was as alien to him as the matter of individuality or self. He focused in it, because though it was vague, it was pleasant. It was another type of patterning. It was what Colene presented as 'emotion': an attitude about things that related to the self. For a hiver, pleasure was achieved by conformance to the consensus of the hive, which was achieved by frequent contacts. To be current was to be satisfied; to lack currency was to be unsatisfied. There were no other significant indications. But with Colene's pattern of self came emotions which related

35

to the individual, and currency was irrelevant. Since Burgess would slowly fade and die without currency with a hive, this alternate system was of interest; could he learn to survive without currency? If so, he would be unique among his kind.

Colene was eager to know more about Burgess and his species and culture. He was as eager to know about hers. Already the alien pattern she transmitted was taking hold, showing him the way to think in her fashion, and he was coming to feel friendly to her. He had never liked another creature before, because such emotion did not exist among floaters except in the sense that each member of the hive needed his hive. Colene, more than the others, was relating to him. She seemed like a discrete entity to him, and he saw himself as a discrete entity in her view. That was something new and valuable. So he tried to obtain more information about her and her kind. Their intellectual pattern was as strange as their physical pattern.

She responded with yet another new emotion: a pleasant, odd, paradoxical mood she called 'laughter.' She would make him a 'deal,' a summoning of chance which would determine who learned first about whom. They would watch the other two creatures of her type, and see which of them was first to move body or limb. If it was the male, then Burgess, being male, would prevail, and Colene would inform him of all he wished, to the extent of her ability. If it was the female, then Colene, being female, would prevail, and Burgess would inform her similarly. This deal was so strange that Burgess did not understand how to decline, so he agreed by default.

They watched, and in a moment the Nona creature rolled over. 'I win,' Colene sent with another thrill of momentary pleasure. 'But I will tell you everything, the next time.' She communicated increasingly in linear chains of thoughts, which were relatively slow compared to floater contact, but seemed to be the key to contact between their species. They were linear creatures throughout, he realized; they applied food to one end of their bodies and eliminated the residues from the other end, and their thinking was similar. But as he came to understand this, and attune, his ability to communicate with Colene improved. Now there were few confusions, and concepts of increasing complexity were being exchanged.

So he gave her the information she desired, and in the process found that he was learning much about her anyway. Every concept she found foreign meant that she had experience of a different nature, and that helped define her. Indeed, she could not exchange the full degree of her recent experience with twenty others of her kind simultaneously, getting current; she had to 'talk' individually with each. Except that she did have an alternate mechanism: the largest creature, with the four feet on the ground, was a 'horse' who was 'telepathic.' He was male, and he could communicate simultaneously with all the others of the group. While in his presence, the others could draw on his ability, so that they could exchange information simultaneously. So they were indeed a hive, by this mechanism, and Burgess could be part of it, if he learned to transmit to the horse without requiring direct contact with a contact point. All this Burgess learned, in the process of answering her questions about the nature of floaters, hives, and individuals.

Communication, though linear, was becoming so facile that Burgess almost forgot the strangeness of the situation. He structured his thoughts to be linear, and paced them, so that though time passed in the transmission, Colene was able to understand his situation.

His kind had evolved, according to hive memory, in that same Cambrian explosion she knew about. This followed the near extirpation of all forms of life, the greatest of three formidable extinctions. The seas had been left bereft of all but single-celled life forms, so many new many-celled forms rapidly evolved. These filled the seas and competed for dominance, and some were winnowed out while others proliferated. Then the second greatest extinction came about 225 million years ago, wiping out nineteen of twenty life forms. But the survivors soon bounced back, forming many competent species. Then the third extinction came, 65 million years ago, again wiping out most life forms. This time the triramous phylum, which had been established but not dominant, expanded to fill the vacated niches. From these came the floaters, who foraged on the surface of the sea, and found it easy to forage also on land. They were just another type on the sea, but became dominant on land, with many species developing. Most lost their multiple contact points, specializing in individual hunting and foraging. But the hivers retained them, and became more closely cooperative, finding security in close numbers. They became smarter together, because of heightened communication. They learned to use the rivers as avenues to reach all parts of the land. By remaining near the water's edge they succeeded in avoiding predators, who were normally either of the land or of the water. Then one species learned to change the land to make better regions for safety at night, and this one flourished.

Burgess had been an external contact entity. Instead of remaining in close communication with his own hive, he acted as liaison to foreign hives, so that the hives could communicate with each other somewhat in the way individuals within each hive did. Each hive had its own nuances, so that a floater from one hive could not readily relate to one from another hive. Burgess had to learn to tolerate and comprehend foreign nuances, and to be able to endure for periods without being current with his native hive. In this manner he helped coordinate the activity of the hives, so that they did not congregate in particular regions and deplete the resources.

But then he had encountered a hive that had gone bad.

38

He picked up some of the poison of its nature, and knew that it had to be isolated from contact with other hives, lest it poison them too. He returned to his own hive and signaled warning: a series of honks. Then he retreated, knowing that he could never return, so that he himself would not infect his hive. It was a tragedy, but there was no alternative.

He was expected to join the bad hive now, since he could relate to its members and had nothing further to lose. That hive would not be allowed to contact any other hive. Any member it sent out would be driven back or killed. But Burgess could not bring himself to join it, because its poison revolted him. He preferred to regress into animalism alone, as would inevitably happen without hive contact. It was a horror, but the alternative was to die swiftly.

But when his native hive saw that he was not joining the poisoned hive, it instituted defensive measures. This was because it feared that he would try to rejoin it, and thus poison it. So it sought to kill him before that could happen. Burgess knew that its decision was reasonable; it had hudnreds of members to protect, while he was only one. The single floater always had to give way to the welfare of the hive. Burgess had attempted to forage and hunt alone, in a remote section of his home hive's province, but this was not allowed. Parties were sent out to kill him.

So he had tried a desperate ploy: he had invoked a Virtual Mode. This was largely a matter of chance. Few of his kind could even sense the Modes, and none wished to explore them. But Burgess' experience as a foreign contact person had prepared him for this yet-more-alien contact. He had tuned in increasingly well, and when a Virtual Mode had come, he had reached for it, using his mind and will to secure an anchor in his Mode. Then he had awaited the contact of whatever creatures inhabited the Virtual Mode with considerable trepidation, knowing that they were likely to be more alien than anything he had encountered. But if they happened to be of his kind, they might represent a new hive,

39

which was not poisoned, and which would not be harmed by his own infection.

'But what is this poison?' Colene asked, concerned. 'Is it a disease that will make us die?'

No, it was not a physical disease. It was a mental one. It was a syndrome known to infect hives that became too small. Their internal contacts became so intense that their members lost their tolerance for any foreign floaters at all. Since it was necessary to share offspring, who went at the outset of their lives to foreign hives, so that there would not be ingrowing, this was an attitude that could not be allowed to spread, lest the entire species fragment and lose its dominance. Burgess himself had not succumbed to it, or he would never have been able to invoke the Virtual Mode. But he had been exposed to it, and that was enough to make him dangerous. Its nature was insidious, and he might at any time be overcome by it. So he was banished from the hive.

'Bigotry!' Colene sent, grasping the poison concept. 'Racism. Intolerance. Prejudice. We have those poisons in our species too!'

They had it too? What had he floated into? He had hoped to find a hive to which he could relate without such contamination, so that he would never succumb to it himself.

'No, we here on the Virtual Mode don't have it,' Colene clarified. 'But it is elsewhere in our species. More prevalent than in yours, I think.'

He relaxed. The aliens had been exposed to the poison, but had not succumbed to it, which was the same as his own state. They would understand his situation. So instead of being a problem, it meant that this was after all a hive he could join. The strangest kind of hive, but not as strange as it had once seemed. The aliens resembled few-legged animals, but understood the dynamics of hive life. The reality counted more than the appearance.

'What about reproduction?' Colene asked, sending a picture of big floaters and little floaters. 'I know you are male and female, because that's the first thing that registers when we make mental contact, but just how do you do it? Do you have marriage or life-pairing?'

Burgess tried to address the matter, because her question implied social aspects that confused him. Mating within the hive was a straightforward act, and the young departed for other hives, while the incoming young from other hives were schooled by the contacts they made with hive members. But it seemed that among the aliens the concept of self complicated reproduction. Colene seemed not to accept the idea of young who had no contact with those who had generated them.

Suddenly there was a crash. Colene jumped up and flashed her ray toward the sound. A huge pincer appeared above the barricade. It came down by one of the angled branches, clamped on it, and crunched through the wood. Then it swept sidewise, knocking other branches out of the way.

It was a crab, a big one, and their defense was inadequate. The thing was coming right through the wood, and the mound of dirt did not inhibit it either.

Colene broke contact and joined the others. Then she returned. 'Can you read me, Burgess?' she asked faintly.

Yes, he received her.

'Good. Seqiro's not carrying me, now; I'm doing it on my own. So we can coordinate like a hive. You too, if you respond to me. To fight this monster. Okay?'

To be part of a hive again: that was what he wanted most. However it was arranged. Especially since only hive action could be effective against the crab.

'We can't stop it head-on,' she sent. 'But we can attack its weaknesses. If we know them. Do you know them?'

Burgess oriented all three mobile eyes on the monster, as it widened its channel through the rampart. It was slow, but

41

once it got inside, it would have no difficulty catching each of the aliens in its pincers and crushing them. It would crunch off Burgess' trunks, rendering him helpless, then consume him at leisure. It was terrible to behold, but it did have some few weaknesses. The eyes and the breathing holes. On the plain, by day, hivers would surround the crab and shoot jets of sand at its eye stalks, forcing them to retract. Then into its holes, clogging its breathing. That would slow it. Then they would try to roll large rocks onto it, crushing it. Or simply flee to their hive, where their rampart of dirt and barrage of stones would dissuade it.

'You're not that sharp against big crabs,' Colene remarked.

That was true. The armored creatures were formidable. The normal way of dealing with them was simply to flee them.

'Well, we can't flee this one. So we'll kill it or drive it away. We're going to blind it first. You fire dirt at its eyes, and keep doing it, so Darius can get close with his sword.'

Burgess sucked up dirt and sent a stream of it at the crab. The crab's eye stalks were small, and hidden behind the giant claw, but the dirt blew in on them. The crab scuttled to the side, trying to get clear of the dirt, but Burgess kept blowing it. Colene and Nona were both shining lights so the crab was clear.

Meanwhile the Darius creature moved right in within reach of the claw, waving a bright stick. He struck down with that stick, knocking at an eye stalk. The eye flew off the stalk. Then he chopped at the second stalk.

But the crab, hurt, scuttled away, and the stick – now Colene's thought clarified that it was not wood, but metal, with a sharp edge, a crafted weapon – struck the shell, denting it but doing no real harm. The claw swung around to grab him, but Colene screamed warning and he dropped to the ground and scrambled away. The pincers clicked together above him, poorly guided because one eye was gone.

Then there came a new emotion: fear. It made Burgess want to turn around and flee, though he had nowhere to go. 'Easy, Burgess,' Colene sent. 'Seqiro's doing that. Ignore it.' She removed her hand-appendage from his contact point, and abruptly the fear was gone. Then she touched him again, and it was back. 'See? It's on our side. I'm feeling it, so you are too, when I'm in contact with you. But I understand it, so I can resist it. For a while.'

He tried to tune it out, and it diminished though Colene's contact remained. What a strange weapon!

The crab turned around and barged back out of the enclosure. Burgess understood why: it felt the fear too, and thought it was its own. The attack-thought of the alien hive had driven it away.

Darius and Nona went to work repairing the damage to the wall, while Colene remained with Burgess, shining the light ray for them. Seqiro merely stood, still sending the fear to the crab. He was able to do it without touching any contact points!

'Well, we won that one,' Colene sent. 'But I think we'd better get out of here, first thing in the morning, and find some place we can defend better. The next monster may not scare as easy.'

Burgess agreed. However, there was still time before dawn, and they would have to wait until then to travel.

'We can not relax,' Darius said. 'The moment Seqiro eases up, the crab will turn around and come back here.'

'Oops,' Colene said. 'Is that true, horseface?'

For the first time Burgess was aware of the four-footed alien's thought: *It is true. I must not sleep.* There was a qualitative difference to it.

'What about when day comes?' Nona asked. 'Will the crab retire then?'

*No.* The crab was aware of prey, and would keep pursuing

it, regardless of injuries, as long as the crab remained hungry. It was not a thinking creature.

'Then we aren't going to be able to sleep again, after this,' Colene sent. 'We'd all better stay alert, to make sure Seqiro does. But we can use the time to talk. Now I'll answer your questions about me, Burgess.'

Burgess was satisfied with that. Where did she come from, and in what ways did her world differ from his, and how had she come to know about the ancient shale? What was the significance of reproducing, among her kind? What had brought her and her companions to the Virtual Mode? Where were they going? Why had they so suddenly fled the Virtual Mode, after going there with him? Why was it easier to understand her than it was the others?

Colene sent the laughter emotion, which was odd against the background of the fear the horse was still sending. 'You want to know everything all at once, don't you! Well, we'll answer you, but it will be better if I show you how it was with me before I ever learned of the Virtual Mode. Then you can pick up on the background, and maybe catch on to how we think. Hang on while I tell you about my crush on Amos.'

Her emotional squeeze on something termed an Amos? This was not necessarily going to be easy to grasp.

# 3

## *Crush*

As she spoke, focusing her thoughts, sharing her memory-experience with the others via Seqiro's telepathy and with Burgess via her hand on his contact knob, Colene pictured herself as she had been barely seven months before, at school's Spring Break. Oklahoma, America, Earth: a world and a lifetime away!

Only three months before that time, during the Christmas holiday, she had gone innocently on a date with a boy she had not known well enough, and gotten herself educated in an adult fashion by four of them. She had learned way too much about alcohol and sex, and finished the night thoroughly sick of both. She hadn't told her folks, but the boys had talked, so that her reputation was sliding. Thirteen years old, in the eighth grade, and already she was a known slut, at least among those who kept track. She was still trying to sort out her feelings on the matter, uncertain whether to shut the whole thing out of her awareness forever, or to commit suicide. As time passed, she was coming to favor both courses. At such time as she figured out suitable means to accomplish them.

However, the teachers knew nothing about it, and no one was about to tell them. The best teacher was a completely ignorant teacher, with respect to real concerns. That made it easy to get along in class. Colene was adept at the art of conforming in nonessential ways, so as to conceal the essentials from irrelevant eyes.

On another plane of her existence, she had normal feelings. Her romantic life was abysmal, and not just because of her reputation. Nothing was as gawky and unwholesome as an eight-grade boy, and the ninth graders weren't much

45

better, and she was not about to trust a high school boy again. But Amos Forell was another matter. He was her science teacher, marvelously handsome, authoritative and mature, and he knew everything. Maybe he could tell her whether hypnotism could enable a person to seal off part of her mind. Maybe he could tell her of the most convenient, painless, sanitary way to die. More important, maybe he *would*.

The more she thought about it, the better she liked the notion of asking him. But she couldn't just blurt it out. She would have to be indirect. How could she get herself into a situation in which she could get the information she wanted, without arousing his suspicion? Because even the nice teachers were part of the administrative conspiracy, bound to blab anything private they learned, causing endless mischief.

Somewhere along the way, as she considered Forell, he became Amos in her mind, and she realized that she had a crush on him. This was girlishly foolish, of course; he was a married man, and distressingly straight. There were stories about certain male teachers who gave better grades to physically mature girls who sat up front in short skirts, especially if they forgot to keep their knees together, but Amos was clean. Either he had no interest, or he was highly disciplined. This was known, because one especially well-developed girl had an absolute flair for stupidity in science, and she had put on a show that should have melted his horn-rims. He had merely murmured in her ear, as he returned her F paper, that perhaps she would be more comfortable in slacks. She had turned on him her loveliest do-what-you-will-with-me wide-eyed stare. Prompted by that, he had explained that perhaps the drafty air-conditioning was distracting her from her classwork. So much for seduction; he had noticed her exposure and demonstrated his immunity. That earned him points.

Of course that didn't stop the girls from trying. Some who

didn't need better grades considered it a challenge. Amos never missed a beat; he was the perfect science teacher, ardent about the wonders of his subject, and his grades showed no sign of deviance. No one could figure it out. Was he a closet gay? Then how to account for his wife and two children? Exactly what was his game?

Then Colene deciphered it: he was a contrarian! He scored by pretending *not* to notice. That way, not only was he technically innocent, he got more and deeper glimpses than would ever otherwise have been offered. What a scheme! He was smart about more than science. She liked that. So she didn't blab his secret. In fact, maybe that secret was what had tipped her into her typical teen crush. It would pass in about two months — they always did — but it added urgency to her quest. She had to get a chance to ask him her questions while she remained smitten, because the experience would be so much more meaningful then.

Then her opportunity came: Spring Break. Students could get spot bonus points by coming in on one of the off days to help the teachers clean up, so she signed up for work on the science lab. She was in luck: no one else signed. She was alone with Amos for four solid hours. He would even have to drive her home, after; it was part of the deal, because the school didn't want to get sued for putting innocent students out on the street when the crossing guards weren't on duty, and maybe fostering an accident. The administration didn't care if it lost a student, of course, but lawsuits were expensive.

She was careful about it: she wore a skirt that came down well below her knees, and a blouse that was fully opaque, and no makeup or fancy hairdo. She was there to get the work done, and she looked exactly the part. Two could play the contrarian game; she would make her impression on him by seeming not to be trying. Her skirt and blouse, though decorous, were quite well fitted, and much depended on the positions a girl had to assume in order to clean under counters or to pick up lab equipment. She didn't have as much body as she could have wished for, but the decorous clothing helped there, accenting implication rather than exposure. She was innocuous and naïvely attractive, she hoped.

And she did work. She made a point of throwing herself into it, doing the best job she could. When there was something to be moved, she tackled it immediately, so that if it was heavy he had to jump to help before she strained some innocent little bone or tendon. Even so, she managed to work into some legitimate heaving of bosom with the effort of the work. She had tied her hair back, but soon it worked its way loose and flopped around her face exactly as she had intended. She was the epitome of the enthusiastic, hardworking, guileless, innocently sexy, sweet little girl.

What did she get for her effort? Not what she had hoped. Amos was a creature of his profession, and he loved his subject. He maintained a constant monologue about the things they were handling, as if it were just another class. He never seemed to look at her; she was nothing next to Science. She was a mere audience for his true passion.

So as they cleaned and put away the astronomy charts she suffered through an extemporaneous lecture on the nature of the universe, and how fascinating it was to see the cracks developing in the Big Bang theory. 'I was an advocate of the Steady State theory,' he said — god only knew what that was, and she knew better than to inquire. 'There was such an elegance to it, both mathematically and philosophically. But as our observations improved, we discovered that the universe conformed to the Big Bang theory, seeming to be a monstrous explosion of matter and energy perhaps fifteen billion years ago. The question became whether it was open or closed — that is, whether it would expand forever, or whether there was enough matter to enable gravity eventually to halt its expansion and draw

48

it back together. I supported the closed model, but it seemed that there was not enough matter in the universe to achieve closure. However, then came the indications of dark matter –'

Colene found herself getting interested despite herself. She had heard of dark matter. It appealed to her sense of the morbid: the idea that the universe was dominated by unseen force. That there was no way to detect the great majority of the matter that existed, except for its gravitational effect. She wished she could invent a telescope that could see dark matter. Maybe it would form the shape of giant animals in space, chasing one another. Maybe Earth and the Solar System and the Milky Way Galaxy were all just fuzz on the tip of a hair growing from a wart on the nose of a Dark Matter Monster.

'So it seems there *is* enough matter to close the universe,' Amos concluded with satisfaction. 'We can't see it, but we do know it's there, and that's what counts.' He glanced at her. 'Am I boring you?'

'Never,' she said immediately. Indeed he wasn't, because she was helping him roll the big astronomy charts so they could be fitted into their casings, and in the process their heads got almost close enough for a kiss. She was developing this fantasy of him glancing up, meeting her gaze, so close to his face, losing control and pressing his lips to hers and then being terribly apologetic and embarrassed and out of sorts until she had to calm him by kissing him again. 'But it's wrong,' he would protest. 'You're only a student and I'm a married man.' And she would say 'There is no wrong in love,' and smile, and kiss him once more. 'But an eighth-grade girl –' 'That's all right, Amos; I've had experience.'

That popped her out of it. Indeed she had had experience – of exactly the wrong kind. She could never be innocent again. She was unclean, unvirginal, undesirable. *Damn* those freaks! They had left her a mere shell of appearance with

49

the core debased, like an oak tree with a rotten heart. Her thrill of first love had been gutted before it flowered. Seduce Amos? If he knew her nature, he would be disgusted.

They moved on to the meteorology charts, and Amos was off again, discoursing avidly about the patterns of weather across the world. He smiled briefly as he remarked on the ignorance of students who supposed that meteorology was the study of meteors. Then on to seasonal patterns, and the significance of El Niño, which was a global effect.

Suppose she got involved in moving a heavy prop, and it snagged on her blouse, and tore it open, and Amos saw her bra? No, scratch that; she simply didn't yet have enough bra-filler. So suppose she had to sit on the floor, spread-legged, to wrestle something into place, and he was helping her, and he got a really close look up under her skirt, and – no, scratch that too; he was immune to bare thighs. He had demonstrated that for years.

So how could she get his attention? There was only one way: by engaging his intellect. That was after all his most appealing feature. So she would have to start really paying attention, and maybe arrange to say something that made him realize that she wasn't just another anonymous classroom face, she was a person with a mind. His first love was obviously science, and so hers would have to be too. Meanwhile she hummed 'Why Was I Born Too Late?' to herself as she worked.

Now they were working on assorted fossils of sea creatures. They were inherently dull, even loathsome, being like squished bugs. 'Ah, the trilobites,' Amos said with satisfaction. 'Perhaps *the* success story of the Paleozoic era. Isnt this a beauty!' He held up a fossil of what looked like the granddaddy of multi-legged under-the-rock creepers. 'This phylum of arthropods didn't disappear until the extinction that ended the era. That means they endured for close to two hundred and fifty million years. The dinosaurs

50

were pikers. Of course then the dinosaurs faced their own extinction at the end of the Mesozoic, ushering in the Age of Mammals, misnomer which that is.'

Colene was getting interested again. Extinctions were wholesale dyings, and she had been pondering death increasingly, since the rape. Was it a way out?

But she wasn't quite ready to bring up the subject of death yet. She preferred to come at it obliquely, so that he never caught on to her real interest in it. So she addressed a secondary curiosity. 'The Age of Mammals is a misnomer?' Misnomer was one of those four-bit words teachers liked to use; it meant that the name was wrong. One of the ways to nail down a good grade was to spot such words early, and get them right.

'Of course,' he said happily. 'The arthropods remain the most diverse and prolific phylum today, with about eighty per cent of all species.'

'Ick!' Colene said, dismayed. 'You mean spiders and flies and beetles?'

'And the crustaceans,' he agreed. 'But even if you limit it to the chordates, even to the vertebrates, the fishes are the most diverse in the sea, and the birds on land. We might as well call it the Age of Aves.'

Now to slide in slantwise to the subject of death. 'And it was the reptiles, until that last big extinction. What killed them?'

He smiled. He really seemed to appreciate her interest. Probably it was rare for any student ever to evince interest if there wasn't a grade on the line. 'That remains a matter of conjecture. Actually that wasn't the greatest of the extinctions. The one at the end of the Paleozoic was, with about ninety-six per cent of all species disappearing. Possibly the one at the end of the Precambrian era, five hundred and seventy million years ago, was worse, but we can't know because the fossil record is insufficient. There did seem to be multi-celled life forms then, none of which survived; life had to rediscover that after the extinction. That ushered in the Cambrian explosion.'

'Explosion? Somebody set off a bomb?' She smiled to show that she wasn't really that dumb, just in case he should forget. Also, it was an excellent excuse to smile at him.

He returned the smile, and she felt like melting. 'Figurative, Colene. New species appeared so suddenly that it seems like an explosive radiation. Most didn't survive, but for a while there was an unparalleled diversity of types. We learn that from the Burgess Shale. There were more fundamentally different types of creature then than now, perhaps. We think it was because the seas of the world were empty of multi-cellular life, so there was for a time completely free diversification. Then the process of selection took hold, and many promising species were winnowed out. It's too bad; there were some really intriguing varieties, like none known ever since.'

'You mean like BEMs — bug-eyed monsters?'

'Yes, though most of these were small compared to the monsters of today. Many were a fraction of an inch long. But strange. Here, look at *Marrella*.' He brought out a picture.

Colene looked. It was a weird bug with long horns extending across its back and sides, and too many legs to count, and two different sets of feeler-antenna reaching out in front. 'Yuck! That's the ugliest centipede I ever saw!'

'But a lovely unique arthropod,' he said. 'Some eighty per cent of the fossils found in the Burgess Shape were of this creature, so it was highly successful in its time. As you can see, it is also quite sophisticated in physical detail, not clumsy or primitive as we might have expected. Note that it is biramous.'

'It's what?' This time he had lost her, but she forgave him that.

'Let me explain,' he said, almost radiating pleasure at the prospect. 'The term means that each leg is divided. One part may be used for walking, in the way we consider normal. The other may be a gill.' He grabbed a pencil and made a sketch. 'Each segment thus has two appendages, and each appendage has two parts.'

'That looks almost like a little man with wings,' she remarked.

'A cute analogy. Early arthropods tended to be this way. But those upper ones are gills. So you might say that *Marrella* breathed with its legs.'

She laughed, not even having to force it. 'What a weird way to do it!'

'But many species lost their biramous features, and became uniramous,' he said. 'Just one part to each leg, as is the case with us. I sometimes wonder what a modern biramous creature would be like, if it had evolved and come onto land with the rest of us. Of course we'll never know, but it's an amusing fantasy.'

'Yeah. Maybe even triramous, or quadriramous.'

He shook his head. 'Three or four divisions to each appendage? I really don't know what a creature would do with such a structure. I suspect it would be unwieldy.'

'Yeah. Fancy two of them trying to make love. He gets his trirames tangled up with her birames.'

This time he laughed. 'What an image! But I doubt that they copulated in any such manner. The arthropods are more apt to do it tail-to-tail.'

Almost before she knew it, she had spoken words she shouldn't have. 'No rapes among them?'

He glanced sharply at her. 'What is your interest in such a subject?'

'Oh, nothing,' she lied quickly, flustered. 'Just foolish curiosity.' She hoped she wasn't blushing.

He shrugged. 'Rape is known among animals, and in some species it's the rule. One has only to watch the way of a rooster with hens in a barnyard to appreciate that. But normally copulation is voluntary on both sides, except that pheromones can make it involuntary. So perhaps it's a matter of opinion.'

Colene looked at another picture, not really interested in it, but hoping to guide the subject safely away from the danger zone. 'What's this — a cutaway view of the interior of a BEM airliner?'

He had to smile again. 'That is *Sarotrocercus*, a tiny Burgess Shale arthropod. It swam on its back, and those "airplane seats" are its gill branches, which we suspect it used for swimming. So if you are amused by legs used for breathing, now you can be further amused by gills used for swimming. These creatures had their own ways. But if you want to see real novelty, let me show you some of the others.' He sorted through the pictures. 'Here is *Wiwaxia*. What does it look like to you?'

'A spiked barbarian helmet,' she replied promptly.

'And here is *Anomalocaris*, a huge Cambrian predator, over a foot long.' He paused, but Colene did not laugh; she knew that these creatures were small. 'It probably swam in the fashion of a manta ray, undulating through the water, a fearsome sight. Note the vicious feeding appendages, and the circular mouth orifice. It probably acted like a nut-cracker, crushing the bodies of its prey.'

Colene was getting into it again. 'That's related to the lobsters?'

'Not at all. It's no arthropod; it's in a phylum of its own. Nothing like it exists today. One of the abiding curiosities of the panorama of life shown by the Burgess Shale is that the most successful creatures of that time disappeared without trace, while comparatively minor lines like the chordates survived to prosper. The chordates, of course, were the ones who later gave rise to the fishes, amphibians, reptiles, birds, and mammals. So the mystery is not so much what caused the extinctions — meteor strikes and global changes of weather can account for them — but why certain obscure species survived. I have pondered that often.'

Colene hadn't thought of it that way. 'You mean it wasn't survival of the fittest? I mean, mammals made it through because they're better adapted than the reptiles, even the big dinosaurs, being warm-blooded and all. It wasn't that way back in the Cambrian?'

'It wasn't that way with the dinosaurs either,' he said. 'They may have been warm-bodied too, and there is every indication that they would have carried on to this day if it hadn't been for a stroke of bad luck. The climate was changing, true, and species of reptiles were declining − but other species were maintaining their vigor. When the meteor came, it was their ill fortune to be large.'

'Huh?' He had caught her by surprise. He was fairly good at that, which she liked.

'We have analyzed it every which way, and the main thing the survivors had in common, through the several extinctions, was their size. They were small. Perhaps they were able to hide in crevices, whether of the land or the sea, until the horror faded. But the big creatures could not hide, so they died. It may indeed be that simple.'

'Gee. Then if there's another extinction, wiping us out, maybe the roaches will survive to rule the earth.'

'That,' he said seriously, 'is no joke. They are even resistant to radiation, and highly adaptable to changing conditions, whether physical or chemical. The roaches are survivors.'

'Let's look at more pictures,' Colene said wryly.

'Are you trying to distract me from the job at hand?' he asked, with mock severity.

'You don't think I could actually be interested?'

He shook his head. 'I always hope a student will be eager for knowledge. I am usually disappointed. Certainly you are interested in something, but I'm not sure it's Cambrian fauna.'

Ouch! 'Do I get a bonus grade for good work here?'

'Colene, you are already making A's.'

'Well, I do have a couple of things I want to know. But I don't know if I want to ask them.'

'Such as whether I really grade classroom legs?'

She paused, astonished. He knew about that story? 'That, too,' she agreed.

'Will you promise not to tell?'

She crossed her forearms against her chest in a cute little girl gesture. 'Cross my heart.'

'I do appreciate what is shown, but I don't grade by it. I never forget that I am a happily married man and that these are adolescents. I am just as glad I'm not teaching at the twelfth-grade level, however.'

He had given her a straight answer! He had admitted that he noticed. 'I wish I hadn't promised,' she said, making a lugubrious face.

'I was glad to see that you are more sensible,' he said. 'You are properly dressed, and you are working well. It's a real pleasure to have a bright student volunteer. If it is information you wish, I shall be happy to answer your questions to the best of my ability.'

There was her opening. But to ask, she would have to reveal her secret concerns, and she wasn't sure she was ready.

Amos did not push her. That was one of the nice things about him. He was generally willing to live and let live. He displayed another picture. 'What does this resemble?'

'A daisy on a Q-Tip?'

'Or a goblet on a thin stem. An inch long, in all. It is *Dinomischus*, a creature of another bygone phylum. See those two holes in the center of what you think of as the flower? Those are its mouth and anus.'

'Side by side!' she exclaimed, wrinkling her nose. 'I'd hate to share its meals.'

'And here is the prize: the strangest creature of all. *Hallucigenia*.'

'You're kidding! Nothing's called that! Scientists are too stodgy.'

'Not always. This has seven pairs of stilt legs, and seven wormlike tentacles on top with tiny pincers. With what may be a bulbous head at one end, and a hollow tail at the other. How do you suppose it foraged?'

Colene squinted at it. 'This is a phylum all to itself?'

'Surely so.'

'So there's no guarantee that it operates any way close to the way we think it should?'

'None.'

'I don't see how it could walk very well. No joints. It sure wouldn't move very fast. And what would the tentacles catch, slow-motion?' She pondered. 'You know, this thing just doesn't make a lot of sense to me, as a stand-alone creature. Could it be maybe part of some other creature, and the head's not a head but the stump where it broke off?'

'Beautiful!' Amos exclaimed. He put his arm around her shoulders, hugging her. 'In one brilliant intuitive flash you have caught up with contemporary conjecture! That's exactly what has been speculated.'

'Gee,' she said, pleased.

Then he froze, realizing what he had done. He had touched a student! He quickly dropped his arm. 'Oh, I'm sorry. I —'

'That's all right,' she said. 'I've got a crush on you anyway.' How delightfully similar that was to her fantasy!

'Oh, no! That was why you volunteered to work?'

'That, too,' she agreed, grinning. 'May I tell?'

He realized that he had not transgressed. She had merely scored a point. 'What, and ruin my reputation?'

She grew bold. 'Aw, they wouldn't believe me anyway. Will you touch me again if I promise not to tell?'

'Absolutely not.'

He was back in Teacher Mode. 'Then I guess we'd better get the rest of the work done.'

They resumed the cleanup. But there was now a certain camaraderie between them. Colene had indeed gotten part of what she wanted: closeness and recognition. She found herself humming 'To Know Him Is to Love Him.'

'What did you come here for, Colene?' he asked after a moment.

'Will you promise not to tell?'

He imitated her prior gesture, crossing his forearms over his chest. 'Cross my sternum.'

'No, I mean really. No private reports, no nothing to nobody. No quiet activity for my own good. You just pretend you never heard it at all.'

He gave her an appraising glance. 'It's that serious?'

'Maybe.'

'I confess you have aroused my curiosity. I undertake to maintain complete confidence.'

That was adult for a promise of silence. He was a teacher, but she decided to trust him, this far. 'I have two questions, but maybe they'll get me in trouble.'

'As I said, I will answer to the best of my ability.'

'The first question is whether hypnotism would help me forget something I want to forget.'

'That perhaps depends on what you want to forget.' He paused, but she did not fill in the information. 'Hypnotism resembles a state of intense concentration; in fact the brain waves of the two states may be indistinguishable. So my guess is that if it is anything of consequence, if concentration won't do it, neither will hypnotism. Also, you might have to tell the hypnotist what it was you wanted to forget.'

'Scratch that, then. My second question is, what is the safest, cleanest, pleasantest way to die?'

He canted his head. 'You are serious?'

'Yeah. Remember, you won't tell.'

'I already regret that commitment. But before I answer, I must know one thing: are you thinking of someone else's death or your own?'

'Oh, I'm no killer!' she protested. 'And not even suicidal, really, maybe. I just want to know, in case.'

'If I told you how to take your life, and you did it, I would not only be deeply disturbed by your loss, I would be accessory to the crime.'

He had a point. 'Well, could you maybe just sort of point me in the direction of where I could find the answer, without anyone knowing?'

'I'm not sure. Colene, you're a bright, seemingly well balanced, and I must say pretty girl. If anything – ' He paused again, but again she stonewalled it, making no response. 'I might just mention that there's a book in my desk, titled *Final Exit*, published by an organization called the Hemlock Society. You know the significance of hemlock?'

'It's what they made that Greek philosopher drink.'

'Socrates. I believe that book is buried under some papers, and it would be a while before I missed it, if someone borrowed it. However, if anyone were to see a girl like you reading a book like that – '

'Discretion can be my middle name, when I choose.'

They continued working, drawing near the end of the job. Amos, perhaps trying to restore some semblance of normalcy, resumed his discussion of paleontology. 'The reclassification of the creatures found in the Burgess Shale forced a reinterpretation of evolutionary theory itself. Originally discovered by Charles Walcott, perhaps the greatest paleontologist of his day, they were considered to be an oddity. He more or less shoehorned them into familiar classifications. This was because the standard model of evolution described early creatures as few and primitive, becoming more varied and complex as time progressed. Thus the greatest diversity and complexity of life should be today, with all prior ages less so. But there is more fundamental diversity of life forms in the Burgess Shale than in all the seas today – and we don't even know what creatures weren't recorded there. We conjecture that most of the creatures lived in shallow water at the base of a sea cliff, in the accumulated mud and sand there. Then that material abruptly slid off a lower cliff and sank into much deeper water, where there was no oxygen. That killed the creatures, and preserved them flattened but almost intact, their soft parts fossilized. It was a bad break for them, but a great break for us, because otherwise we would not have known that most of them existed. But they were from the earliest time of multi-cellular life, and therefore were supposed to be primitive. In fact they are extremely diversified and sophisticated. When these fossils were reclassified and correctly placed, it became apparent that they simply did not fit the standard pattern.' He paused. 'I don't mean to lecture. Stop me, if —'

'No, I'm interested,' Colene said. 'Now.' And she was, because the weird creatures had captured her fancy. She wanted to know more about them, and their significance. They were coming alive for her, in their fashion, there in that ancient mud.

'We now conclude that evolution, instead of being a constantly expanding cone of diversity and complexity, is actually a process of explosive radiation and subsequent winnowing out. That is, a great many types of creatures appear early, trying every ecological niche, and then competition eliminates many of them, leaving relatively few major trunks. These may in turn radiate and be winnowed. But the most surprising and uncomfortable message of the Burgess Shale is that this winnowing process appears to be largely random. The fittest, by any measure we conceive, do *not* necessarily prevail. The most successful creatures of the Cambrian period did not survive, while some of the least promising endured to form the greatest arrays of creatures in ensuing eras. How can we account for this? Only by saying either that we hardly understand the true criteria for long-term survival, or that they were lucky.'

'Lucky!'

He nodded. 'It is true. We can not claim that mankind

is the absolute summit of an inevitable evolution. Our dominance may have been the result of pure chance. The large extinctions, especially — our ancestors may just have happened to be in a spot that was shielded from the worst of the effects, so scraped through while less lucky species took the fatal brunt. If it were to be run through again, the chances are that our kind would never have arisen. It's a humbling thought: that chance, more than anything else, accounts for us.'

That was an awesome thought. 'Pure chance — and I might never have existed.'

'As we now see it. Some scientists object, of course. But the evidence of the Burgess Shale is persuasive.'

Colene thought about it: how she might so readily never have existed. The notion had tremendous appeal — and was simultaneously frightening. Was there after all any point at all to living?

Suddenly all her swirling thoughts, past and present, coalesced into unbearable grief. She burst into tears.

In a moment she found herself sitting in Amos' office chair, and he was handing her tissues from a box so that she could mop her face. 'I'm s-sorry,' she said, trying to get control. 'It's nothing you did, Mr Forell. I just — I don't know.'

'Call me Amos,' he said. 'And don't tell.'

She had to laugh through her tears. 'Thanks, Amos. It's just that nonexistence — it gets to me.'

'So I gather. Colene, it is evident that you have more on your mind than incidental chores. I have promised not to betray your secret, whatever it may be. I am beginning to suspect what it is, but I would rather have you tell me.'

'I was raped!' she blurted out. 'I was such a fool! I went on a date with this high school boy, and I was sort of flattered he had asked me, and he took me to an apartment, and there were three others, and I had a drink, and then another, and I don't know how many, and then — it disgusts

61

me, so, but I can't ever quite wash it out, and I don't know what to do.' She mopped her face again.

'When?' he asked, and indeed he seemed unsurprised.

'Last Christmas. Three months ago. I guess I really asked for it, because –'

'Who?'

She snapped to. 'I can't tell you that, Amos! 'Cause I know you'll have to do something, and you promised –'

'I promised,' he agreed tightly. 'I'm sorry I did, but I did. Very well, no names. You didn't report it?'

'I didn't know how. Besides, I was so ashamed. I mean, I walked right into it! I should have known –'

'Certainty is easy in retrospect,' he said firmly. 'If we all could see ahead as readily as we do behind, we'd never make any mistakes. Consider yourself foolish if you ever walk into such a situation again. But not for your past judgment. You trusted your date to be honorable, and he betrayed that trust. The fault was his. It is obvious that he set you up for it, by getting you to the apartment, then by plying you with alcohol so as to muddle your judgment and resistance. Even then, he used force. You were the victim of a carefully laid trap. You have grounds for outrage, but not for shame. You didn't ask for it; you were chosen for your naïveté. It happens to young girls, too often. They are even encouraged to blame themselves, as if they have sinned. So that they don't report it.'

'You mean – it's a regular thing? It happens to other girls?'

'It does. Because they are what they are: inexperienced and trusting. I suspect that some of your classmates have suffered similarly. I see the signs in them. But I must say you fooled me; I never suspected. You have remarkable poise in adversity, Colene.'

'Gee.' She was really flattered by his compliment.

'So if you don't want to turn them in, that's your decision. I won't push you, on that; it's not an easy route. But don't blame yourself to the point of becoming suicidal, when you were guilty only of innocence. I can't tell you to feel good about it, but you have to understand that you were the victim, not the perpetrator, and that it is wrong to blame yourself.'

'You mean it?' It had never occurred to her that she might *not* be guilty.

'I mean it. Do what you must, but don't accept the blame.'

'Gee,' she said again, feeling a deep relief. Then she lurched up and planted a kiss on his mouth.

She sank back onto the chair. Then she realized that he hadn't dodged back, as he could have. He had accepted the kiss, pretending to be caught by surprise.

He winked. 'Promise not to tell.'

'Promise,' she agreed.

They closed up the lab, and he took her home. She felt a whole lot better. Only as she watched his car drive away did she realize that she had forgotten to borrow the death-book. But perhaps it didn't matter. She no longer wanted to die.

Amos didn't tell, and neither did Colene. They treated each other with almost complete indifference in class, both knowing how to keep a secret. She made an A in science the next semester, but knew she had earned it. Her crush faded, but she retained considerable respect for the man. He was a straight player.

Her suicideal inclination had been beaten back, but as her crush departed, her depression returned. She started scratching her wrists and watching the blood flow. So she hadn't really accomplished anything by her encounter with Amos, but she didn't regret it. As far as she knew, no student had ever kissed him. She probably held the record, as far as making an impression on him went. She liked him, and knew he liked her, and perhaps that was the thing that kept the balance slightly to the side of life instead of death.

In such manner she had come to appreciate the significance of the Burgess Shale — and now she was extremely glad of it. Because it enabled her to understand the nature of this new anchor reality they were in. *Thank you, Amos*, she thought.

When she was fourteen, at the depth of her depression, Darius had come from his other reality, looking for a woman to love and marry. That had been Colene's salvation, because there was nothing left for her in her own reality of contemporary Earth. Indeed, it turned out that he had come because she was one of the few people who could be taken from her reality without affecting it — because she was going to die soon anyway. She had loved him instantly, seeing in him a man like Amos, only more so, and he had loved her — until he learned that she was not only underage by the standard of her culture, she was depressive. He needed a woman of age and full of joy. She had also doubted him, thinking that he was imagining his fabulous magical home reality. So they had parted — and realized that it was too late. All either wanted was the other.

So Darius had tried to repair things the hard way: by setting up a Virtual Mode, where there were no restrictions on what could be done in another reality. But the Virtual Mode was not a direct connection between their two worlds; it was a reality in itself, set as it were crosswise to the layered other realities. It was anchored in five realities, to keep it stable as a four-dimensional temporary entity. Darius had to walk across it to reach Colene's anchor reality, crossing other realities at intervals of ten feet, and everything could change with every invisible boundary. He had a long trek to undertake.

Colene, discovering the Virtual Mode from her own anchor, had set out to join him. She had found the traveling rife with danger. But she had also found Seqiro, the telepathic horse, who sought adventure and a girl to love. Colene loved horses. It was a match made in heaven — or the Virtual Mode.

But when the two had finally met, they were trapped in one of the other anchor realities: the DoOon Mode, where the Emperor Ddwng had sought to use them to enter the Virtual Mode and conquer the other realities. They had barely escaped, and found themselves in the Julia Mode, with Nona as the new anchor person. Nona was everything that Colene wished to be: lovely, nice, full-breasted, magical, and Of Age. Both Darius and Seqiro liked her. So now Colene wanted to get man and horse rapidly across the Virtual Mode to Darius' home reality, before either changed his mind about Colene.

'And that is where we stand at the moment,' Colene concluded. 'We'll be happy to take you along, Burgess. We'd be on our way right now, if that damned mind predator hadn't zeroed in on me and forced me to get off the Virtual Mode. But it should lose interest in a few days, and then we'll resume our trek. We're ordinary folk, like you, just with different bodies and metabolism. By the time we get back on the Virtual Mode, we should know each other well enough to be a decent team, so we can handle whatever other surprises it has for us. I think we'll get along just fine. Just don't try to charm my horse and my man from me.'

Then, as an afterthought to Nona: 'No offense, damsel.' Because Colene liked Nona too, and knew the woman did not wish to be the threat she was to Colene's future.

# 4

## Anomaly

Nona was amazed. She had had no idea that Colene had such a history. No wonder the girl had such a complex array of traits. Even in the ambience of mind-sharing that Seqiro the horse provided, so much was omitted, because it didn't come to the surface. For example, this was the first time that Colene had spoken directly of her introduction to Darius and Seqiro.

Colene was indeed depressive, and she tended to see and express things with almost painful candor. Though she addressed Nona as if she were a rival for the love of horse and man, it had been Colene herself who had asked Nona to join them on the Virtual Mode, instead of vacating her anchor and remaining in her Julia Mode. And Colene was not an inferior person. She thought her age to be a liability, but that was only in one particular culture, and in any event she would outgrow it, inevitably, in time. She thought her appearance was modest, when she was actually a lovely young woman. She thought she wasn't nice, when in fact she had qualities Nona envied, such as intelligence, courage, and generosity. She thought she was in danger of losing the love of Darius to Nona, but Nona had no wish for that sort of relationship with a man. In fact, she had come on the Virtual Mode to escape the need to settle down, marry, have babies, and lose her magic in her home Mode. Nona wanted adventure, and when they reached Darius' Mode, Nona hoped to remain on the Virtual Mode and continue exploring other realities. She hoped Colene would come to believe that.

By now dawn was showing, and they had to start moving. They didn't want to sit and wait for another monstrous crab to attack. They had to get to some place that was secure from predators, so they could sleep without having crabs move in.

They consulted with Burgess, with whom Colene had established the best rapport. Increasingly the creature's thoughts were becoming part of the mind net made by Seqiro. Burgess was alien, but he seemed to really want to communicate, which helped. He normally belonged to a hive of his kind, and needed constant interaction. Now he wanted to interact with them, and this was his right, because he was this reality's anchor creature. Nona had so recently become part of the Virtual Mode that she appreciated its novelty and promise, and understood why any creature would desire it. She also understood the appeal of joined minds; insecurity faded and confidence increased, because of the constant support by the others. Five minds were much stronger than one.

Burgess did not think linearly, but in three-dimensional bursts of information. He was learning to squeeze it into the form they could comprehend, but Colene still had to translate. Thus his input seemed like Colene's thoughts, and there was a slight delay while she organized it. In time that would change, and he would communicate directly, but it was all right for the interim.

'We have to stay in the wilderness,' Burgess (Colene) said (thought). 'Because the floaters of my hive mean to kill me, and will kill you too, now that you have associated with me. They govern the plain by day.'

Because he had contacted the poisoned hive, and then not joined it. They thought of him as a traitor they could not trust. Nona wasn't yet clear on this attitude, but it probably made sense in terms of their values.

'We have already experienced their hostility,' Darius said. 'Fortunately we can throw rocks farther than they can.'

'But we'll have to pass through their lines,' Colene said for herself; there was a different inflection to her thought, and of course she was also speaking verbally now.

'They'll be massed and ready for us, and we'll have to go well within their range. That's no good; just that blowing sand could blind us.'

Nona agreed. She never wanted to get into one of those sandblasts again. There was nothing like that on her home world. But of course this was a different world, in a different reality, where there was no magic. She was constantly running afoul of that, expecting to shape things by magic, or to fly from one place to another, or to transform things into the materials or food she needed. She felt rather helpless, here, and looked forward to their return to the Virtual Mode, where her magic worked.

But the mind predator had attacked Colene, forcing them to flee the Virtual Mode. Colene had mentioned the predator before, because it had attacked her friend Provos when the two traveled the Virtual Mode. Now Provos had returned to her own reality, and severed her anchor, so was permanently beyond its reach. So it was coming after Colene instead. Colene belived that it would give up after a while as it had with Provos, but this was not certain. So they had reason to stay off the Virtual Mode for a few days, and then to hope that the predator was gone.

Unfortunately the big crab was still lurking; its hungry malevolence was a constant presence, because Seqiro remained attuned to it, and the rest of them could pick up that tuning. Worse, the horse was growing mentally tired, because he had been awake a long time and the continuous broadcasting of the fear was draining him. As his power weakened, the crab was losing its fear and moving closer. In time that defense would be gone.

So they decided to travel deeper into the wilderness, until the hivers lost interest. They would wait out the hivers the same way as they waited out the mind predator. They hoped to find a place where they could finally relax, where there was food and water, so that they wouldn't have to use their carried supplies. It was always best to eat at the anchors,

Nona understood, because what they ate that came from any of the worlds of the Virtual Mode would not remain with them. They had to eat only on an anchor world, or food carried from an anchor world.

But forging a level path for Burgess to float along was bound to be tedious and slow, if they had to go any distance. It would have been easier if Nona's magic worked in this reality , but her ability to relate to a creature as a familiar was diminished, and none of the rest of her magic seemed to work at all. She felt helpless.

Then she saw something scuttle across the remains of the dirt barrier they had made. It was a multi-legged bug, with long antennae trailing to the sides. It was small enough to hold in one hand, but moved very quickly.

She had an idea. 'Seqiro, stun me this creature,' she said.

The horse oriented his powerful thought on the creature, for just a moment, and the bug stopped where it was, stunned. Seqiro had not been able to relate well to Burgess at first, but had done better as he tuned in, and now contact was good, if Colene was there to interpret. This bug had a much smaller mind, and was easier for the horse to overwhelm. As he learned to relate to the minds of Burgess and the crab, he learned to relate to all the minds of this reality, to a degree.

Nona nerved herself, and picked the thing up. It had four bony extensions extending back from its head that shielded its body; it was by this armor she handled it. She set it in her other hand and held it close to her face. It seemed to have about twenty-five pairs of legs, the largest to the front, diminishing to tiny at the rear. Each leg had six jointed segments. There turned out to be four antennae: two were very long and smooth and flexible, while the other two were shorter and furry. Between the legs and the bony shield projections were weblike lines . What could they be?

Well, perhaps she could find out. She focused her mind, reaching into the mind of the bug and seeking to tame it.

She hoped to make it a familiar. It was working; that part of her magic was working. She had doubted, when facing the challenge of trying to relate to Burgess, but with this smaller-minded creature she was having no more difficulty than she would have at home with an ordinary bug.

Colene came over to see what she was doing. 'Oooh, ugh!' she said. 'You're holding a fat six-inch-long centipede!'

'I'm taming it,' Nona explained. 'It moves very quickly. Perhaps it can explore the way for us, and warn us of danger ahead.'

'Good idea,' Colene agreed. She bent to look more closely. 'Say – that's biramous! See, each segment has a pair of legs and a pair of gills. In fact – in fact it's *Marrella!* Or his distant descendant, adapted to land. I'll never forget that arthropod, after that session with Amos.'

'Gills?' Darius asked, getting interested. 'Do they work in air?'

Colene returned to the floater and touched a contact point. Burgess' thought came: 'The creatures with external gills do use them in air. My gills are protected under my canopy, drawing nourishment from the air with which I float. *Marrella* does not float, but does use its gills to breathe and to enhance its travel.'

Nona remembered the discussion of uniramous, biramous, and triramous. 'It travels with its gills?'

'It moves them to enhance the take-up of what you call –' Burgess hesitated, then continued when another mind supplied the concept. 'Oxygen. When it is in a hurry, this movement of the gills also enables it to be lighter and faster on its feet. It can not float in the manner I do, but perhaps some millions of years hence it will evolve to that degree.'

'Gills becoming wings,' Colene murmured, intrigued. 'I guess it wasn't just the triramous line that survived, here; Mary Marrella didn't leave any descendants in my world.'

Nona set Marrella down. 'It is my familiar now,' she said. 'It will be my antenna, and show me the best route.'

70

'That would be good, if I could conjure us to the safe spots it locates,' Darius said. 'As we did in Julia, your reality. But I can not, here in Shale.'

'And it would be nice if I could fly, here,' Nona agreed. 'But my magic is almost as diminished as yours.'

'Sometimes I feel lucky I don't have magic,' Colene said. 'At least Seqiro's talent is full-strength, here, so we can coordinate.'

'Yes,' Nona agreed. 'Seqiro helped me get Marrella.' She glanced down. 'Go, friend. Spy the way.'

Marrella shot off into the forest, its legs moving at blurring velocity, its gills buzzing. It scooted over the dirt, stirring up a little cloud, and under twigs and leaves. Its body armor knocked obstructions out of its way.

It was not fleeing. It was moving under Nona's direction. It was her familiar, and its senses served her mind. It had no eyes or ears, but its antennae picked up the vibrations in the air, and the smells. This provided it with an excellent awareness of its surroundings, which Nona tried to translate into a mental picture. But the needs of Marrella and the needs of the party did not match, and the picture was so foggy as to be useless.

'Maybe if Seqiro routed Mary's impressions through to Burgess, he could shape them up for us better,' Colene suggested. 'Because he understands this world.'

Seqiro connected Marrella's awareness to Burgess' mind, via Colene's. Burgess had both hearing and sight, so understood the need. He translated the foggy sound/smell picture into a clearer sight picture for them all.

Now Darius and Colene saw the scene as Nona saw it. The ground was passing rapidly under the fifty-two little feet, and the various smaller bugs, worms, and roots that Marrella fed on were all around. None of the predators Marrella feared were close, because Marrella was staying well out of their way. There was a gentle wind, bringing news of the plants and animals upwind, shaping a picture of some depth.

There was a thick tangle of vegetation near the party, but the giant crab had forged a partial channel through it. Beyond was an aisle formed by a huge tree which had crashed down and rolled to the side. Beyond that was deeper forest where the undergrowth was slight. And beyond that was water.

'I think we've found a way through,' Colene said. 'We just have to get Burgess to that aisle, and he'll be fine.'

Darius looked at the crab's trail. 'This is good enough for us to use, but it would take a lot of work to make it level enough for Burgess.'

'Why make it level? Just carry him over.'

Darius considered. 'Pick him up? He must weigh four hundred pounds!' He used Colene's system of weights.

'You take one end, Nona and I take the other, and he lightens himself as much as he can with his air cushion. It'll work, for a few feet. Seqiro can strengthen us for the occasion, too.'

Burgess was alarmed. 'Lift me? This has never been done.'

'You never became an anchor for a Virtual Mode before, either,' she reminded him. 'You can keep your canopy stiff enough to bear your weight?'

'I do this whenever I settle on the ground. My canopy is formed of what in earlier creatures were legs, with my gills now under my body and my contact points above. But I have always lifted myself on air.'

'Except that you can't rise more than maybe an inch,' Colene said. 'We can heave you up maybe three feet, to get you over that brush and root tangle. Once you're over, you'll be on level ground again.'

Nona felt Burgess' doubt. She searched for a suitable analogy, and found it: she would have similar doubt if alien creatures proposed to carry her by her breasts and knees.

Colene laughed. 'Well, you have better handles than I do!' she said. Then she had to pause to explain that to Burgess. 'We girls don't like to have our breasts touched, unless we

72

decide it's okay. Or even other parts of our bodies. But men keep trying to do it. It's a bad scene.'

Burgess concluded that the aliens understood his situation. He agreed to be carried.

They rehearsed it with a heavy branch, tramping along the ragged path to the aisle beyond. They set the branch carefully down. Everything seemed to be in order.

They approached Burgess. Darius put his hands on two of the floater's front canopy-scales, and Colene and Nona did the same with rear scales. They were bone-hard and smooth, easy enough to grip. But could Darius actually heave up two hundred pounds, and each woman one hundred?

Then strength surged through Nona's body. She heaved, and the body came up. The three of them were perfectly coordinated. They marched in step along the path, then set Burgess down in the aisle.

Nona's surge of strength left her as she let go. 'What happened?' she asked, amazed.

'Seqiro governed us,' Colene said. 'He can make a person very fast and strong, for a while, and he made us all act in synchromesh. It's part of his telepathy. He's used to managing our kind.'

'Then next time we have to fight off any predators, he must do it again,' Nona said, impressed.

'Say! Good idea.'

But something huge loomed ahead of them now. 'The crab's back!' Darius cried.

Indeed it was. The thing looked worse by daylight than it had at night. It had fresh scars and a missing antenna, but its huge claw remained devastatingly functional.

'Because poor Seqiro can't fend it off when he has to concentrate on stunning Mary, or rerouting Mary's impressions through Burgess, or giving us temporary strength,' Colene said. 'Gee, I'm sorry, horsehead; I just tend to think of you as all-powerful.'

*For you, I try*, Seqiro answered her in pure thought. *But I am near the end of my resource.*

Colene looked at the crab barring their way. 'Well, we've just got to help you out. Darius, can you advance threateningly on the thing, while Seqiro gives it a little bit of fear? Maybe the combination will make it think it's more afraid than it is, and it'll back off again.'

Darius took his axe and strode forward. 'Hoo-hah!' he yelled loudly. At that moment Seqiro sent a terrible jolt of fear that made Nona wince, until she realized that it was actually Darius' yell that accounted for much of the effect.

The crab scuttled back, and in a moment was gone. They heard the noises of its retreat. The ploy had been effective.

'Now ease up, Seqiro,' Colene said. 'Conserve your strength. It should be a while before the stupid thing realizes that it's not scared any more.'

Nona knew that she herself would not have thought of that device to spare the horse. She envied Colene's practical sense.

Colene glanced at her. 'I'd trade you for some of your measurements.'

'You would be foolish to do so, and you aren't foolish.' Then they both laughed.

Now they were on their way. Burgess pumped up his air and floated along the aisle, and the others followed. Soon they were in the deeper forest, and had no further difficulty.

Marrella was waiting at the bank of the lake, hiding under some brush. Nona would never have been able to find it, if she had not had mental contact.

The lake itself was wide. It extended to the sides, Burgess indicated, until it intersected the plains where the hivers lurked, effectively isolating this section of the wilderness. Burgess knew that the greatest part of the wilderness lay beyond the lake; they could traverse much of the continent without leaving it. The crabs were not there, as far as Burgess knew; apparently they preferred the isolated niches. He

74

floated out on the water, dipping his intake trunk for a drink.

But how were they to cross the lake? They could swim, but it was a fair distance, and Nona hesitated to trust unknown water. Something else bothered her, and she chased it down, in case it was important. Then she had it: 'The floaters,' she said. 'Why aren't they on the water, cutting us off?'

That triggered a memory in Burgess. 'The water predator! We can not cross that water.'

Colene focused on him. 'We *have* to cross, Burgess. Because Seqiro can't stay awake forever, fending off the crab. What's with this predator, that the whole hive stays off this water?'

Burges made a picture of a huge, flat swimming creature with tentacles in front, eyes on the sides, and a circular mouth below. 'That's *Anomalocaris!*' Colene exclaimed. 'What's *it* doing here in the present?'

'The same thing *Marrella* is,' Nona said.

Colene nodded. 'So several of those early lines carried through, instead of just one. Of course they really aren't the same as the Cambrian creatures, any more than we're the same as the first chordate. But we can see the family affinities. I'll just bet we don't want to meet up with a modern Anomaly the size of a horse. No offense, Seqiro.'

'We don't want to swim here, certainly,' Darius said. 'But if we try to go around the lake, we'll have to cross a section of the plain. Perhaps if we wait until night —'

'We'll have to rest and sleep before then,' Colene said. 'Seqiro can't go forever on alert. He feels more crabs lurking already.'

'Suppose we build a raft?' Nona asked. 'If we make it solid enough, it should be proof against attack from the water. Perhaps, also, Seqiro will be able to send fear to the water predator.'

'Worth a try,' Colene agreed. 'I'm tired, and I guess everyone else is too, but maybe we can drag stuff out from the forest and lash together a raft.'

Darius lifted a hand in a no-way gesture. 'A raft sufficient to support a horse? That's an all-day project at least. Ask Seqiro how he'd like to stand on vine-lashed logs, too. What's good enough footing for a human being may not do at all for hooves.'

Colene didn't need to; the horse was already sending a strong disaster signal. 'But then what can we make?' Colene asked. 'There must be something. Something simple, easy, fast, and strong, I hope.' But her accompanying mood was depressive; she knew there was nothing like that available.

There was a stirring in the forest behind them. There was the crab again. 'Okay, all together, now,' Colene said. 'On three. One – two – THREE!'

Darius and Nona joined her in the shout, while Burgess fired a stone at the crab. The jolt of fear was weaker this time; Nona realized that Seqiro had not been exaggerating about the exhaustion of his mental resource. He had to get some rest.

The crab retreated again, but not as far as before.

'If only my magic worked, I could make a boat,' Nona said. 'Just by transforming material.'

Colene pounced on that. 'Some of your magic works, Nona! You made a familiar. So maybe some of your other magic works, too. Did you try all of it?'

'Yes. I tried levitation, telekinesis, transformation, shape-changing, and illusion. The illusion was just a bit of fog, with no control. I haven't tried healing, because nobody's been hurt, but –'

Colene held up her left arm. There were scars on her wrist. 'See if you can heal my scars.'

That was a good way to test it, because Nona's magic did work on scars too. She took the girl's arm in her hands and concentrated. She knew right away that it wasn't working, but she kept trying, just in case.

Colene glanced at her wrist. 'No good, huh? Too bad. And that's all your magic?'

'No, it's not,' Darius said. 'You can change the size of things, too. Remember how you expanded the size of that dulcimer?'

'Why so I did!' Nona agreed, remembering. 'That's so recent, I had forgotten.' She paused, realizing how odd that sounded. 'I mean, it's magic I didn't know I had, and so I tend still to think I don't. Let me try.'

She picked up a twig of wood and concentrated. In a moment it expanded. It was working! She continued to focus on it, to be sure that there was no limit to this aspect of her magic, and it became so large she had to set it down. With the magic, its mass increased in proportion to its size. Still it grew, until it was a log, and then a large log, and then a veritable fallen tree trunk.

'You know something,' Colene said. 'That could make a barrier to hold back Crabface, there.'

'But there's plenty of wood here anyway,' Nona said, giving up. The trunk did not shrink; it remained as she had left it.

'Yes, but your talent should work on other things too,' Darius said. 'Such as a model boat.'

Of course! She had overlooked the obvious. Darius was already carving on another piece of wood. He hollowed it out, then flattened the bottom, and thinned the sides. Soon he had a tiny flat-bottomed model boat. 'Is this seaworthy?' he inquired.

Colene laughed. 'Better carve a keel on it. And make oars or paddles, so we can move it across the water. I don't think we're experienced enough to handle a sail. But maybe we should have a net too, so we can dip for fish.'

Darius made the keel adjustment, then carved several tiny paddles and poles. He set them in the boat.

Nona dug out her handkerchief. 'This will make a net, when expanded.' She cut out a tiny swatch of the material, and set it in the boat with the other artifacts.

Then she took the model and set it at the edge of the water. She concentrated on expanding it, and it started to grow. Soon it was large enough for one person to get into, so she shoved it further into the water. When it was full size, it might be too heavy for them to move, and she didn't want to have to shrink it again so they could launch it. How fortunate that this one other aspect of her magic worked, here.

But she did wonder about that. In the Julia Mode there was a current of power which the magic drew, because no person could provide the enormous energy needed to do something like this. Was there a similar power current here in Shale? Though the creatures here did not seem to have magic of their own? If so, why was it available for only two of her several types of magic? That seemed to suggest that there was some other factor operating.

'Don't look a gift horse in the mouth,' Colene said, responding to that thought. Then, again: 'No offense, Seqiro.' She seemed to like teasing the horse, and the horse liked her teasing; Nona could feel the currents of good feeling passing between them. Seqiro shared his mind with everyone, but Colene was his truest friend.

'There are sources of power in my reality, too,' Darius said. 'And some of my magic worked in Julia, and some did not. The same was true in the DoOon Mode. There must be natural power flowing through these realities, or perhaps some trace coming through the anchors, so that parts of our magic are operative. If we understood more about the Virtual Mode, we might be able to predict how our abilities would be affected.'

'Yes, Seqiro's telepathy seems to work everywhere,' Colene said. 'But it was diminished in Julia. Meanwhile I started to get a little bit of telepathy, maybe, in DoOon, and more in Julia, so maybe a Mode can enable a person to have power or magic she doesn't have at home. Maybe the magic current in Julia is polarized, so it works only one way or the other, while in the other Modes it's natural, so it's not as strong for Nona but more general.' She looked at the boat, which was now huge. 'Anyway, I'm glad Nona hung on to that type of magic, because it sure makes it easier to cross this lake.'

The crab was approaching again. 'Look out, Seqiro!' Nona cried, for the horse was closest to the crab and facing away.

'Say,' Colene said. 'You're mentally tired, Seqiro, but not physically tired, right? Suppose you kick the crab in the snoot?'

*Tell me when*, the horse replied.

They watched as the crab came up behind Seqiro, lifting its huge claw to clamp on the horse's rear. The claw seemed almost as big as the horse, but this was deceptive, because it was narrow in cross section.

'Now!' Colene cried/thought.

Seqiro kicked hard with both hind feet. One hoof struck the side of the claw, knocking it away and perhaps cracking it. The crab scuttled back again.

'All *right!*' Colene exclaimed happily. 'That'll give it something to think about for a while.'

Meanwhile, the boat continued to grow. At last it was large enough for everything. In fact, Nona was concerned that they would not be able to move its mass across the water. She consulted, then reversed her concentration and made it slightly smaller.

Darius stepped aboard first. He picked up a paddle. 'Ooof!' he exclaimed.

No wonder! The paddle was monstrous. They would not be able to use such tools effectively; each one would weigh more than the person wielding it. Darius, working with a tiny model, had misjudged the scale.

'I can fix it,' Nona said. She stepped onto the boat, put her hand on the huge paddle, and concentrated. It diminished, until it was of about the right size. She did the same with the other paddles, and with the poles. She saw that at this scale they were crudely carved, as was the boat; the magnification exaggerated everything. But everything was serviceable, which was what counted. Except for the swatch of handkerchief cloth, which was now like a net fashioned of ropes. It wouldn't be much good for catching fish.

Colene led Seqiro onto the boat. Nona was surprised by that, but Colene's thought clarified it: the horse was attuned to their minds, but tricky things like stepping over the gunwale onto a shifting deck could be troublesome. So Colene led him, guiding him, so that her senses rather than his prevailed, and he handled it without stumbling.

Then it was Burgess' turn. He floated across the water to the side of the boat; then Darius got out and stood in the shallow water to lift one side, while Nona and Colene reached over the gunwale. Seqiro took over their minds, and with great strength and perfect coordination they heaved Burgess over and onto the deck. Burgess pumped air as they let him go, and floated to the rear center of the craft.

Now Darius and Nona poled off, and the boat slid into deeper water and floated. 'Uh-oh,' Colene said.

Nona looked. Crevices that had been invisible in the model now showed clearly; they too had been magnified in proportion. Water was leaking in to flow across the bottom between the horse and the floater.

'What we need is a bilge bucket,' Darius said.

Nona set down her pole and fetched a cup from a pack Seqiro carried. She magnified this until it was the size of a pail. Colene took it and began dipping and tossing. The leakage was not extreme, and she was able to keep up well enough.

As they got into deeper water, Darius took up a paddle,

and Nona took another. They stood at opposite sides of the clumsy craft and stroked the water. Slowly the boat moved forward.

'Well, we're on our way,' Colene said. She glanced at Nona. 'What happened to Mary?'

'Oh, Marrella? I let it go. It wouldn't be happy across the water. Perhaps I can tame a new familiar on the other side.'

As they got toward the center, their boat's motion became imperceptible, but they kept paddling. Unless there were an adverse current, they were surely forging toward the other shore.

She looked back. There where they had been was the huge crab. Seqiro had stopped sending it the fear, and it had evidently discovered that they had been mostly bluffing it, so it had come after them immediately. But it was a land crab, and could not pursue them in the lake.

*Predatory presence.* That was Seqiro's thought, which Nona preferred to hear as speech though it really wasn't. There were aspects of danger, concern, warning, and mystery: something large and menacing.

'The big crab?' Colene asked.

'No. In the water.'

Then Nona saw it. A huge flat thing was gliding close. An eye on the head part gazed at them. She and Darius ceased paddling.

The *Anomalocaris.* That was Burgess' thought. The creature did not know what the boat was, Burgess concluded.

'Well, let's hope Anomaly doesn't find out,' Colene said, pausing in her bilge bailing.

Nona stared at the thing. The eye stared back at her. 'Do you think our paddling will disturb it?' she asked.

'If we don't paddle, we won't get across,' Darius said. He put his paddle back in the water.

Reluctantly, Nona did the same. The end of her paddle

81

was close to the glistening hide of the creature. She moved the paddle through the water, stirring up a ripple.

The creature oriented on the paddle. Suddenly a nose-tentacle hooked on to the paddle, wrenching it out of Nona's hands. The end of it disappeared under the Anomaly, and there was a crunching sound. Then fragments of the paddle floated up around the head.

Darius studied the situation. 'I think we aren't going to get far, poking at this thing. But if it won't let us paddle, how are we going to get on across the lake?'

It would be best not to provoke it. That was Burgess again. It preyed on anything in or on the water. It was once a bottom feeder, but it had adapted to consume surface creatures too. Burgess thought it could not harm this craft, but it could surely harm the living creatures.

Darius considered further. 'Nona, can you grow something big enough to block it off from us, so we can paddle?'

Nona reached over the gunwale and caught a floating chip from her former paddle. She concentrated, and it grew.

But the lake monster didn't wait. It shoved its nose up over the gunwale. The two tentacles cast across the deck. Each was segmented, with a spine projecting from each segment. It was evident that these tentacles didn't grasp, they stuck, holding the prey with many hooked barbs.

'Get to the far side,' Darius said tersely. Nona retreated, with Colene, standing next to Seqiro and Burgess.

Darius fetched his axe. He was a handsome man as he stood there facing the monster, in his green tunic from the Julia Mode, and boots she had made magically for him before they set out on the Virtual Mode. He was, in the fashion of men, determined to defend the women and animals against the common threat. There was something almost quaint about it.

'You bet,' Colene murmured.

Animals? That was Burgess.

'Companions,' Nona said quickly.

Nona continued to make the wood chip grow. But she wasnt sure how to use it to block off the Anomaly, now that the creature was hooking on to the boat. Maybe try to get the monster back into the water, and then try to keep the block floating between it and the boat?

Darius stepped toward the Anomaly, eyeing its head. But the creature was eyeing him back. 'Oh, I don't like this,' Colene murmured. 'That's no lunatic monster; it's *aware*.'

Darius decided that the eyes would be the best targets. He swung the axe. But as he did so, the Anomaly moved its head lower, using the leverage of the mass of its body, and depressed the entire end of the boat so that water slopped over the gunwale.

Darius, caught by surprise in midswing, missed. Then the force of the missed swing pulled him off balance, and his feet slipped as water sloshed over the rim. He fell on his back. Nona screamed. Her block of wood was now so big that she was holding it against her chest with both arms, but she still didn't know what to do with it. She felt supremely ineffective, in the midst of an ongoing disaster.

The Anomaly followed up its opportunity instantly. A tentacle slapped across Darius' left boot. It didn't coil; the spines dug into the mock leather and held it firmly. Then it curled in toward the head, pulling Darius with it.

Darius sat up and swung his axe at the head. But the tentacle jerked, making him miss again, and in any event he lacked leverage to make an effective strike.

Now Nona saw the monster's mouth. It was circular, with bony plates that overlapped around the center hole. Where were the teeth?

'Pull your foot out of the boot!' Colene shouted to Darius. 'Get away from that thing!'

Darius, startled by the obvious, braced his right boot against the tentacle and shoved. His left foot came out of the boot. He tried to scramble away, crablike, but was jammed against the gunwale behind him. He couldn't retreat further, and couldn't move to the side without risking getting snagged by a tentacle again.

The tentacle drew the boot to the mouth. The mouth irised open. The teeth showed at last: circular rows of them behind the plates. The tentacle fed the toe of the boot into the hole. The plates shifted, and the orifice became smaller. The toe of the boot was constricted.

The orifice opened again. The toe of the boot was gone. The teeth must have chewed it off while the nutcracker mouth held it.

Nona started, horrified, not knowing what to do.

'You block off its eye with the wood,' Colene told her. 'I'll get the axe.' Then, to Seqiro: 'You make us fast and accurate, when.'

Numbly, Nona did as she was told. The Anomaly terrified her, and she felt naked without the main part of her magic, but she knew that something had to be done. She walked forward into the water by the monster's head.

The tentacle threw the rest of the boot to the side. Evidently the Anomaly had concluded that it wasn't edible. The two tentacles quivered, ready to snag something else. Darius was still stuck against the gunwale, holding the axe defensively.

Then the horse's mind took over. Nona leaped to the side of the head and jammed her block of wood right up against the eye, blinding the monster on this side. Meanwhile Colene swooped down to take the axe from Darius' hands. She set herself before the irising mouth and swung the axe with savage force at the base of one of the tentacles.

But the Anomaly, with uncanny prescience, flinched away, and the axe struck the impervious plates of the mouth. The tentacles whipped around and caught the head of the axe. It was clear that Darius had not been clumsy; the Anomaly had been apt.

Then the power left Nona. *I am sorry*, Seqiro's thought

came. *I have no more strength*. After that the ambience of his telepathy also faded.

Colene muttered something, but it was unintelligible. The horse was no longer translating.

A hand fell on Nona's shoulder. She jumped, but it was Darius, who was now back on his feet. He held a knife. He pointed to the block of wood.

'The eye!' Colene said. 'Stab the eye!'

The girl's own telepathy was coming into play! Nona lowered the block, and Darius lunged over it, thrusting the knife at the eye.

And yet again the Anomaly reacted too swiftly for them. It pulled back, sliding into the water. They had repelled it – but the boat was sloshing with water, and riding low.

Colene fetched her bucket and started bailing. Nona looked around for another bucket, but there was none.

Then Burgess floated back. He dipped his intrunk in the water, pointed his outtrunk, and started pumping. The water streamed out.

Colene stopped and watched. So did the others. This was far more efficient than any effort they could make. Soon the boat was almost dry again, and riding high.

But the Anomaly was circling them. It had tried a direct frontal attack and been beaten off, so it was now more cautious, but it had not yet decided that they were not prey. This was a creature like the huge crab, with hardly more than one thing on its mind: hunger. They had barely stopped it, and they remained far from the shore. What should they do?

Nona looked at Colene. Colene looked at Darius. Nona knew what the girl was thinking: she wanted Darius to be the leader, though Colene herself, with her limited power of telepathy, was the most likely leader. Nona had seen Colene in action in her own reality of Julia, and knew that the girl was a natural fighter in her fashion. But she loved Darius, so wanted him to lead.

Darius seemed to come to the same conclusion. But it was evident that he had little notion how to proceed. He had tried to brace the monster, and Colene had had to spring to his rescue. He evidently did not feel much like a hero.

Then he got an idea. He pointed to Burgess, who was finishing up the bailout, leaving the deck clear. Burgess knew more about Anomaly than they did; he might have advice.

Colene nodded. Darius had made the decision; now she could act. She went to Burgess and put a hand on one of his contact points. Nona could not overhear their dialogue, but knew that Colene's limited telepathy was getting through.

Unfortunately, the news seemed to be bad: Burgess had no experience fighting the Anomaly, and none in boats. All he knew was that the Anomaly would make short work of Burgess himself, if he tried to float out across the water. Nona could see that those mouth tentacles could hook on to the floater's canopy, disrupting the flow of air, and quickly swamp him; then it would be easy to grind him up piecemeal.

Then something occurred to Nona. When she flew — Colene called it levitation — she moved across the land by magically moving some fixed object — Colene called it telekinesis. Since the object could not move, Nona did; thus she came toward or away from it, or passed beside it, using its resistance to propel herself. The process was automatic, and she seldom analyzed it. But now she realized that when she did this, she was applying what Colene called a scientific rule of action and reaction. When Nona pulled, either the object came to her or she came to it. That was true whether she pulled magically or physically. So suppose that were done here: would a person be pulled or pushed the same way?

She went to her block of wood, which now lay at the end of the boat. She picked it up and heaved it away from her. She almost fell over. It did seem to push her the other way!

Darius looked at her, curious about what she was doing. Nona couldn't explain to him, with the language barrier, so she went to Colene. She took the girl's free hand. 'Reaction', she said, focusing the thought.

'Yes,' Colene replied, understanding the concept. 'So what?'

'Burgess – throw water – reaction – move boat.' It was hard to convey her concept, because it was new to her.

'Yes!' Colene cried, suddenly understanding. 'Burgess – when you fire things out your trunk, you get pushed back, right? So push us with water!' She made a mental picture.

Burgess floated to the back of the boat. He dipped his intrink in the water, and fired a jet from his outtrunk. The boat began to move, turning slowly around.

Colene grabbed the remaining paddle. She dragged it in the water behind the boat, and it served to steady the craft, so that instead of turning it moved forward. They were traveling toward the far shore again.

The Anomaly realized this. It swam close – and Darius drove the end of the long pole at its eye. He missed, but the monster sheered away.

Nona found a splinter of wood and concentrated on expanding it. They could have another pole, in case Anomaly crunched the existing one.

Anomaly was not so dull as to miss the implication: the prey was escaping! It circled the boat more swiftly, agitated. Then it moved away, turned, and came rapidly straight toward them.

Nona screamed warning. The monster was going to swamp them! Then it could consume what it wanted, as they floundered in the water.

There was no time to act, even if any of them had known what to do. Helplessly they watched Anomaly come at them, broadside. The creature lifted its head – then launched into the air.

Nona threw herself flat, trying to avoid being struck. The dark shape hurtled just above her.

There was a splash. Nona looked up. The Anomaly was swimming away on the other side. It had passed right over the boat!

She realized that it had misjudged, because of the boat's low profile. It had intended to sweep one or more of them into the water, or to land across the boat and swamp it, but all the other people had been at the ends of the boat. Seqiro and Darius were at the front, Burgess and Colene at the back. But if the monster tried again, at one of the ends, it would catch one or more of them.

Colene pulled in her paddle and hurried to join Nona. They clasped hands. 'Grow. Boat. Fast.'

What did the girl have in mind? Nona didn't argue. She put her hands on the gunwale and concentrated with all her might. She could make the boat grow, but it would not affect the people on it, because her power did not extend to living things.

Meanwhile Colene went on to Darius and told him something, making gestures to augment her limited telepathy. She gave him the paddle. The two of them grabbed the net grown from the swatch of handkerchief and spread it out across the empty center of the boat. Then she ran back to rejoin Burgess. Nona's wonder grew; this just did not seem to make much sense as a defensive measure.

The Anomaly was circling again, assessing the situation. Then it made another pass, this time not quite as swiftly. It intended to leap and catch one end of the boat or the other, and make a meal of the creatures there. Nona was expanding the boat, and it was already significantly larger than before, but the monster would still be able to clear it.

Darius took the paddle and stroked vigorously in the water. The boat began to turn, not getting anywhere but changing its orientation.

Burgess aimed his trunk to the side. This caused the boat

88

to turn faster, being pushed from each end. But it remained right in the path of the monster. Had they gotten confused, so that instead of the paddler balancing the floater to propel the craft forward, they merely spun it around?

The Anomaly launched into the air just as the rear of the boat was swinging toward it. This caused it to miss the end and land at an angle in the center. The shock was violent; the entire body of the monster was on the boat. But the boat was half again as large as it had been, and remained firm.

Then Darius and Colene ran in from opposite sides, picking up the ends of the net. They charged the Anomaly with seeming fearlessness. This was crazy!

They met, putting their ends of the net together over the body of the monster. They quickly knotted these, and stepped back.

At last Nona saw what they had done. They had trapped the Anomaly! The creature was now on the enlarged boat, trussed in the net. It was unable to return to the water, because it was not equipped to crawl on land. It couldn't pull itself along with its mouth tentacles, because they too were wrapped. It was, in effect, a fish out of water.

Nona stopped expanding the boat. She started contracting it, so they could move it more rapidly. They had defeated the monster, and had only to move along to the far shore. Thanks to Colene's brilliance.

Nona really was jealous of the girl's intelligence. She would have to tell Colene, knowing how pleased she would be to hear it.

# 5

## *Hallucigen*

Darius was glad to reach the shore. The crab had been bad, but the Anomaly had been worse. He preferred to have his feet on the ground, so that he could at least fight or flee in good order. He had hardly covered himself in glory on the boat!

The boat scraped against the shallow water at the edge, and wedged in place. Now the humans and the horse could get out — but what of Burgess? They had lifted him in, but the special strength and coordination had been provided by Seqiro, who had governed their minds. Now the horse's mind was exhausted, so they couldn't do that. Seqiro, resting as they forged slowly on across the lake, had recovered enough to link them telepathically, but that was all. Probably the telepathy extended only in the small space they occupied, being at low ebb.

'Will we need this boat again?' he inquired, looking around.

Nona shrugged. Colene, as usual, made the decision: 'No. We're getting well away from here.'

'Then we can destroy it.' He took the axe and started chopping at the gunwale, after Colene had led Seqiro to the shore.

'Hey, what are you doing?' Colene cried. 'It's a nice boat!'

'I am making it possible for Burgess to float his own way out,' he replied.

She was quiet, recognizing the sense of it. Before long he had two cuts through the gunwale, and was able to bash out the intervening section. Burgess floated through and onto the water without difficulty.

'What about Anomaly?' Nona asked.

'Say, yes,' Colene agreed. 'We can't just let it die like that.'

So Darius cut the strands of the net, and pulled it clear, freeing the monster. In a moment Anomaly used its tentacles to haul its head over the remaining gunwale. Then it gave a great heave and splashed into the water. It swam away. Darius wouldn't have cared to say so, but he was just as glad; the thing had been a terror, but he had no stomach for killing a creature already rendered helpless.

'I guess it'll know not to bother us again,' Colene said, almost wistfully.

'We should move on into the forest,' Darius said. 'But if there are no crabs here —'

'Yeah, we're all so tired,' Colene agreed. 'Say! Suppose we made a fire? Most wild creatures are afraid of fire, aren't they? Maybe we'd be safe beside it.'

Darius considered that notion, and liked it. He brought out one of the magic firesticks he had gotten from Colene.

'Uh, wait, Darius,' Colene said. 'Those matches don't set fire to just anything. You have to have dry tinder. Anyway, we shouldn't waste them, because we don't know when we'll ever get more. We should save them for real emergencies.'

Darius, about to protest that he did know about tinder, stifled it, realizing that she had a point. One of those matches had enabled him to escape captivity in a foreign Mode, and might be needed for that again. 'How can we make fire?'

That stopped them. There were supposed to be ways, but none of them seemed to be proficient in such techniques. Colene sent out a mental picture of rubbing two sticks together, but without much hope. Probably early man got fire by saving it from a natural blaze started by a lightning strike.

And there was an idea: once they had a fire, they should

save it. Except that they weren't quite sure how to do that, either. If they had the right ceramic container for a firepot, and the right slow-burning material, and could stop it from smoking too badly —

'Maybe Nona can make fire magically,' Colene suggested wryly.

Nona shook her head. 'This was beyond the power of the despots of my Mode,' she said. 'They could make the illusion of fire, as could we all, and could transform materials, so that it looked as if they had been burned, but —'

'So that's what the Knave did, when he was trying to rape me!' Colene said indignantly. 'He made it seem as if my clothing was burning off, but there was no heat. He must have transformed my clothing to dust, with the illusion of flames.'

'Yes. I believe that much of despot magic was actually the appearance of other magic. So my own powers must be similarly limited.'

'How can you be sure?' Colene asked.

Nona paused. 'I suppose I could try it. My other magical powers manifested over time, surprising me. There might be another one forming. But even so, it might not work in this other reality.'

'Try it,' Colene said. 'Just focus on something flammable, and try to light it.'

Nona looked around, evidently somewhat at a loss. Darius saw the chopped remnant of their boat. 'Try that,' he suggested, pointing. 'It's wood.'

'Yeah, try that,' Colene agreed, smiling.

Nona squinted at the boat. Suddenly there was a fireball, and sparks flew out. In a moment Darius saw that the boat had become a bonfire.

He looked at Nona, who stood openmouthed. 'I was joking,' he said, after forcing his own mouth closed.

'So was I,' Colene said.

'I – I knew that,' Nona said. 'I didn't think – the dry tinder – big wet boat – I just made a huge and futile effort, only –'

'Only it wasn't futile,' Colene finished. 'You figured that even if you could do the magic, it would be just a little-bitty spark.'

'Yes.'

They stood and watched the boat burning, awed.

'I hope you never get angry at me,' Darius murmured.

'Oh, I would never –' Nona said, horrified.

'He's teasing you,' Colene said. 'But I guess we don't have to worry about carrying fire.' She turned to Nona. 'But maybe you should see if you can tone it down a little, because if we needed a candle lit, and you made a fireball –'

Darius had to laugh. But Colene was right; Nona's magical pyrotechnics could be dangerous. He gathered some sticks, chips, and dry grass, fashioned a small setting, and showed it to Nona.

Nona squinted. Nothing happened. Then, after a moment, there was a faint curl of smoke. Then a little flame appeared. She had it under control.

'So we'll sleep right here,' Colene decided. Then she did a double take. 'Hey! We're communicating again! Seqiro's recovered.'

'In a small radius,' Darius said. 'He still lacks the strength for more than that.'

Colene went over to hug the horse. 'Don't strain yourself, hoof-foot,' she said. 'We can get along without you for a while.' Then she said something else, but it was indecipherable: the horse had taken her at her word, and was resting.

They foraged for fruits and nuts, which were plentiful, and leveled a section of the shore so that Burgess could move comfortably. Nona got a long branch and used it to knock down more fruits, which she offered to Burgess and Seqiro. Darius dug a shallow trench around their camping site, and piled branches in it for Nona to ignite, once they settled down for the night. With this ring of fire, they should not need much else for protection. Nevertheless he intended to keep watch, if no one else did. The business of the crab had satisfied him that this world was not to be trusted.

When night came, the others did sleep, using a tent made from material Nona expanded for the purpose: more handkerchief laced with leaves. But later Colene roused herself, came to him, kissed him, and indicated their tent: it was his turn to sleep. He knew she would stay alert, because she understood the danger as well as he did. He went to the tent and flopped down gratefully beside Nona.

He woke later, to find the figure touching him. In fact, she was kissing him. What was this? 'No, Nona!' he protested.

He was answered by a laugh. Then he realized that it was Colene, who had finished her turn and taken Nona's place in the tent. Embarrassed, he gave her arm a squeeze, and returned to sleep.

But later yet he discovered himself between two human figures. Both women were there. Then who was keeping watch? Alarmed, he crawled out — and saw Burgess floating along his path. The floater was taking his turn.

When dawn came, Burgess had settled back, air quiescent, eye stalks retracted. But Seqiro was pacing the region. *My fatigue of the mind has recovered*, he thought to Darius.

That was good. They were now reasonably rested, and back to strength, and could continue. As he understood it, they would have to survive in this Mode for several days, to give the mind predator time to forget about Colene. Then they would have to return to the anchor point and cross. With fortune, the hive floaters would also have forgotten about them by then.

Meanwhile, during their enforced stay in this Mode they had gotten to know Burgess, and Nona had discovered a new ability, fire. They could have gotten by without it, because of the matches, but what she could do was better and could well be useful in an emergency. Since the Virtual Mode could be dangerous, this was good.

They foraged for more food and took care of personal incidentals, then got together to decide on their course. Burgess had no idea of the landscape or animal life here; no member of his hive had penetrated even this far, so there was no currency on it.

'Let me get this straight,' Darius said. 'Your kind, the floaters, gather together in tribes called hives, and you constantly exchange information through your contact points, so that every member of the hive knows what every other member does. So if any member of your hive had ever been in this wilderness, and lived to rejoin the hive, you would know it?'

Burgess signaled agreement. With Seqiro back on duty, increasingly able to fathom Burgess' thoughts, there was hardly any confusion now. The floaters were creatures of currency: they had a need always to be current on hive knowledge, and suffered if they lost currency. That was why Burgess had invoked the Virtual Mode. He had to find another hive with which to be current. They were the weirdest kind of hive he could have imagined, had he been a creature of imagination, but he could relate.

'So no other floaters will follow us here, but you have no good information for us,' Darius concluded.

That was true. Since Burgess could travel here only with difficulty, he was a liability to the party.

'That's not true,' Colene said. 'Burgess knows a lot about this world. We aren't going to be in the wilderness forever, and the moment we get out of it, he's going to know what we need to know. We're not dumping him.'

'That was not the nature of my thought,' Darius said hastily. 'If Burgess doesn't know anything about the inner wilderness, then neither do any of the hivers. They won't know whether we're alive or dead, or deep inside or just at the edge of the region. So we don't have to go far. In fact, we don't have to go anywhere, now that we've found a relatively safe spot to camp, here.'

'Hey, that's right!' Colene agreed. 'We can dig in and be comfortable.'

Nona was gazing at the sky. 'Do you know the flying creatures, Burgess?' she asked.

Burgess oriented his eyes. Yes. Those were predatory creatures that needed to be fended off. He floated to a sandy patch and lowered his intrunk, ready to send a blast of sand up.

'They look like birds, from here,' Colene remarked.

They were not birds. Burgess had no concept of birds, because they were vertebrates, none of which existed here. Neither were these insects. They were of another phylum. They were dangerous, and it would be necessary for the others to hide from them.

'From little birds?' Colene asked incredulously.

But the growing picture Burgess was sending made her turn quickly serious. The most descriptive term was shears: they had mouths which sliced or cut the flesh of their prey, swiftly. They tended to attack in swarms, so that it was hard to defend against them all, and flesh was usually lost.

'We had better stop them from touching us,' Darius said, as the swarm of shears loomed closer. 'Nona, if you can grow some shield material –'

Nona caught up a chip of wood and started expanding it. Darius himself went for his sword, then reconsidered; against a flying swarm it would be almost ineffective. Instead he donned heavy gloves, and Colene did the same. Then they put on heavy jackets from their supplies, and took one to Nona.

The shears did not give them much time. Several of the creatures swooped down, making a peculiar buzzing sound. 'What kind of wings do they have?' Colene demanded.

Burgess provided a picture: two paddlelike projections, which angled into the air, moving in opposite directions. They were like propellers, except that each had only one extension, sweeping in almost a full circle clockwise, then counterclockwise, so swiftly that the pair of them blurred into fuzziness.

One came straight at Darius. He batted it away with one fist — and felt a flare of pain. His glove had a gash, and blood was welling from the side of his hand. The creature itself spun to the side and then zoomed on away.

Another came at Seqiro. It smacked into the frame of Colene's bicycle, which was one of the many things tied to the horse's harness, and dropped to the ground, stunned.

The third went for Burgess — who fired a small rock at it, and a blast of sand. The rock missed, but the sand bathed it, and the shear fled.

Colene pounced on the fallen creature, pinning it to the ground with a forked stick. Now they could see it clearly. The shear was about the size of a robin, but there the resemblance ended. It had small overlapping scales which flared at the back to serve as a rudder, the two propeller-paddles toward the front, and a head consisting of several recessed, armored eyes and the scissor beak. Each blade of that beak was knife-sharp, and stout muscles around it suggested the power of its shearing action. Taken as a whole, it was an odd and ugly thing.

But more were coming. 'Shield me, Nona!' Colene cried, still pinning the fallen creature. Nona brought her expanded chip and held it before the two of them.

Darius, seeing that his hand injury wasn't serious, still recognized that gloves alone were not sufficient. But he lacked a shield. So he scrambled for stones and sand, scraping them into the range of Burgess' trunk. 'I'll try to keep you supplied; you shoot them down,' he told the floater.

This time a larger swarm of shears came down. Several banged off Nona's growing shield and spun away. Several more tried for Seqiro, and there was a mental flash of pain as one scored on the horse's flank. But at the moment Darius had to focus on the ones coming at Burgess and himself.

There were about five of them, each a buzzing blip coming rapidly closer. Their motions were erratic, as their alternate paddle strokes jerked them around in an irregular spiral flight pattern. That made them almost impossible to shoot down at a distance. But a scattershot approach might do it. 'Sand,' he told Burgess, touching a contact point. 'Fire a wall of sand at them.' He concentrated his scooping on that, getting just as much sand into the floater as he could.

Burgess obliged. He blew out a spreading jet of sand, moving it around so that a fair-sized region between them and the shears became a cloud of it. The shears sheered away from it, perhaps having had prior experience with this tactic. Probably it was what a defensive contingent of hivers used. There was security in number, certainly!

But then they veered back in, from the sides. Darius grabbed at the bodies, trying to catch them from behind, but his reactions were too slow. Then he got smart and grabbed at where they were heading, which was Burgess' eye stalks. This time he managed to catch one. He threw it down and stamped on it as he grabbed for another.

Then the swarm was gone, and the party was left to tend its injuries. Darius went to see what he could do for Seqiro and himself. The horse's gouge was painful but not serious, as was his own; salve and bandages helped both.

Meanwhile Colene and Nona were busy. 'Here's your next familiar,' Colene said. 'Tame it, and we'll have a flying spy.'

'That's wonderful!' Nona agreed.

But more clouds of shears were appearing in the distance.

'This place is too exposed,' Darius said. 'We have to get some natural cover.'

Colene looked up, seeing the threat. 'That's for sure! At least we can get in among the trees.'

Hurriedly they extended Burgess' path so that it went into the forest. They found a place under a spreading tree, so that there was a network of branches and leaves walling off the sky. The trunk served as a backstop, so that they could cluster around it, having only one direction to defend. Darius took the wood shield Nona had grown; Nona was busy taming the shear, which she now held in her hand. It no longer looked so ugly, now that it was going to be their ally.

The shears did attack again, but now they had to come in along Burgess' path, and Burgess was able to shoot them down with stones. They couldn't stray from that narrow way without running afoul of the tree branches. Soon they gave it up.

'I guess now we know why we can't camp on the shore,' Colene said regretfully. 'If we try to hide from the shears in the water, Anomaly will get us, and if we don't, we'll get sliced up.'

'They do not like the forest,' Nona agreed. 'I am receiving that from this one's mind.'

'Oops — does that mean it won't fly for you in the forest?' Colene asked.

'No, as my familiar it will do what I wish, and feel no fear. But when I release it, it will flee the forest.'

'Then let's have it explore nearby, so we can find the best place for our camp.'

Soon Nona did just that. The shear flew up from her hand and navigated between the trunks of the trees, flying low. Then it angled up into the sky, so that it could see over the forest.

The creature's impressions came to Nona, because of her magic, and Nona's impressions came to the rest of them, because of Seqiro's telepathy. Thus Darius was able to close his eyes and see the world through the beady eyes of the shear. It was an interesting experience.

He (Darius) seemed to be flying just over the trees, feeling the comforting beat of his props. He saw the region where the lake cut through the forest, and the region where a slope led up to a higher level. He followed that slope, and saw that above it was a mesa: a flat and almost treeless expanse, covered by short grass.

'Say, I think that's our camping site!' Colene exclaimed. 'If the shears don't go there.'

'They don't,' Nona agreed. 'Because there's no game there. At least, not now.'

Nona focused, and the others did with her. A picture of something huge and serpentine formed. But it was not a serpent. It was something that slid across the plain and ate the grass. It was armored on top, so that the shears were unable to cut much flesh. Once the grass was gone, the grazer slid off the mesa and moved to another mesa. In the course of a season the grass grew back, and then a grazer would come again. Part of this Darius worked out for himself, as the shear did not think in this manner. It merely had an impression of the big grazer, and of absence of grass.

'That should be a pretty safe place,' Colene said. 'And ideal for Burgess, because it's flat and firm.'

'But there's nothing to eat there,' Darius pointed out. 'Nothing to drink.'

'Nona can magnify a fruit, and a cup of water.'

They hadn't occurred to him. 'You can do this, Nona?'

'I suppose I can,' Nona agreed, surprised. 'I would not try it with living things, but perhaps a fruit would work.'

'So all we have to do is get up there. That's apt to be a problem for Burgess, because he doesn't float well on a tilt.'

Darius considered the practical aspects. The mesa did seem to be a good place. How could they make a path

Burgess could travel, if it had to be almost level? Then he had a better notion. 'A sledge,' he said. 'Seqiro could haul a sledge with Burgess on it.'

'Say, yes!' Colene agreed so enthusiastically that Darius had a suspicion that she had planted that notion in his mind. She seemed to want him to be the leader, and when he faltered, she nudged him with ideas. He wasn't sure how he felt about that, but this was not the time to protest.

They went to work making the sledge. This was easier than it might have been; Darius simply carved Nona's shield chip of wood into a platform with two runners below and a surrounding ridge above, and then she expanded it magically until it was large enough to support Burgess. Meanwhile Colene explored to find the best route for the sledge, accompanied by Seqiro, who kept a mental lookout for any possible predators. There were, indeed, no big crabs here, which was a relief. In due course they had a route marked to the slope; that was about as far as seemed feasible for this day.

They dug a shallow pit into the slope, and shored that with branches to make their shelter. They made a fire, and arranged it to burn low in a shallow ditch half circling the shelter, so that it would protect Burgess and Seqiro too. They found a fruit, and Nona magnified it so that it would serve them all for the evening meal. But that wasn't successful: the fruit expanded its fibers and cells too, so that it resembled a magnified image, and did not taste good. With wood it didn't matter, because they didn't care if it became coarser, so long as it was solid and strong. With metal it didn't matter, for the same reason. But with food it did. They had encountered a limit to Nona's magic. So they had to borrow from their carried supplies, this once. However, Seqiro found that he could tolerate his grain expanded to double size, and that did seem to be nutritive, so at least the magic could extend that type of food. Burgess, also, was relatively adaptable; since he sucked in and ground up his food anyway, a coarseness was not much of a problem. So he consumed the expanded fruit. Also, the shear was not choosy, and would eat fruit as well as a blob of expanded blood Nona made from the sodden bandage she changed on Seqiro. The shear, now tame, was satisfied to clamp its beak on the pole supporting the top of the tent and hang there, sleeping; it needed no feet. That was just as well, since it had none.

Again they took turns walking guard. Darius was first. He made sure the fire was continuous, if low; the smoke helped drive off the nocturnal bugs. He fashioned a route that passed the dug-in tent, Seqiro asleep on his feet, and Burgess settled on the ground at the end of his path. There was a slight susurration from Burgess; he still pumped air, in order to breathe with his nether gills, but not enough to make him float. His eye stalks were retracted, but the light-sensitive patches around his rim remained open. Darius was surprised at how readily he had come to accept the alien structure of the floater as routine. Probably it was because of the connection between minds. That was not operative now, because Seqiro was asleep, but in the day Burgess' mind was part of their network.

Actually the floater's mind was being defined in terms of the human mind, in much the way as was the horse's mind, because Burgess did not have intelligence of his own. He had tremendous storage capacity, remembering virtually all his own experience and that of all other floaters in the hive, but he did not normally reason things out for himself. When a human mind reasoned something out, while being connected to Burgess' mind, then it seemed as if the floater were thinking similarly, but that was illusion. That made Burgess more compatible than he might have been otherwise, because though his nature was alien, his thought patterns were becoming human, learned from the human minds. It was like one of the computers in Colene's thoughts: programmable.

Colene — and there was another matter to be thought out, now that the others were sleep and his thoughts were private. He loved her, foolishly perhaps, but firmly. He wanted to marry her, and could not. Because she was a creature of depression, while he required a creature of joy. This had to do with the nature of his duty as Cyng of Hlahtar, in his home Mode. He had to draw from his wife all the joy she possessed, and multiply it, and send it out to all those in the vicinity. That spread joy to everyone, and made life worthwhile despite its often menial nature. His wife, too, would get her joy back — but it was never quite as much as it had been at the start. So with each repetition, at each new community, her joy was further depleted, until it was too low to be of value. Then he had to divorce her and marry another woman, so as to start the process over. For this reason, the Cyngs of Hlahtar seldom married for love. Instead they married for joy, in an unromantic sense: the joy they took from their wives. They seldom bothered to have sex with their wives; that was reserved for their romantic interests, their bed maidens.

Darius had hoped to merge marriage and love by finding a maiden he could love who was filled with joy. So much joy that he could never deplete it. This was not a matter of feeling good, but of having a certain indefatigable power of joy. This simply would not work, with Colene; he could draw only dolor from her. The irony was that in the course of his quest for Colene, he had found a woman who would make the ideal wife. That was Prima, whose powers of multiplication of emotion were equivalent to his own. He could marry her, and draw from her without ever depleting her. She was a generation older than he, and not physically attractive to him, but that didn't matter. If he went the normal course, and married her for her power of joy.

The trouble was that he wanted to marry Colene. This was a foolish desire, and he knew it, but that was the way it was. He could love her, but he couldn't marry her. She understood this, and accepted it, now. But he didn't.

A further irony was that she was too young for sex, according to the dictate of her culture. So the other part of his potential relationship with her was in a null state, too. He could neither marry her nor take her for a mistress. Yet he loved her.

When their journey was complete, and they reached his home Mode, what would happen? He would have to marry Prima, but who would he have in his bed? Colene was fiercely jealous of any sexual expression he might have with any woman other than herself. This put him in an awkward position, since the standards of his own culture differed. He wanted her to be happy, but she would not be even remotely happy if she were neither his wife nor his mistress.

It seemed to be an insoluble problem. Maybe they would be better off if they did not reach his home Mode soon. Yet that, too, was problematical. He wasn't sure how long he could resist her blandishments. She wanted to seduce him, and her attempts were both subtle and unsubtle, and the plain fact was that he found her little body enormously appealing. She thought that her lack of breasts the size of Nona's made her inferior, but the truth was that he liked women whatever way they came, and could derive as much pleasure from a slender one as from a voluptuous one. Attitude really made a greater difference than body, and Colene's attitude was the height and depth of intrigue. So it was not safe for him to remain with her too long in the present manner. They had to complete their journey and get off the Virtual Mode.

Darius paused. Had he heard something? There did not seem to be anything in the forest; their smoldering fire seemed to be an effective deterrent. It probably wouldn't stop a big crab, but that wasn't the problem. Suppose something came that wasn't afraid of fire?

104

Yet the sound didn't seem to be from the depths of the forest. It seemed to be close, within the fire enclosure. It was also too faint to hear. Was it merely the embers settling?

Darius got down and put his ear to the ground. Now he heard it more clearly: *click-click, click-click*. From within the ground. What could it be?

He scuffed the dirt with a foot, making a shallow excavation. He uncovered something. He took a stick, touched it to the nearest fire, and brought the crude torch across to illuminate the spot.

Now he saw thin projections rising from the scraped earth. He relaxed, relieved. Worms! These were little worms coming up to forage at night. They clicked as they moved. Did they have jointed shells?

He reached down to touch one. But as his hand approached the worm, it whipped to the side, its pointed end stabbing into his finger. Pain flared.

He jerked his hand away. But now the worm came with it, the head still burrowing into his finger. He had to grab its body with his other hand and yank it out — and that hurt again, because its head was barbed. The thing was a bloodsucker!

He dropped it on the ground and stomped it. Then he stomped the other heads showing. He put his finger in his mouth, trying to stop the pain, but it kept hurting and bleeding. The little monster must have injected something to stop the blood from coagulating.

Then he realized what this meant to those who were sleeping. The worms would come up under them, burrow through their clothes, and —

He ran for the tent. 'Wake! Wake!' he cried, reaching in to grab an ankle. It turned out to be Nona's; her shapely leg lifted as she sat up. 'Get on your feet,' he said urgently. 'Quickly!'

In a moment both women were standing beside him.

105

'Worms,' he exclaimed. 'Bloodsuckers. Coming up through the ground. One stabbed me on the finger, and it won't stop bleeding.' He showed his finger, which indeed was still leaking blood. He supplemented this with a mental picture of his experience.

Both women were staring blankly at him. Then he realized that the horse remained asleep; there was no translation. Colene could do a little, when she tried, but she wasn't trying at the moment.

Actually Seqiro could be at risk too, and maybe Burgess. He walked to the horse and touched him on the shoulder. 'Wake,' he said. 'We have trouble.'

Then the minds of the others tuned in. Darius quickly rehearsed the matter for them all.

In a moment Colene had a torch and was looking inside the tent. 'Ugh!' she exclaimed. 'They're coming up! Some are already in the bedding.'

'Now we know why other creatures aren't sleeping here,' Nona remarked. 'Those bloodsucker worms must be all through this forest.'

'But they weren't by the shore,' Colene reminded her.

'Maybe there's too much water there,' Darius offered. 'Waterlogged soil drowns them out.' But of course the shears ranged there, by day.

'Will they be able to get through your hooves, Seqiro?' Colene inquired.

*Three are trying, so far without success*, the horse responded.

'What about you, Burgess?' she asked.

Burgess rested on the hard rim of his canopy, with none of his softer parts in contact with the ground; the worms could not get at him.

'And I guess they can't get through our boots, either,' Colene concluded. 'So we're safe as long as we stay on our feet. What delight.'

'We can fashion an elevated bed,' Darius said.

106

'Say, yes! Because by the look of it, the worms can't climb or jump; they just bore up through the sod and into any flesh that's there. So we can balk them. Still, I'd rather be out of here. The forest has too many ugly surprises.'

Darius was in hearty agreement. He had felt safer on the Virtual Mode, despite its myriad traps.

Nona expanded the wooden sledge, until it was large enough for all three of them to lie on. 'You take it now, with Nona,' Colene said to Darius. 'I'm wide awake anyway.'

She kept putting him with Nona. He knew why: because it was Colene's nature to take suicidal risks. He wished he could reverse that, and make her become a vessel of joy. But, with the worst irony yet, he feared she would then lose her fascination for him. He seemed to have as much of a destructive impulse as she did, when he related to her.

He climbed onto the sledge beside Nona and closed his eyes. Nona, appropriately, kept her thoughts blanked. It was an ability she had been practicing. Actually it was one they should all practice because it was better to have control than lack of control. So he concentrated on that. *Nothing against you, Seqiro*, he thought to the horse. *I just want to know how.*

In the morning he found Colene beside him, cuddling close. She was asleep; he could tell, because Nona's awake thoughts came to him, while Colene's were of scattered bits of dreams. Impulsively he lifted his head and kissed her on her sleeping mouth. Somehow they would work things out. They had to.

She woke. 'Hey, did you kiss me?' she demanded.

'I confess I did. I didn't mean to wake you.'

'Can't think of any way I'd rather be waked.' She lifted her head and kissed him back, hard.

They got through their morning routines, and got to work

on the path up the slope. By noon they had something suitable. Then Nona shrank the sledge down to its prior size, and they put Burgess on it. Just to be sure he stayed put, they passed a cord up over his canopy, tying him down.

Darius expected difficulty, but it was surprisingly straight-forward. Seqiro was a very large, powerful horse, eighteen hands, which meant that his shoulder was as high as the top of Darius' head. When he set out to pull, he hauled the sledge and its burden up as if it were inconsequential. Before long they made it to the mesa. Darius hoped this would turn out to be a safe retreat for them.

And so it turned out to be. The predator worms evidently couldn't get through the rock underlying the surface, and there were no creatures there. It was a vacant plain, as if just waiting for them to use it.

Nevertheless, they made a camp resembling a small fort, with an earthen rampart around it, and a fire trench. They dug down deep, looking for worm holes, just to be sure, then set the expanded sledge in place. None of them cared to take any further chances.

Nona expanded some water, and this at least turned out to be potable. Perhaps that was because it lacked any fibrous structure. Obviously the mass of an expanded object increased because it weighed more; it was just that if it had a rigid structure, it maintained it. That suggested that it was the internal structure of food that caused the problem, rather than the substance itself.

Their night was uneventful, though they kept guard as before. There were no worms, no flying predators, and no land-crawling monsters. Nona's tame shear explored the mesa and the slopes around it, spying nothing. They foraged for fruit and nuts by making excursions down the path. They agreed that no one should go below alone, so they went as pairs selected from among Seqiro and the three human folk. Burgess could float freely across the mesa, but could not get off it by himself. Desiring to contribute sufficiently to the hive, he offered to do all of the night guarding, so that the others could sleep. But floaters could not move with confidence in darkness. They solved that problem by making several limited fires ringing the edge of the mesa; when Burgess knew it was level and safe within that broad circle of blazes, he was able to cope. If any monster came up on the mesa, he would be able to see its silhouette against one of the fires.

They remained for several days, getting thoroughly rested. Communication with Burgess improved, until problems were infrequent. Burgess, like Seqiro, required the contact of a human mind, in order to think like a human being. Unlike Seqiro, he also needed to be touched on a contact point, to establish mind contact. The horse and the floater together had no mental rapport; there had to be a human touching Burgess, who then brought the floater into the telepathic environment. Once they had worked out the exact nature of the limits, it became easy enough to maintain contact. Since it was the floater's nature to constantly exchange information with each other person he encountered, for mutual updating, the three humans simply put their hands on his contact points, rather like the custom of shaking hands in Colene's Earth Mode. Sometimes they all joined him, so that there were multiple contacts. It was possible for each of the three humans to communicate with him without Seqiro's telepathy, but this was more limited, and of three different types. Colene did it with her own limited telepathy. Nona did it by relating to him as a familiar. Darius did it by doing a limited drawing and return of joy. Burgess could even serve as a partial mental linkage between humans when the horse was asleep. So their time on the mesa was well spent, in this respect. Now they could relate well to each other, and that could be important when they encountered some problem and had to react swiftly and with co-ordination.

The question was, when should they return to the Virtual Mode? They had no way of telling in advance whether the mind predator remained lurking, but judged that it should have given up by this time. They had less concern about the hivers by the Mode anchor: they did not understand its nature well, and after a few days had stopped watching it. Nona had learned this by sending the shear there to spy. However, the moment their party returned to the main plain and headed for the anchor, the hivers would be alerted and would try to intercept them. This was no good; they didn't need Burgess' warning to advise them that they would get stoned to death in short order.

The answer, they agreed, was to go to the anchor at night, when the hivers would be sleeping within their ramparts. But that had its own problems, because of the terrain and the nocturnal predators. They wouldn't be able to use fire, because that would alert the hivers, who might then come out; Burgess remembered examples of hive action at night, when there was a threat. Floaters did not like to travel at night, but could do so in familiar territory. How, then, could the party make a quiet, safe transit at night?

They held several communal sessions, the three humans holding on to Burgess' contact points while also being in telepathic communication. As a linked group, with some practice, they became a fairly powerful hive mind themselves. They decided on two things: to move by day to the edge of the wilderness closest to the anchor place, so as to have a relatively short journey the rest of the way by night; and to try to capture a night creature for Nona to tame, who could help them see in the darkness. That combination should enable them to reach the anchor safely.

But what night creature could they catch? Burgess had little information on that, because night predators were things of mystery and horror to hivers, to be kept constantly at bay. Some were creatures of the ground, some of water, and some of air. Other predators quickly hauled away the bodies of those brought down by stones, so that there was nothing to examine in the morning. Of one thing Burgess was sure, however: there were quite a number of creatures of the night. More than there were by day, perhaps because the hivers had eliminated most of the serious day predators of the plain. So they would have to have good information before they made that final trek for the anchor.

The trouble was, they couldn't decide the kind of night creature they could catch, because of their ignorance. It was likely to be dangerous to go hunting for one.

Then Colene had one of her bright notions. 'Armor!' she exclaimed. 'We can put on armor, so nothing can get at us. No predators, no sand, no stones. Then we won't have to worry what's out there.'

'Where would we get armor?' Darius inquired, amused.

'We'll make it, silly! Out of wood.'

He shook his head. 'That could be a great deal of work.'

'Not if we do it small, and have Nona expand it to fit.'

He stopped being amused. She was right: they could be armored. If the panels were solid enough, they would be proof against the stones the hivers could hurl.

'In fact,' Nona suggested, 'we might even make an armored wagon, with wheels, for the plain.'

'Wheels!' Colene exclaimed, thrilled. 'Big ones, so it can't get bogged down in the dirt. Seqiro can pull it. He'll have armor too, of course. Then we can travel there by day.'

Burgess demurred. The hivers would not know what was happening, but they could hurl so many rocks and pile so much sand that it would be impossible to get through.

'At night, then,' Colene said. 'An armored wagon at night, to stop the predators without stirring up the hivers.'

They discussed it, and concluded that it was worthwhile. Darius started carving solid wood chips for the protection of arms, legs, and torso, while Colene set about designing panels for a wagon that could be assembled to make a solid container at the edge of the plain. Because they would not be able to fit that wagon through the forest full-sized, and it wouldn't be much use undersized. With panels, they could use the wheels and base of a reduced-size wagon to carry full-sized panels, then have to enlarge only that base when they got there. Efficiency was the keynote; once they started moving, they didn't want to delay.

Nona enlarged Darius' body-armor sections, and he did some additional carving. They used cord enlarged from thread to tie them to his body. When he stood in his full armor, Colene looked at him and laughed. 'You look like the Tin Woodman of Oz!' she exclaimed.

'The what?'

'It's a fantasy story,' she said, making a mental picture. 'Never mind. I guess you're more like a wooden tinman, anyway. I pity the poor monster who tries to eat *you*!'

'I hope to be too tough a morsel for a monster to swallow, in this armor,' he agreed. But he realized that he must look strange indeed. The curved wooden sections covered his calves, his thighs, his torso, his forearms, his upper arms, and projected up behind his head. There were no joints; the sections simply didn't connect directly with each other. But they overlapped enough so that no part of him was badly exposed. The wood was not unduly heavy, but he would be glad when he no longer had to wear such equipment.

They agreed that Darius and Seqiro would have armor, while the others rode in the wagon. Even Burgess, who could travel well on the plain but would be exposed. Also, if he were hidden in the wagon, the hivers might not realize he was there, and wouldn't pay much attention.

Darius carved miniature panels for Seqiro, which Nona expanded. There was a problem, since the horse was already covered with bags and items attached to his harness. They decided to cover every section not already protected to some degree. So Seqiro got neck panels and head protection. He preferred to leave his legs exposed, because armor would interfere with his walking.

Meanwhile Colene completed her wagon design, and demonstrated how the little panels had projections which poked through holes around the edge of the base so that they would be firm. The roof panel had holes which held the upper projections, so that it too was firm. Of course the wagon was larger, now, but the panels would be expanded to fit it, when. The wagon itself had four fairly nice wooden wheels on wooden axles lubricated by grease expanded from a drop they had in the supplies. It was crude, but it should work for the two hours or so required. Colene was pleased with what she called her technology, and Darius was pleased too.

They set a day for their travel, when everything was prepared. They started at dawn, hoping to retrace their path through the forest, cross the river, and get past the crab section without stopping, in one day. After all, the way was familiar, and the path had been prepared. The sledge had become the base for the wagon, but still served to carry Burgess.

They started backwards, because the wagon had no brakes. Seqiro was harnessed to it, and he then backed it over the edge of the mesa and strained to prevent it from drawing him down after it. Darius, in his armor, stood at the horse's head, watching the wagon and track closely, so that the horse could draw both the picture and the best way to react from his mind. Colene and Nona stood at either side of the path, holding poles which they used to block the progress of the wheels. It was a clumsy process, but they were well coordinated by the mental linkage and did manage to get the wagon down the slope without mishap.

Then Darius led Seqiro around a circle they had prepared, and they got moving forward. Their path led between escarpments at the base of the mesa, before bearing away toward the river.

'Okay, we're ready to move,' Colene said. 'But we'd better check for bogies. Anything to worry about, horseface?'

*There is a predator near*, Seqiro thought as he checked for minds. His concentration on the tricky descent had distracted him from this check before.

'Where?' Colene asked.

*On the path ahead.*

'Uh-oh. We'll have to scare it out of there, because we need that path.'

'I will send the shear,' Nona said. The shear launched from her shoulder and flew in its winding way down the path.

Then, abruptly, there was a thought of alarm. It was followed almost immediately by a flare of pain. Then nothing.

'Something killed my familiar!' Nona cried, falling back against a tree. Darius, connected to the shear's mind through her mind and Seqiro's, was already aware of that. Death had come with stunning suddenness.

This was serious. The shear, though tamed, remained a vicious customer when encountering others, and was more than competent to avoid what it couldn't handle. What could have happened?

'I don't like this,' Colene said. 'You have any idea, airfoot?'

Airfoot? But Burgess, like Seqiro, seemed to like her nicknames. However, he had no idea what the shear could have encountered.

'We shall have to go look ourselves,' Nona said.

Darius was already marching ahead, down the path toward the escarpments. He carried a spear and had the axe strapped to his back. He knew that if he had to fight, Seqiro would enable him to do so with devastating efficiency.

As he rounded a turn to where he could see between the escarpments, he spied something odd. It seemed to be a mass of legs and tentacles, unlike anything he had seen on this world before. He tried to form enough of a mental picture so that the others could make sense of it, but there was a patch of vapor in the vicinity that interfered with vision.

Something struck Darius on an armored leg. Before he could react, his leg was yanked out from under him. He was dragged rapidly toward the thing on the path, sliding along his back. The axe was ripped away, and his spear caught against a tree and was yanked from his hand.

Then he was on his back amidst the mass of tentacles, and they were clamping on his armor. He was several feet above the ground. The monster had gotten him!

He struggled, but the tentacles held him down. He couldn't turn his head to see exactly what it was that held him. But it had to be what had killed the shear.

There was a hissing near his feet. Darius strained to peer down and saw a tube there. Vapor was issuing from it. As it spread out to envelop him, he started coughing; it was putrid stuff which stung his eyes and nose.

'Hallucigen!' Colene exclaimed. 'So *that's* how it feeds!'

'Never mind how it feeds!' Darius cried. 'Don't let it catch you!'

'Fire!' Colene exclaimed. 'Fire will stop it! Nona —'

There was a burst of flame nearby, and smoke billowed out. Nona had magically ignited the brush near the monster.

The tentacles quivered. Then the monster moved. It backed away from the fire, carrying Darius above it.

'Hit it again, Nona!'

There was another burst of flame, so close that Darius winced from the heat. This time the tentacles convulsed, letting him go. Darius rolled to the ground, landing among flames. He scrambled up and charged away. His armor had protected him from actually getting burned, but he knew that wouldn't last.

When he was clear, he turned and looked back. Now he

115

saw the monster clearly. It had seven pairs of stiff rodlike legs, and seven tentacles above its long body. Each tentacle had small pincers at the end. Those were what had held him so firmly. But it was the head that appalled him. It had one corrugated snout with hefty toothed pincers at the end that were almost jaws, small eyes circling the snout's base, and a cruel mouth orifice facing back toward the tentacles.

Suddenly the snout lengthened, the pincers shooting outward. They clamped on Colene's pole and jerked it out of her hands.

Now he realized what had happened. Those pincers had shot out and caught his leg. Then that snout-tentacle had contracted and hauled him in, dumping him on the monster's back — where the tentacles had caught him. But why the noxious vapor, and how did the thing eat?

More fire flared. The Hallucigen dropped the pole and backed away again. Then it turned and scrambled fourteen-footedly away.

Colene ran up. 'You okay, manface?'

He embraced her as well as he could, considering his armor. 'Bruised, singed, battered, choked, humiliated, but otherwise satisfactory, girlface,' he said, kissing her.

'Then let's get moving before the Hallucigen decides to come back,' she said, turning businesslike.

They resumed their march. As they moved, they pooled their information, with Nona putting a hand on one of Burgess' contact points so that he could participate. Soon enough they worked out the nature of the thing they had just driven off.

The monster was a long-descended variant of the Cambrian Hallucigen, the creature Colene had thought might be an appendage of a larger creature. It had evolved to come on land, breathe air — Colene had noticed a set of air gills projecting down from the head — and had grown enormously in size. So now it was a monstrous land-predator, as they had discovered. That pincer-snout had

116

snapped the shear from the air and brought it in for swift destruction. Darius, considerably larger, and boxed in by his armor, had been more of a chore, so the monster hadn't been able to dispatch him before the counterattack commenced.

The Hallucigen's mouth orifice was in no position to snap at anything in front of the head. But it didn't need to. Instead the snout whipped the prey onto the back, where it was held, then shoved forward into the orifice. 'Like a pencil sharpener,' Colene remarked, clarifying her mystifying reference for them so that her analogy made sense. 'You would have been jammed in headfirst, Darius, ground up like hamburger. So maybe it would have taken some time to reach your feet; that was all right, because Hallucigen had you secured. It might simply have eaten another segment each day, until you were gone. Nice system.'

'Very nice,' he agreed wryly. 'But why the vapor?'

She had an answer for that too. 'It's digestive, I think. Probably sort of pacifies the prey and softens it up, so the mouth can grind it in better. I mean, why make the meat grinder work harder than it needs to?' She had to clarify her analogy again, but again it was apt.

'It must also drive away other predators,' Nona offered. 'So that none will try to take away the meat.'

'Yeah, like a skunk,' Colene agreed. 'With the prey held right there, it probably just puts the tenderizer right on it, neat as you please. I'm sure glad I found out how the head works; it was a real mystery. The thing must have stood in a current, so nobody would smell it, and hauled in any creatures drifting in that current. It didn't need to move fast, because the current would bring prey down to it. It just had to be sure it was secure on its feet. It's a pretty neat design, really.'

'Neat,' Darius agreed, echoing her colloquialism. 'I am just glad that Nona knew how to make fire.'

'I never thought of it,' Nona protested. 'Until Colene told me.'

'Actually we might have put a block in its pincers and then beaten it off,' Colene said. 'It doesn't have other offensive weapons. It's just snatch and hold and eat. But I'm glad it didn't eat you,' she said to Darius.

He was glad too.

They continued along the path, making good progress. At this rate they would indeed complete their trip in one day. If they didn't encounter any other ugly surprises.

# 6

## *Modes*

Burgess rode on the wagon, not comfortable but satisfied to be transported in the way that was feasible. Without this arrangement, he would not have been able to travel through the wilderness or to remain with his adopted alien hive.

His original hive rejected anything alien. It even rejected any thought patterns that were too extreme. That was the cause of his rejection: the possibility that he had been infected by the poisoned hive. He had accepted that rejection, because of his loyalty to the hive. But now he realized that there was an irony. The same restrictions which protected the hive also limited it. No hiver had ever explored the wilderness, so the hive was ignorant of its wonders. No hiver had invoked a Virtual Mode, so those wonders too were not known. Yet the aliens had abilities which could benefit the hive. Such as this concept of 'magic,' by which they could change the size of objects, or make fire appear. Such as 'telepathy,' which was like the touching of contact points, but from a distance, and with the barriers of contact conventions reduced. Such as 'technology,' which enabled them to conceive and make this wagon, so that he could travel with them despite his inability to float here. So though he was having to adapt far more drastically than he had anticipated, he was also benefiting more than he had expected.

He had, so far, taken more from this little hive than he had given to it. It was his nature to try to be an asset to his hive, rather than a liability. Perhaps his time would come to make his contribution.

In due course they came to the lake. This time the ingenuity of the smallest and smartest of the human aliens, Colene, provided them with a new way to cross. They expanded the wagon to large size, so that all of them could stand on it, including Seqiro Horse. They pushed it out into the water, using the poles, until it floated. They fashioned paddles, which they fixed to the wheels. Then they stood one to a wheel and pushed each forward on top, so that its bottom moved the other way and stroked against the water. It was what Colene called a paddlewheel boat. It moved slowly, but they were able to steer it, and it seemed secure from the Anomaly predator.

The Anomaly did appear, but this time it did not attack. It seemed that it learned from experience, and what it had learned was that big wooden craft were not fit prey. Nevertheless, protective nets were set up along the sides, and there were a number of sharp spears ready. The humans did not leave things to chance, if they had a choice.

Across the river they got on land and diminished the wagon until it was possible for the armored horse to carry it. Burgess could float on this path, so he did, sparing them the burden of transporting him. They made good progress.

Then the crab came. It was not as smart as the Anomaly, and did not learn well from experience. But this time they were ready for it.

A fireball burst right in front of the crab. A patch of forest brush blazed. The crab retreated, not liking the fire.

The party continued along the path. After a while the crab came crashing through the brush again, following them. Another fireball appeared, making another temporary barrier. The crab desisted.

They reached the spot where the path was too narrow and rough for Burgess to float across. The three humans picked him up again, strengthened by the horse's mind, and carried him beyond the obstruction.

The crab came after them again, still refusing to learn from experience. One more ball of flame balked it.

'Say, I wonder whether Nona could stop the hivers the same way?' Colene inquired.

Burgess considered drawing on the human qualities of the hive mind, because by himself he could not reason well. No, he concluded that the hivers would simply put out the fire with sand. If fire struck one of them, they would think it was a natural fire expanding suddenly, and would not be balked. Since there were many of them, they would attack from all sides. Even if a ring of fire were instituted, they would fire rocks and sand in from beyond it.

'Got it,' Colene agreed. 'Fire doesn't balk a sandstorm or a rockfall. But night and armor may.'

They moved on past the site of their first camp and reached the verge of the wilderness. Here they stopped. It was late afternoon, and they had succeeded in making their trip in one day. They had eaten their middle-day food while waiting for the wagon to expand for the river crossing; now they ate their end-day food. They expanded the wagon again, and installed the sides and top, and tinkered with it to make sure it was ready to move. They fixed the harness so that the armored horse could haul the wagon without complication. By the time it was dark, they were ready to go out on the plain.

This time Colene and Nona joined Burgess inside the wagon. They had slit-apertures through which they could peer to see the darkness beyond. Burgess' own eyes would not extend that far, so could not see out. However, with the linkage to the horse's mind, he could see all that he required. There was some faint light, after all, because of the moon. It did not show any detail, but the outlines of large things, such as trees, could be made out.

They started moving. Darius walked in his armor beside Seqiro in his armor. Darius guided the horse and kept watch, so that Seqiro could concentrate on his hauling and on the minds of all of them. It was a useful collaboration and separation of contributions that represented the proper functioning of the hive.

The wagon ride was somewhat bumpy, but they were

moving slowly and could handle it. While they rode, they conversed.

'Burgess, did you ever have a girlfriend?' Colene inquired.

Contact with a female hiver? It had been constant, when he belonged to the hive, since all members updated regularly. There was no distinction between males and females in this respect.

'No, I don't mean routine social dates and updates,' Colene said. 'I mean going steady, falling in love, having sex, having babies, being a family, not necessarily in that order.'

Love? Sex? Family? These were alien concepts.

'Okay, let's get down to basics,' Colene said, while Nona remained carefully neutral. 'Love is like being just so wrapped up in one person it changes your whole life. Like me with Darius. Show him, Seqiro.'

Suddenly a strange, pleasant, encompassing emotion came, tinged with excitement and fear and desire. Burgess had never experienced anything like it. His closest approach was his devotion to the hive.

'No, that's patriotism, not love,' Colene decided. 'Okay, so you don't know love.'

'Neither do I,' Nona said.

'So let's tackle sex,' Colene continued. 'How does your kind do it?'

He understood that what she meant was how floaters reproduced. They contributed to the central nest, each blowing seeds of itself into the nutritive substance. The males blew many seeds, the females few. When the seeds encountered their opposites in the nest, they merged and began to grow. Eventually they became large enough to leave the nest. Then they emerged and learned to float. When they floated well enough, they were dispersed to other hives.

'Wow, it really *is* a hive,' Colene said. 'No family life at all. No child rearing. How do you stand it?'

It was the way it was, and that was sufficient. However,

122

the rearing of young floaters did occur. It was spread throughout the hive. The little ones made contact first with selected nurse-floaters, who familiarized them with the conventions of the hive. Then they circulated more widely, learning more with each update, until they were fully current. That was it; they were full members of the hive, and would remain so until they lost air and expired.

'What happens then?'

The expiring hivers went to the nearest burial bog and let themselves sink in. It was bad form to expire either in the main camp or on the plain, because then the hive had to go to the trouble of moving or of burying them in dirt.

Colene sighed, which was a way to express resignation. 'I guess it's no worse than what our kind does. We mostly pickle our dead and bury them in boxes. But I'll bet you find life with us on the Virtual Mode more interesting.'

It was already more interesting.

Suddenly it became too interesting. Through Darius' eyes they saw something rise up from the ground. A pit worm! They had to be avoided!

The wagon lurched as the horse skittered to the side. But the monster's snout oriented on the man, and began to suck. Air whistled into that mouth, and a short distance away there was a jet of air carrying out the exhaust. The principle was similar to the way the floaters used air to float and to bring in food or blow out stones. But here the suction was what counted, for the pit worms swallowed their prey whole. Then they closed their aperture shells and digested what they captured. A few days later they would blow out whatever remained undigested. In the interim they were invisible, because their shells covered the two ends of their burrows and dirt settled over them. A floater could float over many without noticing. Since they did not hunt by day, it didn't matter.

Darius was drawn into the mouth. It was just a round hole, with dust sucking in. The suction was so strong that the man was in the mouth before he could flee. But he held his pole crosswise, so that it came up against the snout. He hung on to it, though his feet were drawn into the maw.

Burgess knew that this was not enough. The worm would simply close its maw on the man and withdraw into its hole, carrying him along. Then it would start digesting his feet. The wooden armor wouldn't help, since the digestion was fluid and chemical. Darius had to get free immediately. Burgess could do it.

Seqiro picked up this assessment. Then the two human women were opening the wagon. They let the back panel fall down so that it formed a ramp. Burgess could not float up an incline, but he could float down one. He sailed out of the wagon and over the ramp, flowing into the dirt beyond. Then he righted himself and moved to the side, where the worm was already withdrawing into its hole, carrying the man's lower body along. He moved up right next to it, poked his outtrunk in next to the man, and started blowing. He shot a steady stream of dirt and pebbles into the orifice.

Colene and Nona, understanding what he was doing, got down and scooped more sand to Burgess' intrunk, so that he did not need to move. Thus bolstered, he poured more through, filling the worm.

Soon the worm, realizing that it was sucking in the wrong substance, desisted. The terrible draft died down, and Darius was able to wrench himself out of the maw. 'Thanks,' he gasped as the worm disappeared and slammed down its shell plate.

Thanks? A member of the hive defended the hive and all its members. There was no other way.

'Are there more of these suckworms?' Colene asked. Her accompanying thought was trying to place this monster among those she had seen in the pictures her teacher Amos Forell had shown her, but she couldn't, quite. She thought there had been a wormlike thing armored at both ends, but that was all.

There were many. They tended to cluster, so it was better to avoid the region. Because they were hidden under the dirt, it was hard to be sure one was near until it lifted its shell and began sucking.

'But trying to circle around something when we don't know where it is will take too long,' she protested. 'It's not that far to the anchor site. We need a better way.'

'Also,' Nona said, 'There won't be any other predators, where there are suckworms.'

'What alerts the suckworms?' Darius asked.

Any weight on the ground close by, or any disturbance. They were sensitive to vibrations and compression of the ground. They remained hidden until the disturbance was close; then they popped up to suck it in.

Darius picked up a rock. 'Then maybe this will do it.' He threw the rock a short distance ahead.

Nothing happened. He threw another, with no reaction. But the third brought an eruption. 'So it's clear up to there,' he said. 'You folk get back in your cage; I can handle this.'

They helped Burgess into the wagon, and joined him there. They closed it up and tuned back in on Darius' perception. He was throwing more stones, verifying the safe route through before leading Seqiro there.

'Hey, horsehead,' Colene asked. 'Can you tune in on the suckworms, so we know where they are more directly?'

*In time yes. Immediately, no. Their minds are small and foreign.*

Slowed by the necessity of checking the route with stones, they proceeded at a painstaking pace. Unable to help, Burgess settled down to sleep, and the women did too, depending on the horse to wake them if they were needed. They lay on the dark floor on either side of Burgess, where they were able to reach up and touch a contact point at need. This was not comfortable for any of them physically, but

125

a certain rapport remained even when they weren't touching, and that made it comfortable emotionally. Burgess was gradually coming to appreciate emotion; it was good to feel good and bad.

Just how slow it was they didn't realize until the three were abruptly wakened. Light was coming; it was dawn.

There was sound. Burgess recognized it: hivers!

'Hey, you out there, get a wiggle on!' Colene cried. 'Hivers coming!'

'It's chancy,' Darius responded. 'We have threaded an interminable bed of worms, and there may be more.'

Not when light came; the worms did not suck by daylight.

'So go, go, go!' Colene cried. 'It can't be far to the anchor, and we don't want to be trapped out here by the hivers.'

The man and horse broke into a run. The wagon ride got considerably bumpier. But there remained some distance to go to reach the anchor point. Burgess had chosen it for seclusion and convenience for himself, not considering how close it was to the wilderness.

There was a honk. That was a hiver, sounding alarm! Now they would come.

The region of the anchor came into sight. Burgess verified it through Darius' eyes. But the hivers were already closing in on it. They did remember where it was, and would cut off the party before it got there.

'Damn!' Colene muttered. 'So close . . .'

'Burgess,' Darius called. 'Have the hivers ever encountered armor?'

No. It was an alien concept.

'So they won't be able to figure its weaknesses in a hurry?'

True. They would blow sand and rocks at it.

'And not try to interfere with the wheels?'

They had never encountered wheels before.

'Suppose we just charge right through them?'

They would get out of the way and blow rocks from the sides.

'Hear that, Seqiro? We'll just gallop right at the anchor and through it. They won't get in our way.'

'But swerve around the bigger rocks!' Colene called. 'We don't want to tip over!'

Indeed, the wagon seemed about to fly apart. But they charged recklessly at the group of hivers near the anchor. Rocks and sand struck the wood panels and bounced off. Darius and Seqiro were struck too, but suffered no damage.

As they came to the anchor, the hivers floated aside, not wanting to be struck. The hivers continued to hurl dirt, but though it made for a choking environment, it didn't stop the motion. They were almost to the anchor, moving at speed.

Then a front wheel struck something. It jumped and came off. The axle dropped to the ground and the wagon plowed into the dirt. The three of them inside were thrown against the front panel. It broke loose and fell outward on the horse, while the two women tumbled to either side and Burgess jetted frantically to keep from being turned over on his top.

The hivers, surprised by this display, halted their firing. But Burgess knew that would not last long. He slid down off the panel and back onto the main body of the wagon.

Darius ran back and put his hands on the fallen axle. 'Give me strength, Seqiro!' he gasped. Then the axle came up so that it was level.

'Haul it on through!' Darius cried.

The horse lurched forward − and disappeared. But his harness still connected, and the wagon moved. Darius staggered, hauling the axle − and disappeared too. So did the front of the wagon. There was nothing there but sand and the circle of hivers.

'Move!' Colene cried, getting to her feet. Nona got up and started forward too.

The hivers realized that the prey was getting away. They

resumed blowing rocks. But they were too late. Both women disappeared, and the rocks bounced harmlessly off the sides of the wagon, which remained erect. Then the rest of the wagon disappeared, with a line across it that steadily erased it backwards. Finally that line reached Burgess, and the wagon reappeared, with its back missing but resuming as the line moved on behind.

The axle dropped as Darius let go, his brief strength exhausted. He sat on the ground, panting. Colene ran to him and flung her arms about his head and shoulders as she dropped to her knees. She hauled the wooden helmet off and brought his head in to her chest. 'You poor, wonderful man!' she cried. 'Your arms must be just about yanked out by the roots.'

Nona came around to Burgess. She got beside him and put her hand on a contact point. That was when he got the update so that he was able to make sense of the expressions of the others; he had heard them but not properly understood them before. Now it was as if he had always understood them.

Indeed, he was understanding them more than before. Colene was hugging Darius, and kissing him, and loving him, and Darius was loving the hug and kiss and her. The emotion was of such intensity that it made Burgess himself want to love, though he did not know how. He felt that he had been missing something wonderful, all his life. But how − ?

'Like this,' Nona said. She got down beside him, leaned forward, put her arms around his top section, and touched her mouth to him, between two eye stalks. 'You have now been kissed.'

It felt very good, in an alien way.

They diminished the wagon and the armor for man and horse, so that they could walk free. But they did not walk. Darius and Seqiro had been up all night, doing hard labor, and both were fatigued. So they slept while the women and Burgess took care of the details and did some preliminary exploration. The plain extended around them, uninhabited. But it might come to life at any time, and the suckworms might come out by night. So they used poles to poke the ground for worm shells, making sure it was safe. Then they made a campsite.

'Now we must eat and drink only what we brought with us,' Colene said.

But there were fruit trees in sight, with ripe fruit. Burgess was satisfied to be sustained by those.

'Nuh-uh, airfoot. You got things to learn about the Virtual Mode, just as we did. Let me show you.' She stooped to pick up a rock. 'Watch where it goes.' She threw it a short distance.

The rock flew through the air and landed on the ground, exactly as it should have.

'Now something we brought,' she said. She took out a round bit of metal. 'This is a coin from my reality. I can't spend it here, so I'll throw it away.' She did so.

The coin stopped in midair and dropped to the ground.

Burgess was surprised. The coin should either have landed beside the stone, or disappeared as it crossed the boundary between Modes.

'Now let's carry stuff across,' Colene said. She picked up another stone and held it out to him. 'Hold this in your trunk, and we'll step across to where that rock landed.'

She stepped and Burgess floated. They moved together across the invisible line. Nona, standing to the side, disappeared.

The scene did not change significantly. But the stone vanished. He had not dropped it; it had just stopped being with him. 'See? You can't carry something from a Mode across the boundaries. Unless it's from an anchor Mode. And look — where is that stone I just threw here?'

Burgess knew where it was — but it, too, had vanished.

'See, it didn't cross either. It stayed in its own reality,' she explained.

They crossed back. Nona reappeared. There on the ground beside the coin was the rock Burgess had held in his trunk. And there beyond was the rock Colene had thrown.

'We see the reality we're standing in,' Colene explained. 'But we can't go more than ten feet across it. Because then we step into the next reality, and leave the things of this one behind. We can't take any of it with us. Now suppose you eat a fruit, and cross the boundary?'

Burgess understood her point. The fruit would vanish in the same manner as the rock, leaving him unfed. But the things of his own Mode remained with him, if he carried them. So his food had to be what they had brought in the wagon. Much had been lost when the wagon started to come apart, but much remained.

'However, we can go as far as we want to the sides,' Colene said. 'Because these slices of realities are sort of two-dimensional. They have width and height, but only ten-feet depth. So if you really want to take a walk without constantly changes Modes, go to the sides. And if you see a monster coming at you, step forward or backward so you can pop out of existence before it reaches you. Even if it's right in front, you can step into it, and vanish. It's important to get your reactions in order, because which way you jump on the spur of the moment can make the difference between life and death. Either way: you don't want to jump into a reality you can't see, because there might be another monster there, or a deep pit, or a forest fire. So you jump *only* when you have to.' She glanced at him. 'Or fast-float. You know what I mean.'

Burgess did. He moved back and forth across the boundary, carrying rocks, and shooting them in various directions, until he understood exactly how it worked.

Nona expanded a fruit, so that Burgess could make a full meal of a single item. Her magic was a useful thing.

'Say, I forgot,' Colene said. 'We're back on the Virtual Mode! You can do all your magic now, Nona.'

'Why, that's right,' Nona agreed, surprised. She rose from the ground, floating, but she did not use air. She picked up Colene's coin and it became a fragment of stone, and then a blade of grass. Burgess was amazed.

'Oh, you ain't seen nothing yet,' Colene murmured.

Nona smiled. Then a tiny plant appeared before her, and grew rapidly until it was as high as she was. It changed color, becoming a tree, and its trunk expanded until it formed a wall. The wall extended to circle Burgess and Colene, and the top leaned over, forming a shelter like that of the closed wagon. Openings appeared in the sides, showing the scene beyond — but every one was different. One was a bright green landscape, with a brighter green sun shining down. Another was a blue chamber with a red creature. The third was white sky with black creatures crossing it. They were not shears, but alien things.

'Blackbirds,' Colene said. 'Birds are creatures who fly in my Mode. Most of them are harmless to us, but they eat insects. You'll see stranger things than that, soon enough, I'm sure.'

The birds turned and came directly toward the window. They passed through it, into the chamber, and became twisting flames. The wall caught fire, and in a moment it was a chamber of fire with a roof of smoke. But there was no heat.

Then the fire lifted, forming a canopy above while the regular land showed below. The canopy diminished, until it was only an insect, which flashed as it flew away.

'A firefly!' Colene exclaimed, delighted. Then, to Burgess: 'That was a show of illusion. Of things which are more apparent than real. Everybody in her Mode can do it. They don't even consider it to be magic, because it hasn't any substance. But it can be pretty impressive, for those who don't realize its nature.' She squeezed his contact point. 'Of

131

course you were never fooled, were you, airhead?' Then she laughed at his confusion, but her feeling was positive.

He would have liked to see more of that 'illusion,' because its nature was hardly clear to him.

Then the firefly returned. It hovered before Burgess' inflow trunk, and became a small round rock. He touched his trunk to it, to suck it in, but it had no substance. It was merely a discoloration of the air.

The rock expanded into a boulder. Still it could not be touched. His trunk passed through it without effect. It caught fire, but there was no heat at all. It became a fall of water, flowing away across the ground, but had no wetness. It simply did not exist, in all its forms.

'There you have it,' Colene said. 'Illusion is something that just isn't there. But it looks so real you think it *is* there, until you try to touch it.'

Burgess was impressed. The powers of these creatures were like none he had encountered before.

'No, the rest of us don't have magic,' Colene said. 'Only Nona. And Darius, only his is different. He can magnify joy, and he can conjure. But it's not safe to conjure on the Virtual Mode, because he can't tell exactly where he's going. And he can't magnify *my* joy, because I'm depressive. So we won't be seeing much of his magic soon. And I don't have any magic at all. Just maybe a trace of telepathy that rubs off from Seqiro. Who isn't really asleep now, because otherwise we wouldn't be understanding each other like this. We're a mixed bag. Now you're with us, and I guess you can't do magic either, but you can float and fire out jets of dirt, so you can do more than I can.' Her emotion turned negative as she finished. He wasn't sure why.

'Because everybody else has special talents,' Colene answered. 'While all I've got is depression.'

Burgess still could not understand that. There was a concept he thought would relate, but he could not form that concept by himself.

132

'I'll help you,' Nona said. 'It's that Colene has what she calls an inferiority complex. But her inferiority is illusion. It isn't there.'

'What do you mean, it isn't there!' Colene protested. 'I can't float, I can't conjure, I can't do magic, and what little telepathy I can do is laughable compared to Seqiro's power. I can't even be happy! So what is there to recommend me?'

'You are our leader,' Nona said.

'I'm what?'

'You are the one of us with the most intelligence, creativity, determination, and initiative. When there's an emergency, you are the one who takes charge. You are the one for whom the Virtual Mode was started, and for whom it continues. Without you, the rest of us would not be here. We have talents; you have the essence.'

Yes, that was it. The strongest member of the hive had a weakness that was illusion. Something she saw that did not exist.

'You *agree* with her, doubletrunk?'

Yes, he agreed. His perplexity had been resolved.

Colene shook her head, a gesture which indicated different things depending on the emotion. 'Wish *I* could!'

The illusion still looked real to her.

Late in the day the man stirred and the horse woke up the rest of the way. They remained somewhat tired; the feeling in their bodies carried through with their thoughts. But neither was concerned with this.

'Hey, Colene, what is our course?' Darius asked.

'You haven't decided on it?'

He smiled. 'Well, what do you think it is?'

'I think we'd better just track on around the Virtual Mode until we find your reality.'

'By day or night?'

'Day, of course! We'll fall in a hole at night.'

'So we'd better start moving at dawn.'

'I agree.'

Again, Burgess saw the way of it. Colene had made the decisions, but attributed them to Darius. It was the way she wanted it.

Nona picked up a leaf and changed it into a piece of bread, which was one of the substances they ate. Then she paused. 'I am working from a substance of the Mode we're in. That means it can't sustain us, even if I change its nature.'

Colene nodded. 'Probably right. We'd better not gamble. We'll stick to what we brought with us.'

Again she had made the decision. At each turn, Burgess saw the truth of Nona's statement.

'Oh, stop it, airsnoot! It's just common sense, is all.'

She was the one with the ordinary sense, yes.

They spent the night behind barricades, taking turns watching. At one point Darius and Burgess were awake, and Seqiro partly conscious, so that they could communicate. 'This is just one boundary away from your Mode, Burgess,' Darius remarked. 'There should be others of your kind here, yet I have seen nothing.'

There were floaters here. Their signs were all around. Burgess hadn't realized that it mattered.

'There are? Then why haven't they attacked?'

Because the nearest camp was a distance away at the moment. Floaters ranged from region to region, so as not to deplete any single area. In this Mode they had camped here half a year before, but now were safely beyond. The remnant of their ramparts was visible beyond the boundary Colene had demonstrated. Unless they were quite unlike Burgess' former hive, none would range here for another half year.

'So I was worried for nothing! What about the suckworms?'

They were surely all around. But the women had made sure there were none close by.

'So actually the worms protect us, because anyone who

comes after us is likely to be nabbed by one of them first.'

That did seem likely.

'But we'll keep watch anyway,' Darius said. 'No telling what we'll find when we travel. Each Mode will be just a little different from the last, in general nature, but the specifics can change dramatically. We can't ever afford to let down our guard.'

That seemed wise.

In the morning they started out. They wanted to be careful, but they didn't want to be too slow, so they moved along boldly. They remained alert, ready to change course or to proceed with excruciating care when there was some hint of potential trouble.

Darius led the way, holding a staff made from a chip of wood from Shale. When he came to a boundary, the forward end of the pole disappeared, being pushed into the unseen reality. Then Darius disappeared, as if passing through a doorway in a wagon. Then the rear end of his pole followed, as if being fed into an opaque sheet of water. If that pole did not jerk or show any other sign of distress, Seqiro followed. He too vanished in a linear fashion, seeming to be a headless horse, a two-legged horse, the isolated tail of a horse, and finally no horse. If that tail did not twitch, Nona followed. She carried a stick of her own on her shoulder, so that the end of it followed her across the boundary. If the position of that end did not change before it disappeared, Burgess followed. He saw his own outtrunk painlessly cut off, and his own leading section. Then his central eye stalks passed through, and it was his trailing end that disappeared. His canopy eye patches helped verify that he remained intact, but they were normally used only for tracking the spot contours of the ground. Behind him Colene walked, with another pole on her shoulder. He kept one eye oriented always on that pole, and if it did anything odd, he would advance just enough to blow out a stone to alert Nona in the Mode ahead, then turn quickly, ready to blow out another stone in the Mode behind. It seemed complicated, but it was just a chain of cross-checks, so that they could all come quickly together in a central Mode if they had to.

They made good progress. Not only did the scenery slowly change as they crossed it, as would be the case in any normal world, its nature changed. Trees were in different spots in each reality, but of the same type — until he saw that their species were shifting. Their leaves had been green, but they became blue. They had been of average tree height; they became taller and thinner. Then their leaves turned green again, but their height continued to grow.

Every so often there was a gap. A Mode without trees. Or with twisted and dead trees. Then the regular Modes would resume. What had happened to those treeless lands?

For a while they found themselves in jungle, and had to retreat, because Burgess couldn't navigate it. They retreated, and moved sideways along a suitable Mode, then tried again, and managed to skirt the jungle. This, too, was a fairly abrupt change, as if a few Modes had richer plant life than their neighbors. What trace difference in their nature accounted for so large a difference in their plants?

Sometimes there were creatures. They were usually in the distance, but sometimes they were close. Once there was a suckworm, but it was much smaller than the ones in Shale, and could not harm them. This must be near the edge of their range. Any creatures appeared suddenly when the boundary was crossed, and disappeared as suddenly when the next boundary was crossed.

Then there was a halt. Not an alarm; it was just that when he crossed the boundary, the others were standing there waiting for him. Colene crossed after him, and they stood aligned sideways instead of lengthwise.

136

The three humans put hands on Burgess' contact points, so that he could be completely current. 'What's up, beardface?' Colene asked Darius brightly.

'Sign of civilization,' he said.

Burgess felt the thrill of alarm that went through the others. He discovered from their surrounding thoughts that civilization meant that there was an organized society, and that could be dangerous. They preferred to travel through wild regions, because animals were less likely to bother them.

In this case the sign was a pit. It wasn't wide or deep, so it would be easy to circle around it and proceed, but Darius was concerned that it was artificial, which meant that someone was digging it. He didn't want to encounter such a person, if he could avoid it. Though nothing from a spot Mode could be taken across the Mode boundaries, any harm they suffered in one would remain with them. Of course Nona had the magic of healing, their thoughts clarified, but it was better not to have to use that.

The sensory line they were following indicated that they were on the route they wanted; if they deviated from it too far, it would be harder to follow. Burgess was learning to pick up the faint rightness of the direction; it indicated where there was another anchor. He could find his way back to his own anchor by tuning in on this, or forward to another anchor. It seemed that each anchor had its ambience extending across the Modes of the Virtual Mode, making it possible to travel without getting lost.

They decided to proceed with caution. Instead of maintaining a walking or floating pace, they went in what Colene termed jerks. Darius stepped across, and Seqiro waited a moment before following. That gave Darius the chance to change his mind and step back if he deemed it wise, without banging into the one behind.

They did go around the pit. It would have given Burgess trouble, though he could have gotten out of it. It was not the kind made by floaters. They seemed to be beyond the floater Modes now. Burgess felt a peculiar emotion as he realized that; now he was truly in an alien realm.

There were increasing signs of civilization as they continued. Then Nona called a conference. 'This is near Julia! My Mode,' she said. 'The hills are starting to assume fractal form.'

'You're right!' Colene exclaimed. 'It's your reality we're coming to. But do we want to stop there?'

'No,' Nona said. 'They will want me to be queen.'

'And you'd still rather be hiking through nowhere with us, than queen at home?'

'Yes.' There was no doubt in Nona's mind; the certainty came to them all.

'I suppose it's not surprising,' Colene said. 'Julia was the closest Mode to Provos' Mode, when she let go her anchor. So maybe the anchors are in the same order. Which means the next one beyond that will be Darius' anchor. Then —' But she did not finish either word or thought.

'Then you and Darius get off,' Nona said.

'Yeah. But what about you? When we started this, you and Burgess weren't along. In fact, Seqiro wasn't along. So —' Again her thought was incomplete.

'I want to explore the Virtual Mode,' Nona said. 'Since my magic works on it, I feel reasonably safe. I would be satisfied to travel with Seqiro and Burgess, if they were interested.'

Colene's shock of concern was intense. 'Seqiro! How could I live without you?'

'You will have some decisions to make, Colene,' Darius said. 'You know that it is no perfect life I can offer you in my Mode. I love you, but if I knew that you would be happier elsewhere with Seqiro —'

'I think I would die without you, Darius,' she said seriously. 'And without you, Seqiro. But unless the others want to get off at the same anchor Mode —'

Now the horse spoke, without making any sound. *I wish*

to remain with you, Colene. And with you, Nona. It is my nature to desire the company of human girls.*

Nona smiled sadly. 'It might be best if Burgess and I wanted to join you in that Mode. But if I settle down, I should do it in my own Mode. Until then, I hope to remain on the Virtual Mode. How do you feel, Burgess?'

This was a surprising and confusing question. Originally it had seemed that the four creatures were a unified hive, but now he understood that they were separate individuals, and that this group was not permanent. That made it difficult, because he needed a hive. A hive of two creatures was too small to be viable.

'Oh, that's not a problem,' Colene said. 'Whenever someone vacates an anchor, a new anchor appears, with a new anchor person. Just as you did. So there'll always be five folk in the group, as long as this Virtual Mode exists. But look, people: here we're off on a discussion, and we really don't need it now. We can make our decisions when we get to Darius' Mode. Maybe we'll work something out by then. Right now we know we're passing the Julia Mode, and we don't want to stop there, so we'll just sashay on by, and Nona's our guide. We can pick up speed, now, because Nona'll know when there's danger. So let's put her in front and move on.'

Colene had exercised her leadership again. Nona exchanged places with Darius, and they proceeded at their full walking velocity. The Modes continued to vary, the configuration of trees and grass constantly shifting. Sometimes they found themselves in the midst of rain, and then as suddenly it would be sunny again. But it was always day, and the same time of day, and the landscape shifted only slightly with each Mode, if at all. They chose a route which enabled Burgess to float across fairly level terrain, traveling, as Colene put it, along a contour. They discovered that it was possible for one of them to push him, on slopes, so that he could ascend, and he could slow his descent by

139

diminishing his air so that his canopy dragged slightly. He was keeping the pace satisfactorily.

Until they came to a wall. It angled across their route, evidently artificial. It was twice the height of a man, and had bits of sharp stone embedded in its hard surface. They avoided it by moving to the side, where it cut off. It looked solid, extending all across the hill they were on and the gentle valley beyond, but vanished when they crossed the Mode's boundary. Those boundaries made even the most formidable barriers easy to pass.

But the next Mode had its own wall, angled differently but just as extensive. They avoided this also, by moving farther to the side. Then they came up against a third wall, and this one was angled so that it was exactly crosswise — which meant it extended along the width of their section of this Mode, and they could not readily get around it.

They halted again for a consultation. 'Your folk responsible for this, Nona?' Darius asked.

'They could be,' Nona agreed. 'In Julia, we reversed the flow of magic, so that it now touches women instead of men. But in other Modes it may not have changed, and the despots may be doing unkind things to the land, or trying to pen up the peons. It is the way their minds work. I think we should get past this quickly and leave it far behind. I do not want to become the captive of despots.'

'None of us do,' Colene agreed. 'They're mean jerks. Okay, I guess you can fly over it, and Darius and I can put wood panels on it and climb over. But what about Seqiro and Burgess?'

'We'll have to build a hoist or a ramp,' Darius said. 'I think a ramp is better, because Seqiro can walk up it himself.'

'But what about the other side?' Colene asked. 'That wall is right up against the next Mode boundary, by the look of it; we'll be dropping off into the unknown.'

140

'We'll check the next Mode, of course. We won't have to jump blind.'

'And what about Burgess?' she asked.

'Seqiro can haul him up the ramp on a sledge or wagon.'

They got to work. Darius carved a wooden structure, a long ramp with supports, wide enough for the horse. Nona flew up and over the wall, to check the next Mode. She reported that it was clear, with a wall that wouldn't interfere with them; they could set the ramp on the far side of this one without a problem. Darius set the model ramp beside the wall, so that it aligned, running in the same direction. Then Nona made it expand. She had already expanded the base of the wagon they had used before, so that it was just large enough to support Burgess.

Meanwhile Colene was busy searching for rocks. 'Come on, airfoot, help me,' she said, touching a contact point. 'We want a good supply.'

What were they for? It was not possible to take the rocks across the boundary.

'Look, you know how your hivers didn't just leave you alone? Well, whoever built or magicked this wall isn't just going to sit by and let folks cross it. We're going to see guards coming by on their rounds any time, and if we aren't across yet, we're going to have to fight. If they use magic, Nona will have to help us. But if they're peons, as seems more likely, stones will stop them. That's what you're good at. So we'll have a good supply for you, and we can throw them too. They'll work just fine, as long as we remain in this one Mode, and once we're out of it, it won't matter.'

Now he understood. She was correct. He got to work finding rocks and sand, and storing them in a wooden box she had gotten. By the time they had a good collection, the ramp was almost full size. Nona's magic seemed to be stronger on the Virtual Mode than it had been on Shale, so she could expand things faster.

Darius walked up the ramp to the top of the wall. He set

141

a wood panel on the wall, making a safe platform, 'Um, I didn't realize this until just now: this wall's only about two handspans wide at the top. Seqiro won't have room to cross.'

'What do you mean?' Colene demanded. 'He can just come up on this side, and step across to the ramp on the other side, no problem.'

'But we have only one ramp. We're going to lift it over after Seqiro and Burgess reach the top. So they have to be off it first.'

'Oh.' Colene pondered a moment. 'We'll just have to make a second ramp.'

'I suppose so.' Darius stepped onto the panel on the top of the wall, making sure it was secure.

There was a chime. It seemed to come from the wall itself.

'Uh-oh,' Colene said. 'That's an alarm. I have a suspicion that we aren't going to have time to carve and expand another ramp.'

'True,' Darius said. 'We'll have to act now. Nona, come up here and expand some more panels for the top of the wall. Those are smaller, so they will be faster to do. Colene, you hitch up Seqiro and Burgess and lead them up the ramp.'

They got to work immediately. Nona flew up to join Darius on the top, and began to expand more panels. Colene hitched Seqiro's harness to the wagon and led the horse to the base of the ramp. Darius came down, and the two of them borrowed strength from the horse and heaved Burgess up onto the wagon. They put the box of stones on the end of it, where Burgess' trunk could readily reach them.

There was the sound of barking. Burgess recognized it from Colene's knowledge: it was the noise made by creatures vaguely resembling the horse, but smaller, with sharper teeth. 'Just in time,' Darius muttered. He got on the ramp and hurried up to rejoin Nona.

'Okay, horseface, keep your feet straight in line,' Colene

said. Burgess was able to understand her increasingly even when she wasn't touching a contact point, and through her, the others. 'Use my eyes; I'm watching the ramp. Ignore all else. Darius and Burgess will guard us.'

Burgess hoped so. His position seemed precarious as the wagon tilted, being hauled up the ramp. But he followed Colene's directions too, focusing only on what lay behind.

That manifested soon enough. Several creatures matching Colene's mental description of dogs came charging along the wall, baying. Their sharp teeth showed at the ends of their long snouts. He knew from Colene's mind that they would attack savagely without hesitation, like land-bound shears.

He oriented his trunk. As the first dog came within range, he fired a stone at the white of its teeth. The stone struck, hard, and the dog made a squeal and fell to the ground.

But the next dog was already there. Burgess fired another rock, which struck the head between the two matched eyes. That dog spun off to the side, stunned.

But more were coming. They clustered so thickly that it was not possible to score on each one, and his third stone missed. His wagon was now halfway up the ramp, but the dogs were coming up the ramp too.

He worked his trunk to the bottom of the box, reaching the sand. He sucked it in and spewed it out into the faces of the three dogs on the ramp. Their eyes were not on stalks, and could not be retracted, so were vulnerable to this. They yelped and rolled off the ramp.

Colene was now reaching the top, bringing Seqiro's head with her. 'Step close, keep your balance,' she murmured. 'Right up onto the wall, here, and along it. We'll just keep going. There's nothing else in the world we need to be concerned about, horsehead.'

The dogs were coming again. But now the length of the ramp between them and Burgess was greater. He oriented his trunk, and when a dog came up, he fired the rock at the animal's head. The dog cried out and fell from the ramp. So did the next, when treated similarly.

But then another creature came into sight. This was a human figure, similar to Darius. That was surely not good.

'Nona, we need your fire,' Darius said from the wall. 'Set fire to the grass, so there's smoke.'

A fireball appeared at the base of the ramp. The remaining dogs yipped and scattered. The grass and dry leaves caught fire, and smoke billowed. There was an exclamation from the man beyond.

Now the wagon was at the top of the ramp. Darius was there. 'Steady,' he said, touching a contact point. 'There will be an imbalance as the wheels cross the angle between the ramp and the wall. Stay quite still; don't react. I will guide the wheels.' He leaned over, putting his hands on the front of the wagon.

It was well that he had given the warning, because the wagon shifted and seemed to be falling. But Burgess prevented himself from making a blast of air to right himself. In a moment the wagon found a new equilibrium, and moved on forward. It was on top of the wall. Darius heaved, making an adjustment to the rear wheels, and then the motion stopped.

Burgess was now on the wall, off the end of the ramp. Seqiro and Colene were beyond him. Darius and Nona were behind him, also on the wall, which was now covered by wood panels. But how were they going to move the ramp? It was too big and heavy for them to lift from their awkward position on the wall.

'You watch for enemy action, Nona,' Darius said. 'I'm going to conjure the ramp to the other side.'

Darius held something in his hand. It looked like a tiny man. He stepped onto the ramp, and lay down on it. Then he moved the little figure he held.

The ramp disappeared. So did Darius.

Then his voice came from near the wall, beyond Colene.

'It's secure. Lead him down.' What had happened? Without direct contact with the man, Burgess could not tell.

The horse resumed motion. Burgess followed, borne along on his wagon. Then Darius was there, quickly updating by touching a contact point, then helping the wheels over the ridge. 'It's clear, Nona!' he called. 'Get off the wall!'

The wall disappeared. They had crossed into the next Mode. Now they were coming down a ramp from nowhere. The remaining stones in the box were gone, as was the sand; it was completely empty.

Nona appeared, floating beside the wagon. 'I don't think they could do the same kind of magic,' she said, touching a contact point. 'That's why they used the wall and dogs. But I'm sure they were dangerous. They were bringing up some kind of device.'

'Maybe a cannon!' Colene said. 'It's a good thing we got out of there.'

'A cannon?' Nona was as perplexed as Burgess was. To understand this he needed direct contact with Colene.

Colene made a mental picture of a huge metal tube, which Nona received and relayed to Burgess. From that tube flew an object like a giant cup with a sealed, pointed front, spinning as it flew. It crashed into a mountain, and the mountain became a ball of flame.

Burgess still wasn't sure what a cannon was, but concluded that he did not want to encounter one. It seemed like an enormous outtrunk with no intrunk, primed with stones that exploded.

They reached the base of the ramp. Then Nona used her magic to reduce it slowly to a size she could carry in her hand. She also reduced the wagon, so that Burgess did not have to be lifted off; he floated off when it was low enough.

'How did you move that ramp?' Nona inquired of Darius. 'I thought you conjured only people.'

'I conjure living creatures and the things they carry,' he said. 'Otherwise I would arrive naked when I conjure myself.

In this case I had my icon embrace a sliver of wood representing the ramp, and then I embraced the real ramp myself. So when I activated the icon and moved it, the ramp moved with me. But this is a tricky, fatiguing device, and I wouldn't care to do it in other than an emergency.'

Burgess realized that there was still much he had to know about these aliens. He hardly grasped what Darius had done, except that it was magic akin to Nona's, and that it had enabled them to cross the wall before the Mode creatures had overwhelmed them.

'Let's find a place to camp,' Colene suggested. 'I've had enough strenuous escapes for today.'

Burgess agreed.

They moved on through the Modes of the Virtual Mode. Burgess followed Colene's thoughts as they traveled. They saw other walls, but none got in their way. The one had just happened to be, in a position that blocked them. Probably the creatures of that Mode had not realized that the party was foreign to that Mode. The wall must have been part of a prison complex, or possibly the border of a military zone.

They crossed a low, grassy hill and a river came into sight. It looked broad and deep. Along it were animals, standing in fields. Those were probably horses or cows, Colene thought.

'Neither,' Seqiro responded with his thought. 'Their minds are other. But they are passive, and will not bother us. We can ignore them.'

'That's good,' Colene said. 'I wouldn't want to meet up with your kind. No offense, horsefoot.'

'My kind would be dangerous.'

'Yeah.'

The animals appeared and disappeared with each boundary crossing, but the river remained constant, shifting only in minor detail. They approached it, and finally stood at its bank. It seemed to have two channels, which interwove. The water was clear, and red creatures Colene thought of as fish were visible. 'Are those safe? I mean, can we ignore them too, and go wading?'

Seqiro's mind reached for the minds of the fish. 'No. They are what you call piranha, or similar.'

'So much for sweet nature!' Colene exclaimed, laughing. Her mind clarified that piranha were vicious predatory fish, much like the shears of Shale or the dogs of the walled Mode, but in the water.

'Is that an island?' Nona inquired, peering across the water.

'It seems to be,' Darius agreed. 'It looks uninhabited.'

'Why don't we cross to that island?' Colene suggested. 'Then maybe nothing will bother us.'

That appealed to Burgess, and to the others. They were all tired of having to be constantly alert for weird menaces.

Nona got ready to expand the wagon into a boat. But Colene had an idea. 'See if you can make those fish afraid of us, Seqiro. Then maybe we can safely swim across.'

The horse focused on the fish. Even without contact, Burgess felt the unease of fear. After a while the fish swam away. Burgess floated out on the water, and found no fish near. He dipped his intrunk and took in water, finding it sweet.

'Hey, you can't have all the fun!' Colene cried. She got out of her clothes, waded into the water, bent down, swept her hand across the surface, and splashed at Burgess.

Even without contact, he understood her intent. She was pretending to attack him, in what in her thoughts was a game. This was one of the intriguing alien concepts he was learning. So he aimed his outtrunk and splashed her back, but without force.

'Oh, yeah, squirtface? Take that!' She splashed him harder. He responded by splashing her harder, but still not with force enough to hurt. That was important.

Then the others removed their clothing too, and waded

147

in, splashing. Soon they were all making such a commotion that the fish should have been frightened away even without the fear the horse was sending them.

Burgess became aware of a peculiar emotion. Then Nona touched him, and clarified what it was: fun. He was having fun. They all were. It was a pleasant experience.

Then he floated and they swam across the river to the island. The Modes changed several times, and the horse had to refocus each time to put fear in the fish, but otherwise there was no difficulty. When they reached the island it was still uninhabited, and still guarded by vicious fish. That was ideal.

They had their evening meal and made a shelter. They decided that this night they would not have to keep guard, because it was unlikely that anything would intrude on this island. In any event, a Mode boundary traversed the length of the island, so they could quickly cross it if they needed to. They felt as safe as it was possible to feel, on the Virtual Mode.

Burgess, despite the awkwardness this travel through hills and forests entailed, and the problems occasioned by organized alien species, was coming to like it here.

# 7

## *Chaos*

Colene woke refreshed. The past two days of travel had been wearing, but they had succeeded in getting out of Shale and most of the way to Julia, and maybe two more days would bring them to Darius' home Mode. If they were going in the right direction. She suddenly realized that they might not be, because they had come from Julia to reach Provos' Mode, and that had been replaced by Shale. They should have gone the other way to reach Darius. This direction might be leading back to Earth. If the arrangement of the anchors was the same. There was no guarantee of that, because everything changed when an anchor did. So they would just have to keep on traveling, and if Darius wasn't the next anchor, well, maybe it was for the best. Because she was in the throes of an emotional impasse. She loved Darius and Seqiro, but she also liked Nona, and Burgess too; they were all good folk. She didn't want to give any of them up.

There was also that business of not actually being able to marry Darius, because his wife was the one he had to draw joy from. He would have to marry Prima, whose joy would never expire, and have Colene for his mistress. Yet that too might be problematical, because there were plenty of juicier girls than herself available, and Old Enough too. Darius loved the look and feel of young women, and who was she to deny him that? So their arrival at his home Mode would be a time of decision, in several ways, and she wasn't yet ready for those decisions. As long as they remained on the Virtual Mode, those decisions could be postponed, maybe.

So they would breeze on by Julia, where Nona didn't want

149

to be queen, and see what they came to next. If it was Earth, well, they could breeze on by that, too, because there was nothing there for her, any more. She had only just barely gotten away from there, last time; her folks had pretended to understand, then had tried to get rid of her anchor so as to trap her there. They had thought it was her shed next to the little dogwood tree, which she called Dogwood Bumshed, so they had taken that away. But an anchor wasn't a thing, it was a place on a world, and also a person of that world. So she had to get together with her anchor place, on Earth; no other Earth resident could use it, and she couldn't enter the Virtual Mode from anywhere else. But she remained mad as hell about her folks' betrayal. They had had police there and everything staking it out. They might *still* have it staked out, since they had seen her pass through it and now knew it wasn't any teenage flight of fancy. So she didn't want to go there again, for sure.

Yet she was sorry, too, because on another level she did love her folks, and knew they loved her. Her mother was an alcoholic, and her father a philanderer, but they had both tried to straighten out when she, Colene, disappeared. Probably they wouldn't be able to maintain the straight life for long, but their effort was touching. At least now they knew that Colene wasn't dead, she was just elsewhere, and happier than she had been at home with her shell of a life. If she had had to stay on Earth, they would have lost her for sure, because she would have killed herself. Somehow. Eventually. She had been playing at suicide, really, scratching her wrists, but there were more effective ways. When she got really serious about it, she would have found a way.

But here on the Virtual Mode she was − dare she think it? − happy. She liked the company she kept, even with problems. In fact, she sort of liked the problems too. When they worked together to get over a wall, or fend off attackers, she really felt with it and alive. She was part of a going concern, accomplishing something worthwhile. Her life counted. That was the key: it made a difference to the universe whether she lived or died, on the Virtual Mode. In contrast to how it was on Earth.

She got up. Darius was still asleep beside her, and Nona on his other side. The thing about Darius was that when he slept, he really did sleep. He didn't try to feel her up in the dark, and he never touched Nona at all. Not even when Seqiro slept all the way, so that there was no mental contact. He had integrity, and it was his pride and her frustration. Because she knew how much he liked women. Because she knew that she lacked that fundamental honesty. She had proved it by checking on him, pretending to be asleep so she could watch him. Anything he did to her, he did openly while they were both awake, like tickling her on the butt to make her let go of him; and anything he did to Nona he did in Colene's presence, like helping her keep steady on the wall. She knew that he did not try to check on her similarly, and wouldn't even if she were with another man. He was so damned straight she felt inferior. He was more of a man than she deserved. She would have felt really insecure about that, except that he said he loved her, and he wouldn't lie.

She crawled out from the shelter. The dawn was forming, and it was such a splendor that she paused for a moment in awe. She had never been one to ooh and aah at the sunrise or sunset, but now she realized that she had never seen it in its wilderness glory. Other mornings had been cloudy or mixed, but this one was perfect, and shades of purple, red, and gold were spreading across the irregular pattern of clouds, with scintillating sunbeams between. This was a natural world, unpolluted by the smoke and light of man's designs, and it shone with preternatural clarity in the cleanness of the new day. Maybe it was her fancy that made it so, but it was nevertheless wonderful.

She doffed the slip Nona had made for her, and walked down to the edge of the water. The piranhas were there, no longer repelled by broadcast fear, but she could handle them. She focused her mind and sent a blast of fear and rage dredged from the depths of her old, buried life on Earth. The fish scattered. She smiled, and dipped chill water to splash on her bare body. She could back the fish off only a few feet, compared to Seqiro's few hundred feet, but she was just a toddler in telepathy. It was great even to have that little bit, and maybe it would grow if she kept practicing.

Just how far *could* she reach, if she tried her hardest? She had been able to communicate with others, one on one, when she had to, but that had been mainly in emergencies. She had gotten stronger, because at first her ability had been so slight she couldn't be sure it was working at all. But she had never tried to measure it. Seqiro could even reach across the Modes, when he tried. He had done so when they first met, guiding her in to find him. Of all the things she could have dreamed of, a friendly telepathic horse was the best. When she was with Seqiro, she felt safe, not only physically but emotionally, because his mind constantly embraced her consciousness. That banished her suicidal aspect.

But the time might come when Seqiro wasn't with her. If she settled down on some basis or other with Darius, and the horse preferred to keep traveling the Virtual Mode with Nona, Colene would have to let him go. She knew she was selfish, wanting man *and* horse, and she would have to choose. Nona would be a more than adequate consolation prize for whichever one Colene didn't choose. Nona would rather actually have the horse. So Colene might have to get by on her own telepathy, and it was important to know just what its potential was.

She took a mental breath, oriented her mind, and hurled her thought out just as far as she could. *ANYBODY OUT THERE?*

She waited. Probably she had projected only about ten feet, not even crossing a Mode boundary. But it had sure felt as if she were hallooing across mountaintops.

Then there came an answer. *HUNGER.*

Colene felt a chill. She recognized that thought. It was the mind predator that had attacked Provos, and then later found Colene, probably because she had been with Provos. They had had to get her off the Virtual Mode to escape it. It had evidently gone elsewhere, thinking her forever lost to it — but now she had foolishly alerted it to her restored presence. And she wasn't close outside an anchor. Oh, folly!

What could she do? She didn't know. She knew she couldn't fight it; the thing was too powerful and awful. It fed on minds the way a cat fed on mice. She was lost.

But she had to try. She lurched up and ran back toward the tent. 'Darius! Seqiro! The mind thing's after me again!'

The others came awake. Their minds linked. 'Can you hold it off?' Darius asked.

'No! It's way too strong!'

'But maybe *we* can hold it off,' he said. 'If we link wills and resist together.'

Then it was as if she were at the center of a tug-of-war. On one side the mind predator was pulling her into its dark maw; on the other, her friends were pulling her toward the light. But the predator was stronger; she felt herself being slowly, inexorably drawn into the horror.

'It's stronger!' she gasped. 'Let me go! So you won't be drawn in too! Get away from it.'

'No,' Darius said. 'You are ours.'

'But I brought it on myself! I asked for it! I sent out a call, and it found me! I was a fool.'

'Shut up,' he said, seemingly from a distance. 'Burgess, you seem stronger. Can you resist it?'

Burgess thought he could, because his mind was not as open as theirs, and was different.

Darius picked Colene up physically and carried her to the floater. He set her two hands on Burgess' contact points. The pull of the mind predator weakened, but did not let go.

'Can you carry her?' Darius asked Burgess.

For a time, the floater thought.

Darius put Colene on Burgess' top, spread-eagled, her hands grasping contact points, her feet braced against other points. She was naked, but it didn't matter. The mind predator was another stage weaker. Her four connections to the floater were somehow channeling her mind through his, and filtering out the mind predator. But the monster still lurked, balked only for the moment, by no means defeated. Like an ocean dammed back by a sand castle, it waited, and pressed forward its tidal waves, certain to prevail in the end.

'Stay there,' Darius told her. 'Keep resisting it. We'll get you safe.'

With most of her mind and will she staved off the monster. Peripherally she was aware of the others breaking camp and traveling on. Burgess carried her, blasting through so much air that the heat of it warmed her. He moved across the water and through Mode boundaries, but the siege of the mind predator never eased; it had invaded the Virtual Mode, and she could not escape it as long as she was between anchors. She knew that the others were trying to get her to Nona's anchor, but she didn't know whether they would succeed in time. The power of the predator was dreadful, and she could oppose it only feebly, only while she focused her whole will. When her mind wandered, the predator pressed closer. What would happen when, fatigued by the effort of resistance, she slept?

Yet her will could not remain firm enough, long enough, even when she was awake. Was there any point in fighting the inevitable? Wasn't it better just to succumb now, instead of suffering the pain of the continued struggle?

But that was the predator's thought, not hers. And this

thought was from Burgess, who was aware of her plight without being able to comprehend its nuances. Because of that objectivity, he understood what the predator was doing: trying to make her capitulate without fighting. That could only be because it feared she would escape him if she staved him off long enough.

'Thanks, Burgess,' she said. 'I won't let it trap me that way. I'll fight just as long as I can.'

There was anger, and she realized that it was from the predator. It didn't like being balked, even to this extent. Still, she felt her ability to resist draining out of her, as if she had cut a vein in her wrist and the blood was flowing in a thin steady stream to the floor. How long would it be before she drained too far, and lost her strenth, and was overwhelmed? A day? An hour? A minute? She didn't know, but feared that whatever her maximum time was, it would take longer for them to bear her out of the Virtual Mode. She was doomed.

Funny thing: she was suicidal, yet now she didn't want to die. Because her suicidal impulse was back on Earth, when she had nothing worth living for. Here on the Virtual Mode she had Darius and Seqiro, and she wanted to live for them. So she wasn't suicidal now. What an irony, that this nemesis was attacking her on this same Virtual Mode that gave her reason to live! Had it come after her on Earth, it could have had her without resistance. But it seemed it couldn't pass through the anchors. It was the reverse of the rest of them; instead of being a creature of an anchor Mode, crossing the imitation territory of the Virtual Mode, it was a creature of the Virtual Mode barred from the portals of the anchors. Where did it come from, and what kind of thing was it?

Suddenly she was tempted to go find it, to satisfy her curiosity. Surely it was a magnificent entity! All she had to do was let go . . .

But that was the mind predator's thought, Burgess reminded her. She must not take it for her own.

Colene rallied her determination again. The predator kept trying to trick her, which meant it was worried. That was a good sign. But she was worried too, because these were merely little waves she was deflecting, not the tide itself. The dark water was rising, and her little sand castle seemed increasingly insecure. Was the thing merely playing with her, teasing her, allowing her to think she could escape, when actually she had no chance?

That was the predator's thought, Burgess indicated.

Damn! She kept being tricked, being seduced into defeatism. She was too ready to believe she was lost — and *that* was her own thought.

She hung on, physically and mentally, falling into a daze. And gradually, insidiously, her reality shifted, and the horror loomed.

'I can't make it!' she cried at last. 'Stop the motion! I'm fading out!'

Darius came and lifted her off the floater. 'You're tired, Colene,' he said reassuringly. 'You can make it. We're going to Julia, where we can lose that thing, as we did at Shale.'

'But it's creeping up on me!' she insisted. 'It's going to get me! The way the fire got those firemen!'

'What?'

'Oh, that's right, you don't know about any of that,' she said, babbling, just wanting to hold his attention, because it was all she had to cling to. 'Back on Earth, before my time, but I read about it somewhere, a real horror story. There was this big fire in the dead of winter, it was way below freezing, maybe down around zero Fahrenheit, and these three firemen got trapped way up high on a ledge on a building, and the fire was coming for them, and no one else could reach them. They could only get one fire hose to play on that section of the fire, and it wasn't enough, and the poor firemen were going to get burned up. But then someone had a bright idea, and he said, "Play the water on the firemen!" and they did, and that kept them cool and wet so the fire couldn't burn them. And the fire raged all night before they got it under control, but all night they kept a steady stream of water on those trapped firemen, protecting them from the heat. And in the morning they got a closer look — and the three firemen were frozen stiff.'

'I don't understand,' he said.

'The fire was hot, see, but the night was cold, and water made it colder. So that water made it *too* cold, but they couldn't hear the firemen cry, amidst the roar of the fire, and they killed those three men, just trying to save them. Just the way you're killing me, just trying to save me. Because my body may be getting carried along, but the predator is reaching my mind, and by the time you get me to Nona's anchor, I'll just be a frozen husk, and what's the point?'

'But we have to help you!' he said.

'There's got to be a better way.'

He nodded. 'Yes. I have a better way. I will hold you close.' He put his hands to his clothing, stripping it rapidly off.

'But you don't need to do that,' she protested. 'Just hold me as you are, Darius!'

'This way is better,' he said, stepping into her, naked. His strong arms closed around her, drawing her in crushingly close. She felt his body growing hot.

'Darius, what are you doing?' she cried.

'I am getting close to you,' he said, bearing her back and down to the ground. His knee wedged against her knees, to force her legs apart.

'But I'm too young for this! You never touch me, because —'

His face came down on hers, stifling her protest with a savage kiss. 'It isn't as if you haven't had it before,' he said, and shifted position on her.

She tried to push him off, but he was too heavy. She tried to fight him, but he was too strong. Suddenly this man she loved had become a monster, stealing what she would gladly have given him at another time. He was raping her — the one thing she couldn't stand.

Colene screamed. Her whole energy of fear and loathing went into it.

Then she found herself riding Burgess, yanking at his contact points. It had been a bad dream. As she should have known, because Darius would never try to rape her. It was beside the point that he would never *have* to.

Nona came to her. 'What is it?' she asked solicitously.

'The mind predator — it sent me a bad dream,' Colene said. 'I'm sorry I screamed.'

'We are getting closer to my anchor,' Nona said. 'There you will be safe.'

'But you don't want to go there! We were going to pass it by!'

'We won't stay,' Nona said. 'Just long enough to get the mind predator away from you.'

'You're awful nice,' Colene said, relaxing. 'Nicer than me.' She let her gaze go unfocused as she rested her head on Burgess' central hump. There was an eye stalk near, which turned to check on her every so often. There was a time when that might have freaked her out, but now it was reassuring. As long as she was close to Burgess, the mind predator was held somewhat at bay.

She saw the realities change as they passed through the boundaries. Trees popped in and out of existence, and sometimes animals too. The weather changed from Mode to Mode. One was foggy, so that they proceeded through an almost nightlike opacity. It went on and on, until she realized that they must have turned, and were traveling crosswise, remaining in a single Mode. Why was this?

Or could it be Julia? Could they have passed through Nona's anchor, and her Mode happened to be foggy, so they had to keep plowing through it? Then Colene was safe, and the mind predator couldn't get her.

They came to a building, and went in. Inside there were rows of seats. Pews. It was a church! Colene took a seat near the rear, and the rest quickly filled in. Then the service started. There was music: the first gentle strains of the Wedding March.

Colene felt a qualm. What was she doing at a wedding? Who was getting married? There was something wrong about this. But she seemed to be the only one concerned.

Then she saw Darius at the front. He was dressed in a suit and looked unbearably handsome. He was the Bridegroom!

And here was Colene, way back buried in the audience. She wasn't the one he was marrying.

The music intensified as the Bride appeared. She was escorted by an older man, who reminded Colene oddly of her own father, and she was radiantly beautiful.

Colene forced herself to look at the Bride's face, knowing who it would be. And it was: Nona. Nona was marrying Darius. Exactly as Colene's nightmare back in the Earth Mode had showed it. Lovely, sweet, gentle, talented Nona, the ideal bride for any man, especially one who had strong magic of his own.

Women around Colene began to cry. It was something women did at weddings. It was sheer foolishness. But Colene was crying too. Not from any appropriate fancy. She was weeping because she was losing the man she loved. Maybe in time she could have married him, but she was too young while Nona wasn't. Yet even if Darius had been willing to wait, why would he take Colene when Nona was so much better?

The Bride swept up to the Groom. The music faded. The accompanying people peeled away like the gantry from a rocket about to take off. The man who had walked Nona down the aisle went to sit in the front pew reserved for the

Bride's family, beside a woman who could have been Colene's mother. Who *should* have been. This whole wedding should have been Colene's!

The Ceremony commenced. Colene was too lost in misery to pay attention to the words. All that she might have dreamed of, gone instead to Nona!

Then it was done, and the Groom kissed the Bride. They were the perfect couple, and it was the perfect kiss.

What was left for Colene, except to die?

Colene screamed. This time her whole energy of despair went into it.

She found herself riding Burgess, clinging to the contact points. It had been another bad dream. She should have realized that it wasn't real, because weddings did not just happen from nowhere. But the dream had carried its own conviction, and she had not questioned it, until the doom of her romance seemed final.

This time it was Darius who came. 'Thing's getting to you?' he asked, concerned.

'It sure is,' she said, trying to smile bravely.

'What is it like?'

She knew he was just trying to divert her from the horror of the mind predator, to make her feel better. But it helped, so she answered. 'It made me think you were trying to rape me.'

'I would not do that!' he protested.

'I know. You wouldn't have to.' She tried to smile, but knew it wasn't coming off. 'Then it made me think you were marrying Nona.'

'No, you are the one I wish to marry. If only –'

'If only I had boundless, renewable joy to give,' she said sadly. 'But I don't, and I never will. Maybe you *should* marry Nona.'

Now Nona appeared. 'What?'

'Maybe you have the kind of joy he needs,' Colene said relentlessly. 'I mean, you can do all these other kinds of magic, so why not that? Multiplying joy?' She looked at Darius again. 'Why don't you draw from her, and send it out, the way you do, and see how it is?'

'Colene, I don't want to marry Darius!' Nona protested. 'I respect him as a man, but I respect you too, and I would never –'

But now Colene's suicidal urge was manifesting. 'Go ahead, Darius. Do it. Draw from her, and send it out. See if it's good.'

'But –' he started, seeming out of sorts.

'Find out,' Colene insisted. 'So you know. So we all know. Is she someone you could marry?'

Darius looked at Nona. 'I suppose I could check. But you have to understand that this is an unsettling procedure. I take all of a woman's joy, and then I multiply it and send it out to all present, including her. So she gets most of it back. But never quite all. So that in time she becomes inevitably depleted. That is why I can not marry for love. I have to marry only for joy, and when it is gone I have to divorce her and marry a new one who has not been depleted.'

Nona looked at Colene. 'This is not the kind of magic I know. I do not think I would be successful at it.'

'But you don't know that,' Colene said. 'You can't know until you try it, can you? You didn't know you could make fireballs, until you tried. So don't you want to know? You can find out just like that.'

'But what would it prove?' Nona asked.

'It would prove you have the power of joy,' Colene said. 'Or that you don't.'

Nona came to a conclusion. 'It would be easier to demonstrate that I lack this power of joy,' she said. 'Darius, test me.'

'I see no point in this,' he said.

'Do it,' Colene said grimly.

He looked at Nona, who looked back at him. Both looked

161

at Colene. Then Darius took Nona in his arms and pressed her close in, as close as was possible. It looked like a love embrace. But it wasn't. How well Colene knew it wasn't! It was a terrible kind of taking, despite the good that it did for the community, in Darius' Mode.

He drew from her. 'Oh!' Nona gasped, appalled, seeming to wilt. He turned her loose, and she leaned against a tree, reeling.

Then he sent out the joy. Colene felt it, suddenly being much improved. And Nona felt it too, recovering. But she looked shaken.

'So what's the verdict?' Colene demanded. 'How is she?'

'I feel the same,' Nona said. 'But that – that was an awful experience. My very being –'

Colene bore on Darius. 'Tell me.'

'It is too soon to be sure,' he said, seeming surprised.

'Not with Seqiro, it isn't. Horseface, is her joy depleted?'

*No.*

'So she can take it without losing joy,' Colene said. 'She's a cornucopia, always full.'

Darius stared at Nona. 'This is my impression. You have some magic of this type.'

'So you could marry her for love, and not deplete her,' Colene said victoriously. But she tasted the ashes.

Nona's eyes widened. 'I never thought – but perhaps –'

Darius nodded. 'It could be done.'

And Colene knew that she had lost again. Because Nona could win Darius' love without even trying. The Wedding Scene was feasible. Once they sorted it through and realized how much sense it made. Colene, lacking both magic and joy, could not cut it. She was doomed.

Then Colene was screaming again – and again found herself riding on Burgess, holding the contact points. It had been yet another bad dream, more plausible than the others.

This time it was Seqiro who checked on her. *Your mind*

*goes opaque when the mind predator gains control. What was the vision this time?*

'I dreamed that Darius tested Nona, and she had enough joy. You know, she wasn't depleted, even a little. You verified that, by checking her emotion before and after. So she *could* marry Darius, and be his ideal wife, because of the joy and because she's beautiful and nice and obliging and magical and all. I mean, why should he want a twisted underage thing like me, a vessel of hurt and depression, when he can have a wonderful creature like her?'

*But he does not wish to marry her, and she does not wish to marry him.*

Colene laughed bitterly. 'Darius would love to have an affair with her, because she's got the universe's most ideal body and she's a good person. But she wouldn't just do that without marriage. So he would do the honorable thing, and marry her.'

*Yes, he would. But not if she did not wish it, and she does not. She likes him as a figure of competence and adventure. She does not wish to settle into marriage with him any more than with a man of the Julia Mode.*

Colene knew that was true. Nona really had no designs on anyone. She just wanted to explore the Virtual Mode forever. But she was such a luscious thing that men were simply not going to leave her alone. And the closest man was Darius. Sooner or later the fox was going to notice the goose. This was the nature of things.

*True. Propinquity causes interest in members of your species. He will become increasingly interested in her, and that will bring her return interest. The passage of time makes this inevitable.*

'And it will happen before I get old enough,' Colene said. 'Even if I could be old enough right now, I couldn't compete with her. My only hope is to get us to Darius' Mode right away, with no delay. But we have to stop at Julia, because of this damned mind predator, and that delay's going to be fatal.'

*Yes, that seems to be the case.*

'Oh, Seqiro, let's you and I just gallop off somewhere and be free!' she cried, knowing her wish was vain. 'You don't care if I'm a vessel of dolor.'

*I don't know where we would go.*

'Just anywhere! Anywhere far away from here! Maybe we can outrun the mind predator.'

*We can try. Get on my back.*

She climbed off Burgess and climbed onto Seqiro's back, using the harness to get up there, because his back was well above the top of her head. Then he started to move, cutting away to the side, across a Mode boundary, and farther to the side. He broke into a trot, and then a canter, and finally a full gallop. Soon they were lost in a jungle, where the ground was almost clear under hugely spreading trees. No one could find them here!

'This is great, Seqiro!' Colene exclaimed. 'Do you like it as well as I do?'

There was no answer. The horse slowed to a walk, picking his way between the trees.

'Hey, what's up, horseface? Why don't you answer me?'

He just kept on walking.

Colene felt a small thrill of concern. Was something wrong? She reached for his mind with hers, using her own telepathy − and found nothing.

Alarmed, she put her whole mental force into it. *Seqiro!* But still there was no response.

She climbed down and jumped off. Seqiro stopped walking. She went to the horse's head, putting her hands on his nose to compel his attention. *Seqiro − where is your mind?*

The horse merely stood there. There was no response from his mind. Indeed, all her mind found was dull equine thoughts of vague hunger and awareness of her hands. He was waiting for her to give her next command.

Seqiro had become an ordinary horse. His telepathy was gone, and with it his seemingly human intelligence. The major companion of her life on the Virtual Mode had become a mere animal.

'Oh, Seqiro!' she said, the tears coming. 'I never meant for this to happen!' Now she realized that she had been concerned about the wrong thing. Darius would not betray her. But if Seqiro had lost his telepathy, so that he could no longer draw on her human intelligence and became equivalently smart himself, her life on the Virtual Mode would become chaos. Seqiro linked them all, forging them into a perfect group, or hive. She had become so accustomed to that mental linkage that now, without it, she felt horribly naked and inadequate. Which was an exact description of her condition.

'Without you, I don't want to live!' she cried. 'Your mind sustains me. You were never just a horse. I can't stand to have you this way.'

Seqiro lowered his head and began to graze.

Colene wept.

She found herself riding on Burgess. This time she hadn't screamed, but it had been another bad dream. The implacable siege of the mind predator remained, still inching up on her consciousness.

'And what if I think about you, Burgess?' she asked. 'Will you, too, turn bad?'

Burgess' intrunk came up. It started sucking air. It grew larger, and more air flowed in. Then it oriented on her head. Suddenly the suction became overwhelming. She was ripped from her hold and drawn into the internal void.

Yes, this was her Burgess nightmare. Only this time she knew it for what it was. So she flowed with it, letting it happen. That made it easier.

In a moment she was shot out through the outtrunk. She

165

flew through the air in an arc. Then she saw the ground coming. It was time to get out of this dream, before she made a bruising landing. But she couldn't.

She crashed into the ground headfirst. Her neck broke, and her skull cracked open. Red blood and gray matter got scrambled with brown dirt and green grass. She was dead, of course, and not prettily. Well, that was one way to end her travail.

The others hurried across. 'Colene!' Nona cried. 'Are you all right?'

Here she was, with her brains stirred into the ground, and the idiot asked that?

'She's unconscious,' Darius said. He got down and wedged his arms under her body, picking her up. Chunks of brainy dirt fell out of her skull and plopped on the ground.

'Is her mind whole?' Nona asked, concerned.

No, it was only about two-thirds there; the rest was in a dirty gray pile on the ground.

*She is conscious*, Seqiro thought. *But unable to speak or move.*

'I must heal her!' Nona said. She embraced Colene, pressing Colene's head to her bosom.

Darius would rather have that treatment, Colene thought wryly. She herself had hugged him so, when he was worn out from hauling the wagon through the Mode anchor, but she simply lacked the volume and quality of upholstery Nona had. And of course she lacked the magic of healing, along with all other magic. But this was no good for Nona to do, because Colene's messed-up brains were leaking out onto her nice clean blouse.

Then Nona's magic took hold. Colene felt herself healing. No, don't do it, she wanted to cry. Let me die in peace. That will solve everything!

But her brains sloughed off the dirt and formed back into their natural convolutions. The crack in her skull diminished into a crevice and healed over, and her blood-sodden hair rinsed itself clean and became its normal lusterless brown. She was whole again.

She opened her eyes. 'What happened?' she asked. She knew what had happened, but wanted to ascertain how they had experienced it.

'You fell off Burgess,' Darius said.

'And bumped your head,' Nona added.

*You were unconscious*, Seqiro thought.

Burgess had tried to catch her with a trunk, but had only succeeded in slowing her fall.

That was all? No flying through the air, no splattered brains? Obviously not. She had suffered yet another bad dream. Even though she had known it was a dream, she had somehow come to believe in it. She hadn't been blown through Burgess' trunk; it was laughable to think she could even fit, since small stones were the largest things he could handle. And that business about her brains falling out! She had a gruesome, self-destructive imagination. What else was new?

But now she saw that there was a pattern to these bad visions. Whoever she focused on became the object of the next bad scene. If she focused on two, then they both turned bad. There was no protection in numbers.

So how could she protect her friends from her warped dreams? Becasue she knew they were all good folk, not deserving of her foul imagination. Darius would never rape anybody; Nona would never try to hurt Colene, whether by marriage or anything else; Seqiro would not turn dumb unless caught in a Mode that prohibited telepathy, which seemed unlikely; Burgess would not suck up anyone through his trunk. They all meant well, and were co-operating to get her to the next anchor so she could escape the mind predator. All she had to do was hang on. Even if it felt as if they were playing a stream of water on her body and freezing it, in their effort to rescue her from the fire of the mind predator's hunger. Hang on. Hang on and on.

And how could she best do that? She was bound to be thinking of something. On what could she focus, without mischief? Probably the mind predator could distort anything; that was part of its strategy.

But what about herself? Maybe even that would be distorted – but at least she wouldn't be wronging anyone else. She herself was the only one she had the right to malign.

So she climbed back onto Burgess, took hold of his contact points, and promised not to fall off again. After all, he was carrying her to safety. She focused on herself, knowing that this was unlikely to be pleasant.

'Come on, mind thing,' she urged. 'Do your worst. I'm calling your bluff.'

Just like that, it happened: she woke.

She was sitting cross-legged in a cold chamber, shivering in a flimsy nightie. There was a chamber pot nestled within the clasp of her bare thighs, and from it issued a stench that stung her nose.

She looked around. It was dark, but dawn was coming and she was able to see that she was in a shed, with an array of things propped against its bare walls. An ancient, battered teddy bear, a Raggedy Ann doll, a couple of books, a guitar, a picture of a horse, an artificial flower. Around her, on the floor, was a tattered blanket she must have had hunched over her body. Also a kitchen knife.

Now she knew where she was. In Dogwood Bumshed, her hideout. Ready to commit suicide. Because she hadn't truly believed in Darius, and he had returned to his distant world, and then she had known the extent of the folly of her disbelief. She had had the chance for the love of her life, and had thrown it away. Had she really wanted to believe? Or had she merely been looking for a pretext to kill herself and be done with the agony of existence?

She had set herself up, ready to slice her forearms with

168

the knife, and bleed them into the pot so as not to mess up the floor. If she filled the pot and wasn't dead yet, she would take it out behind the shed, empty it by the roots of the dogwood tree, and bring it back in for another filling. In due course she would be all the way dead, and it would be done at last. At least the dogwood tree would have good fertilizer.

But she had chickened out. She had sat here with the knife in her hand, and her bare arms over the pot, and not been able to make the cut. So she had sat here, her bare bottom getting creased on the floor, trying to force the courage to do what she had come to do — and instead had gone into the most wonderful of dreams.

She had dreamed that she had heard a thought in her mind: *COLENE! Wait for me!* Then, after a pause, *Take hold!* And she had reached out with her mind and taken hold of the Virtual Mode, and had become an anchor person, and had gone out across the realities to meet Darius. And on the way had found Seqiro, the magnificent telepathic horse. And later the others, and adventure galore. They had gotten trapped in the DoOon Mode, where the Emperor Ddwng wanted to get hold of the Chip Darius had used to send up the Virtual Mode, and wouldn't let them go until he had it. He threatened to slaughter Seqiro, to make Colene cooperate, and he threatened to cut out Colene's ovaries for their eggs, to make Darius cooperate. But they had escaped, by tricking Ddwng into freeing his anchor, and found themselves in the Julia Mode with Nona. That was another whole adventure, because those folk could do all kinds of magic. Finally they had won free of that and found the Shale Mode, and the adventure continued.

Until the mind predator had come after Colene, and now it had done its worst: dumping her back here in dreariest reality. Costing her everything. All the wonderful adventures, all her hopes and fears along the Virtual Mode, all her love for horse and man.

So had she really dreamed it all? Or was *this* the bad dream? How could she know? Because if the whole Virtual Mode were a dream, she was doomed. But if the mind predator was doing it, then she was locked into its power, and was doomed. Because she knew without trying that this time she was not going to be able to snap herself out of it by screaming or crying. The grip of the mind predator had been growing stronger, and now it was too strong.

So was there any point in being concerned about it? She was locked into destruction either way. If she had dreamed it all, then it was time to kill herself, because Earth had nothing for her. If the mind predator had her secure, then she might as well kill herself too, because life in its embrace was too horrible to contemplate.

Could she kill herself in a bad dream? Would that kill her in reality, depriving the monster of her mind and emotion? For the thing fed on her fading dreams and fears, as worms fed on a decaying carcass, and if she died there would be nothing for it.

There was one way to find out. She took up the knife again and oriented it above her left arm. This time she wouldn't chicken out!

Yet there was a faint demurring thought. Not hers; it was Burgess. It didn't make sense for her to die, when she was so close to the anchor and freedom. If she died, the mind predator would have beaten her.

Beaten her? No way! She was going to beat *it*, by dying and leaving it nothing to feed on.

But that faint thought hung on. This was the predator speaking, not Colene. It wanted her to give up all resistance, because then not even her friends could help her, and the anchor would be too late.

Ludicrous! It wanted to feed on her living mind, destroying it stage by stage. Only by killing that mind could she balk it.

Still that faint nagging thought. She could not truly kill

herself in the dream, she could only acknowledge the mastery of the predator by giving up all hope of escape. Death in the dream was captivity by the predator.

Which was right? She was sure that death was the correct course, but was there a reasonable doubt? If so, was it rational to commit suicide?

Reasonable doubt. Rationality. Life. Death. Chaos.

She cudgeled her brain, trying to make it think logically instead of with pure feeling. Did death make sense, or life with the risk of awful captivity? Should she trust her own, strong thoughts, or that faint nagging Burgess thought?

And there was the key: her own thoughts had been ranging all over everywhere, always winding up in disaster. So she couldn't trust them. While Burgess was the only one who could help her against the mind predator. He was not subject to human thought processes, because he was alien. He was not subject to human distortion. Thus he could be trusted. Maybe. If it really were his thought she was picking up.

And what he thought was that in human terms Colene seemed to have a good existence ahead. She was with a good little hive. All of the others were working to bring her to safety, and there was not far to go. They all needed her and wanted her to survive.

They needed her. From out of chaos, a thought to warm her soul. She made a difference to others.

'Airfoot, you'd better be right!' she exclaimed, throwing away the knife.

The scene exploded, literally. Bumshed flew apart, the walls flying out across the dawn yard. Colene's precious things were scattered in a circle. The floor dropped out from under, leaving her sitting cross-legged in space. A draft froze her legs, blowing her nightie up and off her body, leaving her naked. The stinking pot before her belched a stench so putrid that she couldn't breathe.

But all this proved was that she had defeated the dream, and now it was coming apart. She had managed to fight off the monster, again, thanks to Burgess. 'Ha-ha, rotmind!' she cried. 'I've beaten you! You can't have me! Nyaa, nyaa, nyaa!'

But she had exulted too soon. The mind predator rallied from its rage, and the siege intensified. It had not lost the game, only an episode, and its resources were relatively infinite. Now it wasn't trying to trick her, it was marshaling its full power for the direct brute kill. No amount of dreaming would stop it this time.

Then there was light. Colene blinked. She was riding on Burgess, and they were on a fair hill. Behind them was the sound of ocean waves breaking against the face of a cliff. She recognized this place, for she had been here before.

They had passed through the anchor, and this was the Julia Mode.

The malignant siege of the mind predator faded. This time it was really gone.

'Oh, thank you, Burgess!' she cried, doing her best to hug the floater. 'You got me through! You saved my sanity!'

They had all gotten her through, Burgess clarified. Nona by knowing the way and making a smooth path by magic, when the terrain became too rough. Darius by drawing joy from Nona and sending it out to Colene, so that she never sank too low to be recovered, and by conjuring them across a crevasse when there was no time to go around it. Seqiro by keeping them all connected, and carrying everything they needed, and sometimes hauling things out of the way so that it was possible to make a path for Burgess. And Burgess himself, by carrying her, and shielding her to some extent from the mind predator.

Colene realized that the others had put forth a heroic collective effort on her behalf. She had thought the battle

172

was all her own, but that was only the inner part of it. Her friends had fought the outer part of it. She felt a terrific surge of gratitude. But when she tried to express it, things blocked up, and she burst into tears.

But it was all right. Her mind was back in full contact with theirs, and they understood. Chaos had been defeated, this time.

# 8

## *Julia*

Nona's feelings were mixed. She was relieved that they had managed to get Colene through the anchor before the mind predator destroyed her. The girl had been writhing and crying out increasingly, and the issue had seemed in doubt. It was impossible to know what she was going through, because when the predator attacked, her mind was cut off. Only Burgess had some limited contact, perhaps because the predator didn't know how to exclude his alien mind. But Colene's moments of rationality between siege had made it clear that she was suffering, and feared that she could not resist the predator much longer.

However, to save Colene they had had to do what Nona least wanted to do: return to Julia, her home Mode. Now they were standing on the hill by the sea, near her home village, on the world of Oria. The fractal outlines of the terrain were evident, though in this region they had been so much worn down that a stranger might miss them. When the villagers saw the party and recognized Nona, they would demand that she remain to be queen of Oria, because she was now the only person who could do full magic. Everyone could do illusion, of course, but that didn't count. The real magic had been the province of the men, and now it was the province of the women, but only those who were born in the ambience of the anima. It would take a generation for the women to achieve their full powers. Except for Nona, the ninth of the ninth, who had brought the anima.

She didn't want to be queen. She didn't want to marry and breed. She didn't want to stay here. Because staying would mean the end of her adventure on the Virtual Mode,

174

which had hardly begun, and every child she bore would draw some of her magic away, until at last she too was left with only illusion. How could she avoid being trapped into this role she so detested, when they recognized her?

'Listen, Nona,' Colene said. 'I really appreciate this. I know you don't want to be here, but I guess we'll have to stay a week or so, here in Julia, same way we did in the Shale Mode. So I guess it's up to me to figure out how to fix it so you won't get trapped.'

Nona had forgotten that Colene was back in the mental network, or as Burgess put it, the hive. So the girl had picked up Nona's thoughts. Nona should have asked Seqiro to limit them. 'This is not your responsibility,' she replied.

'Oh yes, it is! I'm the one the mind predator was after, and you're the one who had to come here to save me. So I owe you. I don't want my problem to become your problem.'

Nona shrugged. 'It can only be my problem, because I am the one with the anima magic.'

'And I'm the one with the animal cunning,' Colene said. 'I'll figure out something. Maybe we can hide you.'

'It's not that,' Nona demurred. 'I would not be recognized beyond this village, physically. But the moment I do any magic, anyone on Oria will know me. Then in a moment, all will know that I am back.'

'Well, maybe if you just don't do any magic, then.'

'I shall have to, to provide food and shelter for us,' Nona said. 'We must not use our carried supplies while in an anchor Mode.'

Colene nodded. 'Um, yes. But there must be a way. Maybe if we stay in the countryside, and you do magic only when no one else is around.'

'We would still have to explain the source of our supplies,' Darius pointed out. 'Lest they think we are thieves. And I am not certain how we can ever explain Burgess.'

'This is true,' Nona agreed. 'There is no creature like

Burgess on this world. He will become an object of cynosure very quickly.'

Colene turned to gaze at Burgess. 'Yeah, I guess he's a freak, here. No offense, airfoot.' She touched a contact point. Then she did a double take. 'A freak! That's it!'

The others all looked at her, even the horse and Burgess' three eyes on stalks. 'Is the mind predator after you again?' Darius inquired with a smile that was not fully humorous.

'No, I'm okay, honest!' Colene exclaimed. 'Tired, sure; I'll have to sleep a day or two pretty soon. But I know what I'm thinking. Back on Earth sometimes they have these freak shows, with a traveling circus or something. A bearded woman, a dwarf, a dog-faced boy, a two-headed snake – that sort of thing. Folks have to pay to see the freaks. It's always a rip-off, but as old Barnum said, there's a sucker born every minute. So Burgess can be our freak, and we'll make folk pay to see him. We'll say he's from a weird distant world, which he is, really: an alternate Earth. But tame, and we won't let anybody hurt him. That should be good for a few thrown pennies.'

'Pennies won't account for our food and supplies,' Darius said.

'So who's to know how many pennies we get? Maybe nickels and dimes, too, or gold pieces, whatever they have here. The point is, it'll explain our livelihood, and no one will question it.'

'An entertainment troupe,' Nona said, appreciating the nicety of it. 'We do have those on Oria. Traveling minstrels, groups of actors who put on plays. I suppose one could be for the showing of an unusual creature.'

'It sure could,' Colene said. 'Darius can be the ringmaster, riding a big brown horse – guess who, horseface! Did you know that Seqiro's the exact age and color I am? Fourteen, and brown hair! We were destined to be together. And you can play music and sing and dance, Nona; the men'll love it, 'specially if you wear a skirt which flares. So sure we can

176

be an entertainment troupe; I like that notion better than freak show.'

'But what will you do?' Nona asked. 'You are definitely not a freak, but – '

'But I don't have a body to madden men's minds, either,' Colene agreed. 'Guess I'll just have to be the hat girl.'

'A girl in a hat?' Nona asked, perplexed.

Colene laughed, and clarified the thought. 'An urchin with a big hat, running around and begging for coins, when the show's done. I'll catch 'em in the hat, see. And I'll do the chores, like cleaning up manure. All-purpose servant.'

'This is obviously your ideal vocation,' Darius said drolly.

'And I'll feed that manure to you, after Nona has made it look like gourmet fare,' she responded with mock sweetness. She turned to Nona. 'So have I figured it out? If I conk out now, can you folk carry through?'

'I believe we can,' he agreed.

Colene went to Seqiro. 'Can you carry me for a while, horseface? Poor Burgess's been doing it, and I know he's worn out too. I've got to sleep safely.'

Seqiro agreed that he could carry her, and Colene climbed up on his harness and half sat, half lay on his back. In a moment she was asleep. Nona knew it, because of the telepathy; Colene dropped out of the net.

'We had better get away from here first,' Darius said. 'So that the folk of your villages don't see us.'

'That is true.' Nona knew that he could conjure them to another place, but this had its complications. It was better simply to walk. 'I will clothe us in illusion. It would be easy for another person to penetrate it, but perhaps none will bother.'

She made Seqiro look like a smaller horse, with no harness and no person on his back. She made Burgess look like another horse. Both wore yellow animal tunics. She conjured a blue tunic for Darius and a red one for herself. These were

177

the theow colors; when the animus had become anima, and the men lost the power of magic, and the despots their authority, the colors had not changed. It was just that blue and red were now worthy colors, instead of indications of servitude. The black and white of the male and female despots had become the lowly colors.

She led the way away from the village. They were lucky; they encountered no one. She wondered about that; normally there were folk working in the fields, and lovers taking walks, and animals grazing. It was odd that things were so quiet.

By early evening they had reached a secluded region shielded from any thoroughfare by an arm of the forest. It was relatively barren, so that no farming was done here. They should be able to camp here without being disturbed.

She took up a stick of wood and transmuted it into a swatch of cloth. Then she expanded the cloth until it was large enough to make a tent, and gave that to Darius to work with. She picked up a stone and transmuted it to crockery, and magically shaped that into a small cup. She expanded the cup into a bucket. She took an acorn and transmuted it into horsefeed, then expanded the feed until it filled the bucket. Seqiro had his meal. She was about to make something for Burgess, but he didn't need it; he was already sucking up more of the fallen acorns and grinding them up inside. Finally she went through a similar process to make bowls of mashed potatoes and cups of milk for the three human folk. It was not, as Colene put it, gourmet fare, but Nona was not an artist with culinary magic; she could produce only type and quantity. However, illusion did serve to improve it.

Colene woke and got down from the horse. She had had several hours' sleep, and remained logy, but was feeling better; her emotion was only slightly depressive now. She was hungry; she gobbled her dish of mashed potato and gulped down her milk.

178

As night closed, they stripped the harness and burdens from Seqiro, and the horse went grazing. Burgess continued to quest for things on the forest floor, quite competent to take care of himself. The three humans settled into the tent Darius had made from Nona's material and planned their tour. Then they settled down to sleep in their normal fashion, Darius between the two women.

This was not, Nona reflected, so much different from their stay on Shale. Except that here they did not need to fear any wild predators; none would venture this close to a human settlement.

'Right,' Colene muttered. 'The only one we have to fear is our own kind.'

Next day their group visited a village that Nona had not been to since her childhood. Darius, the nominal master of the troupe, led Seqiro the trained horse, and Nona, her hair concealed by a cap, rode somewhat regally on the horse's back. A closed wagon was hauled along behind, containing the Monster from Afar. The last was the hat girl, looking somewhat woebegone. They had rehearsed their parts, and hoped the villagers accepted the show for what it was intended to be.

The village seemed normal from a distance, but the closer they got the stranger it became. Instead of a reasonably neat array of modest houses, there was a collection of shells of houses, with rubbish littering the street. A barricade had been placed across the street at the edge of the village, and several grim-looking men were guarding it.

'I don't like the look of this,' Darius said mentally. 'This looks more like a military camp than a hamlet.'

'I don't understand,' Nona said. 'It looks as if there has been fighting here. Where are the women?'

'Methinks this region of Oria isn't as peaceful as we thought,' Colene said from within the closed wagon. 'We may have to beat a retreat.'

They stopped, but it was too late to withdraw. The men were coming to them, carrying clubs and pitchforks. They looked mean. They wore black tunics. Nona didn't want to use her magic, but if the men attacked she would have to hurl a fireball. What were the despot men doing here in a theow village like this?

*I will project caution to their minds*, Seqiro said, also in thought, which was always his way. *And fear if necessary.*

The men came to stand before Darius. 'What's your business here, stranger?' one demanded.

'I have an entertainment troupe,' Darius explained. Nona knew that he was a stickler for honesty, but they had indeed become such a troupe. 'Our maiden plays music and dances, and our horse is trained to do tricks. We also have a strange monster from afar. We ask only pennies from the audience, to defray our meager expenses.'

'Mister, where you been the last month?' the man demanded. 'Didn't you know there's been a revolution?'

'I have been isolated, far from here, with my troupe,' Darius said. 'What is this about a revolution?'

'Some bitch brought the anima,' the man said. 'The current changed, and now we can't do magic. The theows got rambunctious, so we had to put the villages under martial law. You're in theow garb; are you going to make trouble?'

'I came merely to entertain, and to earn a few pennies in payment,' Darius said. This was the truth, as far as it went; he would not have told a lie even to an enemy. 'I thought my troupe would be welcomed in any village. If it is not, I will depart. I wish no trouble.'

The man looked at the other men. Seqiro projected a thought of acceptance. 'Well, if you've got a good show, we'll let you in. But you'll have to be out of here by dusk.'

'I think I have a good show,' Darius said meekly.

They moved the barricade aside and let the party pass. Now the women appeared, coming out from the battered houses, their children following. They were in red. They did not look happy.

'What has happened here?' Nona demanded mentally. 'Where are the theow men? This is not at all like the land I left!'

Seqiro explored the nearby minds, slowly gaining their thoughts. 'The theow men were driven away,' he reported. 'The women could not escape, and remain here as hostages so that the men will not attack. The despot men govern here.'

'But the despots have no magic any more!' Nona protested. 'How can they govern?'

'By strength of arm and viciousness of will,' Darius explained. 'They may lack magic, but so do the theows, so those with weapons and the will to use them remain dominant.'

'Oh, it wasn't supposed to be this way!' Nona thought. 'This is worse than before I brought the anima!'

'This is revolution,' Colene thought. 'It's usually this way, I think. The new order is supposed to solve all problems instantly, but it can't, and the older order gets mean when it starts losing its power. I guess it will take a generation to settle down, when the children grow up with their magic. We should have realized that before we left here.'

'But it was peaceful when we left!' Nona reminded her.

'Because you had all the power,' Colene responded. 'But then you left, and no one had magic to fill it. So instead of a new order, it's winding down into anarchy.'

'I never realized!' Nona thought. 'I should never have left! I was so selfish, thinking only of myself.'

'I don't think so,' Darius replied. 'I fear you might have been killed, as the visible agent of the revolution.'

Nona shut down her protest, realizing that this could be true. Things had taken a terrible turn.

But at the moment there were villagers to entertain. They

181

stopped in the center of the village and proceeded with their show. Nona dismounted, and Darius made the horse do tricks, such as tapping his forehoof once for Yes and twice for No. Soon the children were laughing, and the despot men, seeing that this really was an entertainment troupe, relaxed.

'Now, horse, are you going to perform?' Darius inquired rhetorically. Seqiro tapped twice.

'Do you want any feed tonight?' Darius demanded. Seqiro tapped once.

'Do you know what you have to do to get it?' Seqiro hesitated, like a bad child, and finally tapped once. That brought the first titter. The villagers knew that the horse could not really respond so accurately, and he couldn't be a familiar, because that magic was gone. They knew that Darius was keying the answers with some hidden signal only the horse understood. Had they known the truth, that the horse was not only reading the man's mind but translating his words for the audience, they would have been amazed.

'What is one and one?' Darius demanded. The horse tapped twice.

'What is three and two?' The horse pondered a moment, then tapped five times.

'What is four apples and five ideas?' The horse turned his head to stare at the man, then stared at the audience, as if baffled. Then he faced away, lifted his tail, and dropped a pile of manure in front of Darius.

Even the despots were laughing then. They laughed again when Colene dashed up with a shovel and scooped up the manure. 'Don't ask him that question again,' Colene told the ringmaster as she dumped the manure in a box. 'He just eats the apples, and they give him dirty ideas.' Then she grabbed her big hat and ran in front of the audience, begging for pennies. She got a number.

After the smart-horse-apple act, Nona brought out her

hammer dulcimer and accompanied herself as she sang a sweet song. She was good at it, very good, because her training had been in music, and the audience loved it. Her two little hammers fairly flew across the strings, evoking the lovely music. For a second song, she removed her red tunic, to reveal a red dress beneath, with a reasonably low décolletage. Colene collected more pennies.

Then they opened the closed wagon to reveal the monster. There was a gasp of awe; this really was a strange one! Darius went into his spiel about finding this alien creature on a distant world. 'Look at the people, Monster,' he ordered it. Burgess extended his three eye stalks and oriented them in the direction of the people. Colene collected a few more coins. It was of course mandatory to squeeze the audience at every stage, milking the maximum amount from each aspect of the act.

'And now, for a few more pennies, I will make the monster float,' Darius said grandly. 'In air, but not like a bird.' He gestured, and Burgess took in air and pumped himself up, floating visibly above the floor of the wagon. Then he sank down again, as if exhausted – and also, the people were sure, because too much floatation would allow them to fathom the nature of the trick. Seqiro, attuned to their minds, planted the correct thoughts as the act proceeded.

It was, overall, a successful performance. Colene had a fair weight of pennies in the hat. They used these to buy some food, and then moved on out of the village, honoring the despot's requirement that they be gone by nightfall.

But as they sought a place to camp for the night, their private dialogue was far more sober than their act for the villagers. They had expected to find a peaceful hamlet with satisfied people. Instead they had found a battle-torn remnant maintained like a prison. Was it this way all across the world of Oria? If so, the least of their concerns was whether Nona would be recognized. She knew she could not leave her world in this state. But what could she do to improve it — without sacrificing her dream of adventure on the Virtual Mode?

'I hate to say it,' Colene said. 'But I guess we were insufferably naïve. We thought that all you had to do was change the animus to anima, so that the despots didn't have any more magic, and everything would be just fine. Instead it brought chaos.' She stopped at a depression leading to a tiny river, a streamlet from a rad, one of the typical projections of the fractal world.

'Chaos,' Darius agreed. 'When we were here before, and stopped at that small world, on the way to find that giant Angus, we saw devastation. We assumed it was because their despots had torn things up while being ousted. We never thought that the same would happen here. Despots and theows constantly fighting. Chaos makes everybody lose.' He squatted, dipping his hand in the cold stream and tasting the water.

Nona felt tears stinging. 'I was so selfish! I just wanted to have my own adventure. I deserted my world.' She also felt physically grubby, and wished she could wash her self-condemnation out of her mind as readily as the dirt from her body.

'That's what you thought before,' Colene said. 'I've been thinking about that, and I think Darius is right: you had at least an even chance of getting killed, if you stayed. Then there would have been the same anarchy, and you'd have been worse off. I think you did what you had to do, bringing the anima, and then your role in the scheme of your Mode was fulfilled and you had to get away and let things work themselves out. At that point, you had earned a shot at living your own life.' She began collecting twigs for a fire. They had evidently found their camping site.

'I agree,' Darius said. 'Revolution is not an easy business. The only way you could have avoided it was by not bringing

184

the anima.' He stripped his blue tunic and stood naked, ready to wash.

'But I *had* to bring the anima!' Nona protested. 'And now I have to help my world.' She removed her own tunic, and then the undergarments Colene had encouraged her to adopt.

'Not by getting yourself killed, you don't!' Colene retorted. 'I'm the suicidal one around here, not you.' She pulled off her tunic and underthings, joining them in nakedness. Such was their familiarity with each other now, because of experience and their constant linkage of minds, that this was routine. Nona noted peripherally that not so very long ago she would have been amazed.

'But I still wish I had your body,' Colene said, answering Nona's thought in that disconcerting way she had.

'There is nothing wrong with yours,' Nona reminded her.

'There is nothing wrong with either body,' Darius said quickly. 'Take my word.' They had to laugh as they proceeded to wash. Darius had asked Seqiro not to relay any incidental sexual thoughts he might have on such occasions, and this gave the man the illusion of indifference. Nona suspected that without that, their camaraderie would have been strained at times.

'For double sure,' Colene muttered.

Burgess had a thought. They had visited only a single hive. Was it possible that other hives were not infected?

'Yes, we need to verify the planetary situation,' Darius said. 'It may be that the transition is more peaceful in other regions. We have to assess the extent of the problem before we consider any action.'

Nona knew that they were trying to make her feel better, and to dissuade her from doing something foolish. It was possible that they were right. In any event, she couldn't do anything immediately, and she did not have the right to get her friends of the Virtual Mode in trouble on her behalf. So until it was safe for Colene to venture back onto the

Virtual Mode, they should continue to look around, not revealing themselves.

So they relaxed, and retired to their tent, and Nona tried to sleep. But her mind would not shut down. 'I had better stand guard,' she said abruptly, getting up and leaving the tent. Neither Darius nor Colene protested, though they already had an alarm wire strung that would alert them if any person tried to approach in the night.

She made a small illusion lamp to give her light, and walked down by the little stream. She loved her world of Oria, and hated to see it in distress. Yet she feared that the others were right: there was little if anything she could do now to ease the transition. Did that justify her desertion of her world?

*Do you wish my company?* It was Seqiro, reaching her with his thought though his body was grazing elsewhere.

'I wish your company forever,' she replied. 'But I fear that is not to be.'

*Before I came to the Virtual Mode, I longed for the company of a girl, a human female who was bound to me by preference rather than by my control of her mind. Colene was the realization of that longing. Now I have you also.*

'You have me also,' Nona agreed. 'But you must return to the Virtual Mode, while I think I must remain here.'

*I, too, am selfish. When I am in contact with a human mind, I can think in the human style. Colene gives me intelligence well beyond my own, and so do you. When we reach the anchor where Darius' Mode is, Colene will go there with Darius. I could go with them, but I think they will have other concerns than horses, and it may be that my power of telepathy will not exist in that reality. Then I would be a mere animal, denied the joy of high intelligence. I would prefer to remain on the Virtual Mode, if I could be with you.*

'Oh, Seqiro!' Nona cried. 'I wish I could be with you!'

*If you and Colene separate, I must go with her. But if I go with her, and then lose her, I will have no girl.*

'I do want to be your girl,' she said, feeling the tears on her face again. 'I don't want to be queen. But I must do what I believe to be right.'

*Yes, this is part of your appeal.*

'Where are you, Seqiro?'

*Follow my thought.*

She followed his thought, and soon found him in the field. She doused her illusion lamp and put her arms up around his massive neck, hugging him as well as she could. She wept, because this was when weeping was proper.

After a bit she made her lamp again and walked back toward the tent, her mind less troubled than it had been. Then she encountered Burgess. 'Hello, airfoot,' she said, borrowing Colene's idiom as she put her hand on a contact point.

Burgess was not fully comfortable on the Virtual Mode or this strange world. But as long as he remained with the hive, he could cope, and the longer he remained the better he could cope. He would feel distress if any creature of the hive were to be lost.

'Oh, Burgess,' Nona said sadly. 'Are you, too, asking me to stay with the group?'

As the floater understood it, two members of the hive would be leaving it when they reached the right anchor. That would leave only three. That was too small. If Nona left it too, there would be only two, neither of whom could generate human intelligence. That would mean the end of the hive.

'Oh, Burgess, I do want to remain with the hive!' Nona said. 'But I must do what I can for my world of Oria. If the hive ends, could you and Seqiro come back here?'

Burgess did not know, but it seemed doubtful, because Seqiro needed a human mind for intelligence and Burgess needed human versatility with wagons and bridges to navigate the difficult terrain.

'But if Darius and Colene left, and shut down Darius'

anchor, there would be a new person with a new anchor. Then you would have a new member for the hive.' But that seemed thin. It was not that easy for Burgess to adapt to new people, and a stranger would see him as exactly the kind of freak he pretended to be for their road show.

Yet Seqiro and Burgess could get along, if Nona were with them. Then a new hive member could be introduced by the horse's telepathy and Nona's intelligence. It was the nucleus that could grow a new hive from the remnant of the old.

Nona realized that Burgess' thought was right. It could be done, if she remained with them. Her magic would also help. Darius and Colene had started the Virtual Mode, but the three of them could continue it. They could have their own adventure of exploration, discovering strange worlds and creatures. Now she knew that this was what both Seqiro and Burgess wanted.

'I want it too,' Nona said. 'But not at the expense of my world.'

She returned to the tent, where Darius and Colene slept beside each other in the night tunics Nona had made for them and for herself. There was no pretense here; they really were asleep, because Seqiro relayed their inchoate unconscious thoughts. The two were holding hands, their fingers loosely interlaced yet suggesting tenderness and trust. They were a couple, for all the difficulties they had relating fully to each other when awake, and she wished them well. Colene thought Darius was too morally rigid, except with respect to other women, where it seemed he had an attitude Nona had not seen. Darius thought Colene was too young, though he desired her body and her love with an intensity that sometimes leaked through despite the way the horse filtered it out. The fact was that Colene was not too young, for experience had matured her rapidly, and Darius' awareness of other women would fade if he simply recognized Colene as a woman instead of an almost-

188

woman. All either needed was to accept what the other offered.

Nona laughed to herself. How readily she could solve the problems of others, when she could not address her own! Perhaps to the others, Nona's problem was as readily soluble. In fact, maybe all they needed to do was address each other's problems and soon there would be no more problems.

Nona lay down on Darius' other side. She liked them both, and regretted being any part of the dissension between them. She had no romantic designs on Darius, but did like him as a person. If she were ever to marry, she hoped it would be to a man like him, but that did not mean Darius himself. Colene understood that intellectually, but not emotionally. Colene feared that one day Darius would simply be overwhelmed by Nona's presence and choose to marry her instead of Colene. But Nona would not accept that, for her own very certain reasons, and she wished she could convince Colene of that. Darius, however he felt about women in general, would never take a woman against her will. Nona represented no threat to Colene's romance. Nor to her horse either; Colene would have to give up Seqiro before Nona took him.

But what kind of a threat did Nona represent to her world? Had she done no more than throw it into chaos? What could she do to redress such an evil?

*I will help you sleep.*

Nona realized that she did need this help. 'Thank you, Seqiro.' Then the horse's mind pressed her awareness gently down, and she slept.

In the morning the others were up before Nona. They were ready to strike camp by the time she woke. 'Seqiro – did you hold me in sleep late?' she demanded as she scrambled up.

*Yes. So we could consider your problem.*

189

'But I didn't ask anyone to do that!' She tore off her night tunic and dropped a red day tunic over her head.

*True. This is why it was better for you to sleep.*

'The rest of you don't have any responsibility for me! This is something I have to do myself.' She was now making her way to their designated latrine area, and was conscious of a possible double entendre.

Colene appeared. 'When the mind predator came after me, did you decide it was something I had to handle myself?'

'No, of course not! We had to get you away from –' Nona broke off, grasping the point. She regrouped her thoughts. 'What did you decide?'

'Seqiro says he thinks you can solve my problem, so maybe I should solve yours.'

So the horse had not told the specific nature of Nona's private thoughts. She was thankful for that. 'If you could solve mine, I would certainly try to solve yours. But I fear no one can solve mine.'

'So let me try to solve yours first, and then if I succeed, you'll tackle mine,' Colene said.

Nona finished her private business and went to the stream to wash. She was not at all sure this was wise. She knew that Seqiro wanted her, Nona, to remain with them on the Virtual Mode, but that was no necessary concern for Colene.

Colene followed her, and put out her hand. 'Deal?'

Why should Colene even want to get involved? Nona was not at all sure that this made sense. But the girl was waiting, and finally Nona took her hand. 'Agreed.'

'Anyway, I might get attacked by that mind predator again,' Colene said. 'They tell me that your magic made the difference, getting me here in time.'

'We all made the difference,' Nona clarified. 'We worked together.' She smiled. 'As a hive.'

'Well, I'm not ready to break up the hive yet.'

'What is your solution to my problem?'

'I'm working on it. This will take more than a minute or three to figure out. So you just relax, and let me stew on it.'

'It may take more than a generation to resolve!' Nona exclaimed, laughing. Now it occurred to her that Colene was simply trying to help her to relax, on the assumption that someone else was taking the burden of worry.

'Now we need you to get a familiar,' Colene said. 'So we can spot a place for Darius to conjure us to.'

Seqiro stunned a passing bird, and Nona held the bird and tamed it with her mind. Then she directed it to fly to a distant village, while she had her morning meal.

In due course, using the bird's eyes, she spied a suitable site. It was near a village that looked peaceful.

They got together, and Darius performed a mass conjuration. He had made icons representing each of them, including Burgess, and touched each with the solid, liquid, and air of the one it represented. The solid was a hair or in Burgess' case a tiny chip from his canopy; the liquid was spittle or the equivalent; the air was breath. He activated these with a thought. Then he moved the group from the region he had designated Here to the region designated There.

There was a stomach-turning lurch. They landed in a sloppy pile at the far site. The others were used to it, but this was the first experience for Burgess, and he looked a bit green around the trunk and sunken of eye stalk. Nona and Colene put hands on his contact points, and Seqiro enhanced their power of communication, so they could reassure him.

Then Nona expanded their equipment and they repaired to the village. There were no barricades here, and no sign of despots. But neither were there any glad or curious throngs of children.

Seqiro, garbed as a show horse, let Darius guide him, his mind tuned to the minds of the villagers. It always took the horse a little while to orient on new minds. Their guise as a traveling troupe gave him time to do this before they came to a stop.

But this time they were surprised. *Keep walking. Do not stop.*

They kept moving, passing right on out of the village without pausing, as if they had always been destined for elsewhere. As they did so, Seqiro clarified what he had discovered. This was a peaceful hamlet only in appearance; it was actually an armed and hostile camp. Men were watching from the windows, ready to emerge and stone any suspicious visitors. Any people in despot cloaks, male or female, would be killed on sight; others were let be if they seemed harmless. So Seqiro had projected emanations of harmlessness, and the troupe had been allowed to depart in peace.

Safely beyond the deadly village, they paused to assess the implications. The revolution had come here, too, and worse than the other village. The despots had been abolished.

'But there was not supposed to be killing,' Nona said, horrified. 'Just a change of authority.'

'It seems that without a powerful force to keep the peace, it will not be kept,' Darius said grimly. 'I suspect that even your magic, Nona, will not suffice to bring order here. The people have tasted blood.'

'I am beginning to wonder whether I should have ever brought the anima,' Nona said, chagrined.

'There must have been similar violence when the animus took over, generations ago,' Colene said. 'This is a lot like my world, Earth. When there's no strong authority, nations fission into factions, and the factions fight. I thought your world was better.'

'I thought so too,' Nona said. 'Now I see that the despots, much as we despised them, did keep the peace. I am very much afraid that my magic will be inadequate to restore order in more than a single village.'

'But I guess you don't want to give it up as a bad job,' Colene said.

'A single village is better than nothing.'

They checked several other villages, performing shows at some and avoiding others when Seqiro verified that they were dangerous. The story was similar throughout: a state of overt or covert war existed. The despots had not released their power gently; they had clung to it by whatever means they could. The theows, knowing that they were no longer opposed by magic, had thrown off the yoke wherever they could. The sides were approximately even, so the issue was in doubt. Men were learning war rapidly.

There wre also collections of brown-tunicked rabble, the folk Nona had released from the underworld; rejected by the folk of the surface, they were forming communities of their own, just as distrustful of strangers.

'Well, I think I've figured out how to solve your problem,' Colene said.

Nona didn't laugh. She was afraid of what the girl was going to come up with. 'It will require a miracle, I think.'

'What we have to do is get some more magic here,' Colene said. 'Not one woman, but a group of them, so they can spread out and establish law and order.'

'But I am the only one,' Nona protested. 'I can not duplicate myself.'

'You are the only one on Planet Oria,' Colene said. 'But there are whole planets full of them elsewhere in Julia. There are lots of anima worlds. All we have to do is get some of those other women to immigrate. It could be a pretty good deal for them, you know. Queen for a Day, or for life. Maybe most wouldn't be interested, but I'll bet some are, and even if it's only one in a hundred, that may be enough. One to a village, maybe.'

Nona listened, astonished. Anima women from established anima worlds! Of course there were many of those.

The universe of Julia had an infinite number of connected worlds, of all different sizes, with their populations in proportion. Many were animus, with the men wielding the magic, but many were anima, with the women having it. And a number of such women were bound to be interested, because instead of being unremarkable in their own society, they would be the wielders of full power on Oria. Some might be bad women, not suitable, but many would be fair. It was, indeed, an answer.

'Two problems I see,' Darius said. 'Selection and transport. We'll need a way to alert them and pick out the right ones, and we'll need to get them here. That may be a problem.'

'Two solutions,' Colene replied promptly. 'We'll go to the amazon leaders and explain the situation. They must have dozens of prospects – women who are capable but not in line for power in that world. Women who want special challenge.' Women who are too ambitious so need to be removed, but who are too well connected to be eliminated without a stink. Sure, there'll be politics galore, but there'll be magic women available. They may not be ideal rulers, but they've got to be better than chaos. And we'll transport them the same way we travel, bringing them along the filaments that connect the worlds, in small bunches. Maybe we can get Angus to help. It may take a bit of time, but it can be done.'

Nona nodded, excited. It could be done. But she had a question of her own: 'What about Burgess? Can he travel the filaments? He won't want to remain here alone.'

Colene went to the floater and put a hand on a contact point. 'Hey, elephant nose, do you want to go world-hopping? It's one weird trip, I promise you!'

There was a pause while she clarified the situation for Burgess. Then she looked up. 'He doesn't want to get left behind. We should be able to bring him along the filaments the same way as we bring him along on a group conjuration. It's better that we stay together, as a hive.'

So it was decided. Tomorrow they would go to the East Sea and set up for their excursion to another world. That would be a horrendous endeavor, but Nona felt relieved. For the first time since she had become aware of the problem on Oria, she had some reasonable hope of remaining with her friends of the hive.

# 9

## *Anima*

Darius lay in the tent, awake between two sleeping women as dawn approached. He hoped they wouldn't regret this. Colene had a positive genius for solving problems, and an almost as strong negative genius for making new problems. Her simple solution to Nona's problem was complicated and perhaps dangerous in its details.

First they had to conjure to the East Sea. Oria was part of the fractal reality of Julia, in which every planet was connected by invisibly thin filaments and the entire universe was a deviously connected mass. Colene's mental image, culled from her research bank in her home Mode of Earth, showed an essentially two-dimensional pattern. Each planet was shaped like a six-legged bug, with the head pointed west, with the filaments entering it at the east and departing in many directions from the bumps called rads – radicals – on its surface. There were smaller rads between the larger ones, in descending subpatterns of increasing complexity. Here in the Julia Mode the pattern was three-dimensional, and the rads projected on four sides. The surface of a pristine planet was a complicated array, but inhabited worlds were broken down by the forces of weather and the depredations of man so that they came to resemble the home worlds known by Colene, Seqiro, Burgess, and himself.

To a degree. Nona was so accustomed to the filaments that she didn't even notice them, but Darius did. From every rad filaments issued, and these formed marvelous recurring patterns that became visible at night. All through the sky the starlike networks showed. They fascinated him in their wondrous intricacy. His eye could trace a pattern through endless loops and whirls and curls, until the fineness of the detail defeated his vision. Not merely in the large sky; the near sky had similar, smaller patterns, right down to the very spot he lay, where the filaments remained though the original rads had been removed. It was as if they were silent ghosts, forever marking the sites of their original bodies. He knew that there were invisibly small planets associated with these patterns, and that many of these tiny planets had populations of trees, animals, and people, much like Oria. Every one was a complete world, in scale, with its effects of gravity, season, and life self-similar. It would be hard to imagine a more remarkable universe than this, yet the locals took it all for granted.

It was this duplication and similarity of planets that Colene depended on to solve Nona's problem. There would not be another woman exactly like Nona elsewhere, but there would be other women with similar attitudes and powers. They could indeed do as well with the world of Oria as Nona could, and probably better, because they would have the motive she lacked, and there would be a number of them. So it was a flash of inspiration to think of that. But what a job it would be to accomplish! It was quite within the realm of possibility that one or more of them would get killed in the process. That was the corollary to Colene's bright notion.

But what could he do except play it through? If it succeeded, Nona would be able to rejoin them on the Virtual Mode, and that was good. His interest might be suspect, for Nona was as lovely a woman in form and personality as he had encountered. She had marvelous musical and magical abilities. It would be easy for any man to love her. But it was Colene he loved, and were it not for her age and inner core of depression she would be ideal. Because she had intelligence, initiative, and courage which could be awesome when they manifested, and she was hardly inferior in other qualities. Now she wanted to help Nona escape the emotional call of Oria, and that was generous of her. Nona was certainly an asset on the Virtual Mode, but Colene also saw her as a threat to Colene's relationship with Darius; that was why he considered her attitude to be generous. There was also something to be said for keeping the group together, at least until they arrived at Darius' home Mode. Thereafter – he did not know. Could the Virtual Mode continue, with Nona, Seqiro, and Burgess, after he and Colene got off? It would be a significant risk to free his anchor, because no one could know what the next anchor would be. But if he didn't, it would leave them with no replacement anchor person, and a group too small to be the hive Burgess needed. So he had no answer for that, yet.

Now the dawn was brightening, and the filaments were fading. They were still there, of course, but invisible and imperceptible; his body passed through them without effect. Filaments of any size were intangible unless special magic was used to address them. Which was what they were about to do. They had to go to the main filament at the east pole of the planet, because that one led to larger planets, and thence to others the same size as Oria. They had to find one the same size, because otherwise the people would be larger or smaller than the natives of Oria, and would not be able to mesh well.

He got up, trying not to disturb the others, but both woke when he stirred. Each was so lovely in her way, Nona a radiant young woman of eighteen, Colene a pretty girl of fourteen. They stretched almost together, their breasts moving under their night tunics. Oh, how he wished he could – but he could not. Because the one who was old enough was not his, and the one who was his was not old enough. It was at times an exquisite torture. At times he really missed his life as Cyng of Hlahtar, with bouncy Ella so eager to warm his bed.

'I caught that, manface,' Colene said, forcing a cute frown.

'You couldn't have. Seqiro –'

198

'With my own mind reading,' she said. 'I'm getting better at it, you know.'

Was she bluffing? If she ever caught on how much he desired her, she would be almost irresistible, because she would have no conscience about her blandishments. She was too young, and she believed that that made her unappealing in his eyes, but it was not so. She was almost the ultimate in forbidden fruit.

'Gee, I am?' she asked, pleased.

She had to be guessing! He turned away, somewhat shaken. Colene laughed, well satisfied with herself.

'What is going on?' Nona asked her. Now it was Seqiro's ambience conveying the communication to him; he did not need to be within earshot.

'He was thinking sexy thoughts,' Colene replied. 'He has this deal with horseface, not to relay them, but I peeped on my own. He thinks you're a beautiful woman, but you're not his, and I'm a pretty girl, but I'm too young. When we both stretched just now, it just about drove him crazy, because of the way our breasts moved. He wished he was back in bed with bouncy Ella, in his own Mode, where the girls wear big diapers by day but can get pretty juicy by night.'

That could not be guessing! She had picked it up exactly.

'This is not right,' Nona said reprovingly. 'You should not tease him, when he is trying to treat you correctly.'

'I don't want to tease him, I want to love him! But he won't touch me.'

'Let me think about that,' Nona said. 'You are solving my problem; I shall have to try to solve yours.'

Darius would have liked nothing better than to have this problem solved. But only time would make Colene old enough, years of time. How was he going to survive that? Colene did not like the idea of him being with any other woman, even one he was not serious about.

'You got that right!' Colene yelled from the tent.

This was going to get more difficult. Her limited telepathy was definitely getting less limited.

*No, I had relayed that thought*, Seqiro thought. *It was situational, not sexual.*

That was a relief! At least he retained some privacy, if he wasn't close to Colene.

But there was no sense dwelling in this, when there was an immediate problem to tackle. He and Nona, working together, could enable the group to travel along the filaments between planets. But that was only the beginning. They had to find one Oria's size, with a human population, and the anima. There might be thousands of such worlds in Julia, but there were millions of planets the wrong size, and it would be easy to get lost in the maze of filaments. How could they efficiently locate an appropriate one?

Then he had it: Angus. Angus was their giant friend on Jupiter, the next larger world up the local filament. They had encountered him when they had been trapped in this Mode, and he had helped them to bring the anima. Perhaps he would help them again. Certainly he should have relevant advice.

Heartened, Darius went about his business. In due course they gathered together for the conjuration. It had taken time for Nona's familiar to fly to the East Sea, to orient on a suitable spot. Darius could conjure only to a known or observed site; otherwise the risk of landing in a tree was too great. In a tree did not mean reclining on its foliage; it meant flesh overlapping with wood. That could be extremely awkward.

He invoked and moved the grouped icons, and abruptly the five of them were on the beach by the East Sea. Now they needed Nona's magic, because the filament connected under the sea. The sea actually filled in the giant dimple on the east side of the planet, and was deepest at the connection. So Nona had to make underwater breathing apparatus for them.

Soon Nona had done that. There was now a giant breathing bell, which would hold a supply of air for them all, constantly renewed by Nona's magic. They changed into brief trunks, which Nona also made magically, and entered the water. Each wore heavy shaped weights on the feet, to keep them all on the bottom. Seqiro took the center under the bell. Nona rode on him, while Darius walked ahead, using a lead rope and halter to guide the horse. It looked much like their road show, except for the water.

Colene walked beside Burgess, to whom she related well, keeping a hand on one of his contact points so that he would remain current. He had his own air bell, because he was too low to use the main one. His gills were concealed under his canopy, and needed a relatively small amount of air, which then was wafted to the rear to provide some forward propulsion. He did not need the huge amount required for floating, because now he was floating in the water. His main propulsion was provided by his trunk, which could process water as readily as air or sand, but he had some difficulty maintaining his balance. So Colene was helping to anchor and steer him, as each jet of water sent him surging somewhat randomly ahead.

They made their way on down, losing track of the time, eating as they went. They took turns sleeping, with Nona first, on the horse. Then she exchanged with Darius. Then they both hauled Seqiro slowly along while he slept. Meanwhile Burgess gave Colene a ride, her weight bearing him down so that he could brace against the bottom and achieve better stability, and she slept. Then she hauled him along through the water while he slept. None of this was perfect or easy, but they managed.

At last they reached the depth and found the filament. It was simply a band of light moving up from the center of the dimple. When he looked closely, he saw that it was not really simple; it was fashioned of a tapestry of finer lines, which in turn were composed of vanishingly thin microfilaments. He knew that if he could magnify it, the lines would become yet finer in their definition, with no end to their diminishing intricacies. This fractal universe of Julia was a wonder in a number of ways.

They gathered together in a tight group, with Nona in the center on Seqiro, who was standing over Burgess. Burgess touched one of Nona's feet with his trunk, while Colene and Darius took her hands. Then Nona invoked her ability to travel along the filament.

The wan light expanded. Suddenly they were sailing up through it, leaving the planet behind. Darius concentrated on the surroundings, trying to fathom their fascinating detail, but as before, he could catch only hints. The mosaic of the massed filaments was too devious to grasp in an instant, and the pattern was continuously changing.

They landed on Jupiter, the next larger planet, about eighteen times Oria's diameter. They could see that they were on a mound, which was on a larger mound, in turn on a larger one, leading into the monstrous world. This was the spike of one of the larger rads at the north side of Jupiter. Here everything was in the larger scale, so that ants could be as long as Darius' foot. But they would not have to deal with ants; they had a friend, here.

*Angus!* Seqiro called mentally. *Nona is here.*

They waited. Soon enough a giant man came flying across the variegated surface of the planet. This was Angus, the friend they had made during their prior stay in the Julia Mode.

He hovered near, and extended an enormous hand. They scrambled onto it, with the three humans guiding the horse, then lifting Burgess across, with the considerable aid of Seqiro's coordination and temporary jolt of strength. Angus had to extend his other hand to hold them all comfortably.

Angus peered at them within his cupped hands. He spoke softly, almost in a whisper, so as not to overwhelm them with his sound, and Seqiro translated his words for their minds. 'One of you has changed.'

'Provos has gone home, with her adopted son and granddaughter,' Nona explained. 'Our new associate is Burgess, from the Shale Mode. He is the product of alternate evolution going back about five hundred million years.' She had learned this explanation from Colene.

Angus lifted, flying out across the tiered rads toward the main mass of Jupiter. Darius had been quite nervous the first time he had been carried like this, but he now had confidence in the giant's competence and consideration, and was only moderately awed. 'And why do I have the pleasure of your company again?' Angus asked.

'We have a problem, again, of course,' Nona said. She smiled. She had a marvelous smile, and its effect on the giant was apparent. 'I would have liked to visit you anyway, Angus, but I needed a pretext.'

'I would accept you without a pretext, Nona.'

Darius knew that was true. Nona had won him with her special playing of her hammer dulcimer, before, and he had been loyal to her since. Darius also knew that the giant's help would be invaluable, and that Angus would give it gladly.

'We did bring the anima to Oria,' Nona said. 'I had no wish to be queen there, so left with my friends, to travel the Virtual Mode. But a mind predator attacked Colene, and we had to exit through this anchor. Then I discovered that my world was in chaos. Now I must try to help it, to alleviate the grief I brought to it. I need to find women of the anima, from an established anima world, to go to Oria and govern it until the new generation emerges.'

'Ah, I had not thought of that,' Angus said. 'You wish to have competent help in governing.'

'No, I wish t return to the Virtual Mode, having no taste for governance, or for marriage and children as yet. I wish to explore, while I have my youth and magic. But I must see to my world's welfare first.'

He nodded as he came to land beside his giant house. 'This is not a suitable world, being both animus and somewhat large. I presume you desire one of the same size as yours.'

'Yes. There should be several such worlds. If you could take us to one of those, it would greatly facilitate my mission.'

'I will gladly take you there. But I fear your disappointment.' He entered his house, then set his hands at his giant table so that they could get off.

'They will not help me?'

'They may be willing, but unable. Their magic will derive from their own worlds, and perhaps will not apply to yours.'

'But your magic worked on Oria,' Nona reminded him. 'Theirs should also.'

'Jupiter is a world in the direct line of descent to Oria,' Angus said. 'The animus travels in that direction, so seems to have force throughout. But the worlds which are equivalent to yours spring from three different rads, and are parallel, not senior. Also, the anima flows oppositely, and may not obey any similar rule. That may make a difference.'

Nona evidently hadn't thought of that. 'Can we verify that?' she asked, concerned.

'Only by trying. Perhaps it will be all right, because they *are* parallel.'

'I hope so. Even if the magic of those women derives from their own world, perhaps it will carry across to Oria. They may not be drawing on Oria's power, but may be much the same.'

'This is possible.' Darius wasn't certain whether Angus was trying to ease her worry, having warned her of the possibility of failure, or really believed in the chance.

'We would like to go immediately,' Nona said. 'My world is in pain, and I wish to alleviate it as quickly as I can.'

'I fear there will be no painless answer,' Angus said. 'But your notion may indeed diminish the pain.'

'It was Colene's notion,' Nona said.

Angus turned his gaze on Colene, who was standing with Burgess, her hand on a contact point. 'Ah, the science maiden,' he said, extending his littlest finger to chuck her under the chin. Darius was afraid she would react negatively, because she did have some odd ideas about the proper interactions between men and women, but she actually put her chin forward to touch the tip of his finger. It was evident that she liked the giant. 'The intelligent one.'

'The depressive one,' Colene said, but she was pleased.

'The traits can go together,' Angus said sadly. 'One pursues the pursuits of the mind when the pursuits of the heart are lacking.'

Darius realized that the giant, for all his formidable powers of magic, was lonely. He could surely find a woman if he chose, but perhaps was choosy. Darius understood about that.

'If I were your size, they would not be lacking,' Nona said. She was actually flirting with Angus! Perhaps that was because during their prior visit here the giant had told them a story, and shown it in illusion-vision, about a man of his world, named Earle, and his impossible love for a woman of the next larger world, named Kara. It had been a charming and perhaps not entirely fanciful legend.

'Surely so,' Angus agreed. 'But circumstance has destined that we both be adventurous in other ways.'

'Yes.' She blew him a kiss. Darius, accustomed to Nona's completely nonseductive ordinary manner, was almost jealous, seeing how she could be when she chose.

'Oh, you are, are you?' Colene demanded, turning to him with a frown.

'I shall have to do something about that telepathy of yours,' Darius muttered. 'Still, I didn't see you turning away your chin when Angus chucked you.'

'Yeah? Find yourself a woman his size, and you can flirt with her all you want.'

'I will take you,' Angus said to Nona. 'Do you wish to go alone, or together?'

'Together,' Nona said. 'I would feel inadequate alone.'

Angus put his hands down again, and they climbed on. Then he took them out and up, flying rapidly across the monstrous countryside. He was huge, but so was his planet, and despite his velocity the journey took some time. They relaxed, having a meal and even snoozing, secure in the gentle hands.

In due course Angus came to a rad which looked identical to the one by which they had arrived at Jupiter. That was not surprising; only its position on the planet distinguished it. He mounted the filament, and they were back in the speeding light of the alternate realm of patterns. Their movement seemed faster than when Nona had brought them, and perhaps it was, being proportional to the scale of the giant.

Then they were in the sea, protected by Angus' magic, which was as strong and versatile as Nona's. It was clear why there had been no revolution on Oria before Nona brought the anima; the men of the animus had had overwhelming force of magic. But if women with that same magic were brought in, then there should soon be peace again, perforce.

Angus bounced out of his landing place in the dimple of the East Sea and reached the surface. He did not bother to swim; he simply rose up into the air and flew above the sea, letting the water drip away from his body. The five of them cupped within his hands were not wet at all. This was certainly the way to travel!

'Now before we approach a community, we must formulate a plan,' Angus said. 'I suspect it will be better if I do not appear, at first. So I will clothe myself in an illusion of nothing.' At which point he disappeared, and the rest of them with him; Darius could not even see his own body. It was as if he were a ghost floating high in the air, alone.

'Yeah, a plan, for sure,' Colene agreed from empty space nearby. 'Here we've been zooming along, and we never thought how to present the case. Maybe just have Nona walk up to the town hall or whatever and talk to the headman?'

'There will be no headman, if it's anima,' Darius pointed out. 'And maybe no headwoman either, if it just happened. This could be another world of chaos.'

'I wish we could tell just by looking,' Colene said. 'But I guess a farmstead is a farmstead, no matter who has the magic. We need to talk with someone.'

Nona considered. He could tell not by sight, which was vacant, but by her thought. Then she came to a tentative conclusion. 'Perhaps Darius and I should approach the leader of a village, or a castle, with Seqiro. Colene can wait with Burgess in the forest nearby, with Angus, and should there be trouble they can decide what to do.'

'Seems good to me,' Colene said. 'I can connect some with Angus, mentally, so we can be coordinated. Maybe we should stay out of sight until Seqiro sends a signal. If there are women ready to volunteer, they still need to be prepared for Burgess and Angus.'

So Angus came to land in a forest glade between a village and a castle built around a suitably sized rad. The terrain of this world seemed very similar to that of Oria, making it parallel in every visible respect. Darius wondered whether there was any cache of giant musical instruments, as there was near the anchor on Oria. That depended on whether the giants of Jupiter had colonized this world, millennia ago, and been unable to use their instruments when succeeding generations grew smaller to accommodate the scale of the planet. Certainly it was possible. It seemed that all the Julia universe had been colonized by the species of man, originating from one world. No one knew which world that had been. The legend Angus had told suggested that it was Oria, but there could be similar legends identifying other worlds scattered throughout this universe. However, the fact that the anchor was on Oria, and its people were the same size as those of other Modes, suggested that Oria could be the origin. Men might have crossed to it via some other Virtual Mode, too long ago for contemporary memory. All the other animals, and the plants, might have crossed the same way, brought by man.

'Yeah, like Adam and Eve,' Colene said as they became visible. 'The Garden of Eden might have been on some other Mode, and the first man and woman came here with a Noah's Ark full of goodies, I mean animals and seeds galore, to be fruitful and multiply across a new universe.'

'Unless man evolved in Julia, and crossed from here to the other Modes,' Darius suggested.

'It sure is a bigger framework than we know,' she agreed. 'Back on Earth, they think Earth is all there is. I'd like to take one of their scientists and give him a taste of the Virtual Mode!'

Soon the three set out, in a reduced version of the traveling show: Darius wearing a blue tunic, leading Seqiro, with Nona riding, her tunic red. This was an innocuous group that should be able to pass muster as either the servant of an animus man leading his master's horse and mistress, or an anima woman with her horse and husband. Darius was armed with a theow club, which he as an animus servant might carry more for show than for use. Not all men had magic, on an animus world; only the firstborn and the firstborn descendants of firstborns. Just as it would be the lastborns of the lastborns who had the most magic, on an animal world. The pattern of magic became confusion to Darius, and he never had figured out exactly how it worked.

At least there were no barricades. Seqiro explored the minds of the inhabitants as the three approached the village, orienting more rapidly because they were quite similar to those he had encountered on Oria. Almost immediately he had the answer: *These are animus.*

'Then there is no point in proceeding farther,' Nona said with regret. 'We do not want more animus on Oria. In fact, we do not want them even to know that Oria has changed, lest they get mischievous ideas.'

Seqiro started to turn, to go back the way they had come without entering the village. But at that point someone came out from the village, hailing them. 'You folk lost?' a man in blue called. 'Who you looking for?'

'We changed our minds,' Darius replied. He had to be the spokesman here, being male. 'We have decided not to visit this village.'

'Where are you from?' the man asked.

'A far village,' Darius said, not wishing to misrepresent their situation, but also not wishing to give it away.

'Have you checked in with the despots? You have to know you can't just come through here on your own without despot approval.'

'We had better do that, then,' Darius said, feeling uncomfortable.

'I will lead you to the castle,' the man said.

'There is no need; we can see it from here.'

'I insist. It is my job to inform the despots of anything that happens in the village.'

Worse yet! Darius had forgotten how tightly the despots of Oria had controlled things, when they had been in power.

Now a blackbird altered course and flew toward them. *That is a despot familiar*, Seqiro thought. *I can stun it.*

'I think you had better,' Darius said. Then, to the man: 'We have decided not to check in with the despots after all. We will simply go away and not disturb your village.'

'You are acting suspiciously,' the man said. He started to raise his right hand.

*Stop him!* Seqiro's thought came. Grabbing his club, Darius leaped for the man. He saw the bird falling out of the sky as Seqiro stunned it.

But the man had a club of his own. He lifted it to parry Darius' blow, and it was quickly apparent that he knew more about its effective use than Darius did.

Then the man leaped up into the air — and didn't come down. His arms and legs flailed ineffectively, unable to gain purchase against the air.

Darius stepped back, realizing that Nona had used her magic to lift the man up. But she would not be able to hold him that way long, because magic did take energy.

The man dropped into a bush. He scrambled up and fled, having had enough. Darius felt fear, and knew that Seqiro was assisting the man on his way. Nona was breathing hard, but was all right. They retreated up the road, leaving the village behind.

'We did not handle that smoothly,' Darius remarked, trying to smile.

'At least we learned what we needed to,' Nona said. 'This world has nothing for us.'

They rounded a turn in the road, about to cut back into the forest to rejoin the rest of their party. But a black-clad man was riding a horse at a gallop toward them, evidently having been alerted. Probably there had been more than one familiar, and a party had been sent out to intercept the suspicious strangers before the first familiar had been stunned. This was trouble.

'Oh, he'll have magic matching mine!' Nona exclaimed. 'I don't know what to do!'

'Try a fireball,' Darius suggested, hurrying back to take Seqiro's lead again.

She tried, but he felt her failure. 'I can't do it, here. It just doesn't work.'

Darius realized that the Virtual Mode had limits which did not perfectly match those of any one of its component anchor Modes. So Nona was actually a better magician there than in her home Mode, while being restricted on other Modes, just as he was. Some day he would like to know exactly what the rules were. They surely had a sensible pattern, if only he could fathom it.

But right now they had a pressing problem, and he had no better idea what to do than Nona did. Colene liked to type him as a leader, but he really wasn't; *she* was the leader. When things got difficult, sometimes he figured out a good course, and sometimes he just blundered through. Colene thought of him as the King of Laughter, as if he had executive power and was happy, but his power was more like that of a public servant, and happiness was not really its essence. Distributing joy had its down side. He really was no adventurer by choice.

Meanwhile the black-cloaked horseman was charging toward them, and now he heard another set of hoofbeats from the village: another despot. They were trapped.

*Oh, for pity's sake!* Colene's thought came. *Let me handle it.*

Darius was glad to agree, and so was Nona. Both of them let Seqiro bring Colene's mind into theirs, so that she could for the moment act for them.

The first despot arrived, his horse coming to a halt with a spray of pebbles from the road. He was a saturnine man with a scar on his forehead. 'Who are you, theows?' he demanded roughly.

'We don't have to answer to you,' Darius said for Colene. It was an odd experience, letting his mouth speak her words. 'We are on a mission for my master, who brooks no interference.'

The despot scowled. Suddenly Darius was lifted into the air, magically. 'Identify your master, or he will lose you.'

Then the despot rose into the air. His jaw dropped; he was not doing it himself. Colene had made Nona do it. 'Does your master care to lose you too, scarface?' his mouth inquired belligerently.

Both men dropped abruptly, as the despot oriented his power on himself to counter the outside force. That meant that Darius was free. He reached for his club, but was abruptly frozen in place. He was able to move only his eyes, and maintain his balance so he wouldn't fall.

'What goes?' the other despot called, arriving on his horse. He must be the one now controlling Darius.

'These theows have magic,' the first replied. 'I think we have a foreign despot here in disguise. His tongue is too insolent to belong to a theow.'

'Then he's not protected by the covenant,' the second said. 'We don't have to treat him fairly unless he identifies himself. He forfeits his rights.'

Colene had only gotten them into deeper trouble! Darius knew that Nona could not hope to prevail against two despots. Darius himself could do nothing; he remained frozen by the despot's magic.

'Then let's take his things,' the first despot said. 'I'll take that excellent horse.' He grabbed Seqiro's halter.

'And I'll take this excellent woman,' the second despot said. He grabbed for Nona, who screamed and sailed up into the air herself.

'That's not this man's doing,' the second despot said, astonished. 'I have him covered. That has to be the woman herself! We have an amazon here!'

'These strangers must be from another world,' the first despot agreed. 'This is several times as remarkable as we thought.'

'Well, she's one lovely creature, and I want her,' the second despot said. 'You hold her while I rape her.'

'I'll take over the man,' the first despot said. 'You hold her yourself.'

Darius felt a subtle change, and knew that the magic freezing him in place was now wielded by a different despot. Meanwhile Nona screamed again, discovering her magic canceled by that of the second despot. That man now grabbed her ankle and hauled her down physically.

Then a burst of terrible fear smote them all. Seqiro had

212

sent out the strongest possible emotion. Both despots fell back, mistaking the fear for their own, not understanding it. Nona, released for the moment, descended slowly back to the horse. Darius, similarly released, quickly brought out his three icons, activated them, put one arm against Nona's leg and Seqiro's side, and moved the icons from Here to There.

But as he did so, both despots grabbed for Darius and Nona. The wrenching came, and the three were back in the forest glade – and so were the two black-clad men.

'Oh, no!' Colene cried. 'The despots came too! And Angus is off in the sky.'

The freeze clamped on again. Darius couldn't act, even to move the icons. He saw that Nona was fighting off the second despot again, his magic canceling hers, making the combat physical. Darius knew that the scene had changed but not the situation: the two despots had too much magic.

Then the first despot grunted and fell. Darius was freed. He saw Burgess moving his trunk to cover the other despot. A stone flew out, striking the second despot on the head. Burgess was taking both men out!

'Okay, conjure us all out of here, Darius,' Colene said. 'We want to lose these despots before they wake up.'

'No, better to conjure the despots out,' Darius said.

'Say, yeah! Do it.'

He brought out two blank human icons. He took a hair from the head of each despot and stuck it onto an icon. He touched each icon to the mouth of each despot, to get saliva, and in the process picked up some breath too. Then he activated the icons, and designated Here and There. He moved the two icons, and the two despots disappeared.

'Great!' Colene said. 'Where'd you send them?'

'Back to their castle,' he said, indicating the castle, whose topmost turret was just visible through foliage.

'But you haven't been there, so you don't have it perfectly zeroed in.'

213

'Correct; they may arrive imperfectly zeroed in. Such as in the moat. It may be uncomfortable.'

She laughed. 'That's right! We don't care if they get bruised in transit. They sure won't mess with us again.'

Darius nodded. 'However, this has been a chancy endavor. If Burgess hadn't taken those despots out, we could have been in real trouble.'

'Such as some of us getting raped or killed,' Colene agreed. 'And never making it back to Oria or the anchor. Yeah, when I saw what happened, I told Burgess to let 'em have it in the heads. They never expected that kind of attack. We're going to have to plan the next planet for less bungling. We sort of did this one by the seat of our pants, and that's no good against despots with magic.'

'At least it reminds us how bad the despots of Oria were,' Nona said. 'I thought that chaos was worse than rule by the despots, but now I think it isn't.'

There was a sound, and the ground shuddered. Then Angus appeared, literally: he had landed while invisible, then stopped the illusion of nothing so that they could see him. 'I gather this is the wrong world,' he said.

'Way wrong,' Colene agreed. 'But we have a couple to go yet.'

'But at least we have ascertained that folk from a parallel world will be able to wield their magic on yours.'

'How do we know that?' Nona asked.

'If your own magic works here, theirs should work there. We have established the principle of transfer of magic between parallel planets.'

Nona nodded, surprised. He was right.

They climbed onto Angus' hands, and he bore them invisibly away. It was a great comfort having him along.

They returned to the East Sea and used the filament to return to Jupiter. Then Angus carried them on around another quarter of the planet to the next parallel rad. Before they used it, Angus had to eat and sleep, because he had been doing all the work of transport and was tiring. He lay down in a low tent he made, and they took turns mounting guard through the night. The Jupiter night was the same length as the Oria night, just as its surface gravity was the same, thanks to the magical nature of the Julia Mode.

They discussed plans for the next planet. They concluded that this time they would simply observe, and if they saw black and white tunics in castles and blue and red tunics in the villages, they would assume it was an animus world. But just to be sure that the colors hadn't changed, they would try to catch at least one man or woman in the act of magic. Failing that, they would investigate a village, with a pre-planned conjuration route out. No confrontations with magic-wielding men, if they could possibly avoid them.

In the morning they traveled the filament to the world. Angus settled gently down near a village, invisible, and they remained in his hands and watched. The people wore blue and red tunics, and there was no evidence of magic. Then a black-tunicked man rode in, and floated out of his saddle when he dismounted. The blues and reds deferred to him.

They departed quietly. This was another animus world.

In due course they reached the fourth world — and it too was animus. Only Oria had changed, thanks to Nona's effort.

'Now what?' Colene inquired, dispirited. 'I thought I had such a great idea!'

'There are other worlds,' Angus said.

'But they won't be similar to Oria, will they? They'll be all different sizes, with different-sized people, and maybe if they aren't parallel, the magic won't cross over.'

'We have only to take Nona there and see whether her magic works,' Darius said. 'Perhaps we can find one that is close to Oria in size.'

'Certainly,' Angus agreed. He took them to a larger planet on a filament from a smaller rad. It too was animus. He went to a smaller one, and it was animus. 'It seems that most of the satellites of Jupiter are animus, Jupiter being an animus world,' he said.

'But Nona can't be the only one who ever brought the anima,' Colene said.

'Surely not,' Angus agreed. 'In time, most of the worlds will become anima. But the pattern of change differs. The animus comes to all worlds at once, while the anima comes slowly, world by world. It seems to have been not unduly long since the animus came, so relatively few worlds have reverted to anima. You are the ninth of the ninth generation, therefore the first woman of your world with magic. On other worlds it may require more generations for a woman to achieve magic, and many of those women may be killed before they succeed. Perhaps on some of the worlds nearer the primary world the process takes fewer generations, but it would be very difficult for us to search beyond the environs of Jupiter, and the magic might not transfer. I think our best chance remains with Jupiter. There are many satellite worlds, and eventually we should find one that is anima.'

'Actually, we found one before,' Colene said. 'When we first came to meet you. But it was tiny.'

'Size is a problem,' he agreed.

They continued to search – and the next world was anima. 'Glory be!' Colene breathed, watching a red-clad woman summon a familiar to her.

But there was a problem: this was a larger world, and its people were larger. Their typical person was a head taller than those of Oria of the same sex. Their women were half a head taller than Darius. This would hardly pass unnoticed on Oria.

Then Colene had another notion. 'Look, people vary, right? I mean, I'm five feet, small for the women of my world, but within the normal range. There must be small women here, maybe like tall women on Oria, who could pass well enough. And maybe some size will help, making them regal.'

216

It seemed to make sense.

They decided to try the woman-man-horse approach again, this time going to a castle where red tunics dominated. But they rehearsed carefully, and Darius had his icons and conjure site ready for quick use. They would conjure out the moment there was a threat. If they were unable, Colene, Burgess, and Angus would come in after them. Angus could, if necessary, lift the roof off the castle and pull them out by hand. His magic was the same as theirs, but he was so much larger that his powers of levitation had much greater effect.

Darius led Seqiro up to the castle. Huge men in blue challenged him at the entrance.

'I bring a woman from another world, who asks an unusual favor,' he said.

'Is she anima?'

'Yes.'

'Then bring her in.'

No verification? But probably that would be the province of the mistress of the castle.

Nona floated off the horse's back and landed neatly on her feet. 'May my companions enter too?' she asked.

'As you wish.' For here an amazon's word governed.

Nona walked on in, and Darius followed, leading Seqiro. The castle was large, being in proportion to the planet and people; he felt dwarfed. There was a stable to the side, with horses larger than Seqiro, but not by much; Seqiro was a very large horse to begin with. Nona indicated that she wanted her horse with her, and there was no protest.

They were met by a giant, regal woman in a palatial anteroom. In addition to her red tunic she wore a red crown. She was direct. 'How did you come here?'

'We flew in, invisible, then walked to the castle,' Nona said.

'From what world do you come?'

217

'We call it Oria. It is on a filament from another rad of Jupiter. It is smaller than yours.'

'Why is the horse so valuable you kept him with you?'

'He has special magic that greatly facilitates communication.'

'Demonstrate this.'

Nona and Darius stood silent. Seqiro spoke for himself. *I am Seqiro. I am from another Mode, which is a separate reality from Julia. My kind is telepathic.*

The queen's mouth remained closed. *Turn and touch the wall*, she thought.

Seqiro turned and touched the wall with his nose.

'Is the man also special?' the queen asked.

'Yes,' Nona said, then hesitated.

*She is not hostile, nor will she violate hospitality*, Seqiro thought. *She has royal honor, needing no subterfuge.*

'This is true,' the queen said. Seqiro had evidently shared his thought with the woman. 'You must have had experience with the men of animus, whose honor is suspect. You may safely answer the question.'

'The man is also from another Mode. He has conjuration magic unlike ours. We depend on it to extricate us, should we encounter danger.'

The queen turned to Darius. 'Demonstrate.'

He brought out his own icon, invoked it, and conjured himself to the other side of the chamber.

The queen faced Nona. 'What is the favor you ask?'

'To bring some of your smaller anima women to my world, which became anima only a month ago and as yet lacks women with magic. It is in a state of chaos, and needs governing.'

'I believe we can arrange this,' the queen said. For the first time, she smiled. 'Now we shall exchange introductions, and you and your friends will share our hospitality.'

'I am Nona, the ninth of the ninth,' Nona said. 'I brought the anima to our world of Oria.'

'Ah, you are the one,' the queen said. 'Your powers must then be great indeed. And your man?'

'He is Darius, a friend. The horse is Seqiro, also a friend.'

The queen nodded. 'I am Hyacinth, governess of this province.' She paused, then, with exquisite timing, added one caveat: 'But what will you offer in return for this service?'

'In return?' Nona asked blankly.

'You ask us to give up a number of our women, with their powers of magic. What do you give in exchange, of equivalent value?'

'I thought that the women would consider it a privilege,' Nona said, taken aback.

'Perhaps. But I shall not be going, and I do not do something for nothing.'

Darius realized that the queen's businesslike approach had been deceptive. She was not a despot who tried to take by force what she wanted, but neither was she a generous spirit. She expected quid pro quo. It made sense.

'What did you have in mind?' Nona asked, shaken.

Hyacinth frowned professionally. 'Perhaps your man of strange magic. We could find uses for him here.'

Nona was appalled. 'But I could not — I have no right —'

The queen shrugged. 'The horse, then. That mind-talk magic is impressive.'

*Get Colene*, Darius thought to Seqiro. But he had forgotten that in Julia the horse's telepathic range was limited. Colene was out of range. They would have to get through this by themselves.

'The horse is not mine to give,' Nona said.

'That is unfortunate.' The queen made a tiny gesture with one hand. Men wearing black tunics approached.

Nona turned a frozen face to Darius. She believed they were being betrayed.

*No. I would stun the queen if that happened. This is merely hospitality.*

The horse had to know. They waited.

The lead man bowed to Nona. 'If it please you, Lady Nona, I will conduct you to your suite. Do you wish to have the man with you, or separately ensconced?'

Again, Nona was set back. But Darius, casting about for an appropriate course of action, had an answer. *If the queen is to be trusted, we should bring in the others. Colene or Angus should know how to proceed.*

Gratefully, Nona turned to the queen and voiced her request. 'We are actually a party of six. May we bring in our companions to join us in dialogue with you?'

'Of course,' Hyacinth said. 'Who and where are they?'

'They would not reveal themselves to strangers. But if you send someone out with us, we will go to fetch them.'

'I will go with you myself,' the queen said.

They exited the castle, the queen walking serenely beside Seqiro. She evidently did not stand on ceremony when interested in something. Nevertheless, she had remarkable poise.

Hyacinth's glance dropped down to touch him. 'Thank you, Darius.'

And she was amazingly swift to catch on to the way of telepathy.

'It is my business to make rapid assessments,' she said.

Soon they came into range, and Seqiro acquainted the others of the situation. Whereupon the huge shape of Angus appeared, floating above the trees, with Colene and Burgess in his hand. He came to land before them, and introductions proceeded.

'You wear green,' the queen noted, gazing at Angus.

'I am a visitor to this fair world.' Green was the color of visitors whose status was not defined. 'I could wear black if I chose, but I suspect this would be meaningless here.' For here black indicated the men of theow status.

'Green becomes you,' the queen agreed. 'I presume that you of the animus have no interest in acquiring this world.'

'None,' he agreed. 'My interest is only in facilitating the interest of Nona of Oria.'

'I fear our castle is insufficient to accommodate you, unless you are able to change your size.'

'I can change the size of inanimate things, but not myself,' he replied. 'But have no concern, Queen Hyacinth. I will remain aloof until my friends need me again.'

'You represent the transport of women to Oria?'

'This is so.'

'Will you accede to showing yourself to our population, that they may this once in their lives appreciate what lies beyond our world?'

He squinted a huge eye at her. 'And what will you offer in return?'

She laughed. 'What did you have in mind?'

'Let me suggest alternatives. It is possible that Nona will deal with you, and you will have the franchise for recruiting small women of your realm and neighboring realms, making what deals please you with other castles, and I will appear in my full size to take these women in my hands and convey them along the filaments to Oria, together with my friends, including the magic man and magic horse, making as many trips as are required. Or it may be that I will convey Nona and her party to the adjacent queendom to see whether they are more amenable to such an agreement, in which case they would have the franchise and if any of your women wish to go to Oria, you will negotiate with that other realm. This seems reasonable to me; does it seem so to you?'

The queen nodded. 'It is a pleasure to bargain with the animus.'

Darius realized that Angus had neatly countered the queen's demand for something of significant value, by threatening to take Nona's business elsewhere.

*Colene thought of it*, Seqiro thought.

It did have the flavor of Colene's nature. Nona had been

ineffective, as had Darius himself, but Colene's sharp intelligence and aggressive nature had found the key. Nona was lovely and nice and talented, but Colene had survival skills they needed. This kept being demonstrated in small or significant ways. If only she lacked her two great liabilities of youth and depression!

They climbed onto Angus' hands, and Darius helped Queen Hyacinth up. It was an honorary gesture; she made herself light enough so as almost to float, and he guided her. On this world men served women in all ways, and the protocol reflected it.

Angus lifted and flew to the castle, where there was now a fine array of people, the red and blue tunics in the foreground, the black and white ones behind. Angus came down on his feet before the rad on which the castle was built, and put his hands out to the castle, so that the party could enter without ever climbing the hill. It was an impressive minor show.

The rest of the day passed in festivities at the castle. Darius knew that Queen Hyacinth was sending her minions out, alerting other queendoms to the situation. It would require a few days to assemble the women, and meanwhile their small group would suffer the castle hospitality. He remembered how seduction, rape, and theft had been the order of the night at the despot castle on Oria, when he had first been there. He wasn't sure whether it was a better quality of ruler here, or that women simply were less interested in such activities, but there was nothing of that nature now. He shared a suite with Nona and Colene, while Burgess and Seqiro were in the stable, by their own choice; less was expected of animals, and it was close enough so that all of them remained in the ambience of telepathy. Angus snoozed invisibly in the glade, making periodic appearances to awe the natives.

In due course it was done. Forty-nine diminutive maidens, their magic intact, assembled at the castle, ready to travel

222

to Oria to be the queens of its various regions. The smallest woman was Nona's size; the others were larger, but still could pass for tall natives. They understood that not all the folk would welcome them, particularly the deposed despots, but they planned to work together at first, securing each kingdom, leaving one of their number there, and going on to the next. They were experienced in the system of the anima, and knew how to govern men. The women of Oria would support them, knowing that this occupation was for the benefit of the following generation. Soon enough the world would be secure and at peace. Certainly these governesses would be far more effective than Nona could ever have been alone.

Angus began the job of ferrying them across. Now the core party had to split, temporarily. Seqiro and Nona went with the first group of seven women, to enable them to communicate with the women of Oria, for the languages were not the same. The first job would be to establish a basis for translation. Nona would explain that these women had come to govern the world and see to the protection of the girls of Oria who would assume power as they matured. They would secure Nona's village and adjacent castle, and Angus would bring the other women there.

Of course the telepathy stopped when the first group departed. But the understanding had been worked out, and Darius, Colene, and Burgess needed only hand signals to indicate their wishes. Burgess had become a creature of some attention; the folk liked to see him float and hurl stones. They brought him baskets of fruit to consume.

On the second trip, Burgess went with seven women. They had learned how to communicate with him, though it was rudimentary compared to what Colene, buttressed by Seqiro, could do. That left Darius alone with Colene for the night, and naturally she tried to seduce him, and as usual he declined. They could converse well enough, because of her developing telepathy, and of course they did know some words of each other's languages. He hoped she did not know how infernally tempting her offers were.

*I love knowing that*, she thought smugly.

He made as if to spank her. She countered his bluff by baring her bottom. The sight was electrifying, because in his Mode women wore huge diapers to conceal their posterior contours. He turned away, lest he lose more than the game. She laughed and hugged him from behind. A stranger would never have realized that she was not a vessel of joy.

*You give me joy, Darius.*

But it was not the same. A transient emotion could not compare to a permanently joyful nature. That had been their problem throughout. If only this vessel of dolor were not the woman he loved!

*I know I shouldn't tease you, Darius. If you want to be with one of the local women tonight, I will understand.*

Yes. And Colene would slice her wrists until he returned to her.

*Touché!*

But some day he would have that cute piece of flesh. Then he would make up for all the blocked temptation she had put him through.

*Why wait?*

This time he didn't threaten her. He kissed her. That ended her teasing. For a while.

On the following day three more groups departed. Then two on the third day. On the next to last trip, one woman returned, bringing a report of the proceedings on Oria: verification that the enterprise was legitimate. Queen Hyacinth had made sure to confirm it, as a smart manager should. The reporting woman took the final trip out, satisfied to remain on Oria, and Darius and Colene went too. There was a date to have regular contact between the worlds at monthly intervals; more women might wish to go. But for now, it was done.

Darius and Colene stood on Angus' hand and made formal bows of parting to the queen. They knew that Hyacinth had made the most of this opportunity, and gained prestige in a global sense. Her people had also been treated to the remarkable sight of a giant from Jupiter. They knew that such folk existed, but seldom was it shown so directly. Hundreds of the local large folk waved farewell.

Then Angus ascended and flew east. Most of the time of these trips was spent crossing the surfaces of the planets: this one, Oria, and Jupiter. But Angus was now thoroughly familiar with the route, and covered it efficiently.

'So are you sad to leave all these big, talented women behind?' Colene asked Darius teasingly. She was a head shorter than any of them, though the same size as they in proportion to her home world. It had been a mind-numbing experience to be among so many women whose magical abilities matched Nona's, and many of them were quite young and attractive. But of course he wouldn't say that to Colene.

'Yeah, sure you wouldn't,' she said sourly. 'But I guess it sort of puts Nona in perspective, eh?'

It sort of did. If he ever wanted to retire with a magical woman, this was the place to do it. However, he amended his thought before Colene could react, he had no wish for such a retirement, and in any event, he was needed in his own Mode.

They rode the filament, and the amazons were just as thrilled and awed as anyone else. None of them had expected to make such a journey in her life, until this sudden opportunity had appeared. What was the point, when most of the worlds were animus, as well as being the wrong size?

They crossed the enormous surface of Jupiter, and the amazons were impressed again. Then on to the other filament, and finally across Oria to their starting point.

The local region had already been pacified. The black and white cloaks were properly subservient and the barricades

225

were down. Tall red-tunicked women were using their magic to generate food and other supplies, and to make quick repairs. Life was already visibly better.

They reached the castle. There they were reunited with Nona, Seqiro, and Burgess, who were being treated as royally here as they had been on the amazon world. Things were looking very good, and Nona seemed much happier.

The mission here had been accomplished, and enough time had passed so that it should be safe to return to the Virtual Mode. Colene was eager to resume their journey. So was he.

# 10

## *Malady*

Burgess liked traveling on the Virtual Mode, but did not like constantly encountering rough or sloping terrain, so that the others had to carve a path for him or haul him along on a wagon. He needed a way to travel without being a burden to the others.

He discussed it with Nona, while they waited for the remaining amazons to be brought across to their new hive. Communication between them was not good, but the problem was evident: he needed a way to traverse irregular ground, and to mount slopes. They experimented, and came up with something promising. Nona generated a long flat piece of material that was light but firm. She laid this on the ground, and he floated along it without difficulty. Then she took it to the countryside and laid it over the brushy, rocky terrain. He was able to float along it, but tended to slide off the side when it wasn't level. She modified it ot have ridges along the sides that enabled him to stay on. She made a second piece, which she set at the end of the first, so that he could cross from one to the other. While he floated along the second, she used her magic to float the first to the front, where it became a continuation of his path. It was working! He was able to traverse much rougher terrain that before, because the smooth, flat artificial path gave his air purchase. This would enable him to move much more readily by himself. Instead of undertaking the tedious job of filling in sand to make a path for him, they could lay down the artificial path.

But the problem of slope remained. The path was no help there; he could not get enough forward motion to propel him up it. He could come down it by pumping through less air, so as to touch the surface and drag, but that was slow. He needed a way to move at normal speed.

Seqiro had a suggestion: the horse could pull him along on a rope. They experimented with ropes, and it helped; Burgess could float on a slope if held in place by the rope. When the horse pulled, Burgess traveled along. He held on to the rope by sucking on a ball at its end; when he wished to let it go, he merely stopped sucking. They practiced and got better. It was easier than using a wagon, and faster, because they didn't need to take time to grow the wagon to size. It wasn't perfect, but would do. Now Burgess could travel with somewhat greater independence.

By the time Darius and Colene returned, they had it working fairly well. Colene was pleased when she learned; she kissed him on an eye stalk. She was supposed to be an unhappy creature, but he was learning joy from her.

In due course they returned to the Virtual Mode. Burgess moved along better than before, because of the path. Because it was one continuous piece, formed from the material of an anchor world, it extended across the Mode boundaries when pushed through the boundary. It was there, beyond, but disappeared, looking as if it had been abruptly cut off, because their vision was limited to whatever Mode they were in. When they came to a hill, Nona fastened the length of rope to Seqiro's harness, and it too extended invisibly across the boundaries but remained firm. Then Burgess floated on up the slope, balancing on his air as the rope provided forward motion. Nona, following, picked up the path as he left it, and stepped ahead to put it down in front. She popped out of view as she went ahead, then reappeared as he caught up to the next joining. The process became automatic, and they moved along well.

Then they came to a broad marshy plain. The feet of the humans and horse sank down in the muck, making progress difficult for them, while Burgess floated along without trouble. Now the situation was reversed; they were the ones who required assistance.

They considered, and decided to make a kind of sledge without runners, that would rest on the surface of the swamp. It would not be exactly a boat, but would serve similarly. They did this, growing a craft large enough to hold the four of them. But when they tried to move it, it wedged in the muck and advanced only so grudgingly that it was evident it would be useless for traveling.

'I wish we could float across, the way Burgess does,' Nona remarked.

'Say, maybe we can,' Colene said, her mind taking hold. 'He floats on a thin cushion of air, never actually touching the gook below. If we could get air like that, we wouldn't bog down either.'

'But he is constructed to pump air,' Darius said. 'We are not.'

'But maybe if we had an air pump, we could do it. Force air down below the sledge, so it bubbles out around, making a cushion. Maybe it wouldn't exactly float, but those bubbles would sure be less restrictive than this muck. Then maybe we could pole it along at a decent crawl.'

'But we don't have anything to pump air,' Darius pointed out. 'That's not the kind of magic I do, and Nona doesn't either. We don't know enough of your science to make such a device.'

Then Colene fixed on Burgess. 'Maybe we could use, you, Burg. How much air could you pump, if you had to?'

There was no answer for that. Burgess moved all the air he needed to, to float.

'I mean, suppose we tied you down over a hole in the sledge, and you pumped air down through that, so it came out around the edges? It might take a lot of pressure. Would that wear you out, or suffocate you or something?'

Suffocate on air? He was learning enough of their concept of humor to know that was funny.

229

They tried it. They fashioned the sledge with a hole in the center, covered by netting, so that air could pass through while the muck was restrained. They made a kind of enclosure so that Burgess could rest within it, and the outflow of air around his canopy would be blocked. They put ropes over him so that when he pumped air he would not rise. It all seemed complicated and ineffective, but he was willing to try what they wanted, especially when Colene requested it.

He pumped air. There was some resistance, so he pumped harder. This forced the air down under the sledge and along its bottom. The air began to bubble out around the edges.

But it didn't bubble evenly. It made a few channels, and burped out through them, leaving the sledge mired.

'Hm,' Colene said. 'We need to make that air more viscous, so it forms a sheet supporting the sledge. Only problem is, how do we do that?'

No one knew. It looked as if they would simply have to slog slowly through the muck for the days or weeks it would take to reach solid land again, or else retreat and look for some other route through the Virtual Mode.

'This is no good,' Colene said. 'We have to keep moving. For one thing, suppose that mind predator spies me again? I'm not using my bit of telepathy at all, on the Virtual Mode, so as to keep a low profile, but it might make a routine check and find me. I need to be able to get to an anchor in a hurry, if that happens. And the rest of you don't want to be bogged down in muck forever, or going back over familiar ground.'

'Those may nevertheless be our choices,' Darius said.

'I don't accept those choices!' she flared. 'We need new choices!'

He shrugged, which was a kind of stretching and relaxation of his upper body in a manner not available to Burgess. 'How do we get new choices?'

'Maybe we should brainstorm,' she said.

The others were not familiar with the concept, and she

230

had to clarify it: all members of the hive thinking new thoughts at a rapid rate, without regard to reasonableness. It was hoped that from such a deluge would come something useful. Possibly something which at first seemed impossible.

They tried it. The three humans touched Burgess' contact points, and the horse strengthened their ability to communicate, making the hive fully current. 'Remember, anything at all can be suggested,' Colene said. 'And we take it seriously. We consider it, and if then it doesn't work out, we go on to the next. Like, I'll suggest we all sprout wings and fly across. What do the rest of you say to that?'

'I don't need wings to fly,' Nona said. 'I can levitate myself or others, but I lack the strength to lift us all.'

'I don't fly, I conjure,' Darius said. 'But it's not safe to conjure blind, or across Mode boundaries. Otherwise I could move us across this bog.'

Burgess didn't fly, he floated; he could not rise more than a trace above the ground.

'You're all being too negative,' Colene protested. 'Don't tell us what you can't do, tell us what we maybe can do.'

But the rest of them lacked Colene's ready intelligence and initiative. They could not have ideas the way she could.

'Burgess is right,' Nona said. 'We need to have Colene's mind, to do this well.'

Darius could multiply joy and other emotions. Could he multiply intelligence? If so, he could give them all Colene's smartness for a while.

'Yes, what about that?' Nona asked. 'Burgess has another interesting idea. Can you multiply Colene's mind, Darius?'

'I doubt –'

'Nuh-uh, diaper worshiper!' Colene said. 'Have you ever tried it?'

'Intelligence is not the same as mood or emotion.'

'How do you know?' Nona asked. 'Perhaps Colene is smart because she feels smart, just as she is depressed because she feels depressed.'

231

Perhaps Colene was smart because she was depressed.

Nona laughed. 'Then I don't want to be smart!'

'I can multiply her emotion,' Darius said. 'But that will bring her depression. If, however, that enables the rest of us to think more clearly −'

'Can you reverse it, after we get an idea?' Nona asked.

'By drawing from a happier person,' he said.

'Who is the happiest among us?' Nona asked.

They considered. 'Seqiro,' Colene said.

She was right. The horse loved being with intelligent and friendly minds, even when they were depressed minds.

'So first you multiply Colene,' Nona said. 'Then you multiply Seqiro, after we have an idea.'

'I think this is foolish −'

He was drowned out by the others: no negative thoughts allowed.

So Darius embrace Colene, and drew from her, then sent it out to all of them. Burgess felt distinctly less positive than he had before, but he also felt the urge to explore and understand the mysteries of things, and a desire to move rapidly on out of this marsh before the mind predator came again. He thought there should be a way, if they could only find it.

'I want to get the Hades out of this hole!' Nona exclaimed uncharacteristically.

*You and me both, luscious body*, Seqiro responded, similarly uncharacteristically.

'Great fishes and little gods, you sound just like me!' Colene exclaimed, laughing.

If Darius could multiply mood and intelligence, could he also multiply magic? Such as Nona's ability to lift things? Because then he could make the sledge with its burden light enough to float on air.

'Why not?' Colene asked. 'Darius uses magic, and Nona uses magic. Maybe they can mix!'

Both Darius and Nona tried to demur − and were stopped by the others, again invoking the no-negative rule.

So Darius embrace Nona. 'I will try to draw and multiply her magic,' he said. 'If I succeed, all of you will acquire it, so all of you must focus on the sledge, trying to make it light. You, Burgess, will know whether it becomes easier to push air under it.'

He drew from Nona, and sent it out. Burgess concentrated on his air pumping, trying to make it more effective by making the sledge magically lighter.

He felt the air moving more readily. The sledge lifted. In a moment the entire sledge was floating just above the surface of the swamp, in the manner Burgess did when unattached. It was working!

'It's working!' Colene echoed. 'I feel it! I'm drawing on Nona's magic!'

*So am I*, Seqiro thought.

'And I,' Darius said. 'I have her magic!'

'Let's see just how strong it is, with all of us doing it,' Colene said. 'Everybody get on the sledge!'

They got on, one by one, until all of their weight was there, and still it floated. It had been made so light that Burgess could lift it exactly as he did himself, with the air no longer bubbling because the sledge no longer touched mud. When it tilted slightly, Burges directed more air that way, and this righted the structure.

However, it was only floating, not moving. Burgess lacked the control to do more than float it.

'That's easy,' Colene said. 'We can pole it, same as a boat, or maybe we can magically pull on something ahead, the same way Nona does when she flies.'

They tried it. The sledge lurched forward − and sank into the muck.

'Too many diverted their attention,' Darius said. 'We need to have one or two do the pulling, and the others do the floating.'

They experimented again, and found that Seqiro had to focus on floating, because he weighed more than all the rest

233

of them combined. He could float his own weight, but none of them could float him. So Nona and Colene, the two least massive members of the hive, concentrated on pulling.

The sledge moved, at first jerkily, then more smoothly. It passed through the next Mode boundary. They were on their way!

The swamp was large, but now they were moving well, and made visible progress across it. The complexion of the plants in it shifted from Mode to Mode, but its general nature didn't change. Some Modes were raining, and in some the marsh became open water, but it didn't matter; Burgess could handle water as readily as solid land. They moved more swiftly than they would have in a boat, because there was no liquid drag. They realized that there might be danger, crossing boundaries so rapidly, but there also might be danger in lingering in any.

Gradually the sledge became heavier. Those wielding the magic of lightening were tiring, and so was Burgess. He normally did not pump air at a high volume for an extended time. But the far shore was approaching, and it seemed they could make it the rest of the way across before the fatigue became too bad.

Then they passed through a region of obnoxious flying creatures. They seemed to be a cross between shears, insects, and the birds in Colene's mind. They spied the sledge as it passed through, and dived in. Burgess had only a few stones to fire at them. Then Darius took up a stick of wood and used it effectively to bat the creatures out of the air as they came close.

The watery marsh became a lake. Things swam in it. Some had fins which projected above the surface. The fins changed size and color with each new Mode, but the creatures seemed to be just as interested in the odd craft. Some showed impressive teeth. This did not seem to be the time to pause.

At last they reached the bank. They climbed onto land, and unfastened Burgess. It felt good to float free again!

They made a quick camp, ate, and settled for the night. But though they were all quite tired, they maintained a watch, because they could not know what lurked on this land. Colene had a small device she called a watch, with a picture of two little sticks on it. Each time the larger stick pointed in a certain direction, it was time for a new person to begin a turn. So the one on watch also watched Colene's wrist, and the picture on it.

Something large did approach during Burgess' watch. But it was beyond the Mode boundary, so could not reach them. Indeed, Burgess crossed the line beside the tent, and the thing disappeared. It was probably walking right through the region of their camp, but in its own Mode, where there was no camp. The creatures who could reach their camp would be those they could see coming from the tent itself. Burgess was merely circling the tent, passing through boundaries on either side of it.

In the morning they assessed their situation. The intelligence and magic had worn off, being temporary effects, as had the depression. That was just as well, because it seemed that their notion of gaining joy from the horse would not have worked well; it would have been an overlay on the two prior transfers. They saw that the new terrain was rugged; the swamp abutted the jagged slope of a mountain range, with snow showing above. But that was the way toward the next anchor, so they had to go there.

They considered, and decided not to try to borrow Nona's magic again. It had helped when they needed it, but the process also depleted her slightly, making her less magical, and that was not good. The same went for Colene's intelligence: they did not want her to become less intelligent. These assets needed to be conserved.

They used their path and rope system to haul Burgess along. Again the others disappeared as they crossed the Mode boundaries, with only the end of the path and end of the rope showing. But the terrain seldom changed significantly between adjacent Modes, so he knew approximately where he was going.

They crossed the foothills, traversed a high valley, and started up the main slopes. Nona made heavy jackets for them, including the horse, but it couldn't be managed for Burgess. He needed full access to the air. So when it became cold, she made some fire to warm the air of the vicinity, and he was all right.

Then the pull on the rope abruptly stopped. Burgess settled to the ground and waited while Nona disappeared ahead. Soon she was back with news that they had encountered a discontinuity: the ground level of one Mode was not continuous with that of the next. This was not natural; something had excavated it. In fact, Darius said it seemed to be a mine: a huge hole left when something of value beneath was taken away. That, Darius said, could be trouble.

The pull resumed, and Burgess joined the others on the chill upper slope. The mountain continued unabated. But when he floated cautiously to the next boundary, the feeling changed; the path had no support there. The mountain had been scooped away, as if hivers had sucked out the dirt. Now Burgess appreciated the problem.

Darius explained that when he had traveled the Virtual Mode with another person, Provos, who had later terminated her anchor so that Burgess could establish his anchor instead, they had encountered pits like this, and fallen to the bottom of one, and had difficulty getting out of it. There had been creatures made of metal excavating the pits. Colene called them robots. They looked and acted like living creatures, but they were not alive. It seemed best not to get captured by such creatures, because they might choose to render living folk dead, to match themselves.

Burgess agreed. The assorted odd living creatures he had encountered (no offense to present company) were

236

sufficient. Odd dead ones might be an experience best left for some other adventure. But how were they to get past the mine pit?

They would have to try to get around it. Unless it happened to be only a single Mode wide, in which case they might bridge it.

Nona went ahead, flying above the slope, disappearing as she passed the boundary. In a moment she returned: the pit was indeed only one Mode wide.

But Darius was not satisfied. The pits he had encountered before had been made Modes wide, with different robots in each. It seemed that there were likely to be similar species in adjacent Modes, who could indulge in similar activities. So it would be better to verify whether any of the Modes beyond had pits.

Nona flew across again, and this time was gone for a longer period. There were two pits: the one in the next Mode, and another three Modes beyond. That seemed to be all. She had not flown up the entire mountain, but had noted that the nature of the rock changed, so that once they were beyond this stratum, there would probably not be any more pits. It was not clear what they wanted from the one type of rock. Colene said it could be anything from gold to uranium.

Nona expanded Burgess' two paths, so that each was more solid. Then they put each across the next Mode, so that one end was anchored in this Mode, and the far end in the third Mode. The humans crossed, and then Burgess floated along, drawn by the rope Darius held, out of sight in the next Mode. Burgess found the sudden chasm awesome and had to retract his eyes and trust Nona and the rope to guide him blind. Finally Seqiro crossed, his right hooves on one path, his left hooves on the other. It seemed precarious, but with Colene leading him he stepped along confidently enough, not looking down.

They were safely across, but Burgess concluded that he

was not comfortable with this region. A broad flat plain would be much more to his liking.

They continued up the slope, then crossed the next pit Mode in similar manner. Now all they had to worry about was the jagged icy ridge of the mountain pass ahead. Burgess did not like that prospect much better than the chasms.

In one Mode there was a snowstorm in progress. The humans bundled up further, and covered the horse with more warm padding. Nona took metal nails from their supplies and enlarged them into pitons to provide firm anchorage. They hammered these in, and left them behind, just in case they had to return this way. The storm was uncomfortable, and it rendered visibility bad, but in a moment they were through it and back in sunlight. That was one thing about the Virtual Mode: if they did not like the weather in one Mode, they could readily change it by going to the next.

There was one benefit of the snowy reaches: Burgess no longer had to use the portable path, because the snow leveled the surface. Now all he needed was the rope. Nona diminished the path segments for easy portability, and they continued.

Burgess began to feel fatigued. But as with the swamp, there was nowhere to go but on, so he did not express distress. However, he could not conceal it, because Nona touched one of his contact points frequently, and soon realized his situation. 'Once we pass the ridge, you can slide down on the snow, with no further effort,' she said encouragingly.

They did pass the ridge, braving the cutting wind which crossed it, and started cautiously down. Burgess did relax as he slid, and Nona continued to heat the air around him with fire, but his fatigue increased. He began to feel negative, as if his system were functioning imperfectly. His eye stalks, already cold, worked poorly. His air lost power, and he dragged in the snow.

Then Colene was with him. 'Burgess, what's wrong? You were tired on the bog — we all were — but not like this.'

Burgess did not know. He seemed to be suffering a malady, perhaps occasioned by the effort of the climb and the cold snow. He had not felt this way before in his life. Perhaps when they reached the foot of the mountain, where it would be warm and green and level, he would recover.

'Level,' she said. 'I wonder — you could be suffering from disorientation. You're a creature of level land, but you've been at a tilt for hours now. Like motion sickness; we can get real sick from that, sometimes.'

Burgess did not know.

'I can make a level sledge,' Nona suggested. 'It will vary some as the slope changes, but it should be an improvement.'

She made it. They put Burgess on it, and now he was level though the slope remained. They let him down on the rope, and he did not even have to float. That helped. He withdrew his eyes and let himself sleep, as his energy was low and there was nothing he could do to assist his own travel.

In time they reached the warmer depths, and finally they were on warm, relatively level land again. In fact it became a series of plains which extended as far as they could see. But Burgess did not feel better. Perhaps it would be best if they left him on a Mode and went on without him, as he seemed to be dying.

'No way!' Colene exclaimed unreasonably. 'Listen, Burg — we're coming onto my anchor Mode. I can tell; the terrain's starting to look like Oklahoma. I never wanted to go back there again, and there could be some real complications, but you're sick, maybe the way I was when the mind predator laid siege to me, and I think we'd better just get you onto an anchor Mode and see if that helps. We aren't going to just let you go.'

Burgess would have appreciated that, if he had had more energy. As it was, he couldn't even float, despite the ideal terrain. It was all he could do to pump enough air to sustain his gills.

Nona put her hands on his contact points and concentrated. He knew that she was exerting her magic power of healing. She had used it to fix the scrapes and bruises they had incurred along the way. But though he felt her magic passing through his body, and it was a warm and comforting thing, it did not make him better. He seemed to be too alien for her to heal.

They reshaped the sledge and put him on it. Then Seqiro hauled it, and Burgess went with them though he did nothing on his own behalf. He regretted becoming such a burden to the hive, but lacked the energy to protest.

Time passed. He was aware of this because once when he extended an eye stalk and looked around it was dark, and another time it was light again. Now that he was using very little energy, he was not growing worse at the same rate as before, but neither was he improving. Colene's efforts had merely extended the time it would require for him to die.

They came to the oddest region of the Virtual Mode yet. It had paved paths which were straight and wide, ideal for floaters to float on. But there were no floaters. Instead there were monstrous hurtling things traveling the paths at extreme velocity. Burgess would have been terrified, if he had had sufficient energy. Colene was careful to keep them to the sides of the broad paths, so as to be clear of the metal monsters, but each time they crossed a boundary into a new Mode, more of the things appeared. Sometimes they came to sudden halts, screeching their protests, then after a brief pause they lurched forward again. This was a region of ferocious madness.

They paused to add wheels to the sledge, so that now it could roll along the side of the path. This made it easier for Seqiro to pull.

Objects appeared along the sides of the paths. They were large and cubic, and seemed to have been fashioned of wood or stone. Some were so high they looked like small mountains. They were in many colors, and patterns of colors, with oblong designs on them.

Colene brought the party to a halt. 'Look, we're not at my anchor yet, but I don't know if it's smart to show ourselves to the natives of these adjacent Modes. Could be trouble. Let's enclose Burgess' wagon, so no one can see him.'

Soon he was inside a box, with openings so that enough air could enter, and Nona was riding with him. Through her, he remained aware of what was going on outside, and did not need to look himself. That was good, because he lacked energy to do so. Nona's communication through his contact point was enough.

At last they came to a longer halt. 'This is it,' Colene said. 'The next Mode or two will be mine. But there is a problem. Last time I was here, with Provos, they tried to stop me from leaving. I just barely made it through the anchor. If we just go through now, someone will see us, and we'll be in trouble right away.'

'My magic does not work, here,' Darius said. 'Remember, at first you did not believe in me, because of that. But perhaps Seqiro's does, or Nona's. If so, we may be able to stay away from trouble.'

'Gee, I hope so! 'Cause we've got to get Burgess onto an anchor Mode and see if that helps.'

*I believe my telepathy will work*, Seqiro said. *I have encountered no Mode where it does not, though it may be limited on some.*

'And perhaps one or two of my abilities will work, as they did on the Shale Mode,' Nona said.

'Well, let's try you first,' Colene said to Nona. 'We'll step across, and you see if you can make the illusion of nothing. Because if you can, we can all go there, and no one will see us.'

Nona left the wagon, and she and Colene stepped across

241

the next boundary. There was a wait. Then they returned. 'It works!' Colene exclaimed. 'All her magic works! Everything she tried, anyway. We were invisible.'

So Seqiro pulled the wagon through the anchor, and they were all in Colene's Earth Mode. They were all under Nona's illusion of nothing, and could not see themselves. This had one small advantage for Burgess: the wagon was also under the illusion, so could not be seen; now Burgess could see outside with his own three eyes.

'That's my house, there,' Colene said. 'Right here is where my hideout, Dogwood Bumshed, was. So if you're staring, Darius, you invisible man, that's why: they took it away, thinking it was the anchor. But the anchor's not a thing, it's a person and a place.'

'I was staring,' Darius admitted. 'I spent some time, confined to that shed, learning to love you.'

'Yeah, that's why I kept you locked up,' Colene said fondly. 'And now you're back here.'

'Is it safe to camp at this site?' Nona asked. 'So we can go back through the anchor if we need to?'

'Should be. My folks never come out here anyway. With nothing to see, they sure won't bother. So it's the best place. I know my way around from here. Can you make material for a tent, Nona? Might as well camp out in comfort.'

'Certainly,' Nona replied.

'Seqiro, does your telepathy work here?' Colene asked next. Then she paused, and burst out laughing. 'Of course it works! We're all understanding each other, aren't we? What an idiot I am! So we have it all: Nona's magic and Seqiro's telepathy. I never wanted to see Earth again, but since we're here, I'm glad it's this way.'

'If you were always this happy, I could marry you,' Darius said.

'If you'd marry me, I'd be this happy!' she retorted.

'This seems like a pleasant enough Mode,' Nona said. 'Except for all those hurtling vehicles.'

242

'Hey, Burgess, are you feeling better?' Colene made her way to the wagon, and climbed in to join Nona and touch a contact point. 'Damn! You're not, are you? But maybe a few hours here will do it.'

They set up their tent and diminished the wagon, so that Burgess could be in direct contact with the ground. But it did not seem to help. He lacked the energy or desire even to eat. He was still sinking.

He faded into uncomfortable sleep. But after the darkness came, and the light again, he was no better.

'Damn, damn, damn!' Colene repeated. 'I thought maybe Earth, so similar to Shale, would be good for you. But it's not, is it? What are we going to do?'

Burgess no longer had the energy to send an answer through his contact points. It was time for him to die.

# 11

## Earth

'What are we going to do?' Colene demanded plaintively. She was such a mixture of joy and helplessness that Nona knew that someone else would have to take the initiative.

She glanced at Darius, who shrugged. They were visible, in the chill early morning, because it was not possible for her to maintain the illusion of nothing while she slept. She knew that Darius was none too comfortable on Earth, being deprived of his magic here. Seqiro never led the way; he always reflected the mind of those he was with. That left Nona. She had her mind and her magic, but now she had to try to be the thing she had never been: a leader. For a while.

'Colene, you solved my problem in the Julia Mode,' she said. 'I said I would try to solve yours. Now I shall make the effort. But you will have to help me.'

'You were thinking of me and Darius,' Colene said dispiritedly. 'Now I just want to save Burgess.'

'Yes. I must borrow from what you know, because this is your Mode. But perhaps I can bring a fresh perspective. In my Mode, we would look for a specialist in healing. I have tried to heal Burgess, but that aspect of my magic does not seem to be operative here.'

'It's operative on the Virtual Mode,' Darius said. 'But it didn't help Burgess.'

'I think it would have, had he had an abrasion or injury,' she said. 'But there seems to be something missing that my magic can not supply. I do not know what it can be. But perhaps a person who specializes in healing would be able to fathom it. Do you have such specialists here?'

'Sure. Doctors. But any of them would freak out, if he

saw Burgess. Even a veterinarian. We need someone who knows Cambrian life forms — say!' The girl's face brightened. 'Amos!'

'Who?'

'My old science teacher. I told you about him. The one I had a crush on. He should know, if anyone does, and he'd be fascinated with this. He'd help if he could, I know.'

'Then we must find Amos, and bring him here,' Nona said firmly. 'Is it a far walk to his residence?'

'We can't walk, for all sorts of reasons. It's too far, and there isn't that much time. Any man who sees you on the street — never mind. We'll have to call a taxi.'

'A taxi?'

'It's a car you rent, sort of, with a driver. Only problem is, we need money. I don't have enough.'

'Describe your money, or show me a sample, and I will make more of it,' Nona said.

Colene laughed. 'I don't think so. That would be counterfeiting. I'll have to borrow some from my folks. I hate to do it, but maybe I can pay it back. Let's check the house.'

'I can not maintain the illusion of nonexistence for the other three, if I go with you to another place.'

'Um, yes. Okay, let's make a tent for them, and leave it in sight. The neighbors will figure it's some project my folks are doing.'

Nona's full magic did seem to be working, here, so she did not have to grow material tediously. She simply scooped dirt from the ground and transformed it to tent cloth, and made pegs and poles similarly. They pitched the tent to enclose horse, man, and floater. Nona also made extra blankets, because it was winter in this region of this Mode, and too cold for comfort. She had used her magic to keep them warm in the night, a mild variant of the fire spell, but that would not remain in her absence. Then they went into the house.

'Sure is neat in here,' Colene murmured, looking around. 'It was always pretty messy when I lived here. Mom was alcoholic, and the details of housework sort of got away from her. Dad was away, mostly.'

'He had a distant employment?'

'That too. But when he wasn't working, he was off with his girlfriend.'

'But if he was married – '

'Marriage in name only, mainly,' the girl said sourly. 'I think I was about the only thing they had in common, and they didn't pay much attention to me. That sort of thing leads to juvenile misfits. Ask any psychologist.'

Unfortunately that reminded Nona of her own family. The despots had destroyed it, in revenge for her effort to bring the anima. That had perhaps been the last straw, leaving her no reason to remain on Oria.

'Hey, I'm sorry, Nona,' Colene said. 'I wasn't thinking.'

'It is not your concern.'

'Yes, it is. Because I'm your friend, and I was there, so maybe I have some responsibility for – '

'No, it was bound to happen, whoever was there. The despots did that sort of thing to anyone who opposed them. I knew that at the outset.'

They came to what Colene thought of as the living room. There on the table was a small pile of papers.

Colene went to it, startled. 'This is money! And a note.' She picked up the note. 'It says "COLENE: anything you want. We want to make it right. Only come back to us." '

She sat down suddenly in the couch. Nona saw that she was crying. Colene had been alienated from her parents, yet she did still care for them.

'I think your parents need you as much as you need them,' Nona said.

'I *don't* need them!' But Colene's pain belied her words.

'They tried to keep you here by force, but lost you. Now

they hope you will return voluntarily. That is not a bad thing to hope.'

'I can't stay here. I have to go with Darius. If only I could marry him.'

Something connected in Nona's mind. 'On Oria, women become marriageable at eighteen. But they can do it younger, if there is reason and their parents approve. Is it that way in Earth Mode?'

'Yeah, I think so. We used to joke about it at school. Some kid looked it up in an almanac, and saw that in New Hampshire a girl could marry as young as thirteen, or a boy of fourteen, if the parents gave permission. A lot of other states have it at fourteen for the girl. Some don't have any age limits at all, even, if it's okay with the parents. We'd tease someone about getting a shotgun and – ' She broke off, startled. 'Fourteen! You know, I *could* get married, if – but no, my folks would never approve.'

Nona touched the note in Colene's hand. She could not read it herself, because it was in the alien Earth script. 'They offer you anything.'

Colene stared at her. 'Even that?'

'Perhaps what they really want is for you to be happy, and to feel good about them. If you were to marry with their approval, and they were part of it, then perhaps they could let you go and be satisfied, their job as parents done. This is the way it is in my Mode.'

'But all they ever had was the shell of a marriage. We all faked it, so the neighbors wouldn't know.'

'Perhaps their desire for the reality was greater, then. They knew that they had nothing, but through you they could have something.'

Colene considered it more seriously. 'Our family was nothing, until I left. Then when I came back, with Provos, I found my mom and dad had almost made it real. She had stopped drinking and he had stopped with his mistress. I thought it was weird, that they became the family I wanted

247

only when I was gone. Like maybe they did it only to spite me. But then they tried to keep me here. I thought that was the ultimate betrayal, and I hated them for that. But now I wonder.'

'They do love you, Colene. They just are not very good at it.'

'And you think that if I played along, doing something really family, like growing up and getting married, they'd let me go?'

'I think you should ask them.'

'You know, by the standards of my culture, a married woman is Old Enough. So Darius couldn't say —' Then she crumpled again. 'But I can't marry him. Because *his* culture says he has to draw joy from his wife, to multiply, and I'm just not any vessel of joy.'

'His culture does differ, yes. But you would not be married by the conventions of his culture. Only by yours. So here you would be his wife; there you would be his mistress. In either case, you would be his love. Isn't that what you want?'

'Oh, *yes!*' Colene grabbed Nona and kissed her. 'You *have* solved my problem, just the way I solved yours.'

Embarrassed, Nona changed the subject. 'But first we must save Burgess.'

'For sure! And now we have the money.' Colene got up and took the paper oblongs from the table.

They went upstairs to Colene's bedroom, where clothing of her Mode's type was hung in a closet. 'You'll have to change, too,' Colene said. 'That red tunic's no good, here. But I don't think any of my stuff'll fit you.'

'I can enlarge it,' Nona reminded her.

'Say, yeah! I keep forgetting that you're magical.' She picked out a red dress. 'You should like this. It's not the color, it's the style. Make this fit you, and some matching shoes, and you'll be a knockout Earthgirl.'

Nona made the necessary adjustments and donned the

dress and shoes, while Colene put on a blue dress. The startled Nona, because blue was the masculine color on her world, but she reminded herself that she wasn't on her world now. Then they arranged their hair in an appropriate way, took up purses — Nona simply duplicated Colene's, in red — and went back outside and to the tent.

Darius stared at them. 'You are two lovely but strange maidens,' he remarked. 'Colene I have seen in this manner before, but Nona seems to be a different woman.'

'We must go to seek help for Burgess,' Nona said.

'Seqiro, if anybody pokes around here, you make them go away,' Colene said. 'Don't make them scared, just make them lose interest. You can do that, right? We'll be back in a couple of hours.'

Nona nudged Colene. 'Shouldn't you tell Darius? I suspect Seqiro did not relay the news.'

Colene was startled. 'Right.' She turned to Darius. 'Oh, just so you know, manface: we're getting married.'

Darius' jaw dropped, to Colene's evident satisfaction. 'Tell him, Seqiro,' she said, and turned to Burgess. 'Burg, we're going to get help for you. So hang on, okay? We aren't going to let you die.'

Then Colene and Nona walked back into the house, where Colene used a magic device she called a phone to telepath a message to a central stable where they had many vehicles. A faint voice agreed to send a cab. They went out the front of the house, and to the street. In a while the vehicle arrived: one of those horrifying self-propelled machines they had seen zooming past at breakneck velocity on adjacent Modes.

'Don't worry,' Colene reassured her. 'I know what I'm doing, in my home Mode. This is no more chancy than riding in the hand of a giant, in your Mode.'

Nona hoped so.

They got into the vehicle, which turned out to be like an enclosed wagon, with comfortable couches inside. 'Put on your seat belt,' Colene said, and showed her how to strap herself down. Yet there seemed to be no danger of flying out, as the vehicle was entirely closed in.

There was a man in the front of the vehicle, who seemed to be directing its motion. He did things with his hands and feet, and the vehicle lurched into motion. Nona, seeing Colene unconcerned, forced herself to relax.

The cab zoomed down the street at a horrifying velocity, then abruptly slowed. Only the seat belt prevented Nona from falling off the couch. Now she knew what it was for.

The ride continued, constantly speeding up and screeching to a stop. Now there were other vehicles around them, moving in similar patterns. They were like horses in a chute, racing against each other, shoving each other aside, and squealing in challenge and protest all the while. The vehicles had funny honking voices, as well as the squeals in their wheels as they turned corners.

They stopped one more time, and Colene gave the man some of her paper money. Then they go out. They were now in another part of the town. 'This is the high school,' Colene explained. Her meaning was not as clear as before, because now she was using her own telepathy instead of that of the horse. Nona suspected that Seqiro's mind could reach this far, but that Colene had told him not to bother; she wanted to make it on her own. And of course she knew the local language and customs, so Nona was the only person who needed the translation.

'Now we need a little illusion,' Colene said. 'I don't want anyone to recognize me, until I find Amos, and they had better not get a good look at you. Can you sort of fuzz my face, and make yourself look, well, less developed?'

Nona used illusion to accomplish these things, and they went on into the nearest building. This was crowded with young folk, both male and female, carrying books. They wore every type of garb except tunics. They all seemed to be in a horrible hurry. Then they squeezed into chambers to the side of the main hall, and a loud clangor sounded, making Nona jump.

'School bell,' Colene explained. 'Ignore it; we're not going to class. I think Amos has a free period now, if his schedule hasn't changed. He's the only one we need here.'

They went to another chamber, where a man sat behind a desk piled with papers. They approached the desk.

He looked up. 'What class are you looking for, girls?'

'No class,' Colene replied. 'I need your help, Amos.'

He removed his glasses and gazed directly at her. 'Your voice is familiar, but not your face. Are you a new student?'

'Oh. Nona, drop the illusion.'

Nona did so. Then the man broke into a smile. 'Colene! Where have you been?'

'You wouldn't believe it, Amos. This is Nona.'

He gazed at Nona, and pursed his lips appreciatively. 'I am sure you are not a student here, Nona.'

'Amos, I said you wouldn't believe me,' Colene said. 'But you're going to have to. So we're going to have to give you a crash course in believing, because we may not have much time.'

Amos looked at his watch, which resembled the one Colene wore. 'About twenty minutes, before my next class. Will that be enough?'

'Maybe. First, I've been to some really weird places. I – I think it will be better if you don't tell. Can I swear you to secrecy?'

'Colene, if you have been involved in something illegal – '

'No, nothing like that! But if folk knew – well, do you believe in magic?'

'No.'

'Nona, here, is magic. If I prove it, will you agree to keep our confidence?'

Amos smiled indulgently. 'Yes.'

Colene turned to Nona. 'Do some magic.'

Nona made herself light and floated. Amos, skeptical, got

out from behind his desk and came around to her. He passed a hand over her head, then got down and passed it beneath her feet. Then he made a hoop of his arms and passed that hoop down around her body. There was of course nothing; she was floating magically.

'Impressive,' he said, unconvinced. 'What else can you do?'

Nona settled back to the floor and formed an illusion of nothingness. Startled, Amos passed his hand through the space at chest height — and collided with her torso. He brought his other hand around, feeling her arms and shoulders and finally her head. 'Amazing,' he murmured.

Nona dispelled the illusion. Amos, finding himself almost embracing her, stepped back. She picked a glass paperweight from his desk and transformed it into a red rose. She proffered him the flower.

He took it and smelled it. 'Can you change it back — in my hand?'

Nona touched the flower, and it became the paperweight again.

'I even felt the mass change,' he said, amazed. 'Anything else?'

Nona levitated the paperweight. Amos felt it tug in his hand, and let it go. It sailed up and circled the room before returning to its original spot on the desk.

'You are good,' he said. 'Extremely good. But a professional stage magician could duplicate those feats. What can you do that such a person could not do?'

'Do you have an animal?' Nona asked.

'You are not speaking my language, are you,' he said.

'Right,' Colene answered. 'She's not. She's from another universe.'

'Then how do I understand her?'

'I am telepathically translating for you.'

He pursed his lips again. 'What does Nona intend to do with an animal?'

252

'She will make it be a familiar. Then she can control it. But this takes a little while.'

'And you are magic too, Colene? You can read minds?'

'I'm learning. I'm not really good at it, yet, but I'm better than I was. I can translate for Nona because I know her well, and I know you. It's really a matter of putting her thoughts into your mind, and vice versa.'

'Tell me what I'm thinking of at this moment.'

'A yellow polka-dot bikini — on Nona.' Nona was not sure of the significance, but gathered that he had thought of an item of apparel.

He looked startled, again, but he recovered. 'And what now?'

'A black spider climbing a curtin. It's got a green eternity symbol on its back.'

'You *are* reading my mind!' he exclaimed.

'You made the pictures very clear,' Colene agreed, pleased. 'You set them up for me.'

'What am I thinking of now?'

Colene shook her head. 'I can't get it. It's just sort of swirling blackness with pink streaks through it.'

'You did get it,' he said. 'Very well, Colene, you have impressed me. I will keep your confidence. What is it you want of me?'

'We have a sick creature from a Cambrian world. You have to find out what's wrong, and try to help him.'

'Do you mean Cambrian as in the Burgess Shale?'

'Right. Only stranger. Can you come to my house after school?'

He looked hard at her. 'You really are serious, Colene? This is not an elaborate prank?'

'Deadly serious, Amos. We're afraid Burgess will die, and he's our friend. You're the only one I can think of who might be able to figure out what's making him sick.'

'I will come with you now,' Amos said. 'Just let me check out.'

253

'Oh, thank you, Amos!' Colene said. 'It means so much to me.'

They went with Amos to another room, where he told a woman at a desk, something about canceling a class because of an emergency. Then they followed him to the school faculty parking lot and got into his personal vehicle. Under his guidance, it moved, following the road, with considerably greater docility than the other one.

'Amos, I can't tell you how I appreciate this,' Colene said. 'What can I do for you in return?'

He laughed. 'Colene, you know better than that! I never accept anything from a student except her homework.'

'And you know me better, too, Amos,' she said evenly. 'I never made the wrong kind of offer. But if you can save Burgess, I'll owe you the equivalent of a life. We won't be here on Earth long; what can I give back that's worth a life?'

'There is a life I would like to recover,' he said. 'But not even magic can do that. So forget it, Colene; you have intrigued me, and I would like to help you if I can. No other deal is required.'

Colene did not pursue the matter, but Nona knew she was not dismissing it. She was reading his mind to fathom the nature of his concern. The odd concept *Sin Eater* appeared. Nona also found that she liked this teacher; he was intelligent and principled.

Nona nudged Colene. 'You must warn him about Darius, and Seqiro.'

'For sure!' Colene agreed. 'As if I could forget them.' She turned to the man. 'Some other things you need to know. All part of the confidence.'

Amos raised an eyebrow. 'Stranger than what you have shown me so far?'

'Equivalently strange. One is Darius. He's my man. Don't laugh; I mean to marry him. Now.'

'Not in this state,' Amos said.

'I'm fourteen. There are states where —'

'Yes, Texas is one. With parental permission.'

'I'll get it. Anyway, Darius is a regular man, but he comes from a magic world, and he doesn't speak our language any more than Nona does. So if he tells you he can conjure himself and others to other places, or multiply joy, believe it. He can, where he lives. He's not crazy.'

'Any more than Nona is,' Amos agreed.

'You would probably think me so, if I told you more about my Julia Mode,' Nona said, laughing.

'Julia? As in Julia sets?'

'Colene calls it the Mandelbrot set. It is the pattern of my reality.'

'Right,' Colene said. 'And Seqiro – he's a telepathic horse.'

He looked at Colene. 'You are asking me to take a lot on faith.'

'It's an overload, all at once,' Colene greed. 'Just take it as it comes, Amos, and worry about faith later. Burgess is the one who counts, right now, and he's so strange he'll freak you out at first, but he's my friend.'

Amos shook his head. 'You always were a remarkable girl, Colene. I'm still sorry I ever agreed to keep your first confidence, months ago. I fear I will regret this one more.'

'Well, after we go, I guess you can say what you want. But I think folk will think you're crazy.'

'I am in doubt about that myself, at the moment.'

They arrived at her house. The tent was visible in back, looking makeshift, as if children had assembled it. It was a giveaway that something was going on, but maybe the neighbors wouldn't pry. As long as Seqiro touched their minds and discouraged them.

They walked to the tent. Seqiro's mind reached out, and immediately understood that Amos was to be accepted. *Hello, Amos. I am Seqiro.*

'You are a horse?' Amos inquired wryly.

The horse stepped out of the tent. *I am.*

Darius followed. 'I am Darius.'

Amos nodded. 'Hello, Seqiro and Darius. I am Amos Forell, Colene's science teacher. I hope I can help.'

*You are in doubt about our validity. I will reassure you.*

'I find myself strangely reassured,' Amos admitted.

Colene opened the flap for Amos. 'Now, remember — '

But Nona had seen something. 'Colene! A vehicle is stopping by the house!'

Colene looked. 'Damn! That's Dad's car! He's home. I can't tend to him right now while — '

The girl was beginning to panic; the turmoil of her mind was coming through. 'Yes, you can,' Nona said quickly. 'Darius and Seqiro can introduce Amos to Burgess, while you and I go to see your father.' She took Colene by th eelbow and drew her away.

'Amos, let me explain about Burgess,' Darius said behind them. 'He derives from a Mode Colene calls the Cambrian, but I think that was a long time ago. He does not speak or think in the same manner we do.'

Their voices faded out as the two women walked toward the vehicle. But Seqiro's ambience remained; he was merely letting Nona and Colene have a separate dialogue with Colene's father. Nona knew she would have no trouble understanding what the man said.

The man had climbed out of his vehicle, which was now beside Amos' vehicle. He was staring at them.

'Oh, God, I can't do it,' Colene muttered. 'This is going to totally freak him out, and I don't want that.'

'I will try,' Nona said. 'If you introduce me.'

They came to stand before the man. 'Hi, Dad,' Colene said tightly. She spoke in her own language, and Nona did understand, as she had expected to.

'Hi, Colene,' he said, just as tightly. Nona realized that Seqiro was reaching to the man's mind, helping him to accept the situation.

'This is my friend Nona.'

256

'What happened to your friend Provos?'

Colene turned away. 'I just can't make small talk,' she said, her mind clouding up with mixed emotions. There was love there, and fear, and anger, and hope. This man had always treated her well, but he had betrayed her by trying to trap her here.

'Hello,' Nona said. 'I will try to explain.'

The man nodded. Seqiro was providing him greater understanding, now, or at least a willingness to listen to what Nona would say. 'Let's go inside.'

They trekked into the house and took seats in the living room. 'I do not know how much you know,' Nona said. 'I think you would find the whole truth to be too strange to believe. Perhaps it is enough to say that Colene has had a most strange adventure, and now requires your help.'

'We just want her back,' he said. 'She can have anything she wants.'

'First she needs your belief and trust. She is your daughter, and she loves you, but has become estranged. Did you know she is suicidal?'

He stared at her. 'No. But I suppose I can't blame her. Her mother and I — we had concerns of our own, and it wasn't until Colene left us that we realized how badly we had let her down. We — we thought she had retreated into some kind of fantasy world, insanity, and we were horrified.'

'It was not fantasy,' Nona assured him. 'She found a way to travel to places almost unbelievably strange.' She did not want to mention magic, fearing that he would never accept the notion. She had seen how difficult it had been for Amos to accept it, and indeed Amos still thought it was some kind of clever act or ruse. But the concept of travel into other realities was necessary, if he were ever to accept Colene's relation with Darius.

'We saw her vanish into the air,' he agreed. 'Then we knew that she wasn't just imagining what we had taken to be nonsense about some kind of Virtual Mode and strange places beyond it. We realized that she was into something strange beyond our belief. But it was too late. We had betrayed her, and we feared she would never return. We could only hope she would. We thought we were doing what was right, but then we knew we weren't. We swore to God that if she ever did return after that, it would be different, and we would never betray her again. Now —'

'Now she has returned, but only for a visit,' Nona said. 'As she did before. She — she feels that you did not treat her fairly, before, but if you are willing to help her this time, there will be no further problem between you.'

He nodded. 'I know I speak for her mother as well as myself. We would do anything to make it right with Colene. We've never been much of a family, but she's the most important thing in it, and we —' He stalled out, and tried again. 'We — we love her, and —' He mopped his face. 'Oh, damn it, Colene, we're so ashamed and sorry!'

*He is sincere.*

Colene got up and flung her arms around her father. 'Oh, Dad!'

Then they were both crying. Nona got up and walked away, knowing that she was no longer needed here.

Outside, in the tent, Amos was kneeling beside Burgess, his hands on contact points.

'Amos is achieving some rapport,' Darius explained to Nona. 'But Burgess can't tell him what is wrong, because he does not know.'

Amos looked up, seeing her. 'His world is like this one? Like Earth?'

'Yes,' she said. 'Except that my magic was far more limited there.'

'And it was on the Virtual Mode that he became ill?'

'Yes, though not immediately.'

'I think I need to know more about the Virtual Mode. Will you take me there?'

'I could, but it would be dangerous for you, because you are not an anchor person. Also, Seqiro would have to come too, because you and I could not understand each other without the telepathy.'

*I can reach across Modes*, Seqiro thought.

So he could; he had been doing so as they traveled the Virtual Mode, because their party had often stretched across three or four Modes. 'In that case, I can show you. But it will not seem much different, across just a few Modes.'

Amos got back to his feet. 'Take me, then. I don't know what I'll find, but since I'm at a loss here, it's worth the try.'

'You must take my hand,' she said. 'And do not let go, because you could be stranded in a foreign Mode. You can cross only when in contact with one of the anchor people.'

He took her hand. 'Have no fear. I have no designs on you. I only want to learn what I can of this situation.'

*True.*

She walked him to the anchor at the end of the tent. As they stepped through it, the tent disappeared. They stood in a similar yard, near a similar house. But its color was different, and there were no vehicles beside it.

'That is some effect!' he remarked, impressed. 'This is another world?'

'Another Mode, yes. An alternate reality. There are boundaries every ten of your feet, and each crossing is similar. Each Mode is different, but usually similar to the ones closest to it.'

'And I can't cross by myself?'

'No. Please do not seek to experiment. If I lost you, you would never get back.'

'How could you lose me?'

Nona showed him the stone trick, having him pick up the stone and hold it in his free hand while they stepped across Modes. The stone disappeared, and was there on the ground when they returned. 'If we walked across, without touching, I would enter the next Mode,' she said, 'while you would continue in this one. If you then fell in a hole and were not visible from where I stood, I could not see you, and certainly I could not reach you. If you were sleeping just beyond the boundary, I could see you but not reach you, because I am in the Virtual Mode, which contains only ten-feet depth of any normal Mode. It is wider to the sides, but still, it is a chance not worth taking.'

'I appreciate that,' he said. 'What about food? If you eat on one Mode − ?'

'We must wait to digest it, or we will lose it. Water, too. Even the air we breathe, I understand.'

'The air!' he exclaimed.

'Yes. It, too, is substance. But our bodies incorporate it very rapidly, so we do not suffocate. Otherwise it would be almost impossible to traverse the Virtual Mode.'

'That may be the key!' he said. 'The air. Burgess breathes it too.'

'Yes. More than we do, because he floats. He −' She paused, realizing the significance. 'He is absorbing the air of the Virtual Mode! And it is not the same as that of an anchor Mode. His substance is being replace by Virtual substance, faster than ours.'

'My thoughts exactly. We don't think of air as nourishment, but it is, and most important. Our lungs − and surely his gills − are extremely responsive to things in the air. A number of drugs are administered by inhalation. Suppose there is some trace substance in the air of the Virtual Mode that is poisoning Burgess?'

'But the Virtual Mode is merely a path across ordinary Modes,' she protested. 'There would be nothing there that the others do not have.'

'Then the reverse case. Some substance that *isn't* there. Or is there, but isn't retained, because it takes the body longer to absorb it, and it is lost as you cross the next boundary. Burgess could be suffering from a trace deficiency. There are any number of trace elements our systems need, but we

260

normally get them in our food and water. If he normally picks up some of those from the air, the deficiency might not show up right away, but in time it would manifest. Then he would gradually fail — exactly as he did.'

Nona was amazed at the simplicity of it. 'But why has he not gotten better, in the Earth Mode?'

'He may be getting better. But it took time to develop the deficiency, and it will take time to eliminate it. Especially since he is not processing air at his normal rate, now, because of fatigue. Assuming that our air has it in a similar ratio to the air of his world of origin, which may be an unsafe assumption. We shall have to find a way to replace it faster. If only we knew what it is!'

Nona was thrilled that a likely answer had come, but also had doubts. 'If there is something, and we make him better — will he not lose it again when he re-enters the Virtual Mode? We do not want to make him ill again.'

'Yes, that is a likely problem. I shall try to find something to replace what he is losing. Then he could take a supply along with him, and not suffer. If only I knew what it might be! Burgess is the most fascinating creature I have encountered, and I have no hope of comprehending more than a tiny fraction of his wonders. A genuine triramous creature, of a completely alien phylum! My ignorance is colossal, and that is the root of the problem.'

Nona discovered that she liked this man. But she did not wish to complicate his life, so she kissed him once, quickly, and led him back through the anchor to the Earth Mode.

'We may have the answer, or part of it,' she told Darius happily.

'I heard,' he said. 'It makes sense to me.'

'I must go home now,' Amos said. 'But I will try to research the matter of potential airborne nutrients. Meanwhile, Burgess should slowly improve, just being here in one place. Take care of him, and give him comfort. I'll return

261

tomorrow, hoping for progress.' He turned to Nona. 'Thank you for showing me the Virtual Mode. It is part of an experience I shall treasure for the rest of my life, even if I don't dare mention it.' He paused, smiling. 'There are ways in which you remind me of Colene, Nona.'

Nona felt herself flushing with pleasure, though she wasn't quite sure why.

Amos returned to his vehicle — she realized now that it was called a 'car' — and drove away. As they watched the car depart, a sudden strong thought came. *Marriage!*

Nona exchanged a smile with Darius. Colene had evidently broached the key subject.

In a little while Colene and her father appeared at the back door of the house. She looked radiant. 'I have permission,' she said simply. 'My folks will take care of it.' Then, almost as an afterthought: 'Dad, this is Darius.'

The two men performed the Earth ritual of shaking hands.

'Look, there'll have to be a license, and a blood test, and we'll have to make arrangements in Wichita Falls, in Texas,' the man said. 'It will take a couple of days if we're lucky. No problem. Anything to make my little girl happy.' He eyed Darius. 'Colene tells me that you two have been together constantly, but you never —'

'Daddy!'

Darius nodded. 'She was too young. But if this makes her old enough, by the standard of her culture —'

'It will.' He shook his head. 'We never thought — but it will, and I suppose that's best. Colene always was a good judge of people, and if she loves you —'

'I do,' Colene said.

'We can make space in the house, so you won't have to camp out —'

'No, they like it out here,' Colene said quickly. It was apparent that she had not told her father about Seqiro or Burgess. 'Well, maybe Nona could come in.'

262

'Of course,' he agreed. 'We have a rollaway couch-bed we can make up. Come on in, Nona.'

Nona took advantage of the moment to relay her news, silently. *Amos may have found out what is wrong with Burgess. A trace substance in the air, because we cross the Modes too quickly for him to absorb it. He is seeking a replacement.*

Colene's radiance intensified. She was far from depressed now! *That's the greatest news! I knew Amos could do it.*

They started in. Then Colene paused. 'Something else, Darius.' She shut her mouth, and thought the rest for them only. *Amos is doing us a great favor. He doesn't want any return favor, but I want to give him one. We need to find out about the Sin Eater. I think I'll be busy, but Darius, if you can –*

*I will try. Where is my source of information?*

*Amos.*

They went on in, leaving Darius to ponder. 'Colene, I need to warn you, this is going to come as a shock to your mother,' her father said.

'Is she drinking?'

Nona understood from the thought that the question was whether her mother was consuming alcoholic beverages. There were some on Oria who did that to excess, and it was not a good thing.

'No. She's in a program, and she's been straight. She prays daily for your return. She's the one who set up the note on the table.'

'That helped,' Colene said. 'I had business to do in town. I think Mom will accept me getting married, if you do.'

'If she knows you truly want it.' He hesitated, then broached another subject. 'The people you were with, last time –'

'Slick and Esta.'

'After the way all of you disappeared, there was publicity. The – the vanishing was dismissed as someone's invention;

they assumed that all of you had managed to sneak out of town. The police grilled us, but couldn't prove anything. It turned out that the man was a gangster, and the girl had been severely abused; her stepfather's awaiting trial now. It seemed that the gangster was the child's uncle; he kidnapped her to save her from further molestation. He had a record a mile long, everything *except* molestation. They concluded that it was the single good thing he did in his life, an act of atonement. You knew that, didn't you?'

'I knew it,' Colene agreed. 'I set it up. They're happy now. He's out of the crime business, and she's got nothing but happiness ahead of her.'

He hesitated again. 'In the course of the investigation, some other things came out. The police − we − I don't like to say this −'

But Seqiro was making his thought plain to them. 'They found out about the rape,' Colene said.

'It was just a rumor,' he said quickly. 'We said it couldn't be true. You would never −'

'It happened,' Colene said evenly. 'That's why I had to get away.'

'There was no proof. They couldn't even identify the perpetrators. No one would talk. Just this ugly rumor, how four high school boys tricked this thirteen-year-old girl into coming to an apartment, and plied her with liquor, getting her so drunk she didn't even resist. You read about that sort of thing all the time, but never believe it could happen to your own daughter. You − you never said anything.'

'There didn't seem to be any point. What would you have done if I had told?'

'I'll do it now,' he said, turning grim. 'Give me their names.'

'Dad, why should you care about any of that? You've had a mistress for years!'

He swallowed. 'It is true. It is not easy to be the spouse of an alcoholic, and I needed something to compensate. But

264

I never raped anyone. Like your gangster friend, I am clean in this respect. I abused you only by my absence, and my ignorance, and I want to correct that now. Give me their names.'

The names of two passed through Colene's mind, so strongly that Nona heard them. But she set her little jaw. 'It wouldn't do any good. I won't be here to prosecute, and anyway they always treat the girl as if she's the criminal. It would just drag me and you and Mom down into the gutter, and those freaks would get off anyway. The judge always believes the liars. I just want to forget about it. I've found a good man now, and good friends, and if that's partly because of the spin that gang rape sent me into, then maybe it was a favor in the long term. Understand, I'd like nothing better than to see those freaks get theirs, but this isn't the way.'

'You want marriage instead of revenge,' he said.

'I want marriage,' she agreed. 'And Mom — if she's straight, now, I don't want to hurt her. So if we maybe could just forget this —'

'If that is the way you want it, it is forgotten,' he said grimly. He glanced at Nona. 'Your friend won't speak of it?'

'I will not speak of it,' Nona said, though she, too, was sorry that the rapists would not be punished. She herself had almost been raped at one of the alternate worlds in Julia, and she hadn't liked the notion a bit. But she was aware that Colene, though still deeply angry about the rape, was being practical; she wanted to marry Darius, and knew that something like this could interfere with that by diverting the attention of her parents at this critical time. Colene knew what she wanted, and was choosing her course to achieve it, realistically. Colene was a tough girl!

*No, not tough. I just don't want to lose sight of what I truly want, and maybe lose it.*

Colene's father chose another subject. 'Now the marriage. I will arrange it. You and your man will have to come in for the blood tests tomorrow; I can get the doctor to cooperate. But Darius will have to show identification to get the license.'

'Uh-oh,' Colene said. 'He's from another world.'

'Seiro may be able to handle that,' Nona said. 'By changing a mind.'

'Say, yeah!' Colene refocused on her father. 'We'll have Darius ride to the license office on a horse. There'll be no trouble; they'll accept his ID.'

'On a horse!' The man smiled. 'And will the horse attend the wedding, too?'

Colene had to smile. 'I think not. Wichita Falls is too far for him to trot, and I need him here. Darius and I will just drive down to the civil ceremony with you, and come back here right after.'

'Civil ceremony? Your mother will –' He broke off. 'There she is now. Perhaps I should handle this. There may be some emotion.'

'You do that, Dad.' Colene smiled. 'Nona and I will just stay here and nod our heads.'

Nona braced for the emotional scene to follow. She was not disappointed.

# 12

## Sin Eater

Darius woke and stretched. *Burgess is unchanged*, the thought came. Seqiro was not in the tent; he was grazing the lawn. He could do this without attracting attention because he simply diverted the interest of any who might notice him. He was good at controlling the minds of human people, especially those who had no resistance to it. He had surveyed the neighborhood, and had no problem with the residents.

'I must learn resistance,' Darius said. 'No affront to you, Seqiro, but if we should have to stop at your Mode, we human folk would be patsies for any of the telepathic horses there, and I doubt you could save us. I understand from Colene's memories that there are other Modes near yours where other animals have telepathy, and that could be trouble too. So we all should learn resistance, if it is possible.'

*Your human mind has reasoned it out as mine could not. I will try to teach you resistance. It will not be easy, because we have much experience in controlling humans. I have refrained from doing it when you do not wish it.*

'And we appreciate that, Seqiro. But now we should learn how to protect our minds. This is a good time to do it, when we are more or less idle.'

*We normally exert full control, so that our servants never realize that any resistance is possible. I will try to exert partial control over you. When you are able to resist that, I will intensify it. It is possible to learn resistance, though we normally seek to conceal that information.*

'Let's choose an action for me to resist, that won't interfere with anything else.'

*I will make you bite your thumb. This is a punishment we use on occasion, its severity depending on the offense.*

'That certainly is not something I would do on my own,' Darius agreed.

*I will not make you do it hard. When your teeth touch the skin, you will know that you have lost.*

'Agreed. Start it slow, and we shall ascertain where my threshold of resistance starts.' As he spoke, he got up, and was getting dressed in the odd clothing Colene had decreed he wear for this day.

Darius felt himself touched, mentally. In a moment his left hand was at his face. Realizing that this was not his own action, he tensed his muscles and drove his hand away. It retreated from his face, but then returned. Again he drove it away, but his arm only quivered, and then his thumb came to his mouth and his teeth touched the flesh.

Suddenly his hand was flung away. Seqiro had let go, so that his failing effort to resist became a violent motion. But Darius had lost. He was shaking with the effort he had made. 'How much of your power was that?'

*Perhaps a quarter. You fought well.*

'Not nearly well enough! I just couldn't seem to get a leverage on my arm.'

*Remind yourself that your arm is your own, and must ultimately obey you. Shut out any intrusion.*

'I will try.' Darius focused on his left arm, trying to will it to obey no one except him.

But his hand came steadily toward his face, and in a moment his teeth touched his thumb again.

'That was faster than before! I'm losing my resistance.'

*No. I used greater power to overcome you, now that I know your level of resistance.*

'So I was doing better instead of worse!'

*Yes. In my Mode we would see that you never understood that, and we would dispatch you before you realized that resistance was possible.*

They continued the exercise while Darius ate. Burgess, meanwhile, neither gained nor lost ground; he was in what for a human person would have been something like a coma.

Then Amos arrived in his vehicle-car. Seqiro was aware of him long before he was close; the horse's range did not seem to be limited in this Mode. *He brings containers of nourishment, but does not know whether any will be effective.*

'Seek his information on the Sin Eater. I will need it later.'

Amos walked directly to the tent. 'I have to go teach school today, but I brought some multi-vitamin and mineral supplements of several brands and types.' He paused, looking around. 'Can you prevent the neighbors from noticing me, Seqiro? I don't think it would be wise to be seen coming and going from a young student's house.'

*They will not notice you.*

'Thank you.' Amos had adapted to the horse's telepathy quickly, because he believed what was in his own mind, and when Seqiro spoke to someone directly, it was in the mind. He went into the tent and squatted beside Burgess. 'But there is a problem. These pills have many things, and most will probably be irrelevant. Some may be what we need. But some may be poisonous for Burgess. It's a calculated risk, and I don't know how extreme it is.'

*Poisonous!* Colene's thought came from the house. *Hold the phone while I get down there.*

Amos smiled, wryly. 'That is one charming little girl.'

'So I have noticed. If only she were a vessel of joy, so that I could marry her in my own culture as well as hers.'

'You can't marry her in yours? Why not?'

'I am Cyng of Hlahtar. I must draw joy from my wife, and give it to all the others. Colene –'

'Is depressive. But couldn't she learn joy?'

'How does one learn joy?'

'How does one learn to resist telepathic control? Yes,

269

Seqiro let me feel your practicing. How does Colene learn telepathy? No person in our Mode has done that before, as far as I know, though some have made claims.'

Darius was surprised. 'She *is* learning telepathy! That is akin to the drawing of joy, in a fashion. If she could learn joy, I could marry her.'

'I heard that,' Colene said, entering the tent. 'Oh, Darius, I'll learn it if I can! But right now we have other business. What's this about poison?'

Amos opened a bag. 'All I could think of was to try multi-vitamin, multi-mineral pills. We don't know what Burgess needs, but there's a fair chance it's here. He may have been picking up trace minerals from the dust in the air. So if he takes one of these, it may be all he needs. But if it gives him a dose of what he doesn't need, it could poison him. Just as an overdose of arsenic would poison us. In fact, an overdose of a *needed* nutrient could poison him, as it is with salt with us. I don't know how to analyze his need, here in the field. It might be possible in a laboratory, but that would have other risks.'

'Such as becoming a freak at a freak show,' Colene agreed. 'That's out. Can we try a little bit of something first?'

'Yes, but that will take more time. How much time do you have?'

'I'd like to be gone from here in a couple more days. But if Burgess needs longer, we'll just have to stay longer.'

'I suggest you have him try a bit of powder from one pill, and wait an hour, then try some from another. In the course of the day you can sample a dozen pills. But it's roulette. If one of them helps, you win; if one of them kills him, you lose. Are you sure it wouldn't be better to let him remain here for longer, perhaps several months, so he can recover slowly?'

'If he does recover,' Colene said. 'The way he's going, he could pass the point of no return first. And what's to

270

stop him from reverting when he goes back on the Virtual Mode? No, we need a cure.'

Amos handed her the bag. 'It is not a risk I care to take. Burgess is the most remarkable creature I've encountered. I have acquainted you with the risk.'

'Yeah, I'm the one who's suicidal,' she agreed, with a self-deprecating little smile that made Darius want to hug her. Once more he realized that the very thing that made her unsuitable to be the wife of the Cyng of Hlahtar was one of her most appealing qualities. That semi-bitter edge, that laughed at death even as it flirted with it.

Colene handed the bag to Nona. 'Darius and Seqiro and I have to go for blood tests and a license. That leaves it up to you. Try him on the tiniest bit you can, and see if he reacts. We're just going to have to hope we win before we lose.'

Darius let it be. Colene had made the decision, and it was probably the sensible one. Amos returned to his car, while Darius went to the house with Colene. Seqiro went to the front of the house and waited.

Colene's mother was inside. She had had a considerable adjustment of information and attitude during the evening and night, but now was stable. It was clear that she intended to do right by Colene, and could now be trusted.

Colene brought out a map. 'This is us,' she said, pointing to a spot on it. 'This is the doctor's office. This is City Hall. We need to go to the one, and then the other. I think you'd better ride Seqiro, so that others think you're a man and a horse.' She flashed Darius a winning smile, again making him want to embrace her. As she was probably aware. 'And nothing more. Tomorrow we'll drive down to Texas and get married.'

'We can fit him in the car,' Colene's father said. 'He doesn't need to ride the horse.'

'And leave the horse in our yard?' Colene asked.

'Well –' The man's brow furrowed. 'Where did that horse come from anyway? I thought it was just you and Darius and Nona.'

'Seqiro is a very special horse,' she answered, sliding by his question as Seqiro adjusted his mind so that he no longer thought it remarkable that a horse should have appeared on the scene. The neighbors had already been given the impression that the tent had been in the yard for some time, and was not at all remarkable or interesting.

They went outside. Colene had projected the image of the route in the map to Seqiro, so that he would know the way. Then she got into the car with her parents. 'We'll wait for you,' she said.

'I don't like this any better than you do,' Darius told Seqiro as he climbed up on the wadded blankets Nona had fashioned in lieu of a saddle. They had removed the regular harness with the supplies, so that the horse was unencumbered. 'I know you are not a servant beast, and I am not a practiced rider.'

*You are lighter than my normal burden. It will be easier for me to divert attention if we look normal by this culture's standards.*

That was one of the things about Seqiro: he never stood on false pride. He simply did what was necessary.

*Because it is your way. Were you to become angry, I would share that emotion. My attitude is defined by that of the human I am with, as is my intelligence.*

They started out. Because the horse was in tune with Darius' mind, there was no problem about riding; Seqiro compensated for any imbalance in his posture automatically, and did not surprise him with any motion. Because Seqiro was a large horse, and in good health, he moved along at a good rate though merely walking. Cars passed them on the road, avoiding them. They had no fear of a collision, because Seqiro tracked the minds of the drivers, making sure.

'Did you get the information on the Sin Eater?' Darius asked.

Seqiro filled him in on it. There had been a rape a month ago. The rapist had not been caught, but an anonymous tip had charged a fifteen-year-old boy called Raphael. The police had picked him up, but let him go for lack of proof. Since then, Raphael, once nicknamed Raff, had been nicknamed 'Rape.' The neighborhood had condemned him. He had not been punished by the law, so the community was punishing him instead.

Amos had taught Raff in a remedial class, so knew him. The boy was slow, with just enough intelligence to get by on a minimal basis, but not mean. He had low self-esteem, and was generally the object of cruel teasing. He was no rapist. When the charge was made, Amos had taken the trouble to verify the police report: Raff had been released uncharged because tissue typing had shown he could not have been the rapist. He had merely had the bad fortune to live in the neighborhood where the rape had occurred.

But somehow the police report had not been publicized, so there had been no direct refutation of the charge. That was the start of the trouble. News of the charge had spread rapidly, but not news of the exoneration. So Raff remained guilty, in the eyes of the neighbors. That guilt was destroying him. Other youths were not supposed to play with him, and no girl was allowed near him. He got spat on when he walked the halls of school, and was regularly beaten up by other youths. When anything went wrong, Raff was blamed. It was a joke, for some of the things were impossible, but there was a large, hard core of belief that he was guilty of anything they thought he might be guilty of.

Amos had tried to tell people that Raff was innocent, but they had brushed him off. They *knew* he was guilty.

In Amos' mind there were three reasons for this. Two of them were simple: Raff was stupid, and Raff was not one to stand up for himself. Thus he was an easy target. But it was the third that really bothered Amos: Raff was a Sin Eater.

There was a Sin Eater in every backward neighborhood. In every small town where the folk ranged toward the lower end of the scales of education, income, and ambition. There was always somebody who was the designated object of contempt. The people needed someone on whom to vent their irritation, anger, or despair. They needed to have someone to blame. For anything. Someone who was plainly inferior. Someone to punish for the frustration of the neighborhood. Raff had become that person.

They didn't accept his exoneration because they didn't *want* to. Never mind about fairness; they needed their Sin Eater. Raff was too convenient to let go. It was simpler to maintain a scapegoat than to address intractable grievances such as inadequate education, low wages, and rampant crime.

That was why Amos hadn't told Colene about it. He saw it as an insoluble problem. He railed against it, but it was impossible to convince people of what was true when they were enamored of what was false. Raff was the victim of the community's need to degrade someone. It was easier than trying to lift themselves out of their own Sloughs of Despond.

'Their own whats?'

Sepiro dug into the voluminous ancillary material he had culled from Amos' pedantic mind. It turned out that this was a classical reference deriving from a work of literature titled *Pilgrim's Progress*, where there were some bad geographical regions, such as vast bogs or sloughs.

'Oh, we passed through one of those on the way here,' Darius said. 'Burgess had to float us across it.'

But the reference was actually religious. A sect called the Catholics applied it to a sect called the Protestants, and vice versa. Amos, however, used it in a social sense: it was as if all the people of this region were stuck in a mire, and instead of seeking positive ways to extricate themselves, they preferred to beat down someone else, preferably one who couldn't defend himself. Amos' disgust permeated the concept.

'I like Amos better as I get to know him,' Darius remarked. 'But I don't see how we can help Raff. He should move to another community.'

But Raff's family was too poor to move. That was part of it: the Sin Eater couldn't readily escape. He was locked in to the position, and just had to accept the abuse.

Seqiro moved along the streets. It seemed there were signals which directed people and cars when to move and when to stop. The horse couldn't see those, but he didn't need to; he picked up the information from the minds of the people, and had no trouble. In fact a number of people admired the huge animal, especially the children, and most of all the young girls. To many of them, a horse was the ultimate creature.

'That is the way it is with Colene,' Darius said. 'She longed for a horse, and you were the horse she longed for.'

*I longed for a girl, and she was the girl I longed for. But it was you she was searching for.*

'She wanted a horse *and* a man. But I think if she had to choose between us, to be with only one of us, you would be the one.'

*Perhaps. But her ultimate loyalty must be to her own kind. She must in the end be with you.*

'Fortunately there is no conflict. She does not have to choose between us. I like you too, and will be glad to have you with us.'

*I think there is no good place for me in your Mode.*

'But you can not stay forever on the Virtual Mode. As you breathe, your substance is slowly replaced by the material of the many Modes we cross, and the time will come when that overbalances your anchor Mode substance, and you will no longer be able to cross the Modes. You must decide where you wish to be, before that happens.'

*That is a hard decision. Perhaps I would remain with you. But what then of Nona and Burgess?*

'That is a difficult question. Burgess really needs a hive of his own kind. Nona wants to explore forever, and does not wish to marry and settle down. I would be happy to have her for a mistress, but Colene would object.'

*Most strenuously*, Seqiro agreed. *She does not appreciate the way of a stallion with mares.*

Darius laughed. 'At least you do!'

*I understand the one I am with, as I explained before. I can then use my mind similarly. This is a pleasure for me, as I am not naturally intelligent.*

'Don't you ever long for your home, with others of your kind, including mares?'

*I was dissatisfied in my Mode. I was not comfortable with the complete domination of your kind by my kind, and I wanted to explore other ways of existing. Therefore I was out of favor, and am not welcome there. As for mares — they are the same as any other horses, except when in heat, and that is quickly attended to. We do not marry in the fashion of your kind.*

'But now that you have associated so closely with us, you must have come to appreciate our ways. You understand the meaning of personal commitment. Of love. You will not be able to throw those concepts away as if they never existed. Wouldn't you like a long-term relationship with a mare who understood you? Suppose there were a mare who resembled Colene?'

*There is such a mare. But she is a figment of Colene's imagination. Colene calls her Maresy Doates.*

Darius shook his head. 'A dream mare! Yet strange things can happen on the Virtual Mode. Maybe she exists in one of the Modes adjacent to yours.'

They resumed their practicing for telepathic resistance.

The horse always won easily, but he assured Darius that his level of resistance was increasing.

They reached the doctor's office. Darius had not had to worry about the route, because Seqiro had memorized the map when Colene had studied it, and had a firm sense of his place on its grid. They went to the parking lot beside it, and Darius dismounted. Seqiro waited beside the cars, tuning in to Colene, her parents, and the doctor. He would make sure that there was no trouble.

*Hi, folks*, Colene's thought came. *Get in here, Darius.* There was a current of joy in her that would have made her marriageable in his Mode had it been permanent instead of the surge of the moment.

Darius went inside, guided by Colene's knowledge, relayed by the horse. There he suffered himself to be stuck by a needle so that some of his blood could be sucked out for their science tests. This would assure that he carried no loathsome disease, as if that were not self-evident. Colene had already given her blood.

'Now we go to the license office,' Colene said. 'See you there, Darius.'

Darius returned to Seqiro, and they set out across the grid of streets again. They continued to practice resistance. This time Colene tuned in on it, realizing what they were doing. *Try me too, horseface*, she thought. *Make me bite my thumb. Ouch!*

But her resistance had been more than Darius' resistance. She had been close to the horse for longer, and she was more truly attuned. This gave her a better knowledge of the ways of his power, and she was able to fashion a more effective defense against it. She also had a stronger motive: she had been stunned by a mental blow from one of the other horses of Seqiro's Mode, and knew firsthand how devastating it could be. She wanted never to be subjected to that again.

In due course they reached the appropriate office. This

time Seqiro had more delicate work to do: he had to convince the clerk that Darius had appropriate identification, such as a 'driver's license,' 'birth certificate' — as if a person needed proof to show he had been born! — and then sign his name on a line of a piece of paper filled with print. Darius took a blank sheet of paper from Colene and showed it as many times as the clerk requested things, and each time Seqiro made the clerk satisfied that he had seen what was required. Darius was not entirely easy about this, yet knew that if he tried to provide the legitimate identification of his own culture, it would not be understood. This was a shortcut through blind bureaucracy, as Colene put it. He filled in the forms with information Colene provided, letting her mental hand guide his hand so that he wrote in her graphics, and it was done. They had their marriage license.

Now Colene had to go with her folks to make other arrangements. Darius had the rest of the day to himself. It was time to deal with the matter of the Sin Eater.

Seqiro's mind ranged out to the region where the abused youth lived. Soon enough he located Raff, and walked toward his neighborhood. Even from a distance, the confusion and self-loathing registered. 'That young man is truly unhappy,' Darius said. 'And he did not even do the crime. He does not understand why they blame him.'

*We might give him understanding, by connecting your mind to his. Would that help?*

'I am not sure it would. It is the community that needs better understanding. It is the community that is doing wrong. If that changed, then the Sin Eater would be freed.'

*I could compel some individuals to change, but that would endure only while I applied mental force. They would revert when I stopped.*

'When we were crossing the bog, I tried to draw and multiply the mental powers of others. I made Nona's magic work for us all, for a while. If I could multiply a change of attitude, it might last for several months, as does the joy I normally spread. But I do not know whether I could do that, and in any event my magic does not work in this Earth Mode.'

*How do you know that it does not?*

'I tried it when I was here. I was unable to conjure myself or anything else, and I could not multiply joy. Certainly I would have used my magic to defend myself, were it possible, when I was attacked by four youths from a car.'

*What happened? I learned some of this from Colene, but now need to know more.*

'I had just arrived here, before we instituted the Virtual Mode. It was a spot crossover, just sufficient for me to find and extract the woman I had come for. I did not realize then that she was extractable because she was destined to have little impact on her own Mode, therefore could be readily removed from it. She was going to die soon, by her own hand. She was a vessel of dolor instead of joy. But at that point I knew none of this. I simply found myself by the street, and I had to step quickly back to avoid being struck by a car. A person in the car made a gesture, which I took to be communication of some kind, so I emulated it. The car then stopped, and four youths emerged and attacked me. I tried to invoke a pacification spell, but it had no effect. I was battered, and left in sore straits. It was Colene who later came and rescued me from likely death by exposure. By the time we came to understand each other, I loved her, and she loved me. But she declined to return to my Mode with me, and I knew she was a vessel of grief, so I left her – and then regretted it, and instituted the Virtual Mode in an effort to find her again and bring her home.'

*Colene has started to learn magic, or at least telepathy, from association with me. Is it possible that my ability could help you similarly?*

'Perhaps. But it is not telepathy I need. It is my own power of magic.'

*I am thinking that association with me might change your ability, as is the case with Colene. Perhaps that was why you were able to multiply magic, on the bog. You might recover some of your magic, when linked with me.*

'I doubt it. I did not have my magic in the Shale Mode.'

*But Nona had some of hers, and you had some of yours in the Fractal Mode. We do not know why the magic patterns as it does. Coudl it be because of the company we keep?*

'Now, that's an interesting notion! Very well, let's experiment.' Darius brought out his own icon, and invoked it. He tried to conjure himself across the street.

There was no effect. The magic wasn't operative.

*Try your mental magic.*

'For that I need a subject from whom to draw, and subjects to receive.'

*Can you try it in a small way?*

'I could try to draw from you, and return it immediately. But you would not care for that.'

*I could tolerate it.*

So Darius focused on the horse, and drew his joy — and felt it working. He returned it.

*I felt it, and not merely through your own awareness. That magic works.*

It did work — when it had not before. It *was* different this time. Because of the horse.

'I think we now have a tool we can use to help the Sin Eater,' Darius said, quick to appreciate the possibilities. 'But we still must discover how best to do it. I wish to bring him joy, but none to the oppressive community.'

After a time, Seqiro had another thought. *The youths who attacked you: they are approaching.*

'Those ones? How can you know that? I don't even know their identities!'

*Your mind has a picture of them. Their minds have pictures of you. As I range through this community, I am*

280

*aware of correspondences. There is an alignment. They are in a car, and they are looking for trouble. This is the way they entertain themselves. They like to insult and hurt other people. I am reading this in their minds.*

Darius considered. He had never expected to have such a meeting, but realized that this was the same segment of the same Mode where he had encountered the youths before. They were traveling in their car, cruising the neighborhood, as it seemed was their wont. So it was not after all surprising that they should pass close to him.

'Seqiro, I am not a vengeful man, but it is in my mind that I owe those youths somewhat. They sought to make of me a Sin Eater, and brought me pain. Would you object if I repaid them for the beating they gave me before?'

*I do not like their minds. I share your anger. I have no objection.*

'In Colene's mind, or in Amos' mind, or in the awareness of others you have surveyed, has there been an indication of especially dangerous folk in this community?'

*There is what is termed a motorcycle gang at its fringe. This is considered to be dangerous to those who annoy it.*

'When I saw those youths — that gesture of theirs I emulated — was that an insult?'

The horse explored the minds. *That gesture is considered provocative. The one who receives it is required to avenge the affront, or suffer loss of esteem.*

'Could you cause the youths to drive past that gang, and make that signal?'

*Watch.*

In Darius' mind appeared the image culled from the mind of one of the riders of the car. The buildings were moving rapidly back on either side of the car, and other cars were being narrowly passed. This was termed Joy Riding, and was the youths' main diversion.

The car swerved around a corner, taking a new direction. 'Hey, watch it!' one of the youths protested as his container of alcoholic beverage slopped over. 'You near rolled us over!'

'I can't help it!' the driver replied. 'Something's making me do it.'

The other three laughed. 'Yeah, sure!' the viewpoint character said. 'Where's this demon making you go?'

'To the Chain Gang.'

There was more laughter, but it lacked force. 'You know we don't mess with those toughs,' another youth said, sounding a bit nervous. 'Those chains they use pack a mean wallop.'

But the car kept zooming in the new direction. Soon it was entering the region of the gang.

'Hey, fun's fun, but it ain't fun to trespass on their territory,' the fourth youth said. 'Lay off, Buzz.'

Buzz continued to zero in on the hangout of the Chain Gang. The main group of motorcycles came into view. Several gang members were standing outside, swigging beer.

The car slowed. Then the viewpoint youth put his head and right arm out the side window. 'Hey, ganglia, suck on this,' he said, lifting one finger. Then Buzz gunned the motor, almost running down a parked motorcycle.

It was like banging on a hornet's nest. There was a yell. Men piled out of the hangout. In a moment several motors were starting.

'Get out of here, Buzz!' a youth yelled, terrified by what they had so foolishly done.

But Buzz just poked along, making sure that the cyclists got a good look at the car. As the first cycle roared into pursuit, another youth released his belt and dropped his trousers and undershorts. Then he contorted himself so as to poke his bare buttocks out his window. The first youth reached out his own window and repeated the finger gesture with an exaggerated upward hooking motion. 'Up yours!' he yelled. 'Sideways! The same goes for your gooney friends!' It all seemed rather pointless to Darius, but the horse assured him that it was effective communication in this Mode.

Then Seqiro released the driver. The four youths were on their own.

*Do you wish to watch further?*

Darius chuckled. 'No. I am not a man of violence, and I fear that some is going to occur.' But he was hardly unhappy about it, remembering the drubbing those same youths had given him for returning their own gesture. 'How did you know those particular words that the gesturing youth spoke? They did not come from my mind.'

*Colene had a fantasy of arranging such a sequence for the other four youths who raped her. I merely applied her scenario.*

The rapists! Darius got a wicked notion. 'Are they in this neighborhood also?'

Seqiro searched. *Yes. This is what is considered to be the bad section of town. Their residence is not far away.*

'I would like to deal with those youths too. Colene does not wish to make trouble, fearing that it will interfere with our marriage. But perhaps we can arrange something appropriate for those young men, also.'

*They caused Colene a great deal of anguish. That rape was the start of her trend toward suicide. I do not regard them as worthy humans.*

'I love her, and wish I could marry her in my Mode as well as this one, but she is now a vessel of dolor and I can not. To the extent that those men are responsible for that, I hate them, and wish them ill. The question is what is feasible and appropriate?'

*Amos knows of the rape. Had he not been prevented by his oath of secrecy, he would have reported them to the police. The authorities would have made things difficult for the rapists, if they were able to prove the case against them.*

'I think we can arrange to prove the case. We shall cause

them to go to the police themselves and confess, and give full details.'

*This appeals to me.*

'Do it, then!'

The horse reached out. In a moment the youths were getting themselves ready to go out. By the time Seqiro and Darius reached the abode of the Sin Eater, the four youths were in the police station making their confessions. In fact, as Seqiro explored their minds, he discovered that Colene had not been the only case; they had done a similar thing with several innocent girls. It was their way of having fun. So their confessions were making extremely interesting listening for the police, who were rapidly becoming satisfied that there was substance here.

Darius nodded, satisfied. 'This is a thing that has been worth doing.'

*I am glad to have been in contact with you on this occasion, because without you I would not have had the initiative or motive to accomplish this action.*

Darius patted the horse on the massive shoulder. 'We make a good team, Seqiro. Now we must address the mission we came for. How can we gain justice for the Sin Eater?'

*We can not benefit him by leading him past the Chain Gang or making him confess to the police. He is now on his way home from school, knowing nothing of us.*

'What of the actual rapist — the one who committed the crime of which Raff was accused?'

The horse quested through the local minds, as they stood there in the street. The houses here looked much like all the other houses they had been passing, only worse. People were coming and going constantly, ignoring the man and horse because Seqiro encouraged them to do that. They were not well dressed, and a number were engaged in what Seqiro fathomed as illicit trade.

*The rapist is a close relative of the girl. He told her he would kill her if she exposed him. So she blamed Raff instead.*

'Would the man have killed her?'

*It is possible. The girl remains afraid of him, and no longer protests when he comes to her, though she has no liking for his brutality.*

'Then we had better make him go and confess too. But that still will not make the community respect Raff.'

*That is true. I find nothing here but closed minds. They do not want the Sin Eater exonerated.*

'They are as bad as the rapist, in their way,' Darius said, angry. 'How do you change closed minds?'

*I can do that only temporarily.*

'I am afraid that Amos is correct. This problem can not truly be solved. We can only enable Raff to go to some other community.'

*He is approaching now, coming home from school. He does not want to leave. He wants only for the torment to stop.*

Darius looked down the street. He saw a youth walking toward them. There were others his age, also coming home from school, but they walked on the other side of the street, emanating contempt.

Then three crossed over to join Raff. But they were not suffering a change of heart. One carried a stick. Raff saw them and broke into a run, trying to escape them, but they pursued him, jeering.

'Do it,' Darius said grimly, sending a thought.

The boy with the stick swung it, striking one of his companions on the shoulder. When the third protested, the boy struck him too. The injured ones screamed with pain and protest.

A man heard the scream and charged out of his house. He saw Raff and grabbed him. 'You hit him! You hit him!' the man shouted, shaking Raff. The man hadn't even bothered to ascertain the truth.

'Do it,' Darius said again.

The boy with the stick came up behind the man and thwacked him across the back. The man, hurt and amazed, let Raff go and whirled on the boy.

But other neighbors were converging now. Several were stalking Raff, evidently intending harm. Raff, not understanding any of this, was trying to avoid them and run for home. He wasn't even protesting; it was evident that this sort of thing happened to him often enough to be routine. He expected to be cursed and beaten, in the name of the righteousness of the community. No one was siding with him, or pointing out that he had done nothing here. He was guilty by definition.

'They are determined to blame the Sin Eater, no matter what,' Darius said. 'When we try to help him, they just go after him more.'

*Raff is feeling truly awful now. Use your magic.*

'It doesn't work that way. I can only draw joy and spread it to the multitude. I can not take away prejudice, ignorance, and mean-spiritedness.'

*Spread his grief to the multitude.*

Suddenly Darius understood. 'Give me all the power you can.' He jumped down and ran to Raff. The people of the neighborhood gave way before him, directed by the horse. He caught Raff and threw his arms around him. He drew from Raff, depleting him of all his misery. The terrible emotion came into Darius.

Then he let the youth go. He multiplied the grief and sent it out to the multitude. Suddenly everybody in the neighborhood was surfeit with the same emotion Raff felt. Raff felt it too, but for him it was familiar, and not quite as intense as before.

Darius walked back to the horse. Raff resumed his dejected walk home. The neighbors, of all ages, stood appalled. They all felt terrible, and did not know why. They would feel this way for several months, as the emotional transfer slowly wore off.

286

Perhaps, by then, they would have learned some compassion.

Darius mounted Seqiro. They set off for Colene's house, some distance away. They, too, were depressed. But they understood why, and knew how to abate it. They were satisfied. It did not matter that the community's mass depression would have no rational explanation. Colene's debt to Amos had been repaid.

# 13

## Wedding

Colene was in a whirl. She was trying to stay current with Burgess, who was trying a new pill each hour, as Nona ground it up and proffered the powder for him to suck up weakly. So far there had been no significant effect, and she was beginning to fear that this was not the answer. She was also trying to follow Darius and Seqiro, who had headed off to the seamy section of town to see about the Sin Eater. They were competent to travel alone, because Seqiro's telepathy was operative, readily reaching across town; in fact it seemed to be able to reach thirty miles or so, here on Earth. Seqiro had long experience controlling human beings, and that's what was here, by no coincidence. Darius provided the human brainpower and initiative and nerve; they would do something for the Sin Eater if it were possible. Amos would be pleased when he learned of this quiet effort, later.

But mainly Colene had to keep track of her mother, who was hyper. She had stayed home from work, to manage this occasion. She was determined that Colene was going to have a perfect wedding dress, come what may. And a grand bouquet of flowers. And a wedding cake. Everything. So she was measuring Colene, and sewing material, and baking, in parallel columns as it were.

'But Mother, it's only a justice of the peace in Texas,' Colene protested. 'A dinky little civil ceremony, no frills.' She didn't have the heart to say that it was just so that Darius would accept her as Old Enough, and not go seek a relationship with someone else before Colene was of age. This really was a case of being born too late. Fortunately a token ceremony would remedy that. Nona really had found the way to solve her problem. She also didn't say that the marriage would be valid only in the Earth Mode; she would be a mere mistress in Darius' home Mode. But this was the necessary compromise she had to make, unless she could learn to be a vessel of joy.

'The bride always has a nice dress, and a corsage, and a cake to cut,' her mother insisted. 'It will be a nice wedding.'

Colene saw that her mother had a fantasy of how a wedding had to be, and was determined that her daughter would fulfill the role. Perhaps she was fulfilling herself, in the manner of a father pushing his son into football, trying to realize the unfulfilled dreams of the parent in the child. And Colene could not say that this was wrong. It was certainly so much better than having her mother get drunk. So if this was what made her positive, it was best to encourage it. Colene could wear a wedding dress for a civil ceremony.

Her father had meanwhile gone off to work, but he was making the arrangements in Texas by phone. Her father had always been competent with details, and Colene had always gotten along with him well enough. She hadn't even blamed him for his extramarital affairs, really. Who wanted to come home to a woman in an alcoholic stupor? Of course there was the nagging question whether her mother would have taken to drinking if her father had been home with her every night. Colene had never been sure which was the chicken and which the egg, in this regard. Probably it had been a messy mixture, like everything else, with her father having a wandering eye and her mother a taste for drink. The two had played off each other, making each worse.

Yet it had to be recognized too that neither parent had ever abused Colene in any direct way. She had never been beaten or fondled or unreasonably punished; she had never gone hungry or inadequately clothed. Not even verbal abuse. Yet she had become suicidal. Now, as she saw her parents

289

being so positive on her behalf, she was moved to wonder why. She had been raped, yes — but other girls got raped without turning suicidal. It had been a shock, certainly, and it had changed her opinion of herself and torpedoed her trust in people and made her extremely wary of strange men. It had left her with an abiding disgust with the whole business: the boys for doing it, herself for allowing it to happen, the society for fostering the attitude that a man was supposed to take whatever he could get away with, and that it was the girl's fault for being the victim. She had indeed lost her innocence, and had never felt fully clean since. But now that she understood the larger picture — why was she still suicidal?

And she *was* still suicidal, she knew. She had not been tempted to try to kill herself since she had set out on the Virtual Mode to rejoin Darius, but she remained, in his parlance, a vessel of dolor. Any time things went wrong, she got depressive. Probably the key factor was Seqiro: within his mental ambience, she was always mostly positive, but without it she would be her natural self. She loved Darius, but she needed Seqiro. She was artificially propped up by the support of the group she had found. By the hive, as Burgess saw it. She needed the hive as much as he did.

So it had to be her family. She had not been conscious of the stress at first, but after the rape she needed the support of a strong family, and it simply wasn't there. Her father was mostly physically absent, and her mother mostly mentally absent. So Colene had wound down, down, into her own private hell, because there had been nothing to stop her. No real family, no close friends.

But now she had friends, on the Virtual Mode. And now her parents were trying to do what they had not done before, being there for her. Rather late, and almost pitiful in their determined sincerity, but they did mean well. It was not their fault that they hardly knew how.

So she would wear her wedding dress, and carry the flowers. Nona would have to make Darius a formal suit. They would go through the motions, to give her parents a memory picture to sustain them when Colene was gone again.

Her father called: it had been arranged, in Wichita Falls, just across the border in Texas. The caterer would have it ready tomorrow afternoon, Saturday.

Caterer? 'Mother, what is going on?'

'For the reception, dear. There is always a reception after a wedding.'

'Not for a civil service!'

'Well, there will be a nondenominational minister. We couldn't arrange a Catholic wedding, on such short notice.'

They couldn't arrange a Catholic wedding regardless of the notice, because they were an extremely poor excuse for a Catholic family, and Darius had no truck with any Earthly religion. But what were they trying for?

Colene realized that she had to get to the bottom of this. She could have Seqiro pry it out of her mother's mind, but that didn't seem quite fair. It was better to make her mother be open. 'Exactly what are you planning, Mother?'

'Well, we thought a nice church ceremony, with music, and a photographer —'

'A photographer! That's only for a fancy full-dress social event! And a church — music —'

'It is all being taken care of. No need to worry.'

'But the expense must be ruinous!'

'Oh, please, Colene, we only want what is best for you. We want you to be married in style.'

Colene opened her mouth to protest this disaster, but saw her mother's strained face and realized that she, Colene, was on the verge of parent abuse. She would be here such a brief time, and her folks wanted to make the most of it. How could she blame them? Perhaps this was their way to sublimate the romance that had been lost in their own marriage. They wanted their daughter to have a romantic wedding. No matter what.

She felt tears. It was touching, in its inadequate way. A brave show now, instead of emotional support back when she had needed it. Her parents just didn't know *how* to relate. 'Thank you, Mother.'

Then she was distracted by something Darius and Seqiro had done. Her mouth pursed in an O of belated appreciation. Males would be males, and the man and stallion were doing something naughty. They had found the carful of punks who had beaten up Darius, the first time he visited Earth. All because one of them had given him the finger, and he, thinking it to be a polite greeting, had returned it. He could have died, if Colene hadn't found him in the ditch near her house and helped him. That had been their first encounter, the beginning of the restoration of Colene's desire to live. But no thanks at all to the punks, because Darius had been looking for Colene anyway, and had not intended trouble for anyone. Colene had had to go to dangerous trouble to get back the key he required to return to his Mode. The punks had stolen it from him, not knowing its nature. The punks deserved whatever they got.

She watched the picture she culled from Seqiro, really enjoying it. The punks drove by the hangout of the Chain Gang and one of them gave a gang member a wicked finger. Another mooned them. Plus a verbal insult or two. Exactly as she had fantasized it for her revenge on the rapists. Seqiro had drawn it from her mind and made it come true, in a fashion. Soon the chase was on – and Seqiro let the punk driver go. The punks would have to get out of it whatever way they could. They had just about the same chance they had given Darius, for the same offense.

But the Chain Gang was not a collection of idle youths seeking incidental thrills. They took their honor seriously.

They radioed ahead, and a barricade was put across the street ahead of the fleeing car. The youths, knowing better than to stop, tried to go through it — and nail-studded boards punctured their tires. They were lucky they didn't roll over.

They piled out of the car as it slowed to a stop. But the cyclists were already there, swinging their mean chains. They weren't out to kill, just to make a demonstration. They were good at that sort of thing. It would take the punks time to recover physically, and longer emotionally, and some of the scars would be with them for life. It would also be some time before anybody else tried to aggravate the Chain Gang, knowing the consequence. That was okay; Colene believed that Slick, the man whose abused niece Colene had helped rescue, had come from the Chain Gang in his younger days, and Colene liked Slick despite his profession.

Colene tuned out, satisfied that justice was being done. There was the sound of a police siren, but in the minute or so it would take for the police to arrive the job would be complete and the motorcycles would be gone. There would be no adequate police report; it was just another incidental rumble. No one would know what had really happened, not even the participants. Except for the members of the hive.

'You must be very happy, dear,' Colene's mother remarked, noting her smile.

'I think I am,' Colene agreed, allowing her mother to believe that thoughts of the wedding were responsible. Actually that too was worth smiling about.

But things were not going as well in the tent. Burgess was having a reaction to one of the pills. His body was shaking and his air was flowing erratically. The calculated risk was miscalculating.

'Mom, let's take a break, okay?' Colene said, shrugging out of the dress-in-the-making. 'I'll be back.' She hurried to the back door.

'But you can't go outside like that!' her mother protested.

Colene realized that she was in bra and panties. 'I'll put something on,' she said over her shoulder as she exited. Then, to Nona: *Clothe me with illusion.*

When her mother looked out, she saw Colene in normal street clothes. The woman turned away, blinking. Why had she thought Colene would go out unclothed?

Colene entered the tent. Nona was sitting with both hands on Burgess' contact points, trying to steady him physically and emotionally. Colene plumped down on the other side, taking hold of two more points.

Now she felt the distress within the floater, which did not transmit well by telepathy. He had indeed been poisoned by the pill; something in it was bad for him. He was sick, feeling somewhat the way a person would when it was necessary to throw up. 'Clear it out, Burgess!' she cried. 'Just blow out the rest of that powder, if you can. We won't give you any more like that.'

It was too late to blow it out, because he had taken the pill most of an hour before. But Colene's presence, physical and mental, calmed him. His shuddering eased, and he became normal. But still very weak. He still needed that missing element.

'I tried to help, but I don't relate as well as you do,' Nona said apologetically. 'When you came, he started to get better. I could feel the change.'

'Maybe it's my telepathy,' Colene said. 'It helps me get in closer touch, when Seqiro's at a distance.'

'Whatever it is, I lack it,' Nona said. 'My magic just doesn't help him.'

Colene let go. 'Let me see those pills,' she said. She took the bottles and scanned their listed contents for common ingredients. 'This is the first one with fish oil,' she said. 'Must be something in it that makes him allergic. We'll set aside any other with fish oil.'

She culled the remaining bottles. 'Keep trying them,' she said. 'Just don't give him these three.' She marked the three with X's and put them aside. 'Now I have to go back inside, before Mom gets upset. But call me if you need me.' She grasped Burgess' contact points again, giving him emotional reassurance, then departed.

She returned to the house. She paused in the kitchen. *Vanish the clothing*, she thought to Nona, and it faded out. Now she could get back into the wedding dress, which was standing on petticoat hoops in the living room.

She had hardly resumed that business when she became aware of more activity by Darius and Seqiro. This time they had found the rapists! The boys who had tricked Colene to their apartment and coerced her into sex. She had known it would be futile to go after them, because it would only be her word against theirs, and the men always won that round. But she had reckoned without Seqiro's power. All four were heading down to the police station to make detailed confessions.

But this was where Darius and Seqiro's inexperience hurt. The police would not just take the word of the four; they would seek to verify it objectively, by interviewing Colene herself — and Colene would be gone. That would deflate the case. Especially since the boys would recant their confessions the moment Seqiro wasn't there to keep them straight. Darius just didn't know how things were, here on Earth; he thought one action would take care of it. There was a certain charm in his naïveté.

Except that it turned out that there had been other girls. Colene hadn't thought of that. *Go after another girl first*, she thought hard to Seqiro. He would see that the first confession featured one of the others, who would still be available, and that might be enough to establish the case. They normally made the case from just one example, so that if that failed, they could take up the next example as a new charge. It made sense. Certainly those four boys would be in for the hassle of their lives before this was done. That was a nice thought.

'You are smiling again,' her mother observed.

'I was thinking of the nice things my friends are doing for me.' Such as diddling the diddlers. There was immense satisfaction in that.

They they worked on her hair. She had always worn her brown tresses loose and shoulder length, trying to cultivate sensual curls, but now her mother bound them up with a sparkling tiara.

The dress was finally ready. Colene had to admit that she looked extremely mature and fetching in it, sort of like a picture. She was small, but some women were. She was young, but women were supposed to look young. The dress actually aged her somewhat, by its conservative lines, and the hairdo transformed her face. The bodice even made her bosom look fuller. She hardly recognized herself.

'Oh, Mom!' she cried, hugging her. She hadn't wanted anything this fancy, but now that she was in it, she loved it. This was just one terrific experience.

'Now you had better rest,' her mother told her, pleased. 'You will have a big day tomorrow, and you want to look fresh.'

She was making sense. So Colene went upstairs to her old room and lay down on her old bed. Everything was charged with nostalgia, now. She couldn't really relax, of course, but this was a good place to be in touch with the others.

Burgess was unchanged, finding neither poison nor cure in the next pill Nona administered. That was getting worrisome. Suppose none of the pills worked? Would it mean that they just hadn't found the right one yet, or that the whole theory was wrong? They just had to find something to make Burgess better, and to keep him better. That was the whole reason they had stopped here on Earth.

She tuned in on Darius and Seqiro. Now they were

addressing their true mission, the Sin Eater. They had learned all about the situation, which was ugly, but were still trying to figure a solution. There didn't seem to be one. Were they going to have to let it go? Darius had discovered that his joy-spreading magic worked on Earth, when he was with Seqiro, but there was no joy to be spread in that neighborhood, only grief. Those miserable folk were as bad as Colene herself, except that they got their kicks from humbling others. That made them worse.

Yet there had to be some way. Colene cudgeled her brain – and came up with it. No misery was worse than that of the Sin Eater, or less deserved. Why not spread that around? At least it might teach that community a lesson. When everyone felt as bad as the Sin Eater, maybe they would stop being so mean to him. It was worth a try. She fired that notion off to Seqiro, and he suggested it to Darius. In a moment Darius was doing it, drawing from Raff, then sending it out to everyone in range. The effect was stunning – for everyone except the Sin Eater himself, who was used to it.

Would it have the desired long-term effect? It would be hard to know. But it was most gratifying for the short term. Darius and Seqiro had done excellent work this day, settling scores with the beat-up punks, the rapists, and the oppressors of the Sin Eater. Now if tomorrow just went as well . . .

To her surprise, she slept. When she woke, it was evening, and not only were Darius and Seqiro back, they were gone again. They had consulted with Colene's parents, and decided to head off for Texas early, so as to be in no rush on Saturday. 'But I wanted to see them!' Colene protested, bemused.

'It is too close to the wedding,' her mother cautioned her. 'It is bad luck for the groom to see the bride right before the ceremony.'

*You let her push you around*, Colene thought to groom and horse.

*She made sense*, Darius returned. *The distance is about fifty of your local miles, and we would like to rest before the occasion, so we started out early. Seqiro will wait about halfway there, because that is about the limit of his range in this Mode, and we need to remain in touch with Nona and Burgess. He should be able to reach both parties, from the center.*

'But my folks don't know anything about Seqiro and Burgess,' Colene muttered subvocally. 'I mean, that Seqiro is a special horse.'

*When we explained it, we made sense*, he replied, with a corollary thought indicating how the horse had touched the woman's mind just enough. Seqiro was proving to be extremely useful in this respect. *You and your parents will rendezvous with us tomorrow morning, and I will then join you for the remainder of the journey.*

It did indeed make sense. 'Okay, manface, horsetail,' she said. 'But don't do it again.' Then she rememberd another thing. 'But your suit! Nona needs to make –'

*She has done so. I have it with me in a bag. Also food for us both. If we need anything else, we shall obtain it on the way. We work well together.*

'Hey, don't get too friendly, and cut me out,' she said.

*Never that, girlface*, Seqiro's thought came.

Colene checked on Nona and Burgess. They were doing well enough, considering. They had tried all the remaining bottles except the three Colene had set aside, with no sufficient effect. But Burgess seemed slightly improved. Perhaps the Earth air was slowly restoring him. Nona was having no trouble, as she was able to use her magic to provide anything she desired. They would be all right for the night, and for the following day, until the hive could get back together and ponder the next step.

\*　　\*　　\*

Early in the morning Colene heard a motor. She looked out the window and recognized Amos Forell's car. She hurried out in her nightie to intercept him, forgetting that Seqiro was not close by to make things seem reasonable. Fortunately it was an unusually warm morning, for an Oklahoma winter.

He eyed her, smiling. 'What mischief are you up to now, Colene?'

'I'm getting married.'

'That's the outfit for it.'

'My mother made me a fancy wedding dress. I'll squirm into it when the time comes. Why are you here?'

'Your horse says that none of the pills worked. I have another idea.' He showed a larger bottle. 'It occurred to me that something ancient might be the key. This is dolomite.'

'You mean now dolor comes in a bottle?'

'Calcium-magnesium carbonate. Don't you remember your science? We need both calcium and magnesium for our bones and teeth, so it stands to reason that Burgess could have some use for some of this too. It seems worth a try.'

Colene warred with herself. She did want to try the dolomite, in the hope that it would cure Burgess. But she was afraid that there could be a bad reaction, and if that happened, she would need to be there to help tide the floater through the crisis. It would be safer to wait until she returned, late tomorrow.

Then her suicidal aspect took control. It was a gamble, but a good one. 'Let's try it!'

They entered the tent. Nona, still asleep, was startled awake, her limbs flashing. Embarrassed, she quickly clothed herself in illusion.

'As if I didn't see enough of that in class,' Amos muttered with mock annoyance. 'I must say, though, it's impressive, considering that you obviously weren't using illusion while sleeping.'

Nona looked blankly at him. Colene, realizing that Seqiro was not on the job, translated. Then Nona smiled.

The dolomite was already in powder form. They put a little bit out, and Burgess sucked it in.

Almost immediately he perked up. This was it! What he needed was here!

'It is?' Colene asked, thrilled. 'Well, have some more!' She poured out another spoonful.

'Caution,' Amos said. 'It is better to give it the time test, before taking too much.'

But Burgess had already sucked up the spoonful. 'Well, we'll stop there, for now,' Colene said. 'No more, for another hour or two, if you're okay. But it sure does look promising.' She turned to Amos. 'I have to go get married. You can stay here with Nona if you want to. But I warn you, she'll hit you with a fireball if you get fresh.'

'I would have the devil of a time explaining that to my wife. I will leave you to it. But I will check again later in the day, to see how Burgess is. It is a phenomenal pleasure to associate with such a creature, and I would like to see him in healthy action.'

'I think you will,' Colene said as they left the tent. Then: 'Damn! I forgot to do it in the tent.'

'Forgot what?'

'This.' She pulled him down toward her and kissed him. 'It would have been better if nobody saw.'

He shook his head, bemused. 'Colene, I think you had better get married quickly.'

'Yeah. That was my last maidenly kiss. I didn't want to waste it.'

Amos returned to his car, and Colene to the house. Her parents were stirring, but she was able to make it back to her room before they realized she had been out.

They had breakfast, and packed the wedding gown. Her

300

mother fixed Colene's hair, complete with tiara, then put a plastic bonnet over it, so that it would keep until the wedding. Her father went out to start the car. Colene went back to check on Nona and Burgess one last time.

As she went, she became aware of something wrong. 'Oh!' Nona cried in her language. She sounded desperate.

Colene almost dived into the tent. Burgess was having a reaction, a worse one than before. Air was blasting down, causing him to float erratically. The substance he needed seemed to be in the dolomite powder, but there was poison too. Now he was in trouble, having taken too much of the stuff.

'I can't hold him!' Nona cried. She was sprawled across the floater, trying to keep him down. 'I'm afraid he'll hurt himself!'

Colene plumped down beside Burgess, grabbing on to his contact points. 'Hey, easy, easy, fellah,' she said, exerting her mind to calm him. 'Try to get the bad stuff out! You can do it.'

'You're helping,' Nona said. 'Oh, I'm so glad. I tried, but I don't have the rapport you do.'

Colene knew it was true. She had the best rapport, and she could help Burgess when others could not. Now she was aware of the agony within him, and knew that this would be no five-minute problem. He was in deep trouble, and it would take hours to tide him through − if it could be done at all. She had made a bad mistake, giving him the extra spoonful of dolomite.

'You must go,' Nona said. 'I think it will be all right, now.'

'No, it won't,' Colene said. 'I can feel his pain, deep down. I'm damping it some now, but if I let go, it will rise up to overwhelm him. I can't leave him.'

'But you have to get married! Everything is ready.'

Colene wrestled with horrible alternatives. She came to a decision. 'I can't let Burgess die, when I'm the one OD'd him. I've got to see him through. You'll have to go instead, Nona.'

'But —'

'It's all set. Seqiro's in range. He'll make you understand the ritual and words. You can make yourself look like me. I can't disappoint my parents. The marriage must go on. Go and do it, Nona. It's the only way.'

Nona stared at her. Then she got up and clothed herself in illusion. Suddenly she did look like Colene, face, dress, and size. Even the tiara and bonnet. 'I will do it, Colene. For the sake of our friendship.' She left.

Colene concentrated on Burgess, seeking the pain in him and suppressing it. The flow of air diminished, and he settled back on the ground. He was still in agony, but it was becoming tolerable, with her help. She hung on, tiding him through, making sure that his fundamental will to live remained. It seemed like hours, but her watch said ten minutes.

She heard the car move out. She tried to reach it with her mind, but her range was too short. She was alone with Burgess.

Gradually in the course of the next half hour, the pain in the floater eased, and she was able to disengage from him somewhat. She sat beside him, one hand on a contact point. 'Well, I did it,' she said conversationally. 'I sent Nona off to my wedding. I wonder if that's what I had in mind all the time? She's really a better match for him. She's older, and prettier, and she has way more magic than I'll ever have.'

Burgess began to be aware of his surroundings and her thoughts. He had not been in a position to understand what was happening in her social horizon. What was Nona doing?

'Nona is marrying Darius, in my stead,' Colene said. 'I told her to. It just had to be done. We couldn't cancel; it would have broken my folks' hearts, after they put themselves in the hole to finance it. The show just had to go on.'

Then she put her head down and wept. The tears flowed, and kept coming, dropping into her lap. She knew she had done it to herself. She had gambled on Burgess' treatment when she shouldn't, and then had to throw away her dream. But if it hadn't been for Burgess, would she have found some other excuse? She had so blithely set up to marry Darius, but she was afraid of marriage, too, because she had seen so clearly what a loss her parents' marriage was. Was she, deep down inside, determined to avoid the married state herself?

Or was it that she remained suicidal in every way? Not merely in the body, slicing her wrists, but in emotion, slicing her potential happiness? So that every time something good threatened to happen to her, she just had to mess it up? Sometimes she had used her nature to beat others, such as when she had won back Darius' Mode-traveling key by challenging the jerk who had it to a bleeding contest. She would have bled herself to death, too, if he hadn't backed off. Because part of her always wanted to die. Did another part of her always want to be miserable?

She remembered telling Seqiro that she wanted everything — and nothing. She was a cipher, even to herself, a riddle never to be understood. Even buoyed by her friends of the hive, she had never truly known her true desire, and she didn't know it now. What did she want, if she didn't die?

'My future is a blur,' she said to Burgess. 'I have no goals, I only want to make my life count. When I think of how short life is I can't accept mere survival as an achievement. If there is nothing after we die, we have to make every second we're alive count. I don't want to be caught in "Mundania." I can't bear to live a dull, gray existence when there are bright glorious adventures to explore. I know they are out there somewhere. Because I can read about them.

303

Perhaps that's my trouble. I read far too much. At least I did before I found the Virtual Mode. How can I help it, though? My life and the life of a fantasy character just can't compare. Before, I was satisfied to live the lives of the people in my books, but now I know that it's not the same. I want to really and truly live. I want so many different things I know I can't have. I'm bright, creative — I could probably choose any profession I wanted, but I don't want any of them. Not here on Earth. I want to roam the universe looking for adventure, never being sure where I'll go next. I want to be a famous artist or musician or something. I want a simple home and family. I want to change the world. I want everything anybody wants — and more. I wish there were no civilization, only nature and living. I want to live in the wilderness empty of people and technology. Yet I love to watch different people come and go. I want to live in a bustling city. I want love, I want hate. I want a cause I could give up everything for. I want to be able to just get up and leave where I am and not worry if I have enough socks and whether I forgot my toothbrush. I want to be organized and under control. Nothing can satisfy me.'

She glanced at Burgess. 'Does any of that make sense to you? Well, it doesn't to me. I'm a bundle of conflicts. No wonder I can't even get married when it's all set up. I have a love-hate feeling about marriage. I want it and I fear it, at the same time. So I guess it's not surprising that I'm sitting here mourning the marriage I didn't make. I really walked out on Darius at the altar. And I shoved Nona into something she really didn't want.'

She shook her head. 'You know, sometimes I even wrote poems in my diary. I would tease Maresy Doates with them. Maresy is my friend who is a horse. Before I met Seqiro. She always understood me. The way Seqiro does now. But still I teased her.'

Colene closed her eyes. She recited the poem from memory.

*I'm really a bug-eyed monster*
*From outer space.*

*I can tell*
*By the way people look at me*
*That wide-eyed wonder*
*That such a creature could exist,*
*Let alone talk to them.*

*But there's something strange*
*About the mirrors here —*

*All they'll show me is a*
*Brown-haired girl,*
*Not too fat and not too thin,*
*With green eyes no bigger*
*Than loneliness.*

'My eyes aren't actually green, in this life, of course, but in my fantasy realm they are. In the ugly real world they're brown, but when I'm exotic they're green. So if you ever see me with green eyes, you'll know I've crossed over. With my loneliness.'

She laughed, verging on hysteria. 'Do you want to know something funny, Burgess? Last year, when I had been raped and was turning suicidal, I was voted the happiest person in my class. That's how well I fooled everybody.'

She thought the floater was laughing, before remembering that he had no sense of humor. He was going into another seizure!

She grabbed on to him. 'Easy, Burg, easy! You got through it before; this one's bound to be easier. Just tide through, and the poison'll be gone.' Her words were more for herself than him; what counted for him was her presence and her emotion. Whatever comfort and hope she had, she gave to him, spreading mental oil on the troubled waters of his malady.

Slowly, it eased, and at last he settled again, his pain diminished. But Colene's pain was increasing. Because more time had passed than she thought, and now the wedding was beginning.

She was at the limit of Seqiro's range. Most of his mental energy was devoted to the wedding, to make sure that the groom and bride did not miss their cues. But there was enough left to send Colene a picture, and snatches of sound. No actual thought, but that didn't matter; the picture was enough.

There was the church, nondenominational but still looking very churchly, with stained-glass windows and pews and a chancel in front. There was an organ. There were flowers. There was an audience: well-dressed people, looking sedate but expectant. Her folks had set it up to be perfect, and the caterer had really known its business. The whole thing had a preternatural familiarity, giving her an overwhelming sense of déjà vu. She had witnessed this scene before!

Of course she had! This was the wedding of her vision! Her nightmare — and now it was happening, exactly as she had seen it. She had seen it coming.

The music swelled. The Bride swept down the aisle, ethereally lovely in the gown that had been made for Colene, and magically grown to fit the other woman. Beside her was a man: Colene's father, impeccably garbed, looking proud. They made a perfect father/daughter couple. Colene felt her face wet with tears, but the vision did not blur. She was not seeing it with her own eyes.

'That should have been me,' she whispered brokenly. 'So close, so close . . .'

The Bride progressed to the front. The view shifted, and now the audience was seen from the front. There was Colene's mother, dabbing her face with a silk handkerchief.

Her father came to join her in the first pew, and took her hand. They looked so much like the ideal parents. Most of their marriage might have been a shell, and this was a shell too, but it was a picture to remember. This was the way it should have been, had there been reality beneath the shell. It was impossible to begrudge them this image. It was about all they had.

Now the scene was the Bride and Groom. Darius was the Groom, looking well groomed (naturally!) and handsome. Nona was the Bride, fair in the sense of beauty, dark in the sense of beauty, the loveliest possible creature. They made the perfect couple. They stood before the minister, and the key words were spoken.

Colene realized that Nona no longer looked like Colene. The illusion was gone. Of course Nona could not have fooled Colene's folks about her identity; not during the hour's ride in the car to Wichita Falls. The moment she opened her mouth, they would have known. Even if Seqiro was able to translate, at that distance. Because Nona was just plain different. So her folks knew, and accepted Nona, so there was no need for illusion.

'Oh, God, I can't stand it!' Colene cried, trying not to listen.

Nevertheless, she heard Darius speak: 'I do.'

'I did want to marry him! I did! Why did I throw it away?'

Nona spoke: 'I do.'

'And what is left for me now?' Colene sobbed.

The picture came, relentlessly. Darius turning to face Nona. Nona lifting back her veil. Colene jammed her eyes closed, but could not shut it out. Nona smiling.

They kissed. There was the flash of a camera's bulb. It was done.

Colene found herself hunched against Burgess, her hands grasping his contact points, her head against her hands. Her hands were wet with her tears.

She had done it for Burgess. To tide him through the reaction. She had given up her important ceremony to save him. She had valued friendship more than experience.

That was Burgess talking! 'Burg, you're back!' she exclaimed. 'You're conscious!'

He was conscious. He had been aware all along, but of too low a vitality to do more than focus on surviving. Now he was improved, though still far from well.

'That dolomite — it did have what you need. But also what you don't need. So it's no good, but it gives us a clue. Is it the calcium or the magnesium you need — or some associated trace element? I wish we had a safe way to tell.'

Colene thought about it, taking her mind off her own misery. 'Maybe Amos would know.'

She knew that her range was too short, but she tried it anyway. After all, when she had sent her mind across the Virtual Mode, asking 'Is anybody there?' the mind predator had heard. So maybe, with a narrow focus, she could reach him. *Amos! Dolomite is halfway there. How do we find what counts?*

There was a silence for a moment. Then, faintly: *Colene!* He had heard her! *Dolomite — good, bad. What next? Idea.*

So Amos had been notified. Maybe he would have the answer. She relaxed.

Then the wedding scene returned. Seqiro was still sending. She saw the wedding cake her mother had labored over. The caterer could have provided a fancier one, but her mother had wanted this aspect to be personal. She saw Nona's hand on the knife, with Darius' hand on hers, giving her strength. They were still following the ritual.

'If only I could have done that!' Colene said, her tears resuming.

She watched the continuing vision compulsively, as she might the funeral of a close friend. It was so perfect,

308

and so dreadful. Like her life. Every time she came close to happiness, she bypassed it in favor of dolor. It was her way.

They even danced. Colene's folks had somehow managed to squeeze a bit of everything in! That, too, was beautiful and horrible. Her man and her friend, so perfect.

There was the sound of a car pulling in. That was Amos. He walked directly to the tent. 'Colene! How did you get back so quickly?'

'I never went,' she said.

'Never went! You're a mess! What happened?'

'Burgess had a reaction, and I had to stay to tide him through. Nona went instead.'

He nodded. 'That must have been a beautiful wedding.'

'It was. Seqiro showed me. I saw Nona marry Darius.'

'That was nice of her, considering her unfamiliarity with the ritual.'

'Yeah, sure.' Colene hoped the irony came through.

'Fortunately Texas is one of the states which allows marriage by proxy.'

She stared at him. 'Proxy!'

He laughed. 'You sound as if you thought *she* could marry him — when all the papers were in your name. It was your marriage, of course, throughout. She was merely your stand-in. An actress, really, going through the motions so that the ceremony could be accomplished with appropriate flair. I'm sure she was a picture to remember! Still, I can appreciate your disappointment at not being there yourself.'

'I missed my own wedding!' Colene breathed.

'For the most generous reason: to help your alien friend. You're a great girl, Colene.'

Colene was awed by the realization. She knew about proxy marriage. She must have known that that was what she was really asking Nona to do. And Nona had known, too. That was why she had agreed. Any why Colene's parents had gone along with it. It was the only way to have the wedding

309

performed on schedule, without sacrificing Burgess. Colene had known — yet hidden that knowledge from herself. She really was a creature of dolor!

'Now let's see about Burgess. I got your message. I was amazed; I thought you were sending all the way from Texas. Then I realized that you would have been using Seqiro to boost your signal. So I brought refined products: calcium supplement, magnesium supplement. One of them should do it.'

Booster by Seqiro. Probably that had been the case. Even at the extreme of his range, Seqiro was so much more powerful than she was that he could amplify her thought, especially when it was narrowly focused.

Amos held two packages. 'Your call, Colene. Which one first?'

She was still dazed by the revelation of her marriage. 'What do they do?'

'In simplistic terms, which may not be properly applicable to Burgess, calcium is the stuff which makes our bones and teeth, while magnesium hardens them.'

'Calcium is more common?'

'Yes. Except in something like dolomite.'

'So maybe it's the rarer element he's missing. Try that.'

'Done.' He opened the magnesium and took out a tiny amount, which he set in a Petri dish he had brought. He put a hand on a contact point. 'Burgess, this is another try. We hope it's the right one. Take it cautiously.' He set it down by the floater's trunk.

The trunk touched it. Burgess sucked in the powder.

'Now we wait,' Amos said. 'If he has an adverse reaction, we'll give him the other, quickly, because that's likely to be the right one. With more of the right one, he should be better able to handle the wrong one.'

'Yeah.'

'A penny for your thoughts, Colene.'

'I'm married. I really am married. To Darius.'

'You really are, Colene. I realize that it doesn't seem like it at the moment, considering what you were doing during the ceremony. But that will pass. I wish you a long and happy relationship, wherever you may be. You deserve it.'

'No, I don't. I'm depressive. I'm unclean.'

'Damn it, Colene, you aren't! You're thinking of that rape, and it's just not so. It was those boys who — you know, something strange happened yesterday. It was in the paper this morning. Four boys turned themselves in for rape. Was that you?'

'Darius and Seqiro did it.' She smiled. 'Not the rape. The mind. They made the boys confess. They'd done it to other girls, so it will be one of those other cases that comes to court. But we're responsible.'

'I'm glad to hear it. So any lingering problem you had with that can be ameliorated. You were a victim, and despite the attitude of too many ignoramuses, it is not a crime to be a victim. So enjoy your marriage, Colene; you have earned it.'

'Yeah, maybe,' she said, cheering.

'And there was something else. Very strange.'

'The Sin Eater,' she agreed. 'Darius and Seqiro gave everyone in that slum the same feelings Raff has. To show them what it's like.'

His mouth pursed appreciatively. 'That should teach them manners!'

'We wanted to make Raff happy, but there was no way. So we made it even. And Darius even got back at the punks who beat him up, by setting them against the Chain Gang.'

'Your friends are amazing!'

'Yeah,' she agreed, pleased. 'They're great. All of them. Including Burgess, here.'

Amos got up. 'I have other business to attend to. But do let me know how this works out.'

'The wedding night?'

'The medication, you little tease! I want to know that this most remarkable of creatures is well again. It has been the experience of my life, knowing him. Knowing all of you.'

'Don't you want to be the first to kiss the bride?'

'Colene, you sneak-kissed me twice, and I'm a married man. The school will think I'm putting a move on –' He broke off. 'That's all of the ceremony you can have, isn't it? You sacrificed the rest. Yes, I'll kiss you, Colene. But don't tell. Others would never understand.'

'Others don't matter.'

He got down beside her and kissed her lightly on the mouth. She felt the tenderness in his mind. He understood so well, and he was genuinely happy for her. It was wonderful.

'Thanks, Amos,' she said faintly.

'You're welcome, Mrs Darius.'

She laughed. The universe was looking brighter. She could make it as Mrs Darius. She would succeed in marriage – or die trying. Ha-ha.

'You will be reconsidering your status, in much the way paleontologists reconsidered the Burgess Shale, and perhaps coming to similarly momentous revelations. I wish you the best on the Virtual Mode, Colene.'

'I think I have the best already, Amos. I'm glad we stopped by here. It was good to see you, and to get other things settled.' That was the understatement of the month.

Then Burgess stirred.

'Oops – it's a seizure,' Amos said.

Colene clapped both hands on contact points. 'No, it isn't!' she cried gladly. 'He's recovering! I can feel the strength surging through.'

Yes, that was what he needed. They had found the elixir of his health.

'That was Burgess talking,' she said. She squeezed the points. 'Oh, airfoot, it was worth it! You're cured!'

Burgess sucked in air, smoothly. Colene let go, and he

312

blasted air out below, lifting smoothly from the ground for the first time since coming to Earth. Then he settled, tired.

He needed more magnesium.

They put more out for him, not too much, lest he overdose. He took it in, and rested, waiting for it to be digested.

'It was worth it,' Amos echoed, watching. 'There should be enough magnesium in that jar to hold him for years. If you ever stop by here again, be sure to look me up.' Then he left Colene to her reconsideration of her status.

# 14

## *Problems*

Nona had to admit that the odd Earth customs had their points. The ritual of the wedding, with the fancy gown, and music, and cake, and dancing — that was nice. It had been a genuinely moving occasion, despite the fact that she was only playing a part. She had been standing in for Colene, the real bride. It was too bad that Colene had had to miss her own ceremony, but at least she now had her heart's desire: marriage to Darius.

Now they were riding back to Colene's kingdom of Oklahoma, from the neighboring kingdom of Texas, where proxy marriages were permitted to girls of fourteen. Colene's parents had been very nice about both the wedding and the proxy aspect, thanks in part to Seqiro's influence. But it was also because the parents had had serious difficulties in their own marriage, and felt guilty because Colene had suffered thereby, and were trying to make it up to her. This wedding was the symbol of their makeup. In this, at least, they could give their daughter the best. Then forever after they could remember that beautiful occasion, and believe that everything had worked out for the best.

Nona had lost her own parents, as a result of the strife entailed in the changing of the animus to anima on Oria. Actually they had not been her birth parents, because of a ruse intended to conceal Nona's nature as the ninth of the ninth. But they had been the ones she had known for all of her life, and she loved them, and only magic grief-healing had enabled her to carry through in the first days after the news of their deaths. Gradually she was eliminating the magic and assuming more of the grief herself; only when she could handle the whole of it would she be emotionally stable in her natural state. Here on Earth, substituting for Colene, she found herself warming to these parents, who were truly hurting, if in a different way. So while Nona was a mere proxy for the wedding, there were aspects of it that were meaningful for her personally.

She had to admit, privately, that it had been fun kissing and dancing with Darius. He was the kind of man she would like to have, at such time as she was ready to have a man. So was Amos, Colene's science teacher. Neither was muscular or physically prepossessing, but both had knowledge and special abilities, and a keen sense of right and wrong. It was intellect and conscience that most truly distinguished one man from another.

They reached the thicket where Seqiro snoozed. The horse's mind remained attuned to the two of them, so that they could converse and understand Colene's parents, but he was otherwise at rest. Darius was about to get out to ride the horse back, but Nona stopped him. 'You have a wife to return to. I will go with Seqiro tonight.'

He looked surprised. Then he nodded. Colene was now Old Enough, by the standard of her culture.

So Nona got out and joined the horse, and Darius remained in the car with the parents. Nona watched the vehicle depart, then floated up to land on Seqiro's broad back. She had been careful not to use her magic during the wedding; though the people had been placed there by the caterer, they would have noticed something that did not follow the normal rules of science. She had been similarly discreet with Colene's parents. Only with Amos, at Colene's direction, had she demonstrated her powers. And during the ceremony, using illusion to make herself resemble Colene. Seqiro had sent the scene back to Colene without the illusion, because Colene understood. But now, alone with Seqiro, she had no need for concealment.

'I wonder how Darius and Colene are doing?' she mused, at about the time the two should be getting together. 'No,

315

don't spy on them, Seqiro! Leave them their privacy. Spy out only one thing: how is Burgess doing?'

*Burgess is healing. They found the substance required. It is magnesium. Amos brought enough of it to supply Burgess for as long as he needs.*

'That is a relief! Burgess is a nice creature, who would not have suffered if we had not brought him to the Virtual Mode.'

*He would have suffered death at the trunks of his former hive. The Virtual Mode was a necessary rigor.*

'That is true. Still, I am glad he is better. It would have been awful if Colene had made her sacrifice, only to lose him.'

It was pleasant, traveling with the horse. It reminded her of the time she had first been with him, in her own Julia Mode, hiding from the despots. They had gone under the water, with the help of her magic. But there was no need for that, here; Seqiro's own magic sufficed to keep the natives incurious. So they proceeded at a leisurely pace, chatting about inconsequentials. They paused to eat, with Nona making him a fine bag of sweet horsefeed and a pail of cool water. Then they resumed, and Nona slept as the horse made his way through the night. This was the sort of life Nona was satisfied to maintain indefinitely: just a girl and horse, crossing an odd land.

By now, Darius and Colene must be indulging in their nuptial night. Colene had been so eager for it, despite her youth, always frustrated by Darius' insistence that she was too young by the standard of her culture. Now that same standard made her old enough. Despite her disclaimer, Nona found herself to be almost unbearably curious. The girl had, after all, despite her youth, had sexual experience. Would that make a difference?

Nona stifled her curiosity as long as she could, but it would not be denied. 'Seqiro, I know it is wrong, but – '

*They are not yet in their nuptial night. Colene's parents*

*have arranged a room for them for the night elsewhere in the town, but Colene will not leave Burgess untended.*

'Then we must rejoin them after all. I had thought they would be with Burgess.'

*The parents are not aware that anything except supplies is in the tent. They do not understand why Colene delays, but I have helped them to be unconcerned.*

So they moved on at a faster pace, and approached the town. Colene, understanding that they would join Burgess within an hour, finally agreed to go to what she called the motel with Darius. The night was now half done.

Nona and Seqiro reached the tent. Burgess was there, much improved. Nona got down and touched a contact point.

At the rate he was recovering, Burgess would be fit for the Virtual Mode again on the next day. He was eager to end this delay, so that Colene and Darius could at last reach the end of their long journey and be at peace.

Those were Burgess' thoughts, all right. He was in no further trouble. Nona set up her bed in the tent and lay down to sleep for the rest of the night, while Seqiro grazed in the gully behind Colene's house. Though well fed on grain, the horse still liked to do for himself, and he was careful not to leave droppings where they would bother anyone. This, he knew, was the place where Colene had once dreamed she might find a lost horse. That gave the region a certain compatibility.

But Nona did not sleep. Her curiosity about what did not concern her surged back. Exactly what went on during a nuptial night? Eventually there would come the time when Nona herself participated in one. She understood about sex, of course, but was that all? What did such folk say to each other? Did they get the sex out of the way early, or were they more leisurely about it? Or did they keep doing it through the night, catching up on formerly suppressed desires? Was each episode swift or slow?

317

She got up and went to check on Burgess again, more to distract herself than for concern for his health. She put a hand on a contact point.

What did two of the human persuasion do when united in a mating agreement? Would that agreement alienate them from the hive? Would it change their personalities? Would Colene no longer come to share thoughts with Burgess? The matter was worrisome.

Nona almost laughed. The floater was just as curious as she was!

That did it. 'Seqiro,' she murmured, 'give us the scene.'

She sat beside Burgess as the scene formed in her mind, translating it for him. It showed the room where Darius and Colene were. They were eating a snack. Behind them a large bed remained undisturbed. They had not yet gotten to it. Nona felt guilty for being relieved.

But how could she see the scene with both of them in it? Seqiro could only animate the pictures in people's minds; he did not do illusion the way Nona's people did. This had to be what Darius saw, or what Colene saw, in which case the view person would be missing from the image.

Then the view shifted, and Nona saw the mirror. Darius had been gazing in the mirror across the table, seeing the reflection of the two of them. Now he saw only Colene.

They continued their eating. This was not exactly what Nona had hoped to see. But she schooled herself to guilty patience. They would surely get to it. Why had they delayed so long already?

They finished eating. Colene went to the lavatory and brushed her teeth. She changed into a sheer nightie. She went to the bed. She looked almost unbearably cute. Then Darius took his turn, taking a shower, emerging naked, drying, and going to the bed. Nona's patience was finally to be rewarded.

'I guess I'm Old Enough, now,' Colene said almost challengingly.

'By the standard of your culture,' Darius agreed.

'So this time when I come on to you, you aren't going to ignore me. You're really going to do it.'

'Yes.' He spoke calmly, but Nona could feel his surging desire. He had wanted this as much as Colene had, and now at last they could have it.

'I guess you think I've been stalling.'

'There is no need to rush you.'

'It's what I've always wanted from you. Full commitment at last.'

'Yes. There are no further barriers.'

He reached out a hand to touch her, under the sheet, expecting her to meet him with an almost savage hunger. Instead, Colene stiffened visibly.

Darius withdrew his hand. 'Is something wrong?'

Colene burst into tears.

Darius was startled, as was Nona, sharing his vision and receiving his emotion. The vision through his eyes blinked. What was the matter?

'Oh, Darius, you're going to have to rape me.'

'What?'

'I just can't *do* it: I thought I could, and I really do want to, but I keep remembering how it was with those four, and I just freeze up.'

'But they are being dealt with, now. They will pay for their crime against you.'

'They can never pay enough!'

'And you have been trying to seduce me all along,' Darius said, perplexed.

'Always before I knew you wouldn't do it,' she said, the tears squeezing out of her closed eyes. 'I was baiting the bull, when the bull was corralled. Now I know it's loose.'

'Then we must wait until you are ready. I did not understand.' Nona felt his terrible disappointment.

319

'No! Do it now! We've got to do it on our wedding night. Everyone knows that. Just rape me. I promise not to resist. I didn't before.'

Even Nona could see that this was just about as appetizing as a slab of wormy meat. What an attitude to bring to the nuptial night!

'No,' Darius said with deep regret.

Colene kicked off the sheet, pulled up her nightie to expose thighs, torso, and breasts, and spread her arms and legs in the manner of a scarecrow. 'Do it, Darius! No resistance. This is as far as I can go.'

'I have desired you from the outset,' Darius said carefully. 'When you first came to me, as I lay beaten on the ground. But I would not take you, because you were not ready. I desired you as we came to know each other, and you tempted me with your tight trousers —'

'Jeans.'

'And your sheer nightie. *This* nightie. I wanted you more than anything. But I did not take you, because you asked me not to. I desired you when we were together in Oria, and you asked me to take you, but then I knew that you were too young, so I did not. I desire you now, more than ever, but —'

'Take me! Take me!' Her eyes were closed, her teeth clenched, as if she were expecting to be tortured.

'But you are afraid. I will not do it when you fear it. Relax and sleep, Colene; I will let you be.'

Her face twisted into the semblance of anger. 'What is it — I'm inadequate? Not enough body for you? Would you hold off if it were Nona?'

Nona jumped.

Darius took the taunting question seriously. 'Yes. I would not do it with Nona, because it is not her desire, and it is not your desire that I do it with her.'

Nona relaxed. He had spoken the exact truth. But her respect for him was increasing, because she knew the strength of his desire and the agony of his decision.

'You didn't answer the right question,' Colene complained. 'Is my body too immature for you? Not like Pussy?'

Pussy? Nona wondered.

*A female feline of the DoOon Mode who tried to seduce Darius. He found her quite interesting.*

'A *cat?*' Nona asked.

*A Null. A human slave, called a feline, with a feline face, but in other respects an extremely well endowed human woman. The DoOons have many such slaves, with the aspects of cats, dogs, horses, pigs —*

'Pigs!'

*The Emperor's Nulls are pigs. They command great respect.*

Nona decided to let it pass, lest she miss the dialogue on which she was so guiltily eavesdropping. Darius had tried to demur, but Colene insisted that he answer the question of bodily endowment.

'You are adequate,' he said, with his precision. 'In fact I like your slender little body very well. But you must truly want the interaction.'

'I *do* want it! I just can't *do* it! Rape me, and maybe I'll loosen up. Just get me past this hurdle, Darius.'

'No.'

'I'll make you do it!' she cried. 'Seqiro! Make him do it!'

*No.*

'Damn it, whose horse are you, anyway?'

Darius smiled grimly. 'Seqiro loves you, Colene, as I do. He will never hurt you, for the same reason I will not.'

Colene lay there crying, the picture of misery.

Darius paused, then spoke. 'I am going to touch you. I am going to bring you to me. I am going to kiss you. I am going to hold you close. I am going to love you. I am not going to coerce you into sexual expression. This is the way

321

it will be, until such time as you truly wish it otherwise.'

She remained frozen. Carefully he reached for her, putting his hands on her shoulders. He brought down her nightie, so that it covered her body again. He brought his body across and brought his head down to hers, kissing her. Then he turned her to face him, and clasped her to him. He stroked her sodden hair, and her back, gently.

'Oh, Darius, I'm so ashamed!'

'No. You have been hurt, and the hurt has not yet healed. I did not properly understand, before. Now I do. We shall heal you, Colene. In time. In time.'

'In time,' she agreed, relaxing at last.

Nona shook her head. 'I did not know how bad it was. How she was hurting.'

*She did not wish to share it.*

'I can heal a person physically, but emotional hurt is beyond my power. I can not help her in this respect.'

*Neither can I. I can only help her to block it out.*

'Is it this way for every girl who is raped?'

*I do not know.*

'It must be, at least to some extent. Some rapes must be worse than others. Some girls must be more sensitive. But it is a terrible thing, regardless.'

*Regardless*, the horse agreed.

Regardless, Burgess agreed.

'But we will all help her to recover, however we can.'

There was agreement from horse and floater. And, perhaps, Darius, whose disappointment was second only to Colene's own.

Nona returned to her bed. 'Help me to sleep,' she asked Seqiro. Then she slept.


In the morning Burgess was so much improved as to be almost at full strength. Nona was somewhat logy, having remained awake too late, to snoop on Colene. Yet she was glad she had done it, though she had not learned what she

322

expected. She had discovered the girl's true weakness, so now knew what was needed. Colene needed the support of the hive, in much the way Burgess did. She would have it.

Late in the morning Colene's father drove his car to the motel to pick them up. Nona cleaned up the tent, getting things organized so that they could travel again. They all knew that Colene wanted to get on with the journey to Darius' home Mode. Nona suspected that Colene would be better off with more delay, while she worked out her scrambled feelings, but it was not Nona's province to make that decision. They would go to Darius' Mode, and then see. Perhaps the others – Seqiro, Burgess, and Nona – would remain there for a while, to be sure that all was in order, before deciding what to do.

Colene's mother came back to the tent. 'Nona – may I talk with you?' she asked hesitantly.

'Of course.' What could the woman want?

'I know you are not exactly what you seem. That none of you are exactly what you seem. Not even Colene, now. But I believe you are good people.'

'I believe we are,' Nona agreed cautiously.

'It was a nice wedding.'

'It was very nice.'

'We really do want what is best for Colene. After she disappeared, before, we realized how poorly we had served her. When my husband had an affair, it drove me to drink. I just didn't think of the effect on Colene, to my shame. My husband loves our daughter too. We were both blind to the effect on our child. We resolved that if God should grant us another chance, we would do better. Then Colene returned, with an older woman, and a strange story of a Virtual Mode. We concluded that she had fallen under the influence of an evil cult, and that the strange woman was preventing her from escaping it. We tried to save her from that. Then she disappeared again, right before our eyes, and we realized too late that she was involved in something beyond our understanding. Whe we learned the story of the gangster and the little girl, we saw that Colene had done something good. So we believed her, too late. We swore to God that if we should ever have yet another chance, this time we would trust in our daughter and do whatever she wished to be done. We swore to lead perfect lives until we had our child back again. And we did so — and Colene did return again.'

The woman stopped, overtaken by emotion. 'You did what Colene wished,' Nona agreed. This family had been dysfunctional; now it was trying so hard to recover. Nona remembered again how her own family had been lost. She was still using magic to stave off the horror of that.

'Now our little girl is married, and she will go her way. All we — all we ask is that she visit us again, when she chooses. We want so much to —'

Nona came to an abrupt decision. 'Let me tell you more about the Virtual Mode,' she said. 'It is a way to cross over to other realities. Other worlds. Darius lives on one; I live on another. Seqiro, the horse, lives on another. Seqiro enables us to talk with each other, because I do not know your language.'

'The horse?' the woman asked blankly.

*Hello.*

The woman looked at Seqiro. He lifted his head to gaze back at her. He projected acceptance.

'The horse,' she said, realizing it was true.

Nona took her hand. 'I will show you the Virtual Mode.' She led the woman through the anchor.

The scene changed. The new scene was similar, but the nearby houses and yards were subtly different.

'This is not our town,' the woman said, looking around.

'It is the adjacent world. Very similar, but different. There are others; the farther we go, the more different they become, until there is no similarity at all. Some have strange animals, or strange machines. Some are dangerous. Some have magic.'

'Magic!'

Nona decided not to confuse the woman with too much. 'Some do. The rules change a little with each Mode. Darius has a special kind of magic. He lives in a nice world, and he wants Colene with him.'

'He does seem like a nice young man.'

'He is.' After last night, Nona realized how much of an understatement that was.

'He seems to be upright.'

'He is absolutely upright. Colene could not be with a better man.'

'I am so glad to know that Colene is in good hands.'

Nona led the woman back out through the anchor. The Earth Mode reappeared. 'So you see, Colene is making a strange journey, but she is with friends. I think she will be happy with Darius. Certainly she is happy with Seqiro.'

'If we can only see her once in a while, to know she is all right.'

'She surely will visit you again. If she doesn't, I will.'

Now the woman understood some of the significance of that promise. 'Thank you so much, Nona.' Then, dazed, she returned to the house.

The car arrived. Darius and Colene walked to the tent, holding hands. He looked so tall, and she so small, but they were married now. Nona resolved to say and think nothing about what she had seen last night.

'Let's go,' Colene said briskly. 'I'll say goodbye to my folks.'

Nona abolished the tent. She helped Darius put the harness back on Seqiro, and load their gear. Burgess floated through the anchor, disappearing.

Colene returned. 'I promised your mother you would visit again,' Nona said.

'I will,' Colene's eyes were wet. 'I don't think I ever really knew my folks, until now. They've been great.'

They move on through. They were back traveling the Virtual Mode. It felt good.

Traveling this segment of the Virtual Mode was easy, because the paved street remained. Burgess had no trouble keeping the pace; this was ideal terrain for him.

They came into a region of animals. The streets and moving vehicles remained, but now the animals were dominant, with human beings serving them. 'Watch out for these,' Colene warned. 'They're telepathic. Like Seqiro. But I don't think they can reach across Modes. So if we get attacked, we just need to step on across. Quickly.'

Indeed, they saw dogs, cats, bears, and other creatures, of all sizes, moving around in their Modes as if they were the proprietors. They felt the touches of the animals' minds. Once Nona received an order: *Stop. Come to me.* Unable to resist, she had stopped, turned, and walked toward the bear. Then she had crossed the boundary, and the bear disappeared, and she was freed from the compulsion.

So it was easy to escape, because of the narrowness of the slices of the worlds. But not pleasant business. Because the bear had viewed her as food.

*I will help you resist, the next time*, Seqiro's thought came.

'Thank you. I don't know how to fight it, when its power bypasses my magic.'

*Darius has learned to resist. He has been practicing. He had stood off two creatures so far. Colene is making a similar effort. Perhaps you can learn to resist, too.*

'I hope so,' Nona said. 'I'll try to fight the next one. Let me do it, and rescue me only if I am in too much trouble.'

'I'm practicing,' Colene said. 'But I can't resist as well as Darius can, now.'

'Burgess has no trouble,' Darius said. 'These creatures can not touch his alien mind.'

'So if we are even in doubt, follow Burgess,' Nona said. The others agreed.

They crossed a boundary — and there was a row of oxen to the side. *What comes into existence?* an ox demanded.

*Just passing through*, Seqiro replied.

Nona felt a mind clamp down on her body. She saw Colene freeze just ahead of her. Even Seqiro halted. Several of the creatures were doing it, overwhelming the single horse.

Darius fought to move. He half fell beside Burgess. One hand struggled to a contact point. That was all he could do.

Burgess his put intrunk down to the ground. There were stones and sand there. He sucked them up. He aimed his outtrunk. A rock shot out and struck an ox on the head, between the horns. Then another rock flew, striking another. And a third.

Suddenly Nona's mind was free. She leaped ahead, across the boundary. Colene was right with her.

In a moment all of them were across except Burgess. Then he too appeared.

*There were too many telepaths*, Seqiro explained. *I could not prevail against several. But they were unable to address Burgess. When he shot stones at them, they concentrated on him, letting us go. But still they could not stop him, without touching his contact points.*

'It's good to have you back with us,' Nona told the floater as she touched a contact point. He kept helping them in unexpected ways.

They found a Mode without telepathic animals, where a river crossed to the side, and made camp for the night. It was early evening, but they still needed to catch up from the prior night.

Nona and Colene went down to the river, careful to remain within the boundaries so that they would not accidentally cross over to the Modes on either side. There

327

had been so many kinds of telepathic animals that it wasn't worth the risk.

'I wonder whether there's a Mode with telepathic humans,' Nona said musingly. 'Obviously humans can do it, because you are learning.'

'I don't want to see that Mode,' Colene said. 'The animals are bad enough.'

'Except for the horses.'

'The horses are bad too, except for Seqiro. He had to leave his Mode, because he wanted to think for himself. They tried to pen him in. We don't want to stop there.'

'There should be no need to, with Burgess well.'

'I hope so.' They stripped and waded into the water, which was cool but not unbearably so. Seqiro had checked it for minds, and reported nothing inimical or dangerous there.

They scrubbed each other off, then emerged, refreshed. They stood by the bank, letting themselves dry.

'About last night,' Colene said. 'Thanks.'

'I don't mind watching Burgess.'

'For not mentioning my shame.'

Nona could find no answer to that.

They returned to the camp, and the three males went down to wash, while Nona took small parts of their supplies and expanded them into a good-sized meal for all. Originally she had been concerned that such expansion, on the Virtual Mode, would be ephemeral, but when she started with anchor material, it remained anchor material, and was all right.

There was the sound of splashing from the river. Burgess was shooting a steady stream of water at Seqiro, hosing him down. 'That looks like fun,' Nona said wistfully.

'Then let's go down and enjoy it,' Colene said. 'We can take another bath if we want to.'

So they put off their clothes again and ran down to the river. Soon they were in the midst of a five-way splashing contest, screaming with the sheer fun of it.

328

When they emerged the second time, Nona knew one thing: she did not want to see this hive break up. She would not interfere with what Darius and Colene decided to do, but she hoped that their time on the Virtual Mode was not soon to end.

*Yes.*

Yes, indeed. This was, taken as a whole, a good life. That was Burgess' thought.

Nona started to make a separate tent for herself, but Colene stopped her. 'We can sleep together, as before. If I ever manage to get my act together, I don't care who sees it.'

'You know, Seqiro could enable you to —'

'But it wouldn't be real. I have to do it myself. And I will. In time. Somehow. Like learning to resist the telepaths. Maybe if I can do one, I can do the other. I dreamed I could multiply joy, a little. Just enough to make me good enough to marry Darius, in his Mode. But that would be no good, if I couldn't give myself to him. So I'll keep trying.'

'It does seem like a good approach,' Nona agreed. Then she had a dazzling thought. 'Maybe you can, indeed!'

'What do you mean? Sheer excitement's coming through.'

'Colene, at first you couldn't do telepathy, but now you are learning it, and getting better. Then you had a vision that I was in a wedding with Darius — and later it happened. Maybe you had precognition!'

Astonished, Colene considered the prospect. 'I did see it coming, only I didn't truly understand it. Like imperfect precog! And now I've dreamed I could learn joy. Could it happen?'

'You must try,' Nona said. 'Because if you could learn joy —'

'I'm going to try!' Colene said. 'I'm going to try everything! Maybe something'll come true!'

'Surely something will,' Nona agreed.

So she slept again by Darius' other side, with Burgess near, and Seqiro grazing outside. Nona had finally gotten smart about that, and grown him a patch of hay to chew on, so that he would not be diluting his substance with non-anchor Mode material.

In the morning, refreshed, they resumed travel. The paved streets became dirt roads, and then open countryside. Slopes developed. They had to help Burgess with the artificial paths again, but this was a practiced system now, and not much of an inconvenience.

'Uh-oh,' Colene said.

Nona hoped it wasn't what she feared it was, but it was. The mind predator had found Colene again. The girl was under siege, and they knew it would not relent until they got off the Virtual Mode. What were they to do?

Colene, dazed by the siege, began to babble, as she had before. But this time it was worse. 'I think I'll never lose the need, to cut myself and see me bleed,' she declaimed, holding out her arm as if offering it for the knife.

She was going into suicide mode!

*My Mode is close.*

'But you aren't welcome there,' Nona protested.

*Colene must be saved.*

Nona had to agree. She had brought them to her own Mode when Colene had been under siege before, though she would have preferred to avoid it. Then when Burgess had suffered his malady, Colene had brought them to her Mode, though she too would have preferred to avoid it. Now it was Seqiro's turn.

Yet in each case, good things had come of those visits to their anchor Modes. Maybe that would happen again.

They put Colene on Burgess, again. Seqiro could have carried her far more readily, but he could not shield her from the mind predator as effectively as Burgess could. They moved as rapidly as they could toward the anchor, while Colene hallucinated and cried out with her internal horrors.

Sometimes she seemed almost to make sense, but then would verge back into chaos.

'Nothing would make me happier than if some big piece of the cosmos just came through the ozone layer and just took me out. God, do I really want to live another year? The snow is everywhere, and life isn't necessarily all that exists.

'When the happiness ends . . . there is life in death . . . and the happiness I feel is the essence of that joy . . .'

Nona looked at Darius. Was Colene remembering their wedding night? Or was she into some deeper misery?

'I see a time when things weren't black or white or red and green but when they were always gray . . . I sit here and think about all the times that have been and all the lost causes, and I wonder if any of it was ever worth it, and these insights haunt my mind . . . as I try to think back to the good times, and the times when all things were good and there was no hate or frustration in the world but I can't remember, when I can only remember now and now is the time for all good men to come to the aid of our enemies – they should pick up guns and kill innocent people to show the loyalty to the red, white, and blue and every blessed child shall wave a flag to let the world know their confusion and when they grow up their lives should end each time they pop a pill to forget the latest problem and soon the nation's children will be grievers of Death and ruin and we shall live long and prosper and father children who have no mothers and they shall rock soulless babies to sleep and fate cuts the threads away and I shall find the magic that will take me away from all the pain and I will remain forever in a place not far from here and in this new existence I shall live . . .'

Nona hurt for her friend, unable to draw her out of her torment. They moved on as rapidly as they could, hoping they would reach the anchor in time.

'And the little boxes will clump together and gather into

331

one giant big box, and I'll be in it, and the lid will clamp down and I will suffocate and it will be my coffin forever and ever, amen . . .'

*We are approaching my Mode*, Seqiro thought. *But there is danger here, too.*

'We must proceed carefully,' Darius said, though Nona saw him wince as he looked at Colene. He loved her, and wanted to get her away from her pain as soon as possible. But they all knew that they could not allow Colene's pain to make them blunder into worse trouble.

As they came to it, they made a plan of approach. The anchor was in Seqiro's old stall, which might be closed or otherwise occupied. It would be disaster to barge through and discover another horse there. They would bounce off the other animal, and have to retreat, but the horse would know that Seqiro was returning.

He could explore ahead, since he could cross Modes with his mind, unlike most of his kind; he had practiced it, in anticipation of his tour on the Virtual Mode. But the moment his mind touch encountered another horse, his presence and identity would be known, and that would be similar mischief.

So they would send another person across first. Nona agreed to do it, as she might be able to extricate herself from a trap with magic. She would cross, look, and cross back to make her report. Then they would know what they faced.

They came to a region of paths and stalls. This was one of the adjacent Modes, similar to Seqiro's but not identical. There were other horses there, but they passed through as quickly and silently as they could, to arouse no commotion.

Then they were at the anchor. It was right at the entrance to a stall. The stall was empty, in this Mode, but that did not mean that the anchor stall was empty. Nona braced herself, and stepped through.

It was empty. In fact it was barred. Its door would not open. If Seqiro entered, he would be trapped.

She returned to report. 'Maybe I can get that door open before you go through.'

*The anchor is just outside the stall. I caught on to it with my head. I will need to enter the stall, then turn and go out beside the anchor. I was trapped before because of the closed gate. So that gate will have to be opened first.*

Fortunately there were no horses near. This entire wing seemed to be empty. She could work on the gate without arousing any creatures.

'I do not trust this,' Darius said. 'Is that wing normally empty?'

'No. It is a confinement section, with difficult horses placed there. That was why I was there. There are usually several scattered through it.'

'That suggests that they have something devious in mind,' Darius said. 'They may be waiting for you to reappear, so as to trap you.'

*This seems likely.*

'We shall need to interfere with that trap. Let me go through, to see whether my conjure magic works. If it does, we can escape readily enough.'

Darius went through, while Nona awaited nervously and Colene continued to groan sporadically. Nona knew that they could not afford to delay long; the mind predator seemed to be making faster progress against Colene this time, as if it had started where it left off before.

Darius returned. 'My magic does not work,' he reported grimly.

'Maybe mine does,' Nona said. 'Let me check.'

She went through again, and tried to levitate. She could not. She tried to make fire, but could not. She tried everything, and nothing worked. Not even illusion. She felt naked.

She returned to deliver the bad news: she had no special powers in the Horse Mode.

'Then we must do without magic,' Darius decided. 'I will explore the region, to find any other horse there, and determine the nature of the trap. I think I can resist a single horse long enough to get back to the anchor.'

*You can. You have done well, and the others will not be expecting resistance.*

Nona hated to offer objections, but had to. 'If Darius discovers the trap, and we avoid it, will they follow where we go, and catch us anyway?'

'There is a wild region nearby, where horses seldom go. If I went there and shut down my mind, they would have difficulty locating me.'

'So we could go there and hide, until the mind predator lost interest again,' Nona said, satisfied. 'Then we could return to the Virtual Mode and move quickly to your home Mode, Darius.'

'That seems feasible,' Darius agreed. He went through again for a longer exploration.

This time he returned with a more complete report. 'The entire wing is enclosed and locked,' he said. 'Each stall, and a stout fence around the whole. So if you thought you were free because you got out of the stall, you would be deceived. There is a mare in the farthest stall, but she seems listless; she did not react to my presence at all, and there was no mind attack. I think they have made this a solid prision, but I can use a tool to pry open the gates. They may think you will return alone, so have no such resource.'

*This seems likely. The mare — no reaction to you at all?*

'None. She seems mindless.'

*I fear she is. Now I appreciate the nature of the trap. They know I could not allow a mind-blasted mare to suffer.*

'Mind-blasted?' Nona asked, not liking this.

*When a horse goes truly wrong, it may be mentally destroyed. This can be done if two or more horses focus*

334

on it, breaking down its defense and destroying its mind. It can also happen when stallions fight. Such a creature is better off dead.

'That's horrible!' Nona agreed. 'But why is her presence a trap? If you can't do anything about it?'

*I would kill her, to end her suffering. Then the others would feel the death, and know that I had returned.*

'Kill her! Is there no alternative?'

*Sometimes a mind can be rebuilt. But there has to be a very specific template. Then the new mind honors that template, and the horse is in effect a new creature. The old mind can not be recovered. I could try that, but I have no template.*

Nona remembered something. 'Maresy!' she exclaimed. 'Doesn't Colene have an imaginary horse named that?'

*She does. But such a horse never existed, so could not be remade.*

'But it might be made new! Colene could give you all the particulars of her perfect horse!'

Darius shook his head. 'Colene is under siege herself.'

'But she won't be, the moment we pass through that anchor. I know she could do this, and would be glad to. We can save that mare, so she won't have to be killed, and there will be no alarm.'

Darius considered. 'This makes sense to me.'

*It may be possible.*

'Then let's try it! Darius, you open that gate, then we'll go through and tend to that mare, and then we'll go out to the wild region to hide. With luck, the other horses will never know, until we are gone.'

*They will realize when minions come to feed the mare, and she is gone.*

'And then it will be difficult to return to the anchor,' Darius said. 'But we face extreme alternatives, and this seems best. Colene is imaginative, and may be able to find a way back, when we are ready.'

'Should we leave our supplies here?' Nona asked. 'Just in case there is trouble?'

'There could be trouble *here*,' Darius said. 'A person of this Mode could pass by and steal our things.'

Nona appreciated the point. They would be safer keeping their supplies with them.

Then she thought of another problem. 'The other horses will know Seqiro's back the moment he uses his telepathy, even if no one actually sees us. So he should go mute, mentally.'

*But I must use my power to help the mare.*

'If you get identified, you will not have time to help the mare,' she said firmly. 'You will have to wait until you are hidden in the wild country to tend to her. One of us can lead the mare there, silently.'

*You could not do so. There must be a mental command.*

'I could not. Darius could not. But Colene could. She has some telepathy, probably too little to alert the horses, but enough to reach the mare for simple commands.'

He nodded. 'You do remind me of her at times. You are thinking of the things she would think of.'

'Thank you,' Nona said, trying not to blush at the compliment.

So Darius went through again, to fix the gate, and then the others, and they were through the anchor at last. Nona was relieved to see Colene relax, and then stir; her mind had not yet succumbed.

But she could not allow anyone to relax. There were essential things to be done. 'Colene,' she said. 'You must help us. We are in the Horse Mode — ' She broke off, realizing that with Seqiro mentally mute, her words were not being translated. This was a complication she had overlooked.

The girl looked at her blankly, then at Seqiro. She said something indecipherable.

'Colene!' Nona said. 'Use your own telepathy!' She pointed to her own head. 'Think at me!'

336

'What's wrong?' Colene asked, projecting her thought.

Nona focused her thoughts as well as she could, summarizing the situation. Horse Mode. Unfriendly horses. Mental silence. Need to hide. Mind-blasted mare.

In a moment Colene understood. 'Thanks, Nona. I'll take it from here. You stay with the boys.'

# 15

## *Horse*

Colene found herself in a horse stall, with Nona talking at
her. But the words weren't making sense. Was this another
bad vision sponsored by the mind predator, with Nona about
to turn into a horse and claim to be Seqiro? Or something
more believable but insidious? Such as offering to enter into
a mutual suicide pact? Colene had been trying to fight, but
the battle had exausted her, and she knew she couldn't last
much longer.

Then Nona pointed to her head, and Colene realized that
she wanted the telepathy. Where was Seqiro? Had something
happened to him? If so, Colene hoped that this *was* a dream,
so she could move on to the next horror, and the horse would
be safe. So she used her mind. *What's wrong?*

Then she got it in a fast summary, and made sense of
the situation. This was reality. They had brought her to
Seqiro's Mode, where Seqiro's enemies held sway, so Seqiro
didn't dare use his telepathy lest it give away his presence
here. Colene understood that problem; she had been
stunned by another horse here before. They had to hide
from the horses here, until the mind predator departed the
Virtual Mode.

But what was this about a mind-blasted mare? Quickly
Colene got the details from Nona. It seemed a lot like what
the mind predator was trying to do to Colene herself. Oh,
yes, she would help the mare!

She went to the mare. The horse was in a pitiful state.
Her dark coat was soiled, her mane tangled, and her eyes
were dull. Every so often she kicked randomly at the side
of her stall, and sometimes she banged her head into it.
Streaks of blood on her neck suggested prior bangings.

As Colene tried to enter the stall, the mare went wild. She threw herself from side to side, and foam appeared at her mouth. Her eyes were wide and her ears flat back. She was a fair-sized mare, about sixteen hands, much larger than Colene, but she was terrified.

Yet there was no evidence of any injury that was not self-inflicted. No one had been physically brutalizing this horse. She was merely in a nearly mindless state, afraid of any other creature. She was not rational. Her awareness was chaos.

She had, in effect, been raped. Savagely.

Colene could relate well enough to that. She started at the beginning. *You are Maresy*, she thought firmly. Because nothing remained of the mare's former personality; she was a frightened foal in a grown body. Like a crashed computer, she had to be restructured, given new organization. She had to be given a new identity, and trained in its ways. Colene had borrowed the name of her imaginary horse from one in an old popular song dating from her grandparents' days she remembered as *Lamzy Divey*, which seemed like gibberish until pronounced carefully: 'Mares eat oats and does eat oats and little lambs eat ivy, and a kid'll eat ivy too. Wouldn't you?' Later she had learned that the name was spelled Marezy, but in her mind it remained with the *s*. She couldn't be responsible for the spelling of prior ages.

The mare had no other source of information She became Maresy.

*I am your friend.*

The mare calmed. She was no longer being threatened.

*Follow me.*

Colene opened the stall and Maresy stepped out. Colene walked toward the other members of the hive. She kept her communications brief, because she wasn't sure that the other horses couldn't tune in on her thoughts as well as Seqiro's. She hoped that her telepathic power was so small that it was beneath the threshold of background mental noise, and therefore invisible at a distance. But she was taking no unnecessary chances. *Ignore all others; just stay with me.*

Darius nodded approvingly as Colene and Maresy joined them. He had opened the outer gate. But before they left, they had to change clothing. Nona was returning with an armful of it; Seqiro must have explained the need to her before they went through the anchor.

They changed, donning loincloths, capes, sandals, and beanie-type hats with tassels. Colene made sure the tassels fell in the right direction; they were an indication of status, and an error could lead to immediate trouble. Such as proclaiming sexual interest in a stranger one happened to pass on a path. Darius and Nona seemed dubious about the clothing, but Colene donned hers, assuring them that this was in order. So they followed her example.

They walked out and away from the prison complex. There were fields of growing grain, with human laborers. They wore similar costumes, vaguely resembling Chinese coolies. Seqiro, Maresy, and the three humans rated only cursory glances; obviously the horses were taking them on some errand. Now if no horse sought mind contact, they might be home free. For a while.

*Who?*

The query was imperative, and not friendly. Definitely not Seqiro. Trouble.

Colene caught Darius' eye. She pointed to her head. He nodded, pointing to his own; he had received it too. It was probably a routine query because someone didn't know what the party was doing in this vicinity.

They didn't answer. They walked rapidly for the edge of the cultivated region. With luck there would not be any quick follow-up, and they could reach the wild section before the pursuit began. As Colene understood it, to exert control a horse had either to know the mind of a person or another horse, or know that person's location. In the wild place, location would be concealed, and the enemy horses would not be able to get a proper fix on strange minds. As long as Seqiro kept mental silence, he remained anonymous, and perhaps almost invisible, in that sense.

*Who?* This time the query was more insistent.

Still they did not answer. It was better to be anonymous than known, however suspicious that might be. A horse was not supposed to mess with the minions of another horse, and as long as they remained anonymous, they could be taken for such minions.

Then a man appeared at the edge of the field. His tassel was in an unfamiliar position. Colene suspected that he was a minion of the querying horse. He would surely recognize Maresy by sight, and realize that the trap had sprung. He had to be stopped before he made that connection and relayed it mentally to his master.

Colene ran to Burgess, who was floating along between the two horses, shielded from general view by their bodies. She clapped a hand on a contact point. 'Burg! Can you shoot that far? Take that man out?'

Burgess lifted his trunk, aimed it, settled to the ground for better purchase, and let fly a single small stone. He had certainly recovered; the stone arced way over the field, and struck the man on the head. He fell.

'Great shot, airhead!' she exclaimed. On Shale the humans had been as effective as the floaters, throwing stones, but this was a shot whose range and accuracy was beyond the power of most humans. Burgess was healthier than normal, thanks to the magnesium. Maybe he was bingeing on too much of it, and should ease off. But not right now!

They broke into a run, because now it was obvious that they were not a routine party on routine business. But the workers in the field ignored them; they must be under the direction of horses who weren't paying attention, or perhaps were working on their own, unmonitored.

They left the field and came to a path leading into a river

valley. Seqiro abruptly cut away from this and moved across a sloping fallow field toward a forested mountain. He knew where to go, and did not need to use his mind to show them.

But here Burgess had trouble. The slope and roughness were too great. They had to pause while Nona expanded the artificial path — and Nona spread her hands helplessly. Oh, no! Her magic didn't work here!

Seqiro cut to the side, finding a contour. Darius took a stick and bashed down weeds and bushes. They made a crude path for Burgess, and the floater was able to use it, slowly.

Men appeared in the field behind. These were definitely minions of a dominant horse. They were armed with clubs and knives and were approaching purposefully. It would not be possible to outrun those, with Burgess so slow, and a beaten path left behind.

Then she had a brighter notion. A river! If there were a river anywhere near, Burgess could float on that, leaving no trail.

Colene went to Seqiro. She signaled to him to bring his head down. She put her head to his. *River!* she thought, in what she hoped was a limited, noninterceptable signal. *Burgess — river.*

Seqiro's ears perked. He led the way down into a winding gully. Burgess was able to follow, because of the downslope. At the base was a section of exposed rock, also suitable for the floater. Finally it led to a river, large enough to have a smooth surface. Ideal!

Burgess floated out on the water. The rest of them made their way along the bank. They melted into the increasingly rugged land. Now it would be difficult indeed for the minions of the horses to locate them.

Indeed, the pursuit seemed to peter out. There was no longer a path to follow, and Burgess might as well have ceased to exist, because the horses would have no idea he could use water as a highway. They had escaped.

But they were hardly out of trouble. They had to maintain mental silence, so couldn't hold much of a dialogue. Nona could not do magic, so they had to use their own supplies and forage from the land. Getting back to the anchor would be a formidable problem, because the horses would certainly be waiting in ambush there.

Colene knew that the others had come here because of the mind predator's attack on her. They had taken an awful risk. So now she had to do her part.

Maresy had faithfully followed her, ignoring the others. Seqiro had known they couldn't leave the mare in the prison stall. It was time to restore her to a fully functional state.

While the others set up camp, Colene tackled the mare. Maresy was a good deal smaller than Seqiro, but still a pretty fine solid horse with good muscle under her matted coat. Her shoulder was four inches above the top of Colene's head, but not above Nona's. Colene put her head up against Maresy's head, so as to fire short-range thoughts into it. She had a mental picture of those thoughts passing through the mare's head and being largely stifled there, like the sound of a gun with a silencer, so that only unrecognizable fragments radiated out for enemy horses to intercept. Maybe that wasn't accurate, but it allowed her to use her telepathy to train the mare.

'Maresy. I am your friend Colene. I will not be with you long, but I will help you to be a full horse again. You have been badly hurt in your mind, but you can recover.' If only Colene could recover from her own hurt, and be a true woman to Darius! 'First I will check you and brush you and see to your injuries. You must not hurt yourself any more. You must take care of yourself, and not be afraid.'

Colene got a brush, and worked on Maresy's coat as she continued talking. Her mental contact with the horse was getting easier, because she was becoming more familiar with

343

Maresy, and because Maresy's own telepathy was beginning to manifest. Colene thought of the computer analogy, again: a blank disk and blank memory did nothing, but a little bit of programming could enable them to start to help themselves. The power was there, it just had to be structured. Colene did not encourage the mare to use her mind that way, because that could alert the bad horses. She just wanted the mare to listen to her thoughts and understand. What she hoped to do was shape Maresy into the horse Colene had dreamed of, before she met Seqiro, because she knew more about that horse than any other. Maresy was, above all, a competent, self-assured, sensible, *nice* creature, very good at listening. Just the way Seqiro had turned out to be.

'Let me tell you about Maresy, before you lost your memory,' Colene said, working a burr out of the horse's mane. 'I am an introspective sort. I like to express my thoughts. But sometimes I have trouble writing fast enough to keep my thoughts going in a straight line. I have so much verbal information hit me at once that I can't write or type fast enough to get it out. And talking just does not work. I can't talk as fast as I think, but I speak faster than I write. Speaking and talking are different. Talking is two-way; speaking is one-way. Your thoughts get interrupted by the other person when you talk. I get the greatest ideas when I'm just lying there on my bed nearly asleep, letting my thoughts wander. They wander where they will. My thoughts are like my hair: they have a mind of their own. I've created whole worlds, then lost the greatest part of my creations when I fell asleep. My shoddy memory just can't get it right the next day.

'But with Maresy it was always all right. Because Maresy heard and understood everything I said, and didn't interrupt. Or forget. Just as you are doing now. She was the ideal listener. Sometimes I did write to her, too, and she never chided me for being slow. It was all right with her how much time I took.

344

'You know, I used to be shy. Then I went from shy to downright antisocial. No one knew, because I pretended I wasn't. I was always pretty good at fooling people, especially myself. Of course it happened gradually, so I could adjust. I know I'm not truly antisocial because I'm lonely as all hell. If I was antisociety I wouldn't give a flying dump about the human race. I do give. So I filled the void with a nonhuman pen-pal, and that was Maresy. I could tell her anything, and she never told anyone else. She always kept my secrets. I discovered I could not relate to your average run-of-the-mill teenagers. Because when I became a teenager I was neither average nor run-of-the-mill. I was the classic description of still waters run deep. School became for me the root of all evil. I tried to forget it existed. But it was hard to do when I did homework for four hours every night. I never could just skim a chapter then say I'd read it. I was honest to a fault. Honest to the point of not having FUN like a normal person. It got painful to hear other kids laugh. It was more painful to see them kiss. The only romance I had was in romance novels, which I read by the truckload. That was my life: schoolwork ('cuz nothing else about the school experience applied to me) and romance novels. I love fantasy, but it's not plentiful in small-town libraries. Romance, on the other hand, was available from anywhere from a nickel to fifty cents at just about any yard sale in the state. I would buy like twenty or thirty at a time, read them, and trade them. I've read so many formula stories I can't keep most of them straight.

'Of course some of what I read did stand out. There was this hardcore erotic novel an old man in a hospital showed me. Now I know I didn't understand it at all. If I had, I would have known better than to let four horny freaks get me alone in an apartment. And I couldn't tell anyone about that, either. Except Maresy. Life sucks. I hate school. I love to learn. This is no paradox. So I learned that honesty doesn't necessarily pay, and I learned to fool everyone. The funny thing was, I became the life of the crowd. A popular girl. A socialite. But it was all a lie, and I was slicing my wrists in the toilet. Just never had the nerve to go all the way and die. But Maresy understood. She understood how life is one long unending irony. Irony is what I live on. It keeps me going. If you can't see the humor in your existence any more, at least look for the irony. As far as I was concerned, for a while, it was reason enough to stay alive, just to be able to thumb my nose at existence. By the way, Alive and Exist are as much alike as Talk and Speak.

'You know, I came to feel that ninety per cent of my classmates were plastic. Shallow as a credit card. I discovered that I'm not a herd animal, and never will be. I also discovered that the key to sanity is to take the entire world with a grain of salt. To have a finely tuned sense of the ridiculous. I'm looking for other people who realize that the universe is one big contradiction, and the only true purpose to life is to smell the flowers and hug your friends. Life can be beautiful if you let it. There was this song by Nirvana, ''It Smells Like Teen Spirit.'' I really liked it, even if the lyrics were senseless. I understand the song got its name from a deodorant commercial, with three or four young women wearing bright but nonthreatening clothing with conservative but bouncy shoulder-length hair, glistening smiles, and peppy attitudes. They liked this deodorant because it smelled like teen spirit. The first time I saw that ad I thought ''this is the stupidest most patronizing thing to grace the small screen I've ever had the misfortune to see.'' I don't think girls like that exist. They're like every suburban mother's fantasy child. Besides, Teen Spirit, if condensed down to a scent, wouldn't be peppy, light, bright, and fresh, it'd be dark, angry, clashing, reckless, sexual, wild — despair and exultation in a bottle.'

Colene paused in her monologue. She had gotten the coat

nicely brushed out, and the mane untangled. Maresy was looking good, now: a mare whose brown hair matched Colene's, just as Seqiro's did. 'Am I boring you? You don't really have to listen to all this, you know. You just have to pick up the way you are from my mind: the perfect mare. I've just come out of a siege with a mind predator, and all this horror of my past life has really been freshened up, because that's what the predator was doing to make me capitulate. But it really helps to have you listen, Maresy.'

Maresy turned her head to nuzzle Colene's cheek. *I understand.*

Colene hugged her around the neck. 'You're back, Maresy. Just like before. Only now there are others. They are all your friends.'

She looked around. More time had passed than she had thought. The camp had been made, and the others were eating. 'Come on, Maresy. I never introduced you to them.'

She did so. Now Maresy did not shy away at all; she was poised and friendly. Darius patted her, and she did not flinch; Nona offered her a carrot, and she ate it; Burgess lifted a trunk, and she touched it with her nose. Then, surprised, she lowered her nose to touch one of his contact points.

The others stared. Maresy was establishing contact with the floater, his way!

Then she met Seqiro. They sniffed noses. Then Seqiro sent a single, amazed thought to Colene: *She has been restored! Without the intercession of another horse.*

'All I did was talk to her,' Colene said. 'And share my feelings. Just as I used to do with Maresy of Earth.' But she realized it had been more than that. She had projected her mind to the mare, in a continuing stream, and the mare had accepted it and been defined by it. Now Maresy was the horse Colene had loved, because Colene had defined her. It had been, in its way, an act of creation.

347

Colene went to have her supper. Nona gave Maresy a dish of feed, and she ate it without concern. Then they turned in for the night, this time with two horses eating hay nearby. Seqiro seemed interested in Maresy, perhaps still amazed that Colene had been able to handle the restoration alone. It had been some time since he had had a companion of his own species, and perhaps he had missed it. Colene remembered that horses generally preferred to associate with their own kind, if they had a choice. Had she been depriving Seqiro, all this time?

It was good to be alive, even with mental silence and a language barrier. Colene had thought that it was Seqiro's mental ambience that made all the difference, but now it was absent, and they were still the hive. With another member, for a while. What more could she ask for?

She reached out to touch Darius' shoulder. She knew what more. But she just wasn't ready for that, yet.

In the morning the news was bad. Darius had been exploring, and had discovered that a formidable party of minions was approaching the wild country. It might be several hundred. He put his head next to Colene's, so that she could read his image directly, and she saw that it was so. The horse masters intended to locate the fugitives physically, so that mental silence would not allow them to hide any more.

What were they to do? Colene knew that this was a dire strait, because the horses meant only mischief to Seqiro. But there had to be some way out. Colene was normally suicidal, but now she was perversely positive.

She put her head next to Seqiro's, using her limited-range telepathy instead of his. 'Why do they hate you? Aside from your independence?'

*I am a potential rival for leadership, because of my size and power of mind. I do not seek it, but the lead stallion does not believe that.*

She knew that Seqiro just wanted to explore and learn new things, and have a sweet human girl or two to dote on him without being coerced. He had found exactly that on the Virtual Mode. After seeing the ways of power in the Julia Mode, she had a better understanding. Small, greedy minds *did* seek power, and believed others were out to take it from them. So this was in that fashion an ordinary situation.

But in that case, all they had to do was satisfy the horses that Seqiro was not going to stay, just as Nona had not stayed in her Mode. 'Can you tell them you're going away again?'

*They would believe it a ruse, or that I would return with formidable creatures from other Modes.*

Um, yes; paranoia had an evil rationalization for everything, and would not be persuaded of innocence. But something else bothered her. 'There must be many rivals for power; why should they be so hot after just this one, Seqiro?'

*There are not many. I am the only one who matched Koturo in mind. If he eliminates me, there will be no real threat to his dominance for some time.*

Koturo. The lead stallion. That figured. But still she wasn't satisfied. 'Do the other horses support him? I mean, don't they have some choice in the matter? Maybe some of them would like you better.'

*Many would. They would not ordinarily support him in this. But he trumped up a charge against me, so I was confined with my minions while they investigated it. It was a false charge, as they must have discovered, but in the interim I escaped to the Virtual Mode with you.*

Okay. So now there should be no charge against him. Yet they were acting as if there were. So a new, worse charge must have been trumped up in his absence. 'And I know what that is!' Colene exclaimed. 'Maresy! They will be saying that you were the one who mind-blasted her!'

*Surely so. It is a serious crime, equivalent to your rape.*

'But you didn't do it! She wasn't there when I came to you, and you couldn't have done it after you went on the Virtual Mode.'

*True. But Koturo will have claimed I did, and his minions will support him.*

'Then you can deny it, and your minions will support you! That would make it your word against his. What happens then?'

*Then it would be a matter of challenge. But my minions will not support me; they were removed when I was confined. That is how I was confined, because only human minions can operate the mechanisms of the stalls.*

'This challenge,' she persisted. 'Exactly what happens there?'

*When there is a question of honor between two horses, they may be obliged to settle it by mental and physical combat. The presumption is that the one who has the right of the case will prevail.*

Colene bore down. 'Exactly what kind of combat? I mean, do you try to mind-blast each other? In which case, why bother with anything physical?'

*One horse can not readily destroy the mind of another. It is easier to defend than to attack, in this respect. So the minions attack the opponent's minions physically, supported by their master, and the minions that prevail then attack the other horse physically. If they can injure him sufficiently, or if he is distracted by having to use his mind to try to wrest control of them from the other horse, he may be laid open to an effective mind attack.*

'Like chess!' she said. 'The king never leaves the board, but if he is trapped, the game is lost. Only the lesser pieces get wiped out. They count only for what they can do to protect their king.'

*Your mind indicates a game situation which is parallel to the case here. The losing horse is seldom killed; his mind*

350

*is restored on another pattern, one which will not be a problem to the winner.*

Colene had one more concern. 'Seqiro, if you had to fight — could you do it? I mean, not get skunked?'

*Ordinarily I could.*

'Okay. So all we need to do is prove to the other horses that you have a case, and then you can challenge Koturo. That should set the matter to rights.'

*But I lack my minions, and without them I would not be able to prevail.*

'Your old minions, maybe. But you have new ones. The four of us. Do we qualify?'

Seqiro was startled. *Your are not minions. You are free companions.*

Colene went to Darius and touched heads. 'Would you mind fighting for Seqiro? If it got us out of this mess?'

*I am not a fighter,* he thought in reply. *But I see little hope in the present situation. If this offers a better chance, I would do it.*

She went to Nona with the same query. *If I had my magic —*

'I wish I knew why you don't. I think it was Seqiro's ambience that brought your magic to Earth, where magic never worked before. So you should have magic here. But I can't argue with the fact that you don't. So it's just you, yourself. Would you fight for Seqiro?'

*I would. But I fear I would be a liability. I am no good with physical weapons, and I lack the fighting spirit you have.*

'With Seqiro in your mind, you'll have it.'

Nona nodded. *I will do it.*

Colene went to Burgess, grabbing a contact point and describing the situation as well as she could, not sure he could grasp it.

For answer, he fired a stone into a tree, hard.

She returned to Seqiro. 'We will be your minions. How do we proceed?'

*One of you must go to establish that the charge is in question, and that I wish to challenge. But it means laying one's whole mind open to the horses, and this is not comfortable.*

'I'll go! It's my idea.'

*Then you must wear your tassel so.* He made a mental picture for her to read, showing the position.

Colene explained to the others. Then she set her tassel and marched toward the enemy.

The moment she was alone, she began to doubt. She knew how strong the mental powers of the horses were, and she knew how many guilty little secrets she had hidden in the cluttered recesses of her mind. Was she doing the right thing, or merely bringing disaster upon them all?

But what else was there to do? They would not be able to hide for long, or to resist after they were located. So she went on, trying to quell her nervousness. It couldn't be worse than the mind predator, after all.

In due course she encountered the first servant. The net was closing in; she had acted none too soon. The man took one look at her tassel, and signaled her to follow him. Soon she stood before a handsome mare.

*Who?*

'I am Colene. Seqiro's minion. I know he did not blast that mare. He was with me on the Virtual Mode when that happened.' As far as she knew, that was true.

She felt the mare's mind exploring hers. Language was no problem to the horses; they read thoughts directly. Truth was no problem either; a horse could read a falsehood as readily as a truth, and know it for what it was. Evidently a horse could lie, and make his minions lie, but Seqiro was not protecting her from this verification by the mare. She hoped that her evidence was enough to satisfy this horse that Seqiro had a case.

*You have some telepathy of your own!* the mare thought, surprised.

'I learned it from Seqiro. Does it matter?'

*You restored the mare! Seqiro could not have taught you that.*

'I guess maybe I have some talents of my own, and I'm gradually learning how to use them. I do love horses, and maybe that helped. But you can read my mind. You can see that — '

*Seqiro has a case. We support his right to challenge Koturo.*

Just like that! But of course with telepathic communication, it could be very fast.

The mare turned and walked away. So did the nearby minions.

'But what am I supposed to do?' Colene demanded.

There was no answer. So she shrugged and went back the way she had come.

When she reached Seqiro, and told him what had happened, there was a sudden change. His mind came back, encompassing hers, and all of them were able to understand each other again. *We must go to the field*, he thought.

'But aren't there arrangements to make, or anything?' Colene asked. 'I mean, they just walked away.'

*My right to challenge was granted. They read your mind and saw that my case was valid.*

'You mean we don't have to hide any more?' Nona asked, relieved.

They reviewed it as they struck camp and walked back down the river to the field that would be the challenge site. A challenge was fair; there would be one horse and four minions on each side, and no other horse or minions would interfere. The winner would have the right of the case. The loser would in effect be dead. The winner would take over the minions of the loser — all of them, not just those participating in the challenge. And that would be it.

The only problem was that the minions could get themselves killed during the combat. Even if Seqiro won, one or more members of the hive might be dead. Colene had found a way out of their predicament, but the cost might be suicidally high. Which was perhaps par for her course.

The details were arranged by the horses, so rapidly that there was no delay. The combat would occur on the following morning, and probably be done within an hour. Meanwhile, they were free; no one would molest them. It was all very civilized, in a medieval way. They even had the use of several stalls for the night, and could fetch water from a nearby cistern.

Colene expected to be too uptight to eat supper, but she wasn't; Seqiro made her mind relax. She feared she would be unable to sleep, but she was slumbering before she knew it. Seqiro again. The funny thing was that he did not seem concerned about the event of the morrow. They did not discuss it, or review tactics or anything; they just ignored it. Seqiro and Maresy ambled out to the field to graze.

Then, in her hidden (she hoped) thought, she realized what Seqiro was doing: he was concealing the devious advantages his minions might have. They knew that Colene had some telepathy, but it was so slight compared to that of any of the horses that they surely discounted it. Yet it might enable her to do something on her own, without having to draw from Seqiro's power. Nona — was it possible that she could find a bit of her magic, when she needed it? That might help a lot. Darius — he was now able to resist the mind control of a horse, which meant that Seqiro might not have to protect him that way. Colene might resist some too, though she had lost her chance to practice when the mind predator attacked. And Burgess was almost immune anyway. So they just might represent a formidable array of minions, freeing Seqiro to act with force where he needed to. They might have a hidden advantage. She hoped.

\*     \*     \*

When she woke, well rested, daylight was firm and servants were arriving in clusters. There were no horses, apart from Seqiro and Maresy — because, Colene realized, they did not need to witness it visually. They could receive it from their minions, sent here for the purpose. They could also tune in on the battling minds of the two participating horses.

There was time for a quick breakfast. Then they took the field without ceremony. It was large, and they were not restricted to it; once commenced, the battle could continue anywhere. But it would not be stopped until there was a victor. It seemed pointless to waste one's energy fleeing, because that would just give the advantage to the pursuit. There was an array of weapons roughly defining the main arena: clubs, knives, pitchforks, crowbars, and stones. It was apparent that no one would be caught weaponless; there would always be another lying nearby.

Nona gazed at the scene, and shuddered. She had no confidence in her ability to wield any of those implements in attack or defense. Colene marked where the knives were; she wanted to be sure to have one at all times, because she was not afraid to use it. The gravity of the situation was clarifying; this was indeed a deadly serious encounter. Yet could it be worse than getting surrounded and attacked in the forest? Better to have a fighting chance, literally.

Koturo appeared, marching in from a farther pasture. He was a large horse, similar to Seqiro, with a black hide speckled with white patches. He looked mean. He was flanked by four minions: two men and two women. They looked mean too. The five of them took a stance in the center of the field, weaponless, about fifty feet away. It was possible that they could conceal weapons under their capes, but Colene doubted it; the horses had control, and any cheating would be noted.

Seqiro stood in the center of his force, facing the other stallion. Nona and Colene were to his right, opposite the two enemy women. Darius and Burgess were to his left, facing the two men. The horses would have gotten Burgess' nature and capabilities from Colene's mind; evidently they felt he was a fair substitute for a human man. There were no rocks in the center, so he was weaponless too. But how was he going to get direction from Seqiro? A person had to touch a contact point to communicate with him, and then it could seem indirect, because of Burgess' fuzzy notion of self.

The four enemy minions reached up and turned their tassels to combat position. Seqiro's three humans did the same, acting on a nudge from the horse. The battle was on.

Neither horse moved. Instead the minions moved. One man kept his place, while the other ran to the side toward the weapons. The women did the same, one standing and watching Nona and Colene while the other went for weapons.

Nona gave a savage cry and charged the standing woman. Colene realized that Seqiro was directing her. But Colene herself felt nothing. Not even a mental suggestion.

She glanced across at the men. Darius was standing guard while Burgess floated toward a region of stones. Seeing that, the standing man was starting to advance to intercept the floater, and Darius was starting to intercept the man.

Suddenly Colene put it together: all Koturo's minions were under his mental control, acting in concert. Some were watching the opposition, while others were fetching weapons. It made sense. But only one was under Seqiro's control: Nona, who needed it most. Burgess was independent, because neither horse could control him. Darius and Colene were free, because they could be trusted to use their own initiative. Thus Seqiro could concentrate his power more effectively. Because his minions served him willingly, while Koturo's minions could not be trusted on their own.

Even as she realized this, Colene was launching herself at the woman going for the weapons. A weapon was too great an advantage; the forces had to stay even, at least until her own side could get the advantage.

The woman, seeing her, ran. But Colene had gotten up speed, and gained on her. As the woman bent to sweep up a club, Colene tackled her. They fell among the clubs in a tangle of limbs.

The woman was no patsy. She rolled over, wrestling Colene down with superhuman strength. The horse was doing that – and Colene lacked that support. She realized that this was because it was going to Nona, so she could try to overcome her minionette, but this left Colene in a bad position. Already she was on her back, pinned at the throat while the woman reached for a club. Why did Seqiro think she could handle this tigress on her own?

Because of her own little bit of telepathy. And her suicidal nature.

Colene went to it. She clapped both her hands on the woman's arm, wrenching it up. It was like moving a branch from a tree, but she did succeed in getting the hand up across her chin as she twisted her neck. Then, quickly, she snapped her head around and bit the hand, hard.

The woman didn't even react. She continued to grasp for a club with her free hand. *Koturo had blocked off her pain!* She probably didn't even realize what Colene was doing.

So Colene chomped down again, as hard as she could. And a third time, gnawing at that hand. She felt gristle and tasted blood as the woman finally got the club and brought it about.

Colene's teeth had taken their toll. The woman's hand was no longer able to maintain its purchase, not because of lack of will or strength, but because the tendons had been chewed and the blood made Colene's face and neck slippery. Colene wrenched her neck free and grabbed for the club. They rolled over, as the woman tried to grasp and hold Colene with her injured hand. The thing about pain was that

357

it warned a person not only of danger, but that an appendage was not up to snuff. This woman still didn't know that her hand wasn't working at a hundred per cent.

The club came up. That could still finish Colene, even if ineffectively swung. So she focused all her mental energy at the woman and thought: *drop it!*

The hand opened, letting the club drop. The woman had taken it for a command from her master, and obeyed, though Colene's own thought could hardly have had strength enough to do it. Score one for surprise.

They rolled again, as the woman grasped for another club. Now they were in a region of knives. The woman reached for one with her injured hand, failed to catch it properly, and for the first time actually looked at the hand. Now she — and her master — realized what had happened. She paused for just a moment.

Colene grabbed a knife, whipped it up, and stabbed it at the woman's face. To her amazement, she scored. The point of the knife plunged into the woman's mouth and through to her throat, inside.

Then Colene realized that Seqiro had lent her a moment's force, guiding her hand with unerring power in that instant of advantage. The woman was dead, or soon would be.

Colene scrambled up, grabbed another knife, and ran back to the knot of bodies that represented Nona and her minionette. They were at an impasse, each controlled by a horse, their special powers canceling each other out. In an ordinary contest, the stronger horse would eventually enable his minions to prevail. But this one wasn't ordinary.

Colene did not hesitate. She came up behind the enemy woman and stabbed for her neck. But the woman twisted aside with an awareness that could only have been that of the horse, and Colene's thrust caught Nona's shoulder. Nona did not react; Seqiro had blocked off her pain. But Colene, horrified, jerked the knife back — and again struck with awesome speed and precision, slicing the point across the other woman's throat. Blood poured out, and the woman lost concentration. Colene used her knee to shove the body to the side, and reached out to help Nona. 'I'm so sorry −'

But this was not the time for that. Nona was injured, her cape soaked with fresh blood, and needed healing − and there was only one place for it. She could heal herself in the Virtual Mode, where her magic worked. Where she would be safe. So Colene led Nona away from the battle, to the stalls, where the anchor was. No one interfered; this was all part of the battle.

But Nona herself protested. 'You can't leave the others,' she gasped, spitting out a bit of reddish froth. The stab must have punctured a lung. 'You have to help them. I can make my own way.'

Colene knew she was right. The stab was bad, but she was able to walk, and could probably manage to cover the distance before losing too much blood. Triage: she was one of the walking wounded. But others might be killed, if Colene did not get back into the fray immediately. 'Go heal yourself − and if we don't make it, go home.'

Nona nodded. Then Colene turned and ran back to rejoin the battle.

She saw the two enemy women lying where they had been downed. What a vicious fighter Colene had turned out to be, with her favored weapon and Seqiro's power to guide her at key moments! She knew she should be appalled and sickened, but right now she was on a suicidal high. A berserker, heedless of the carnage.

The males were still battling. Burgess had reached the stones, but the minion had reached Burgess, and was tipping him over. Burgess weighed about four hundred pounds, but the man heaved with superhuman strength, and the floater went over on his top. For the first time she saw his underside, with the gills waving like fine foliage.

The man used stones to prop Burgess upside down, then

snatched up two clubs and headed back to join the other minion. It was about to be two against one, with the two armed and the one unarmed. That made sense; the man probably didn't know how to kill Burgess quickly, so saved time by taking him out of circulation while he went after the more dangerous one. Burgess' mental independence had proved to be no avantage. The enemy horse had figured out how to handle the alien creature.

But Colene was charging across the field while she observed. She would not let Darius fight alone!

Then she felt a nudge in her mind. Just enough to signal her the way Seqiro wanted her to go. Not toward Darius. Toward Burgess.

But Darius could be killed in the seconds she took to try to help Burgess!

Yet despite that, she yielded to the judgment of the horse, and swerved to go to Burgess. She had to trust Seqiro to know his tactical situation best. The two men closed in on Darius, the one tossing a club to the other.

Then the men hesitated. Colene felt the periphery of a terrible mental battle. The two horses were struggling for mental control of the two minions. Koturo had the advantage, because they were his minions, but Seqiro was able to reduce their efficiency so that they staggered and fell before straightening out and stalking Darius. Darius, however, was free to move at full speed. He could disarm one, or run for his own weapon.

But Darius did not. He too staggered and fell. Koturo was trying to take over his body. Then he stood straight, flinging out his arms in a gesture of defiance. He had blocked the enemy horse's attack! Which meant the home team had taken the advantage, because Koturo was struggling to control three men, while Seqiro could focus on two.

Colene reached Burgess. He was in a sad state, with his trunks flattened under his own weight, his contact points jamming into the turf, and his eye stalks retracted. She swept out the stones propping him, then bent at one side, grasped two contact points, and heaved. He was four times her weight, but Seqiro gave her a flash of strength, and the floater went up and over. He landed with a muffled whomp — because he was frantically pumping air as he came down, cushioning the shock.

Colene grabbed on to two more contact points. 'Pump rocks, Burg! We need you!'

The floater extended an eye stalk. Colene saw with horror that the other two had been squashed, and were useless. The third was operative — but the eyeball was unable to travel to its end. He was blind.

'I'll be your eyes!' Colene cried. She focused on the three men, who were doing an odd dance: Darius was unarmed and fast, the other two armed and slow. Darius could avoid them, but could not disarm one without getting smashed by the other. It was a standoff, for the moment. 'Can you see the targets?'

No. Colene's mental picture was fuzzy for him, so that he could not distinguish one vague shape from another.

'Then let me call out the shots, like a cannon with a surveyed site,' she said. There was a large artillery base near where she lived, so she had picked up a bit about what the big guns did and how they oriented. 'Just get these straight: range and direction. Fire where I tell you. But first go to the side for ammunition.'

Burgess pumped more air, and lurched to the side, finding the rocks. His two trunks seemed to be functioning, if slightly squashed. He sucked up a rock and fired it out. It struck the ground not far away, and in the wrong direction.

'Next shot,' Colene said. 'Quarter turn to the right, and twice as far.'

The next rock fell near the three men. It was working!
'Next shot: just a bit farther, just a bit left.'
The third rock struck one of the minions on the leg. He

did not react; his pain had been blocked. That was fine with Colene. She didn't want him hurting, she wanted him incapacitated or dead. With no pain, he would not take evasive action. 'Next shot: same direction, little bit higher.'

The next rock missed, because the man had moved. But it was right where it belonged.

'Hold it, now,' Colene said. 'Fire when I tell you.' She watched the men move. When one minion started to go back to the key spot, Colene called the shot. 'Now.'

The rock struck the minion in the head. The man went down, unconscious. Great!

Now Koturo recognized the threat. The remaining minion broke away from Darius and ran toward Burgess, dodging. He would be almost impossible to hit.

But Darius was chasing him. In a moment the two men were locked in hand-to-hand combat, fighting for the club. A rock could hit either one, so was too risky.

Colene thought of something else. 'Eighth turn to the right. Double distance. Fire.'

The rock sailed out — and just missed the enemy stallion. The pieces were putting the king in check.

Now Koturo moved. He started toward Burgess. The horse might weigh a ton, literally; he could trample Burgess in short order.

But Seqiro also moved, to intercept the enemy stallion. It was going to come to direct physical combat between them.

Colene pondered her course, quickly. With the two horses together, stones were too risky. Darius remained locked with the other minion. But Colene was free.

'Stay here, Burg. You're out of it, for now.' She let go of his contact points and stood.

She grabbed another knife and ran for the horses. No mind interfered with hers. She saw Seqiro and Koturo squaring off, turning to face each other.

Then the two horses squealed and reared up, striking at

362

each other with their forehooves. Two hooves met with a thud; another struck a shoulder, bashing the flesh so hard that a wide gash opened. Colene wasn't even sure which horse was hurt; the two were moving so quickly despite their size that her eye hadn't quite caught the skin color.

It looked like an even battle. All the minions except Colene had been neutralized, one way or another, and she was physically and mentally insignificant. But she was not about to leave the outcome to chance.

She came up to the horses. Each stood higher than her head normally, and when they reared they were twice as high. But she never paused. As the two reared again, she ran in under Koturo and stabbed into his lower belly with her knife, driving it in with both hands.

Suddenly the terrible force of Koturo's mind smashed into her mind. Colene reeled back, falling, helpless. She was done for, she knew. As she hit the ground, she felt the sledge-hammer blow of a killing strike. Then mental fireworks radiated out, and something struck the ground beside her. She waited for death, helpless to move. She had done what she could, and it hadn't been enough.

Hands came down to touch her. It was a man. She knew she was part of the spoils of the victor; now she would be raped and killed. It hardly seemed to matter. But she forced her eyes open. She wanted at least to see who did it.

It was Darius! He was kneeling beside her, feeling her body for breaks. Could they have won?

Darius helped her sit up. Dazedly she gazed at the scene.

The body beside her was that of Koturo. His belly was gouting gore, but he was oblivious; he was unconscious. Seqiro stood nearby, breathing hard. The victor.

'You distracted Koturo,' Darius said. 'He stunned you – and in that instant of his distraction, Seqiro blasted his mind. Seqiro was waiting for that key mistake, knowing what you would do on your own.'

363

'Gee,' she said, able to think of nothing more cogent.

Then Darius kissed her. She kissed him back, so glad for his presence and his love. Then she passed out.

When she woke, it was a new day. She realized that Seqiro had put her to sleep, and kept her asleep, so that she could recover from the mental bolt she had received, unprotected. It seemed that only that little bit of mental resistance she had practiced, a shadow of what Darius had managed, had saved her from destruction. Koturo had swatted her as he might a fly — but what would have blasted a normal minion had not quite finished her. The horse had used enough of his power to leave him open for Seqiro's timed, savage counterstrike, and that had done it. She had indeed made it possible, in her suicidal fashion.

Nona had taken Burgess to the Virtual Mode and healed them both there. Burgess now had all three eye stalks back in good working order, and Nona's lung and shoulder were whole. Seqiro had a bad gash on his shoulder, but that too would heal soon enough. He had won his case, and there was now no charge against him; indeed, he was in a position to assume the leadership of the local equine community. Koturo's minions had become his.

But Seqiro did not want to be a leader. He wanted to return to the Virtual Mode with the hive. So he was assigning the minions to Maresy, who would now have a good life as a restored horse.

But Colene, suicidal even in her caring, had to raise a point. 'Seqiro, you know you aren't in trouble here, any more. You can stay and not be hassled, and have a good life. Are you sure you want to risk the Virtual Mode again, where you could get killed or stuck in some foreign Mode with poor grazing and no horses with your type of mind?'

*On the Virtual Mode I have you.*

That was hard to disparage, for a number of reasons. But

she tried. 'You know I'm headed to Darius' Mode, to be his love mistress, the moment I can get over my ludicrous fear of sex. There's just not a whole lot to interest you there, Seqiro.'

*I could go with Nona.*

'And she would be good for you, too,' Colene agreed. 'Your mind and her magic could go far. I would be horribly jealous. But she won't stay on the Virtual Mode forever either. Neither will Burgess, I think. While here you have Maresy. You have learned the emotions and concerns of free human beings, and Maresy is now patterned after my favorite horse, before I met you. There's a lot of me in her, now. And you could breed with her, if you wanted. So you could sort of have me and the good life here, without risk. And if we kept the Virtual Mode open, I could come and visit you regularly.'

Seqiro considered. Maresy, nearby, raised her head to gaze at them. Colene knew the mare wanted Seqiro to stay, for she too now understood the human way as well as she understood the equine way. She too loved Seqiro, as Colene did, but with the additional quality of sexual awareness for a stallion of her kind. Maresy, now well, was a fine figure of a female horse, worth a stallion's attention.

*I would like that*, Seqiro admitted. *But I want to be with you more.*

That was it. The hard decision had been made, and Colene had done her duty by giving him the chance to seek his own life. She hugged him.

Then she went to hug Maresy. 'What I said to him goes for you too. I will come to visit you. Maybe we all will. We will know the route.'

*Thank you, Colene. I love you.*

Surely true, because she was what she was. But Maresy could not travel the Virtual Mode. Not without extreme hassle and danger that would not be worth it.

Now at last Colene unwound enough to assess her own

feelings. What had she done? She had butchered two women and stabbed the guts of a horse! What kind of a freak *was* she?

But Darius cut her off with another thought: 'How is it that you can fight like that, and not tolerate loving sexual expression?'

Colene's jaw dropped. She knew it sounded like an ugly taunt, but knew also that it was valid. Surely she *could* get over her hang-up about the rape, if she truly tried to. She would have to think about it, and come to terms with herself. Meanwhile, her horror of her own actions had been countered; she couldn't feel properly sick about it until she knew how she felt about the rest. Darius had thrown a block into her horror.

And maybe Seqiro was shoring up her mental balance, too, so that she would not go plunging off the deep end quite yet. Being in the ambience of his mind was like coming into the wonderful warmth of a house, after braving the wintry storm outside. The storm was still there, but it no longer had the power to hurt. Telepathy made all the difference.

That brought her another realization. 'Nona! Your magic — could it have worked on Earth because Seqiro connected us to the Virtual Mode, where your magic remained? And Darius could start to do some of his magic, for the same reason?'

'But our magic does not work, here,' Nona reminded her.

'Because this is home to Seqiro. He's not extending any part of his awareness through the anchor. But if he did — '

Startled, Seqiro extended his mind.

'Now try your magic,' Colene said.

Nona rose up in the air. She flew to the side. A pink cloud appeared over her head, shaping itself into a parasol. A fireball burst in the air to the side. 'It's back!'

Darius brought out the icon of himself. He moved it — and suddenly he was across the field.

'We could have had the magic — if we had realized,' Colene said. 'But I guess it worked out okay anyway. We were lucky.'

They agreed that they had been lucky. Perhaps not all of their magic would work in each Mode, but there should be enough to add considerably to their safety and comfort. They would be sure to have all their assets with them, when they came to Darius' anchor. Nona could join them there with her magic intact.

Buoyed by the discovery, they went to the anchor. Maresy saw them off, sadly. The others stepped through, disappearing. Colene, the last, gave a weak wave to Maresy. Then, with tears in her eyes, she stepped through herself.

And the mind predator clamped down on her mind. She screamed as she was drawn helplessly into that dread maw.

In a moment she was out; Darius had simply picked her up and carried her back through the anchor. Now they had a formidable new problem. Instead of departing, the predator had remained to catch her immediately. There was no certainty that a longer wait would be effective. Colene could no longer travel the Virtual Mode.

*I will free my anchor*, Seqiro thought. *That will disrupt the old Virtual Mode and form a new one. It will take the predator some time to reorient. By then you can be at Darius' Mode, and safe.*

Colene knew it was true. It was the practical thing to do. yet she protested. 'But I'll lose you!' she wailed.

He did not answer. There was no need. Colene herself had just presented the case for him to remain here with Maresy. Now he had a compelling extra reason to do it. She could not turn this down. The alternative was to remain here and let the others travel, and that would cost her everything she wanted from the Virtual Mode. It wasn't that being here with Maresy would be bad, but that Darius had to return to his Mode, to be the Cyng of Hlahtar, so she would lose him.

She had a choice between her man and her horse.

She knew what that meant. The greater good for the hive lay in accepting the horse's offer. They would lose magic in other anchor Modes, but they weren't planning to go to any except Darius' Mode. So maybe it didn't make a lot of difference.

Colene wept. But all her grief could not change the awful nature of the choice.

She did what she had to do. She firmed her resolve and bid farewell to Seqiro. Then she turned to Darius. 'Do it.'

Darius carried her back onto the Virtual Mode, while Seqiro stood at the stall. Then, as the mind predator clamped down, Seqiro vacated his anchor. 'But I'll still visit you!' Colene cried as the predator was yanked away from her mind. 'Your Mode will remain. It just won't be an anchor Mode. We can cross it for ten feet! And maybe later you can latch on again, and make a new anchor, and we'll all be together again!' She knew she was babbling, but she couldn't help it.

*Yes.*

Then his thought faded, for the realities were whirling. It would require a search to locate the Horse Mode, but she would make that search. She just couldn't give Seqiro up forever.

The whirling stopped. They had a new anchor. Someone from another Mode had latched on in the moment the opportunity had come. There would be a new person, animal, or thing to get acquainted with. Someone who was desperate to travel the Virtual Mode.

The outline of a palatial chamber formed. Within it stood three human figures with the faces of cats. One was robustly masculine; one was lusciously feminine; the third was neuter.

'Oh, no!' Colene cried. For she recognized them. These were the three feline Nulls who had served Darius in the DoOon Mode: Tom, Pussy, and Cat. Now, obviously, they would be serving the evil Emperor Ddwng, who wanted to get Darius' Chip so he could use it to take over all the alternate Modes. The three of them, cloned from a single zygote, were the new anchor figures.

Before, Colene had tricked the Emperor into vacating his anchor, by having Seqiro send him a forceful thought to that effect. But this time Seqiro was not here.

There was going to be hell to pay.

# Author's Note

No, we surely have not seen the last of Seqiro. By the ineluctable logic of this series, one major character is lost at the end of each novel, and a new anchor is introduced. The choices are becoming more difficult. But Colene simply will not accept the loss of Seqiro for long. She's a pretty feisty girl who doesn't necessarily settle for what is destined. We shall see.

As I completed this novel, writing the chapter titled 'Horse,' I suffered something devastatingly relevant. My daughter's horse Sky Blue died. Penny bought her in the spring of 1978, a registered hackney mare, a former harness racer, then twenty years old. She was black, with two low white socks on her hind legs. She was a small horse, just fourteen hands high, but healthy. It was the happiest day of Penny's childhood, and Blue was the ideal horse for her: well trained, obliging, and old enough to be philosophical about things. Blue's former owner had been ten when *she* acquired the horse, and now at fifteen was passing Blue along to the next ten-year-old girl. As I liked to put it, Blue's business was raising girls, teaching them what they needed to know in life. So Penny learned to ride, to care for a horse, and know the special type of companionship a good horse represents. We hoped Blue would live for at least five more years, but she lived for almost fourteen, being a scant thirty-four when she died on the third day of 1992.

Blue was Penny's horse, but I was the one who fed her. Penny grew up and went to college and became an adult, but Blue remained with us, with several companion horses over the years: Misty, who died in eight years after foundering so badly she could not stand; Fantasy, who died

370

in four months because of a heart condition; and Snowflake, the white pony who survived her. So it was that Blue had perhaps as much impact on my life as on Penny's, and her loss grieves me deeply. She entered my fantasy fiction, in the form of the Unicorn Neysa in the Adept series, who looked exactly like her except with a horn, and also Night Mare Imbri of Xanth, who lacked the white socks. Thus many of my readers know Blue, indirectly. She was a wonderful horse, and we loved her, and she will always be in our thoughts.

There are some credits for contributions. As I have done before, I will simply list the contributors alphabetically by first name, without identifying their entries, perserving partial privacy.

*Amy Tanner*
*Cricket Krishelle*
*Jessica Timins*
*Margaret McGinnis*

*And Colene's poem was actually written by Kira Heston.*

There was some feedback relating to the first volume in this series, *Virtual Mode*. One woman had lost an acquaintance by suicide, and was spinning into chaos herself when the autographed copy of the novel arrived, containing her contribution. She said it gave her a lift at a critical time. Another recognized herself in the Author's Note, and wrote to tell me that she had survived her suicidal inclination and was doing much better. But one contributor criticized the novel as, in essence, sexist. Maybe so: a man wrote to say that Colene was an almost perfect description of his girlfriend. He was in prison for statutory rape. Several wrote to say that they resembled Colene, and that she spoke some of their thoughts. And a woman wrote, excited about the prospects for a new character mentioned at the end of the novel; her name is Nona Colby. Well, there should be a number of Nonas in the various similar Modes; she could be one.

My reference for the nature of the Cambrian explosion and some of the creatures in it is *Wonderful Life* by Stephen Jay Gould. Because the world described in the novel is parallel in time to our own, I did not render such creatures literally; they had half a billion years to evolve. Thus they moved onto land and grew considerably larger, as did the chordates of our own Mode. But they retain their fundamental differences from our familiar forms of life. Readers who wish to see the origin of some of the named creatures, such as *Anomalocaris* or *Hallucigenia*, should read this book. It does indeed present a persuasive revision of the nature of evolution. The notion that chance determined that our kind evolved, instead of something like the floaters, awes me. Yet it may be so. But one correction: it was later concluded that *Hallucigenia* had been viewed upside down. Those were protective spikes, not legs. Too late for this novel, alas.

As those who have read the novels of this series know, there is generally something socially serious afoot when Colene returns to Earth. There will be some problem which cries out for redress and isn't likely to get it without Colene's help. Well, there was a case that occurred in real life that was about as outrageous. I will refer to the participants by their first names only, without reference to their city or state, so that only those already conversant with the case will be able to identify them. The names hardly matter, but the principle does.

As readers of my autobiography, *Bio of an Ogre*, know, I had trouble with schools from the outset. In my day there were no dyslexics or learning-disabled students, there were only stupid or lazy ones. So it took me three years to get through the first grade, and longer to satisfy teachers that I wasn't subnormal. I was later a teacher myself, though

I regarded some of the required material as irrelevant, and later still a parent with a hypersensitive, dyslexic, learning-disabled child. I became militant when the teacher was yelling at my daughter Penny from the first day of first grade. To make a seventeen-year story short, Penny did make it through to her college degree, and is today a well-adjusted adult. I fear she would not have made it, had I not fought throughout to ensure fair treatment for her. I thought my quarrels with the school system were over.

Not quite. When the first novel of this series, *Virtual Mode*, was published in hard cover, a reader who was Penny's age named Jessica bought it, read it, and liked it. Jessica's seven-year-old daughter Samantha, also a fan of mine, saw the book, and asked to take it to school so she could read it during her free time. Now these Mode novels are adult, and I don't recommend them for children. Had I been on the scene, I would have urged that she take a Xanth novel instead. But some children are more mature than others, and can handle adult material. Indeed, even Xanth may not be safe, as I had discovered two years before.

On that occasion, a Florida grade school student, Tommy, had taken a Xanth novel to school, because he was hyperactive and his counselor recommended that he take something interesting to read instead of running around. So he took a copy of *Heaven Cent*, a humorous fantasy about a nine-year-old boy, and was reading it in the cafeteria when a teacher approached, looked at the book, and took it away from him. The book was not returned. When Tommy's mother protested, she was lectured; apparently the school administration felt that it owed no accounting to the child's parent. Now I once taught school in Florida, and I know the general procedure: if a book is inappropriate, the teacher takes it from the student, but returns it at the end of the day with the admonition not to bring it to school again. Policies may vary from school to school, but this is really all that is required for a first offense. One might ask why the schools are not the first place where reading should be encouraged, and censorship discouraged. But if there is too much freedom, the kids will be bringing in whatever they believe will freak out the teachers, including wild pornography. So there do have to be reasonable limits. A Xanth novel is hardly a taboo-breaker, however, and many schools encourage the reading of Xanth novels because they do get students interested. Xanth has taught many folk to read. Also, this was not just any trashbin junk; this was a copy specially autographed to Tommy, of some personal value. When I learned of this, I wrote to the principal. 'What is the difference between this and theft?' I inquired. But the principal fudged the issue, claiming that books weren't allowed in the cafeteria. The counselor, whose advice Tommy had been following, pursued the case, challenging the teacher, in the presence of the principal, to establish why the book was forbidden. Well, it seemed there was a picture of a naked man in it. The counselor had a copy of the novel: Would the teacher show the bad picture? Of course the teacher could not. Could it have been the cover, which does show the back of a bare boy? No, it was an interior illustration – though there are no interior pictures in that novel. Still the book was not returned, and no apology was forthcoming. Probably the teacher, with the arrogance of a minion almost impervious to accounting, had simply thrown the copy away. Yet there was no recourse; I saw that the principal was covering for the teacher's mistake, stonewalling it, and would fudge the truth as far as necessary to avoid admitting error. Florida education is not first-rate; I knew that from my own days as part of it. Many teachers are dedicated, but the bureaucracy too often weeds them out while protecting the inferior ones, because a dedicated teacher is apt to be the first to protest injustice. By the bureaucracy's definition, that's a troublemaker. I sent Tommy another autographed copy, with the note 'Some battles need to be fought.' Even when, as in this case, they

374

are lost. Virtue is not necessarily rewarded, and truth is too often secondary to convenience.

So this time, with *Virtual Mode*, I would have recommended caution, because that is a novel of a different nature. It is, in its way, an exposé of the reality of too many public schools, where drugs abound and girls get raped in stairwells while the administration covers up.

However, I was not there, and it is the parent's prerogative to determine what type of reading is appropriate for the child. Jessica had read the novel, and knew her daughter, and judged that Samantha could handle it. Samantha was a bright girl, with advanced reading ability and maturity. If the school disagreed, there are procedures to clarify such things, even if they aren't always honored. So Samantha took the book to school. And — how did you guess? — she got in trouble. The principal sent Samantha home three hours early, and suspended her for a week, because she had been caught reading 'such immoral trash.' Jessica went to see the principal, and — I see you're ahead of me, here! — got lectured herself. In fact, the principal suggested that her daughter should not be allowed to read any more Piers Anthony books. Because, he said, they contained such things as rape, suicide, bodily functions, and sex. Perhaps it was incidental that this novel also poked fun at stuffy principals. A child, he explained, might be harmed by such material, because at that age they can not distinguish fantasy from reality.

I have to say that the man did have a case. *Virtual Mode* does contain such elements, and some children might indeed be harmed by such exposure. I would question whether children are not more likely to be harmed by the endless violence they watch on television, but that does not justify harming them in school. Yet the principal hardly buttressed his case by condemning all my work outright, attributing elements to it which are not found, for example, in my Xanth series. He should have informed himself, before making a statement which could be regarded as slanderous. Unfortunately, ignorance of this type abounds in the school system and in communities at large, with even classic works of literature getting banned for spurious reasons. The principal also erred when he attempted to preempt the parent's authority, and to dictate what a child might read in her free time − and indeed, to punish the child for what was at worst an error in judgment by her mother. The moment any person outside the family or legal guardian attempts to ban certain books from being read within the family, that is censorship, and I believe unconstitutional. The principal had far overstepped his authority.

But the principal did not stop there. He filed a report with the local Social Services, charging Jessica with negligence for giving questionable reading material to a minor. Because Jessica was a single parent with little formal education, he questioned whether she was capable of raising a child with above normal intelligence. Never mind that she was obviously doing so, for Samantha was doing well in school. It was evident that the man had a private agenda, and was determined to punish mother and daughter yet more for the nominal crime of bringing *Virtual Mode* to school.

You might think that such a vendetta would be laughed out of existence, the moment the basis of it was discovered. Not so. An investigation was made. This led to court proceedings. In the preliminary hearing, the judge decided that there were sufficient grounds to remove both Samantha and her five-year-old brother Joshua from Jessica's custody. They were placed in a foster home, and Jessica was forbidden to visit them. How could this happen? Well, Jessica had to work to support her family, so she had a full-time job. But she was also trying to improve herself, so she was taking classes three nights a week. She couldn't afford a day-care center, so a neighbor took care of the children before and after school, until Jessica got home from work in the afternoon. She couldn't afford a car, so time was also lost with the bus schedule. The Social Services folk made six surprise visits. Four times, Jessica wasn't home, being at work or school. Once they came on Saturday, which was her cleaning day. So the beds were apart, the children's room had toys scattered across it, the kitchen sink was piled with dishes, and the living room was turned upside down so the children could play and watch TV there while Jessica did the other rooms. Her clothes dryer wasn't working, so she had strung a rope up in the bathroom and hung the wet things there. That was when what looked like southern dowagers, complete with white gloves, walked in unannounced. There was Jessica in this mess, wearing a T-shirt and cutoff shorts, and her children still in their pajamas. She was horribly embarrassed.

Now you might think that the Social Services folk would have some inkling what real life is like. That they would see that there was no neglect or abuse here, but simply a typical housecleaning in progress. I was once a social worker, and I visited homes to be sure that children were being properly cared for. I would have understood, as I think would any normal parent. If the visitors had found the mother drunk, and bruises on the children, they might have had a case. Instead Jessica was doing exactly what she should have been doing: catching up on everything that there hadn't been time for during the hectic weekly schedule. But on the basis of such visits, and the fact that Jessica's bookshelves were full of science fiction, fantasy, romance, and horror genre books, including some Piers Anthony novels, they concluded that the children should be removed and visitation rights denied to the mother.

Remember, all this started because a child brought *Virtual Mode* to school. Does this seem stranger than fiction to you too? Do you wonder at the evident priorities of our schools and social services? Or is this sort of thing already all too familiar in your own community?

Jessica borrowed money from friends so that she could

hire an attorney. He was amazed. He went into action. He filed for another hearing, where he gave the judge Jessica's work schedule, school schedule, and bus schedule. He brought in the baby-sitter, who was licensed as a day-care worker, and he documented everything, showing that in no way had Jessica been a neglectful parent. The neglect had been on the part of the Social Services investigators, who had not bothered to get the facts before destroying a family. The judge yielded somewhat. He granted Jessica visitation during the week, and let her children come home on weekends. This continued for six months. Samantha made it through okay, but Joshua couldn't handle the disruption – remember, he was five years old, suddenly taken from his home and mother – and wouldn't do any work at school. He was removed from kindergarten.

Meanwhile the battle continued. Jessica wrote letters to the newspaper, the school board, the television station, the city prosecutor, and even the mayor. Her attorney brought to court a book reviewer, a child psychologist, two analysts, the school director, a teacher from the school for gifted children, Jessica's family, neighbors – everything.

Finally justice was served. Jessica got back custody. The principal who had started it all was removed from the school board and forced to retire. Jessica received formal apologies from the school board, Social Services, and the mayor.

Now Samantha is in a school for gifted children and loves it. Joshua is at a new school and is excelling. Both of them are running and laughing again. Jessica got her GED and a license for nursing, and is making more money than before. She is buying a house in the middle of an apple orchard. The family has a cat, a hamster, a goat, and three little pigs. Jessica now has more faith and confidence in herself. She fought through and won, and now truly appreciates what happiness is. 'It really is true,' she says, 'that you don't realize exactly what you have, until something is taken away.' (Later the cat got at the hamster. Sigh.)

So good triumphed over evil, this time. But isn't it sad that Jessica ever had to go through this ordeal, and see her children suffer — because she let her daughter take the first Mode novel to school. Isn't it a shame that it took six months before this obvious wrong was righted. Colene is a fictional character, based on a composite of real ones. Jessica is a real person. I believe Colene would like her. Colene did, after all, affect her life. I think we need more people like Jessica and Samantha, and fewer like that principal.

So, once again, the writing of a novel has brought me experience and emotion. This one more than most, because of the evidence that this series is affecting real people. I hope those of you who are not suicidal, and who are not in danger of losing your children for reading it, also find it meaningful.

As usual, my notice: those who wish to subscribe to my personal Newsletter, or to find a source for any of my in-print titles, can call my troll-free number 1-800-HI PIERS.

# Mouvar's Magic
## Piers Anthony and Robert E. Margroff

### FINAL FRAME

As soon as the vile witch Zady has grown herself a new body,
Professor Devale sends her back into the frame to flush out
Mouvar and the Opal – and kill everything Kelvin Knight
Hackleberry holds dear. By now Hackleberry is almost a
grandfather; Charles is in love with Glow, nursemaid to the
slow-growing twins Kildee and Kildom; Horace the dragon
is in love with Ember, another dragon, equally telepathic;
and, although Merlaine doesn't yet know it, her true love,
whose name is Glint, is just about to come into her life . . .
unless Zady gets to him first. The stakes are high. The last
battle is on.

ISBN  0 586 21674 X

# Beauty
## Sheri S. Tepper

Brilliant, unique and unforgettable. The first great fantasy achievement of the 1990s.

Winner of the Locus Award for Best Fantasy Novel.

On her sixteenth birthday, Beauty, daughter of the Duke of Westfaire, sidesteps the sleeping-curse placed upon her by her wicked aunt – only to be kidnapped by voyeurs from another time and place, far from the picturesque castle in 14th century England. She is taken to the world of the future, a savage society where, even among the teeming billions, she is utterly alone. Here her adventures begin. As she travels magically through time to visit places both imaginary and real she eventually comes to understand her special place in humanity's destiny. As captivating as it is uncompromising, *Beauty* will carve its own unique place in the hearts and minds of readers.

'*Beauty* lives up to its name in all ways. It is a story of mankind and magic, fairies and fairytales, future and fantasy all intertwined into a complex collage about the downfall of Earth . . . It is a story you can float away in. The writing is beautiful and the storytelling immaculate, so get it' *Time Out*

ISBN 0 586 21305 8

# Thebes of the Hundred Gates
## Robert Silverberg

'A master of his craft and imagination'        *Los Angeles Times*

### WHEN ANCIENT EGYPT WAS YOUNG . . .
### AND DANGEROUS

Two time-travellers from the 27th century go missing in ancient Egypt. Edward Davis, a promising rookie in the Time Service, is sent back in time to find them . . . back much farther than he has ever been before. Reeling from the time jump, he arrives in Thebes, only to discover that his training for survival is no protection against the intoxicating magic of *Egypt* . . .

Pyramids and obelisks, snakes with legs, winking sphinxes, birds with the heads of women, women with the heads of birds, forests of fat stone columns, lapis lazuli and gold, plump Pharaoh on his throne beneath the pulverizing sun.

Davis has thirty days in which to get a grip on his senses and find the missing time-travellers. Instead, he is taken in by a temple priestess, befriended by a beautiful slave girl, and tricked into crossing the Nile to the City of the Dead. As the hour of his scheduled rendezvous with the time field approaches, Edward Davis is brought face-to-face with the shattering truth behind the fate of his former colleagues, and the prospect of sharing that fate.

'Silverberg is our best'        *Fantasy and Science Fiction*

ISBN 0 00 647646 5

| | | | |
|---|---|---|---|
| ☐ | MAGICIAN Raymond E. Feist | 0-586-21783-5 | £6.99 |
| ☐ | SILVERTHORN Raymond E. Feist | 0-586-06417-6 | £4.99 |
| ☐ | A DARKNESS AT SETHANON Raymond E. Feist | 0-586-06688-8 | £5.99 |
| ☐ | THE SILVER BRANCH Patricia Kennealy | 0-586-21248-5 | £4.99 |
| ☐ | THE ELVENBANE A. Norton/M. Lackey | 0-586-21687-1 | £5.99 |
| ☐ | MASTER OF WHITESTORM Janny Wurts | 0-586-21068-7 | £4.99 |
| ☐ | THE DRAGON AND THE GEORGE Gordon R. Dickson | 0-586-21326-0 | £4.99 |
| ☐ | BLACK TRILLIUM May/Bradley/Norton | 0-586-21102-0 | £4.99 |

All these books are available from your local bookseller or can be ordered direct from the publishers.

To order direct just tick the titles you want and fill in the form below:

Name: _____

Address: _____

_____

_____

Postcode: _____

Send to: HarperCollins Mail Order, Dept 8, HarperCollins *Publishers*, Westerhill Road, Bishopbriggs, Glasgow G64 2QT.

Please enclose a cheque or postal order or your authority to debit your Visa/Access account –

Credit card no: _____

Expiry date: _____

Signature: _____

– to the value of the cover price plus:

UK & BFPO: Add £1.00 for the first and 25p for each additional book ordered.

Overseas orders including Eire, please add £2.95 service charge.

Books will be sent by surface mail but quotes for airmail despatches will be given on request.

24 HOUR TELEPHONE ORDERING SERVICE FOR ACCESS/VISA CARDHOLDERS –

TEL: GLASGOW 041-772 2281 or LONDON 081-307 4052